Vestments

Vestments

John Reimringer

milkweed
editions

The characters and events in this book are fictitious. Any similarity to real persons, living or dead, is coincidental and not intended by the author.

Published 2010 by Milkweed Editions
Printed in Canada by Friesens Corporation
Cover design by Christian Fuenfhausen
Cover photo/illustration "Everyone's Still Asleep" by Paul Robertson
Author photo by James Peters
Interior design by Connie Kuhnz
The text of this book is set in Baskerville
10 11 12 13 14 5 4 3 2 1
First Edition

Please turn to the back of this book for a list of the sustaining funders of Milkweed Editions.

Library of Congress Cataloging-in-Publication Data

Reimringer, John.
    Vestments / John Reimringer. — 1st ed.
       p.   cm.
    ISBN 978-1-57131-080-4 (alk. paper)
    1. Self-realization—Religious aspects—Fiction.   2. Temptation—Fiction.
    3. Priests —Fiction.   I. Title.
    PS3618.E564536V47 2010
       813'.6—dc22
                                                        2010007143

This book is printed on acid-free paper.

For Katrina, my love, who sees things whole

What did I know, what did I know
of love's austere and lonely offices?

—Robert Hayden
"Those Winter Sundays"

Vestments

On a loud and sweltering city day, in a Catholic church on a downtown street, heavy wooden doors close out the traffic noise. Here are cool shadows and silence and stone, tile painted by the fall of light through stained glass. On the walls, Christ's passion and death play out again in plaster, while in banked rows of votives, scattered candles flicker with the intentions of the prayerful. A confessional door opens and an old man comes out. Above his head a red light blinks to green. In the nearest pew, a young man of thirty or so—blue-eyed, slope-shouldered, curly-haired—glances around, then unfolds big-knuckled fists and stands. He wears a pair of paint-spattered jeans and a light blue sport shirt that matches his eyes and is open at the neck. The man enters the confessional, and the door clicks shut on the ritual words: "Bless me, Father, for I have sinned."

I

1

SATURDAY MORNING IN SAINT PAUL, church bells ringing the hour. I was in the dining room of my mother's house, celebrating Mass, when we heard my father arrive—the rattle of a rusted exhaust, the backfire of a badly tuned engine. He'd come to drop off his alimony. For a moment I lost my place in the small sacramentary that lay open on the dining-room table. "It's just the old man," I said, then put a forefinger on the words of the Eucharistic Prayer and went on. *Take this, all of you, and eat it: this is my body, which will be given up for you.* My mother's eyes rose with the Host. *My Lord and my God,* she mouthed.

At breakfast, she'd asked me to say Mass: "It's your first weekend home, let's make it special," and we left it at that. I stood at the dining-room table—its scarred walnut top cleared this morning of Mom's fabric patterns and sewing machine—with my mother in her bathrobe for a congregation and the neighbor's teenage son out front on his skateboard. The back-and-forth rumble of the wheels and the clatter of the board when the boy tried a jump kept interrupting the introductory rites and the readings, but with the consecration of bread and wine the sounds outside faded. I set the chalice back on the corporal—*In memory of his death and resurrection, we offer you, Father, this life-giving bread, this saving cup. We thank you for counting us worthy to stand in your presence and serve you—* and at that moment I could have been back on the altar at Saint Hieronymus.

Of course, I wasn't, and now my father was getting out of his old Buick and coming up the walk. He stopped to make a gruff joke to the neighbor boy, and I turned a page and intoned: *Through him, with him, in him, in the unity of the Holy Spirit, all glory and honor is yours, almighty Father, for ever and ever. Amen.*

"Amen." Mom bowed her head for the Lord's Prayer, and in the middle of it, we heard Dad's heavy steps in his work shoes cross the front porch. Then he barged through the open screen door without knocking and came to a stop in the living room, taking in Mom and me facing each other across the dinner table.

The skateboard rumbled down the sidewalk. Dad glanced over his shoulder. "Goddamn, Maura, don't you ever get tired of that fucking noise?"

Mom shook her head. "He's not out there much these days," she said. "He's got a car and a girlfriend now."

The old man frowned. "Hell, I'd've known that was all it took, I'd've bought him a whore down on University about four years ago."

"Deliver us, Lord, from every evil, and grant us peace in our day," I said, raising my voice to remind Mom we hadn't finished. Dad started, then came and leaned in the dining room archway, burly forearms crossed, pale eyes following my every gesture.

At the Sign of Peace, after I'd hugged Mom and kissed her on the forehead, I offered a hand to my father. His eyes flicked about, over my outstretched hand and Roman collar and red stole—red for today's feast of Saint Matthias, the apostle who'd replaced Judas—then back to my hand. We shook. Dad's face was puffy, cheeks and nose blotched by broken veins. He wore a dark blue T-shirt starting to pull apart at the collar, a pack of cigarettes rolled in one sleeve, exposing the Marine Corps anchor-and-globe tattooed on his bicep. I glanced from that to the blurry tattoo of the

Crucifixion on his right forearm. "The Right Fist of the Lord" my father calls it when he holds court in the neighborhood bars. He stood too close, an ex-Marine and onetime Golden Gloves boxer.

"You're looking good." The small lie came easily, and I chucked him on the shoulder, then stepped back to the table. Two consecrated Hosts lay on the gold paten; I took Communion and held the remaining Host up to my mother, then pressed it into her cupped palm.

"Guess I don't get fed," the old man said.

I hesitated. The Host lay in my mother's hand.

After their divorce, my father briefly remarried, a union that lasted all of six weeks. By Church law, he couldn't receive Communion, though in this, as in so many things regarding my father, the facts were murky: he was no longer living with the woman, and he might or might not have bothered to get a second divorce. His answers about what had happened changed depending on his mood, and here at home, where the act wouldn't be a public sanctioning of the adultery of a second marriage, uncertainty and mercy might well have prompted me to give him the Sacrament. I could have picked up the wafer, broken it in two, and given Communion to each of my parents. But at ordination I'd taken vows of obedience, and, however confusing the old man made things, as a priest I represented the Holy Roman Church. That had always been my compass.

"No," I said. "I can't." Satisfaction and shame wavered over my mother's face in turn. She hadn't remarried, only slept with a man *now that I've been abandoned by your father, and I confess that to Father Phil every Friday, though the Good Lord knows I'm not the one ought to be in that confessional.* Then she put the Host in her mouth, lifted her chin, and smiled at the old man. I shook my head and finished Mass. *Go in peace to love and serve the Lord.*

"Thanks be to God." Dad murmured it in unison with my mother, his voice solemn with a cradle Catholic's reverence for the Mass. I realized I hadn't heard the skateboard in a while. Guilt at denying my father the Eucharist caught me by surprise, and I busied myself with lifting the stole from my shoulders and arranging it over my forearm as I passed him in the living room. I had a foot on the stairs when he called out, "Always good to see you too, Father," and I paused, then walked deliberately up the stairs, wondering how it was that the old man could so reliably manage to make me feel like a prick.

In my room, I looked in the mirror and rubbed both hands over my scalp. I hung the stole with the rest of my vestments and changed from clerical black to a T-shirt and gym shorts, meaning to slip out the front door and go to the park to shoot baskets, leave my parents to each other. By now they were arguing, angry voices rising up the stairwell and spilling into my room. I'd moved back from my parish last Sunday, had boxes of books stacked along one bedroom wall. In two weeks, I was to celebrate my brother's wedding Mass, my last official act as a priest for a year, and I had expected the old man to have something to say about that. Instead, he and Mom were fighting about her boyfriend. I listened for a while, then sighed and padded downstairs barefoot, stopping on the landing at the bottom.

They were in the dining room. The old man had taken my place at the table, and he leaned on it with both hands, head and shoulders thrust forward. I'd left the paten and chalice and cruets of water and wine out. "You bring that asshole to my son's wedding," my father said, "and I'm not responsible." Between his hands, the paten made a gold circle on the walnut table.

Mom set down her coffee cup. "Your other son just got home," she said. "He said Mass at this table, and this is the way you act?"

Dad straightened, hands fisting. "Don't you disrespect me—"

I stepped into the living room, meaning to put the sacred vessels out of harm's way. "Why don't you leave Mom alone this morning," I said.

Dad turned on me. "You're getting a mite big for your britches," he said. I started toward the table, but he moved to block me. "Don't tell me what to do in my own house."

"It's not your house anymore," I said.

"He pays his alimony," Mom said.

I cast her a look, then the old man stepped forward with his chin tucked. He gave me a little stiff-fingered shove to the chest.

I put up my hands, palms out. "I'm just asking you to leave—"

"You can't throw me out of this house." He shoved me again, then harder. I pushed him away and he came back in a rush, working in close with his hands, slapping, wrestling me out the screen door and onto the porch, his face a jerking blur of bristles and washed-out blue eyes and curling gray hair.

The screen slammed shut behind us. Dad sent me skidding backward with a last shove and smacked his hands together. "I'm throwing you out, is what's happening here."

Forgetting myself, I balled my fists. He stepped in close again, eyes bright. "You want something, son?" He smelled of unfiltered Camels, last night's bourbon, Old Spice.

"No, Dad, nothing."

After he'd held me like that an instant, he smiled, satisfied, and turned to Mom, where she stood inside the screen. "I can see what it's gonna be like around here this summer," he said. "The goddamn money's on the table. You need anything, you give me a call."

Then he was down the steps and across the yard to his car. I gripped the porch rail and watched him go, noticing the way the broad V of his back disappeared into the roll of fat around his waist. Behind me, the screen opened and Mom came out. "You shouldn't have done that," she said. "Joseph Dressler's not gonna show me anything new."

I started to say something vicious and not fitting from either priest or son, but instead reached inside the screen for my socks and basketball shoes, then sat on the porch step to put them on. My hands shook with the laces, and I steadied them by rubbing at a mark on the toe of my sneaker.

Mom stood beside me, chipping paint off the porch post with her fingernail. "I'm sorry," she said. "I guess everyone's surprised at your being home."

"That's not it," I said. She wanted to talk; I wanted to get out of there. I stood and picked up a basketball from the torn couch that shared the porch with rusting bicycles, broken chairs, and a greasy charcoal grill. "Where's Jacky keeping himself?"

"I imagine he's at Mary Beth's."

"If he calls, tell him I'm at the park." I left her on the porch and dribbled the basketball across the postage-stamp yard, mostly dirt under the dense shade of the boulevard maple. At the corner of our lot, the neighbor's lilac hedge hung over a chain-link fence, twisted trunks the size of small trees, deep green foliage nearly obscured by heavy clusters of dark purple blossoms. It was the middle of May, and the low sun threw long shadows from the maples and elms across the pavement. The air was cool and the world was raw against the scent of the lilacs. I was aware of the grit of the basketball in my hands, of the tense muscles in my legs and stomach beginning to relax, and of the sharp stink of fear.

For a moment downstairs, I'd thought to reason with my father. I'd run a small parish for two years, presided over the rituals of other people's lives and deaths as a priest now for four, and I'd forgotten that the king of the Gossip Inn, John's Tap, and the Florida Tavern was a man who acted out of instinct, moving always against perceived threats to his sovereignty, threats that were real enough in his world. Mom had worked him up with talk of her boyfriend, and I'd been stupid enough to walk into the middle of it. Used to be I knew better. At the basketball court, I planned to forget again. I would practice my jump shot. I would chase rebounds until I was sweat soaked and breathing hard.

The park was empty. Two muddy ball diamonds, a hockey rink with a wooden fence around it, a playground, and a tennis court cracked by frost heave. The basketball court was bordered by small pines and oaks. Puddles of rainwater flagged low places in the concrete, splashing my ankles and calves as I dribbled. My aim was off at first, jumpers spinning out, bank shots banging off the front of the iron. When I warmed up, the shots started going in, the ball hanging in the back of the net for a satisfying instant before dropping. After a while, there was nothing to hear but the hollow sound of the ball, the scuff of sneakers on pavement, and the *bang, rattle,* and *whoosh* of shots falling; nothing to see but an orange rim, a white backboard, and the green-black tops of the pines against a high blue sky. The scent of resin washed the air.

I'd been at it like that for half an hour or so when the ball lodged between rim and backboard. I jumped to punch it free, and when I turned back to the court there was a group of Mexican teenagers standing at the far end. We stared at one another for a moment, then a tall, thin kid nodded and dribbled a ball onto the court. While I shot, more deliberately now, catching my breath, I watched them warm up, horse around, choose teams. When I was in high school, Mexicans wouldn't have come to this park. There wasn't a lot of violence, but certain lines were seldom crossed. The lines had blurred, but still there was tension when I walked down the court.

"Even your teams?" I offered. They fell quiet, exchanged looks. An older white guy wanting to play ball. Still, one team was a player short. Someone shrugged. Sure. Why not?

We started, and I ignored the extra elbows. I'd been too busy in my parish for a game at the gym this past winter, and the whole physicality of the game—the jostle of bodies, the drive of a dropped shoulder, the slash of one forearm across another—was something I'd missed without knowing it. Soon enough, though, I realized I was going to be plenty sore tomorrow without the added bruises of an inside game played against younger men. In high school I'd been a shooting guard, so I drifted out of the mix under the basket to the open edges of the court. After I sunk a couple of step-back eighteen-footers over the thin kid, Hector, he grunted "motherfucking Larry Bird here," and I had a nickname.

The team I was on took the first game easily, then the second. We were ahead in the third when suddenly I could no longer keep up with those tireless seventeen-year-old legs and my shots started hitting the front of the rim again. Bent over and catching my breath afterward, I watched the kids shove each other around. Hector caught my glance and said, "Good shooting, Larry Bird." I lifted a hand from my knee and gave him a little wave in return. When I had my wind back, someone tossed me my ball, and I caught it and spun it and joined the talk about the game. Then someone asked what I did, and I said, "I'm a priest." There was a stir among the boys as they remembered the language they'd used during the game—tough, crude talk about faggots and pussy and cutting a guy a new asshole—and I felt the distance come then that always comes between people and a priest. "Good game," I said, and walked away.

Walking home, I could feel the slow ache of long-unused muscles. I dribbled the ball lazily from one hand to the other, enjoying the time to myself and the echo of the ball off the brick apartment buildings and the glass storefronts I passed near the park. I'd lived alone in the rectory of a country parish the last two years, and I felt crowded in the house with my mother.

By the time I'd showered and eaten lunch, though, Mom had gone up to Roseville to visit my sister, Anne. I watched college baseball on cable all afternoon, settling into the hollows in the couch that marked my father's spot. The old man had moved out two years ago, but little else had changed. Stacks of yellowing newspapers still staggered against each other along the walls, and Mom's fabric-covered sewing box sat open on the lamp table under the piano window, a few spools of thread scattered about. The only new addition to the room was an ashtray stand from my grandfather's house, its bottom now crowded with Mom's women's magazines. The ashtray brimmed over with cigarette butts ringed with her lipstick, mixed with the half-smoked off-brands that belonged to her boyfriend, Samuel, and the room smelled of stale smoke.

After the baseball, I felt the buzzing drowsiness that comes from losing yourself to a book or the television on a sunny afternoon, as if a piece of glass had dropped between me and the world. I went out for air and ran by the dry cleaner to pick up my best priest's suit, laundered and pressed for Jacky's wedding. When I got home, Mom was setting the table, and I hung the laundry on the coat tree and went into the kitchen to pour milk while she dished up chicken and mashed potatoes.

"How's Anne?" I asked, after we said grace. My sister had five children. Just catching me up on the kids would take Mom most of dinner, I figured, and leave the unpleasantness of the morning behind us.

"Worried about you. I told her not to, but I wasn't very convincing." Mom gave me a weary half-smile.

I patted her hand. They say behind every good priest stands a worried Irish mother. Mine is black Irish, and she has the moods and wary pessimism of Irish women, a look in her eyes that says she expects the worst. Being married to my father for a quarter of a century didn't help this. Their fights in my childhood followed a predictable pattern, a few days of Irish squalls from my mother, then a German blitzkrieg by the old man.

"You know," Mom said, "we all have to do things we don't like for our jobs." She nodded at me, then added in a resigned voice: "You sure gave me a lot of explaining to do."

"All you have to tell your friends," I said, pressing the serving spoon down into the bowl of congealed mashed potatoes until it bent a little at the handle, "is that I'm teaching at Saint John's this fall and took the summer off." It was probably all she had told them.

The full story was not that much more interesting, although it would have given her friends enough to talk about. There'd been, briefly, a woman. It was a serious transgression, but one that might well have gone unnoticed. When it didn't, the archdiocese tried to transfer me to a hardship assignment, and I'd chosen instead an offer from the Benedictines to teach history. The fact that it was May of 1994, with the newspaper stories from Boston getting worse and no one wanting to see a priest in doubt for any reason, made the timing awkward, but there wasn't anything I could do about that. I dished up a second helping of potatoes and straightened the spoon.

Mom gave me a sharp look. "What do you want, James?" she asked.

The direct question startled me, and I snapped back: "Want? I want to be back at my parish. I want not to have fucked up. I want Granddad at Jacky's wedding. I want all sorts of impossible things."

I shoved aside my plate and got a beer. When I sat down again, Mom had sunk into her own thoughts. We finished our dinners in silence. The only sounds in the kitchen were the clink of Mom's silverware and, through the open window above the sink, the shouts of boys playing street hockey on Rollerblades. After dinner,

Mom sat at the table and paid bills with a big glass of sherry at hand while I put away leftovers and washed dishes. By the time I dried the last coffee cup and sat down with another beer, she had started dealing a game of solitaire.

She'd been using my closet and chest of drawers for storage and hadn't cleared them out; when I moved in I'd carried armfuls of winter clothes, extra linens, and boxes of Christmas ornaments into Anne's old room. "You know, I could find someplace else to stay," I offered.

"Oh no, honey," Mom said. "You have a place here as long as you need." She moved a file of sequenced cards onto an ace. "Samuel stays over sometimes," she said.

"How's the old man feel about that?" I asked.

"How do you think?" she said. Then: "Your father comes by Saturday mornings. You'll notice Samuel wasn't here last night."

"There you go." I slid my chair away from the table. "I'm getting together with Jacky tonight," I said. No answer. I rinsed my beer can and dropped it in the recycling bin on my way out. Behind me, the sherry bottle rang the rim of Mom's glass. It was going to be a long summer.

In the fall, though, that history lectureship was waiting for me up in Collegeville, where the Benedictines were willing to take in a wayward diocesan priest. I pictured myself moving into a monastery room in August, unpacking my clothes, arranging my books. I saw a simple chest of drawers beneath a crucifix on the wall, and a study desk at a window overlooking a walled garden and the blue waters of Lake Sagatagan, one bough of a tree crossing the window's upper left-hand corner. There would be a twin bed with a ticking-striped mattress, a set of crisp white sheets neatly folded at its foot, and a single pillow at its head. I'd make the bed, take a nap or read at my desk until the abbey bells rang for vespers, then hurry across the lawn to join the rest of the community at prayer.

In the fall there would be Johnnies football games. Jacky could come up, or some of my priest friends.

But as I walked out of Mom's kitchen, my father's angry face blocked out the ticking-striped mattress, the lake, and everything else. The old man named me and Jacky after the Apostles James and John because Jesus called those brothers *Boanerges,* meaning *Sons of Thunder,* in reference to their passionate tempers. When we were boys, the old man would sometimes call us "my *bone*-urges" to make us laugh. More often, though, he called us "my Sons of Thunder," making us proud and a little afraid. That our father was the thunder was not lost on us.

2

I MET JACKY FOR BEERS at John's Tap. He nodded at the bar when I came in, but I'd already seen the old man's Buick in the parking lot. Our father sat hunched over the remains of ribs and fries, a fresh beer at one hand, an ashtray full of cigarette butts at the other. While I watched, he shook a cigarette from his pack, clamped it in his teeth, and cupped his hands to light it. The Twins were on the TV behind the bar, and the old man nudged the guy next to him, gestured at the game, and said something ending with "Haw-haw." His neighbor, a compact man in a Ford cap and company shirt, muttered something and stared into his beer. The old man leaned back and smiled at him. I held my breath, and then my father returned his attention to the game.

I sat down across from Jacky. Dad would figure out I was here soon enough.

"Heard you had a run-in with him this morning," Jacky said.

"I got between him and Mom. He shoved me around a bit."

Jacky toyed with a beer coaster. "I always thought he'd leave us alone someday."

"Fat chance," I said. Dad had tipped his big shoulders into Ford Cap's space again, his cigarette waving over the other man's beer.

"One of these days I'll make him pay," Jacky said.

"If you do," I said, "it'll just mean he's gotten old. There won't be any pleasure in it."

Jacky took a sip of beer, licked foam from his mustache. "I never thought of that. Shit." He shook his head. "That's you, James, always seeing things cockeyed."

The barmaid brought out an iced mug and poured me a beer from Jacky's pitcher. I ran my thumb through the frost on the glass. "Do you and Mary Beth have everything straight with the parish?" I said. "Did you pass Pre-Cana class? Get the license?" Jacky was liable to forget things like that.

He ignored me and punched in selections on the wall-mount Wurlitzer, its chrome dull and greasy with fingerprints. John Prine started singing "Angel from Montgomery," his scratchy voice tinny on the cheap speakers.

Jacky sat back. "This gonna take with you quitting?"

"I'm just going on leave."

"Sure," Jacky said. "You get your wick dipped, and you're gone for good."

I laughed. A priest's life is full of people who apologize if a *hell* or a *damn* slips out. And my rougher parishioners—corn farmers, grain-elevator workers, long-haul truckers, even the guys I played ball with—made the apology into a slight with a condescending grin: *Sorry, Father, didn't mean to offend you.* But I didn't have to worry about that with Jacky.

"Let's talk about the wedding," I said. "Father Phil did your Pre-Cana. You've got the license for me to sign? Everything's in order?"

"Yeah, yeah." Jacky glanced around the bar. "Mary Beth took care of all that shit."

"You should have a hand in this." I leaned forward so he couldn't look around me. "Conflict resolution, handling money, how you're gonna raise the kids—you want to think about all of that now."

"And you're the expert?" Jacky took a drink and eyed me over the rim of his glass.

"C'mon, Jacky." I sat back. "I know Phil went over this. I'm just asking."

"I didn't come here to talk with a priest." Jacky dug a finger in his ear. It felt like we were in junior high again and I was trying to help him with his homework.

"Then we'll sit down with Mary Beth next week," I said. "As the officiating priest, it's my pastoral duty."

"Pastoral who?" Jacky gripped his beer. "That's bullshit talk."

"Shit." With my fingertips, I traced initials someone had carved into the table and inked in with a pen. My ordination might not have made any difference to my brother, but my education had. It filled me with ideas, gave me ways of talking that angered him.

"What's the matter?" Jacky said.

"Forget it." At the bar, the old man swiveled on his stool. Great. Now he'd be over in a minute. "I'm going to the john," I said. I walked past the bar and nodded at the old man, who turned his attentions back to Ford Cap.

Down the hall in the back room were a pool table with worn felt and one leg shimmed, the door to the men's toilet, and empty beer kegs stacked at the screen that opened on the alley. The bathroom was cramped and smelled of urine. Paneling warped from the walls. I checked the mirror, pulled at the shoulders of my black T-shirt, too small now because I'd lifted weights all winter. I fingered the skin of my throat above the soft neckband and missed the harsh white square of the Roman collar. More and more these days, young priests wore civilian clothes, but Father Phil, the priest of my childhood, had taught me that it was a priest's duty to be a public and available representative of the Church. So I'd made a habit of clerical black, one that ended when I came home last weekend. On leave I couldn't say public Mass without permission, and my collar felt like false advertising.

Someone tried the bathroom door, rattling the knob. "Just a minute." I splashed water on my face and went back out front. At the bar, Dad had turned full on his neighbor, expansive, talking, laughing, gesturing with cigarette and beer glass. Ford Cap glowered, leaning as far away as his bar stool would allow. Jacky was watching them with his feet up in the booth.

"That's Terry Doolin's dad," he said, as I slid in across from him. "Pop better lay off."

Above the old man's head there was a Hamm's beer sign that scrolled at a glacial pace through a northern scene of river and waterfall with a tent and a canoe on a gravel beach. It used to remind me of childhood trips to cabins offered by one or another of Dad's friends or Mom's supervisor at the bank where she worked as a teller. I stared, waiting for the tent, until I realized the sign wasn't moving, the motor apparently having broken since I'd last been in.

Mr. Doolin stood suddenly, threw a bill on the bar. He said something sharp to the old man and walked out fast, settling his cap over his eyes. Dad, quickly on his own feet, watched him go, the corners of his mouth working in amusement. Then he caught my eye and came our way, carrying his beer mug, shoulders back and gut out, pleased as punch. "Uh-oh," I muttered.

The old man loomed over our booth. "That Doolin," he said, swaying slightly. "I been listening to him run at the mouth for years."

"Yeah, Dad," I said, "you never run at the mouth."

Dad sat down beside me. "What's this I hear about you giving up being a priest?"

"Damn it," I said. "I'm on leave."

The old man tilted his head back and peered at me. "Little sensitive, ain't ya?"

"Lay off, Dad."

He nodded at Jacky. "Your brother," he said, "I get on his nerves."

"You get on everyone's nerves," Jacky said.

Dad reached across and cuffed him gently on the side of the head, the table tilting under his weight. "Watch it, Jackyboy."

Jacky smiled, and Dad turned back to me. "I always raised you to stick with shit."

Here it comes, I thought.

"But—" he took a swig of beer, "I reckon you're old enough to know what you want." He smirked. "Giving up pussy's got to have been hard."

I drew in a breath, thought better of it, and had a long pull at my own beer. "Sure," I said. "Real hard."

The old man leaned into me, dropping his face next to my shoulder and staring at the tabletop. "You know what's white and moves across the sky at five thousand miles per hour?" He squinted up slyly.

"The Coming of the Lord! Haw-haw!"

Jacky spluttered beer over the table. I frowned, which wasn't enough for my father. He stood. "Christ, it's a terrible joke," he said. "Blasphemy. I'm going to the Gossip." He went to pay the barmaid, who paused in the middle of wiping down a table. She laughed at something he said, swaying against him and shaking her hair. Then he walked out, stopping at the cigarette machine on the way.

As the door closed behind him, Jacky and I looked at each other, then cut our eyes back and forth. We heaved heavy sighs at the same time, which set us to laughing.

"What's with the Gossip all of a sudden?" Jacky said.

"Beats me," I said. "The old man's like winter: you can try to predict him all you want, but in the end you just hunker down and dig out after he's gone."

The Gossip was the roughest bar around here, and we knew that if the old man went there he was looking for a fight. That he would sit at the bar, smoking one cigarette after another, holding them like darts, knocking back whiskey with beer. That he would argue religion or sports or city politics with someone at the bar, and that, late in the evening, a point of argument would grow into a physical challenge. The old man seldom lost, and if he did, he'd fight the guy again until he beat him or the man found another place to drink. "You don't fuck with Joe Dressler unless you want to go to war" was the common wisdom of the Gossip's regulars.

Jacky said something I couldn't hear. "What?" "Nothing." The bar was getting crowded and noisy with softball teams coming in after practice, and the beer was making me sleepy. "You want to shoot some hoops tomorrow?" I asked. "About ten?" I gave myself time to go to early Mass.

"Sure."

I finished my beer. "I'm going home."

"How's Mom?"

"Moody."

"Wait'll you meet Samuel."

"I have. He's a piece of work."

"Like a nasty old woman." Jacky yawned, stretched, and glanced around. "Think I'll see if Cheryl wants to play some pool."

Cheryl, who waitressed here sometimes, was sitting at the end of the bar smoking a cigarette, a screw-together cue in a case at her elbow. "Don't put too much on it," I said.

"Hell no," Jacky said. "Don't tell Mary Beth. She's a little jealous."

With effort, I kept my mouth shut. Last spring, after years of dating Mary Beth on and off, Jacky had cheated on her with Cheryl. That's when Mary Beth asked for a diamond.

I looked at Cheryl, who was wearing black leather pants. Once this winter, when I was having a beer with the old man, he'd claimed to be sleeping with her. I thought about hitting Jacky with that one, then settled for "You'd best take your vows seriously, little brother." The old man had likely been lying, anyway.

"Mary Beth can take care of herself," Jacky said. "I mean, would you cross her?"

"You did," I said. "Anyway, I wouldn't cross either of 'em." Mary Beth rode her own motorcycle, and Cheryl was a tall, raw-boned girl who entered and won men's pool tournaments. I stood and lifted my denim jacket from the hook between the booths.

"James," Jacky said.

His voice made me pause, the jacket on one arm. "What?" I said. I took out a bill for my half of the beer.

Jacky hesitated, then shook his head and waved off the money.

"Thanks." I put my billfold back. "I'll see you tomorrow."

Jacky hopped out of the booth and walked to the bar. He's lean, a welterweight, with Mom's dark complexion, high cheekbones, and Irish temper, but he swaggers just like the old man. Me, I've got the old man's bluff German face and blue eyes, and a sweet nature all my own.

On the way home, I drove down University by the Gossip Inn, wedged between a Vietnamese take-out place and a head shop. Through the grated front window, I could see my father's bulk at the bar. It occurred to me that he was there, looking for a fight, because he was still worked up from this morning.

The Gossip's the kind of place that gets its windows shot out, where the guy on the next stool might carry a gun or a knife. Twenty years ago, some men pulled a gun on my father as he sat at the bar there. They took him out back to the alley lot, where they beat him with a baseball bat. They took turns, the old man said later, passed the bat around like a grudge. After he heard the bat clatter into the bed of a pickup truck, after he heard footsteps and tires grind away over gravel, the old man pulled himself into his car and drove home. He drove by clinging to the steering wheel to hold himself up, while streetlights and the headlights of oncoming cars split and drew back together, half the world a dark pink haze because his right eye was filled with blood.

When the old man appeared at our back door, he was swaying, ready to topple, gravel from the parking lot ground into his swollen face and forearms. I was ten, sitting at the kitchen table eating a bowl of cereal before bed, and I yelled in fright, only half-conscious that what was in the door was my father. Then Mom was there, holding the door open, reaching for him and drawing back, unsure where to find an unbroken place to support him. "They hurt me bad, Maura," he said.

He had broken ribs and a broken collarbone. The thick muscles of his upper back and his shoulders were a mass of bruises, and once, when he'd rolled his head from the protective cradle of his forearms to cry out, the bat had caught him just forward of the right temple, cracking the bone at the outer orbit of his eye. To this day, his vision is bad in that eye; he misses objects, movement, to his right.

But he refused to stay at the hospital for observation after the doctors set his breaks, and that summer he lay on the couch, using first his sick leave and then his vacation. Mom was working two jobs, and it fell on me to tend him, rubbing salve into his muscles and watching his back turn from blue and green to sickly yellow, shot with the purple of burst veins. It was hard to look at and harder to touch. I'd never been this near my father except when he taught Jacky and me how to wrestle. Up close, his skin was old and oily and darkened by years of working shirtless in our backyard, and there was a strong smell to him. My hands seemed small against his broad back and sloping shoulders, and it scared and thrilled me to know that someone could beat him up. I thought the men from the bar might come to our house, and I rehearsed how I would lock the door and run to where he kept his handgun. And when the men broke down the door, I would point the gun steadily at their leader. "If you take one more step, I'll kill you," I'd say, and he would know I meant it.

My father didn't know how fiercely I meant to protect him. He bullied us from the couch, kept us all running to the kitchen for cigarettes and beer, changing the channel on the TV. He flew into rages, screaming and cursing if he were left alone in the living room, even if he woke by himself in the night. "Where the fuck is everybody? I could die down here while all you sleep."

In the evenings, though, as I sat on the floor by the couch watching the Twins, he would tap my shoulder and point to the TV. "Look at that young Blyleven's big curve," he'd say. "When it works it's great, but if he hangs it, it's gone. Fucker'll give up a lot of home runs." On those nights, locusts hummed outside, the cooling evening air came through the open screens into our close living room, and the smoke from my father's cigarette drifted out so that you could smell it if you were sitting on the front porch with a book, half-listening to the game inside. That summer, he taught me how fielders shifted depending on the batter, how the middle infielders called the pitch to first and third behind cupped hands. Watching boxing, an obscure middleweight match or a rerun of Ali and Frazier, he showed me how smart boxers adjusted to their opponents from round to round, how they used their thumbs and elbows in a clinch. When he tired of TV, he read passages from the Bible and we argued. I was getting a 1970s Catholic grammar school education, and the old man was pre-Vatican II at best. I know now that his thinking was more that of a fundamentalist, primitive and contradictory, but he was not a stupid man, and

I learned a lot from dealing with his shifting arguments, which roamed from salvation to theories about how Zoroaster was actually Satan. One night he told me how sorry he was that he'd fucked up and couldn't get to my Little League games that summer. And when Mom tired of his slow convalescence and said that maybe she ought to find a man who could provide for his family, I stood next to the couch and cried out that I was sticking by him even if she wouldn't.

3

AFTER DRINKING BEER WITH JACKY, I slept well and woke Sunday to green light slanting through the oak leaves outside my window, stirring finches and house sparrows loose from the night. I knelt by the bed and said my morning office, trying to ignore the closeness of my childhood room and the sour, ever-present stench of cigarettes that hung over the house like a dirty blanket.

I remember waking in the dark once, a Sunday before Christmas in seventh grade. Mom and Dad had yelled at each other until late the night before. Anne was learning to make dinner, spaghetti and meatballs, and the old man, just home from a bar and not knowing that, had been angry about how spicy the meatballs were. "Christ, Maura, do I look like a dago?" Mom let him go on about it while Jacky and I exchanged glances and Anne's face whitened, her mouth tightening until it almost disappeared. When Dad threw down his napkin and said, "I can't eat this crap!" Mom turned to Anne and said sweetly, "I'm sorry, honey, you did your best." The old man froze in place, standing at the head of the table with his chair pushed back. Then he turned on Mom. "You fucking bitch," he said. Years later, I can still remember the low pitch to his voice, the unsurprised venom in it. The fight that followed was vicious, Mom going at the old man from all sides like a terrier and him blundering around like a bear, angrier and more helpless by the moment, until he finally put his fist through the paneled wall alongside the stairs.

At dawn, I lay in bed dreading the tense ballet that would go on in the house all morning, the two of them tiptoeing around each other and we kids tiptoeing around them. Mass might break the tension, but Mass was a sometimes thing in our house. More often than not, if anyone took us, it was our grandparents. My grandfather Otto, the old man's old man, would call Mom Saturday night and announce: "We're taking the kids to Mass tomorrow, Maura. Have 'em ready by 9:30."

That morning, with the Advent wreath my father had placed on the dining-room sideboard a month before dropping needles, unused candles tilting now at odd angles, I decided to go to early Mass on my own. Maybe Father Phil would need an altar boy. In the dark, I dressed in my best Sunday clothes, even putting on a tie, tightening the knot before the mirror like my grandfather had taught me. Going downstairs, I kept close to the wall where the steps were quieter. The old man would be sleeping on the couch.

I lifted my parka from the coat tree on the landing and wrestled into it. A few feet away, the TV hummed with a test pattern and my father snored, the coffee table littered with empty Grain Belt cans and an ashtray full of cigarette butts. The dead bolt squeaked when I turned the latch. Behind me, the snoring stopped. I dared a glance over my shoulder. Dad turned on his side and snorted, but didn't wake. The doorknob rattled under my hand, and I paused, then eased the door open and was ready to slip out when I heard a floorboard creak and was caught by the biceps in a hard grip.

The old man swung me back against the wall. He peered at me, breath stale with beer and tobacco. "The hell time is it?" He shook me by the arm.

"I'm just going to early Mass."

He stared, puzzled, gripping my arm hard enough to bruise. I shivered, trying not to let fear make me look defiant, and noticed for the first time that his right eye had been skewed by the damage the baseball bat had done two years before. He shifted his hold, then shoved me toward the door. "Jesus, I'm raising a Holy Joe. Get the hell out of here."

The heavy wooden door caught me in the ear, and I scurried onto the porch. Halfway down the block, I stopped, looked back at our house. It was stinging cold out, and I rubbed at my ear with a mittened hand, then pulled my hood tighter. I wanted to be back in bed. But by now the old man would have the percolator going and be sitting in the dark in the living room, brooding over the orange glow of a cigarette. I started walking again, which made me feel better. I crossed the railroad overpass, face lowered against the north wind, then slipped on a frozen patch of sidewalk and looked up; ahead, the church's blocky red-brick bell tower and tiled roof rose among the morning trees.

In the chill vestibule, I dipped the tips of my fingers in holy water, breaking a thin film of ice. The church was almost empty, lights dim, and I sat in the shadows in one of the side pews with my coat on. The scent of candles drifted from the altar, along with the turpentine smell of sap from boughs newly cut to freshen the Advent wreath. A kneeler thudded, and, reminded, I knelt, easing my weight slowly onto my knees because that was the year I had a knee condition called Osgood-Schlatter. It was common in growing boys and eventually it went away, but at the time, even on a padded kneeler, it felt like kneeling on bone bruises. When I served Mass and had to kneel on the marble altar steps, I offered the pain for Jesus.

Votives flickered, and the stained-glass window beside me was deep blue and red, like night and wine. I tried to pray, but kept remembering the old man's bad breath in my face, last night's shouting, my sister crying. It amplified the dull ache in my knees until I couldn't think. Then the lights came up. Father Phil entered from the door behind the altar to the ringing of small bells, and I found refuge in the litanies of the Mass—*I confess to almighty God, and to you, my brothers and sisters, that I have sinned through my own fault, in my thoughts and in my words, in what I have done, and in what I have failed to do*—until my mind slipped again and I had shoved my father up against some wall, any wall, and was hitting him with little slaps to the face the way he did with Jacky and me sometimes when Mom wasn't around: "Listen to me, you listen to me—"

"Deliver us, Lord, from every evil," Father Phil said. "Amen," I said. "This is the Lamb of God, who takes away the sins of the world," Father Phil said, and, far away, the Host shimmered in his upraised hands. Father Phil, who was good and strong and happy in the Lord. "Happy are those who are called to His supper." "Lord, I am not worthy to receive you," I whispered, "but only say the word and I shall be healed." I found myself moving up the center aisle with the other people to take Communion. "The Body of Christ, James." Father Phil held the Host before me. "Amen." I let him place it on my tongue and swallowed without chewing. I, too, could be whole. The dry taste of unleavened bread lingered in my mouth as I returned down the aisle, renewed. I knelt with my back straight, ignoring the pain in my knees, and turned my eyes to Father on the altar, purifying his fingers with wine and water. I imagined myself like him, robed in white, pure and strong.

My mind had drifted from my prayers. I was thirty years old and there was no one fighting. I got off my knees and went to shower and shave, then dressed for Mass in slacks, a sport shirt, and loafers. Before leaving, I made coffee and leaned against the kitchen counter, drinking it black while I woke up. The house felt strange without the old man's presence, though, as he'd made clear yesterday, he was still very much around. The house was also empty: Mom hadn't come home last night, not wanting, I guessed, to sleep with her boyfriend under the same roof as her priest son. After

Jacky's wedding, I'd sublet an efficiency or see whether I could move up to Saint John's early.

Halfway to church, I remembered how Father Phil felt about priests in civvies. I wasn't ready to see him yet, and so I decided to go to Guadalupe, the Mexican church across the river. I hadn't been there in years, but in high school I'd dated a Mexican girl, Betty García, and we'd attended Mass together. I liked the simple, open church. I'd be anonymous enough there.

The streets were empty, and I took the long way to Guadalupe, driving over the sleek new High Bridge, climbing toward bluffs and memories. The old bridge, dynamited and rebuilt a few years ago, had figured in the nightmares of my childhood, a spidery iron structure that seemed to rise a thousand feet above the Mississippi. One morning in high school, I walked home across it after spending the night with Betty García at her grandmother's house off Concord Street. I remember the brilliant January wind, the plummeting flutter of a knotted condom onto Mississippi ice.

Early for Mass, I knelt near the side chapel of Our Lady and said the Rosary with the old Mexican women there. As I began reciting the mysteries, I twisted my rosary around my hands so that the beads dug into the tendons and flesh. In the shadowed chapel, votive candles lit jewel-colored glass holders, but the sun was up and the church—a cinder-block rectangle with high clear windows—was filling up with light like a sand-bottomed pool in spring sun, wavering shafts where dust motes turned in air currents like tiny fish. I turned my forearm and watched light slip over my skin, so tangible it nearly tickled the hairs there. The air was cool, full of whisperings. This time of the morning was for the old, for those who went to bed early or slept badly or woke alone.

The church of Betty García. The deep scent of her body, twisted sheets, the squeaks and rattles of the different beds and couches and backseats where we made love. We were high-school lovers, frightened and made passionate by the delights of sin. I had other lovers after Betty; my vocation came late, during the fall of my senior year of college. After that, I'd been celibate for eight years, had, in pride, thought I was past temptation, and then in an unguarded moment betrayed my vows, my Church, and my congregation. I prayed for forgiveness, fingering Our Fathers and Hail Marys, while people drifted into the church in ones and twos.

When Mass was ready to start, I left my spot near the chapel for a pew midway up the aisle. The turnout for the early service was sparse and I was the only Anglo there besides the priest, one I didn't know, a bull-necked man with crewcut black hair. His homily was from the old school, popular again with conservative young priests: he lectured the congregation about the things they'd let get between themselves and God. There was a satisfied glint in his eye, and no hint that his own relationship with the Lord had ever been less than exemplary. Maybe it hadn't. When Communion came, I found myself trembling in the slow line. I stepped up in front of the priest and cupped my hands to receive the wafer.

"Body of Christ."

"Amen." I met his eyes, worried against all reason that he'd recognize in me a troubled fellow priest.

He turned to the server, exchanged the paten for the chalice. "Blood of Christ."

"Amen." I'd held his gaze an instant too long. There was a hint of alarm in his eyes now. What kind of needy soul was I? Would I bother him after Mass, disturb his routine? A priest's Sunday afternoons are sacred—time to watch sports on TV, have a few beers, maybe talk on the phone with old seminary buddies scattered across the diocese, sharing complaints about bad pastors or the latest special fund-raising campaign ordered by the Chancery.

I returned to the pews and knelt and bowed my head. This was my first Sunday not giving Communion. For years, I had looked forward every week to the quiet shuffle of long lines of communicants, the solemn exchange. If a small child accompanied his mother, I would make the sign of the cross on his forehead with my thumb, saying, "May the Lord bless and keep you," and watch him swell with importance. The young and middle-aged received by hand, but old people—thinning World War II veterans like my grandfather—still received by mouth, ecstatically, sticking out their tongues with heads tilted back and eyes shut. In the pew at Guadalupe, I made my hands into the steeple the nuns had taught us in first grade and closed my eyes.

After Mass, I paused in the parking lot and watched families on their way in for the next service. Near me, a Mexican teenager shuffled his feet and tried to talk to a black-haired girl, who answered him in a clear voice—that Mexican lilt—tucking a stray bang behind her ear with a nervous hand. The boy was as awkward as I had been and the girl's gestures were familiar shadows of Betty García. I watched them with affection and said a prayer that they would be happy and chaste—or at least careful—and make no mistakes that couldn't be undone. Back at the church, the priest stood on the steps energetically shaking hands. My hand closed briefly over the rosary in my pocket, then I got out my keys and went on to the car.

"Dad said you wouldn't give him Communion." Jacky brought it up on the court later that morning, hunched over the basketball, elbows out. Sweat dripped from the ends of his mustache.

"You gotta be kidding," I said. Home again after years of purposeful distance, I kept getting caught off guard by how quickly word passed around my family, how easily sides were taken and quarrels started and forgotten.

Jacky swayed, and his eyes darted back and forth. He was going to drive to the basket. Right or left? I leaned one way, and when he drove the other I reached out and flicked the ball out of bounds.

He chased it on the grass. "I just think," he said, picking up the ball and catching his breath, "that you're getting a little high and mighty."

"You sound like the old man," I said. "Dad goes to Mass a few times a year. He's like a little kid; he only wants it because he can't have it."

Jacky walked back to the edge of the concrete. "What do you care?"

"I'm a priest, remember? Who if not me?"

My brother nodded, looked from me to the basket. He was still thinking layup; his jump shot hadn't worked all morning. Then he said, "You're a bigger pain in the ass than Father Phil and all that Pre-Cana crap."

He drove left, and I bodychecked him under the basket, hard into the creosote-blackened telephone pole the backboard was mounted on. The ball rolled across the court.

"Fuck me," Jacky said. I saw the change in his eyes too late, and he popped me in the nose. I tackled him, and we grappled and rolled around in the grass at the edge of the court for a minute before separating and sitting up, breathing hard, brushing grass trimmings off our arms and legs. "Okay, maybe that was a foul," I said. My nose was bleeding, and I swiped at it with my wrist.

Jacky rubbed his shoulder. "Yeah," he said. "A foul."

That afternoon, I called Betty García. We'd been friends since a few years after our high-school breakup, meeting once or twice a year over coffee to talk Church and city politics, discuss our professional lives, and, lately, to lament Clinton's problems. Betty was a labor lawyer who knew the ins and outs of local politics much better than I did, and sometimes she had inside news from the archdiocese.

She answered on the third ring—"García," she said, and then: "James. Mary Beth said you were in town," and we started talking about Jacky and Mary Beth. I told her about scuffling with Jacky on the basketball court. "Don't know whether he's wound up about the wedding or I'm pissy about being around the family so much," I said. "Probably both."

"Understandable," Betty said. She knew my family.

"I can't believe Jacky's finally tying the knot," I said.

"I can't believe Mary Beth waited so long," Betty said. Betty had been engaged in college, married while in law school at William Mitchell, and had a five-year-old son.

"She had to catch my flighty brother," I said.

"That's what I mean," Betty said, and I laughed, then told her about playing basketball with the Mexican kids the day before.

"I'm surprised you didn't recognize my cousins," Betty said, a long-running joke about her large family. We visited a while longer, the talk disjointed because I was trying to figure out how to bring up being on leave. When Betty suddenly went silent on the other end of the line, I thought she'd caught on that my mind wasn't on the conversation. Then I heard the click of a lighter and the sound of Betty taking a drag on a cigarette. She wasn't a smoker, but she kept a pack of cigarettes in her purse. "For my nerves," she always said.

"Ethan and I—" Betty said, and I heard her exhale, "—are separated."

I pressed a hand against my forehead. "God, I'm sorry," I said. She hadn't said a thing about her marriage in the fall. But then, why would she? There was only one answer a priest could give in that situation, and people tended not to talk to me unless they wanted to hear it.

"Maybe we should have coffee," I said, studying the calendar of holy days Mom had thumbtacked to the wall above the phone. Epiphany, Ascension, Pentecost, Assumption. . . .

"Just what I need," Betty snapped, "to talk to another god-damned priest."

My head jerked back a little at the profanity. "Betty——" I said.

"I'm ending my marriage, and I don't need your pity." She took a deep breath. "Look, I'll see you at the wedding.". Her voice softened. "I've never seen you say Mass."

"That'll be nice," I said. The anticipation of saying Mass filled me, again and as always, with a sense of light and air. Then I said good-bye, hung up the phone, and put my fist into the wall, which hurt like hell and knocked a chunk of plaster loose. I moved the church calendar to cover the hole until I could repair it.

II

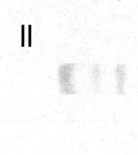

4

BETTY GARCÍA AND I GOT TOGETHER at a National Honor Society party during the autumn of my junior year of high school. Neither of us belonged there. A freshman, Betty had come to the party with an older cousin. I wouldn't be in the honor society until the end of the year, but I'd been invited by one of my friends from the track team. Nick lived on Summit Avenue and hung with a group of kids who looked like they'd just walked off a tennis court.

Before the party, I pulled on a striped, V-neck sweater and parted my hair neatly with water. Then I went downstairs to get my letter jacket off the coat tree. The old man and Jacky were sitting on the couch watching football, Minnesota at Illinois.

"Joe College," the old man said. He nudged Jacky. "Where's Joe College going?"

"Some party on Summit," Jacky said. "Hey Jimmy, you got real purty hair."

The old man grinned and pointed at me with a beer can. "They'll arrest you down there, boy. Bring us home some silverware."

Nick lived in a Tudor near the College of Saint Thomas, where Summit ran on either side of a wide median shaded by cotton-woods in the summer. Mr. Hawthorne answered the door. He had a golfer's tanned face, a flat belly, and wore a forest green sweater with embroidered autumn leaves drifting across the front. "Straight back," he said. "Can I take your coat?" I shook my head, mumbled, "No thanks." My footsteps felt wealthy, sinking into thick off-white carpeting.

The party was in the library, which jutted from the back of the house. The room was reflected in tall, many-paned windows, and the deepening dusk outside made it seem all the more bright. A couple dozen kids were scattered on leather sofas and ottomans, talking and toying with swizzle sticks, heads and drinks cocked at careful angles. Mickie Malone tossed her red hair and laughed.

"Hey, James." Nick left a circle of people by the fireplace. "Take off your coat and stay awhile. Didn't my dad let you in?" I left my jacket on and got a beer, then sat on the edge of a group of seniors who were talking about college visits and scholarship offers. I didn't know to be interested in that stuff yet, so I watched Mitzi Barnard, who had makeup you didn't notice until you looked at her for a while and a cashmere sweater that hugged her breasts in a way that made it clear no boy was worthy of them. When the talk turned to Homecoming dinners and the food at a new place on Nicollet Island, I got up to thumb through albums by the stereo: *Rocket to Russia. London Calling. My Aim Is True.* I didn't recognize any of them. A thin-shouldered, pinch-faced young man in nerd glasses stared at me from the last album cover. I had the quick urge to punch him.

Nearby, a Mexican girl in jeans and a maroon cowl-neck sweater stood looking up at the bookshelves. She wore her hair in a French braid, with silver hoops in her ears. I recognized Betty García, a freshman who'd been the team manager this fall when I ran cross-country. She felt me watching, glanced over and smiled, and looked back up at the books. I leaned against a set of Dickens. "Hi," I said.

"Hi, James." Her face was sharp, with a pointed chin and nose, intelligent eyes. Dark rouge highlighted her cheekbones. Her smile pulled at one corner of her mouth.

"Having a good time?" I asked.

She glanced around. "I don't know any of these people. My cousin Linda brought me and then took off with this guy she likes. My Uncle Hank's strict."

I looked out the windows. It was full dark outside. "You wanna take a walk?"

She studied me for a moment. "I could use a cigarette."

I got us beers and helped Betty into a navy-blue wool coat, short and belted to show the curve of her hips. We walked toward the river. When Betty stopped to light up, I handed her a beer. She took a swig and offered me her cigarette. I shook my head.

"I forgot," she said, "you're a jock. How come you don't play football?"

We were walking again, the cigarette tracing an orange arc between us in the dark. "My old man won't let me," I said. "He says he doesn't want me and Jacky getting busted up in a game we'll never take past high school."

"Jacky's in my class," Betty said. "He cracks me up."

My brother was a charmer, all right. He'd lost his virginity in the seventh grade with a high-school girl who lived with her baby in Frogtown. Jacky would go over to her apartment after school, and the old man would stop on his way home from work and drag Jacky out of there. He didn't mind the sex, but he didn't want Jacky getting killed walking out of Frogtown at night. What bothered my father—us maybe getting hurt playing football—and what didn't—Jacky getting laid regularly at thirteen—never made much sense. When Jacky and I left for parties, the old man would say from the couch: "See if you can get your brother's cherry popped tonight, Jackyboy." I would duck my head, and Jacky would grin and punch me in the shoulder as we walked out the door. "Everybody loves my brother," I said to Betty.

We passed the stone chapel near the corner of the Saint Paul Seminary, its Celtic cross rising against the starry sky, and stopped at the corner of Mississippi River Boulevard. The ground sloped to the river overlook, and the oak grove to our right rattled its dry leaves in the dark. In front of us, the granite pillar of the DAR World War I memorial ended in another cross; Father Phil always said that Saint Paul was a city of crosses and so we were never far from God. In the west, beyond the cross, the skyscrapers of downtown Minneapolis glittered.

We went to the overlook and sat on a bench. Betty talked about her family and her Uncle Hank, who was a labor lawyer, and told me that she was going to be a lawyer, too. Then she ground out her cigarette with the toe of her little black boot and said, "But I've been talking too much. What are you going to be?"

Father Phil had me thinking about the priesthood, but now was not the time. Instead, I told Betty about getting lost in the big public library downtown when I was a little kid. My German grandfather, Otto, had found me in the stacks, staring at the ceiling, trying to sound out the foreign names carved like maps into the beams: *Voltaire, Descartes, Galileo.* That Christmas, he bought me a set of World Books that was still on the shelf in my bedroom. I didn't tell Betty that I had one of the old man's *Playboys* hidden behind them now.

I kissed Betty. She drew away, then put her arms around my shoulders and kissed me back. Her breath was rough with beer, coppery with tobacco. The moon sunk huge and orange over the Minneapolis skyscrapers, and the skyline and the moon together made it feel as if I'd never seen either of them before. Betty drew her feet up on the bench and curled against my chest, and we kissed until the night air chilled us. Then we headed back to Nick's. What was left of the year's first snow lay in shards along sidewalks and in the lee of north-facing houses. It looked like whitecaps in the moonlight. Because it was clear that she liked smart boys, I told Betty about the stars as we walked, outlining for her Orion, which had just risen in the east and now was staggering, tilting north.

"He's drunk tonight," I said. Betty stopped and turned her face up to mine, and we kissed again. We were in front of one of the big houses on Summit now, and a woman, pausing at a window, watched us before drawing the curtains.

A week after Nick's party, I called Betty and asked her out.

"I can't date until I'm fifteen," she said. "But that's only three weeks. I'll see if you can come to my quinceañera." She paused. I could tell I was supposed to ask.

"What?"

"It's a Mexican debutante ball. There's Mass and dinner and a dance. Every night before my dad goes to the plant we practice waltzing, and I've been rehearsing my speech with Uncle Hank. I'll have all of my cousins and best friends, and a white dress and high-heeled shoes, and—oh, James, you don't want to hear me talk about all that." She paused again.

"The boy's going to a greaser hoedown," the old man said when Mom told him why I needed a suit. "Hey, don't look at me, I ain't prejudiced. Married your mom, didn't I, and her black Irish. 'Course, I didn't know that the first time I saw her walking down Selby, all blonde hair and hooters out to here." He raised his hands about a foot in front of his chest, shook them. "I thought I was bringing a good German girl home to my momma."

"With this skin and these eyes?" Mom touched her face, then shook her head, the corners of her eyes crinkling a bit. "I should've left that bottle of peroxide on the shelf at the drugstore."

"Can I have the suit?" I said. I'd heard all this before, but it meant the old man was in a good mood. If Mom hurried, we could buy the suit this afternoon, before the stores closed. Tonight Dad would be at his taverns, and tomorrow he might change his mind. Then Mom would light into him, and he would say he worked his ass off and wasn't a goddamned savings and loan, and in the end I'd never get a suit.

The old man leaned back on the couch, his gut lifting before him, and pulled out his money clip, the one with the buffalo nickel inset in the back. He snapped off several crisp bills—he always insisted on new bills when he cashed his paycheck—and smiled as he handed them to Mom. "Buy the boy a good suit. Can't have them fancy-pants greasers looking down their brown noses at him. Get it? Brown noses! Haw-haw." I went for my jacket.

The quinceañera Mass was at Our Lady of Guadalupe, the first time I'd been there. I felt conspicuous—blond, a head taller than most of the grown men in the pews. Across the aisle, a middle-aged man with a handlebar mustache and a thick turnip-shaped body caught my glance and stared back, a fleck of blood in the white of one eye. I busied myself with studying the church, the cinder-block rectangle with its clear windows so different from the arches and stained glass I'd grown up with. In the center of the altar where I expected to find Jesus there was a statue of Our Lady in a turquoise shawl with gold stars on her shoulders.

Mass started like a wedding, with a procession of young couples in black tuxedos and purple satin dresses, followed by Betty in white, carrying an armful of roses that she laid at the feet of the Virgin. The Mass itself was like any other until the sandy-haired Irish priest gave his homily, which was about Betty becoming a young woman. "In today's world, there are people, so-called feminists, who object to telling a young girl to 'act like a lady,'" he said. "But those people, out there, are mistaken. Ladies respect God's gift of modesty. . . ." He went on like that for a while, until I began to worry that Betty wouldn't want to make out with me again.

At the end of Mass, the priest led Betty by the elbow to the center of the altar, and she made a little speech, her chin in the air, her voice earnest and precise. "Standards are important," she recited, "but, if women have more opportunity to err in today's world, we also have more opportunity to lead, and we must make the most of it." Everyone applauded, led by the priest.

In the parish hall afterward, Betty hurried about, but she stopped long enough to introduce me to her parents. Her father was a short, barrel-chested older man with a broad grin—he'd started out as a line mechanic at the Ford plant, then been promoted to foreman, Betty had told me—and her mother was a tiny woman with quick, birdlike eyes and dyed-black hair. "I'm so pleased to meet you," Mrs. García said, glancing around my shoulder, then pulling Betty away to greet an aunt from Texas.

Mr. García shook my hand, then introduced me to a big man who had come up beside him: Hank, the labor lawyer. Hank was huge for a Mexican—well over six feet and pushing three hundred pounds, I guessed. He had a big belly, but the vest of his three-piece suit was cut to hide it. The suit's charcoal-colored wool shone, and under it Hank wore a gray button-down shirt with a pink silk tie done up in a fancy knot. A matching handkerchief pointed out of his coat's breast pocket. I caught myself staring, but it wasn't at his size or the clothes—I knew him from somewhere. Then I remembered: he umpired American Legion baseball. My family had had trouble with him, of course. With Dad in the stands and Jacky on the field, we had trouble with most umpires. Hank looked down at me, recognition dawning. He didn't offer his hand. "You're the quiet one," he said.

Mr. García told Hank I was a starter at shooting guard for Central and asked whether the team would be any good this year.

"We'll win some games," I said.

"You're starting," Hank said, "so it won't be five niggers on the court for a change."

"No sir," I said, surprised to hear a Mexican using that word.

"Fucking Roberto Duran," Hank said. There was liquor on his breath. "Letting that pussy Sugar Ray beat him. '*No mas!*' Worst thing to happen to Panama since United Fruit."

"Sugar Ray was tearing him up, sir," I said. Dad had taken Jacky and me to a closed-circuit showing of the fight at the civic auditorium.

"The hell he was," Hank said.

Mr. García laughed. "Duran didn't know whether to shit or go blind, Hank. You said it yourself."

"He shouldn't have quit," I said, trying to ease things. The old man had been livid when Duran threw in the towel.

"The hell you know about quitting?" Hank said.

Mr. García grabbed his elbow and steered him away. "Hey Hank," he said, then looked back over his shoulder. "You enjoy yourself tonight, James."

"Thank you, sir," I said. At dinner, seated with several of Betty's cousins who were around my age, I imagined kicking Hank in the knees—the best way to take a big man down, the old man always said—or maybe just telling him he was a lousy umpire. The cousins were talking about Leonard-Duran, too; it seemed like every Mexican in Saint Paul was pissed at Duran for letting a black man beat him.

Dessert was cut from an ornate white cake topped with a Mexican doll in a little dress that matched Betty's. I was eating the icing off my piece when the band struck up. Betty walked out onto the dance floor in front of the head table, and one of her attendants brought her a chair. *"Es tiempo de vivir,"* the band's singer wept while Betty's parents came out together, her mother carrying a pair of white high heels on a satin pillow. I sat up, noticed Hank watching me from a nearby table, and shifted my back to him. Betty had on flats, and her father knelt and removed them, then fitted a white pump onto the curve of her foot.

Betty pointed the other foot, and I saw that her toenails were painted bright red under her hose. I glanced at Hank, but he was watching Betty.

She stood, twirled into her father's arms. The song ended, and the band shifted to a slow waltz. Betty danced with her father, her feet moving quickly and expertly in the new heels. The tempo picked up, and a slim, handsome Mexican boy cut in. I watched the familiar way she moved with him, the ease with which he held her, and felt vaguely jealous but told myself I was glad not to be at the center of attention. Betty danced with boys in tuxedos, uncles in suits. She was tiny in huge Hank's arms, and his face was the face of a father as they danced and talked. At last she stood in front of me, flushed with excitement and exertion. "Dance with me?"

We turned about the floor. "Having a good time?" she asked.

"Sure," I said. Her perfume wafted around us. She had dusky powder over her cheekbones, and red lips and nails. A gold cross with a diamond in the center that she'd been given at Mass hung in her cleavage, and I could feel the boning of a long brassiere under my hand at her waist. I imagined Betty dressing with her cousins: a cramped changing room in the basement of the church, crowded with bawdy black-haired girls. I imagined undoing Betty, laying her down on a big bed somewhere, all of those fancy clothes strewn about us.

"James?" Betty's face was close to mine, and the grown-woman smell of perfume and powder mixed with sweat made the pulse pound in my temples. "A penny for your thoughts."

"You and that first guy danced really good together."

She rolled her eyes. "We practiced. Ramón's as boring as they come." We neared Hank's table; he sat flat-eyed, watching.

"Come meet my favorite uncle," Betty said, pulling me off the dance floor before I could tell her that I already had. She went on:

"Hank's the only one in the family who doesn't expect me to get married right after high school."

Hank stood. "That's right," he said.

I stuck out my hand.

Hank took it, and I felt bones grind together. "Pleased to meet you, sir," I said.

Hank released my hand and turned to Betty. "And how did you two meet?"

"At that party of Nick's you had Linda take me to," Betty said.

Hank's eyebrows went up a little. "You a friend of Nick's?" he said to me.

"Yes sir," I said. "We run the medley relay. I'm a half-miler."

Hank nodded. "That baton pass is tricky," he said. "I threw the javelin myself. 'Course, I was thinner then." He touched Betty's shoulder. "You have a good time tonight, Bettina," he said. "Make sure to dance with everyone."

He bent down, and Betty reached up on her tiptoes to kiss him on the cheek, then led me back to the dance floor. "Isn't Uncle Hank wonderful?" she said. "He's my mom's little brother— though he's not so little—and he understands me. He made Father Shannon give him that homily and helped me write my speech to go with it."

"That's great," I said. The song was already ending.

"Hank's right, I've got to dance with everyone," Betty said. "But there's a party after at my cousin's. We can be together there."

The party was a few blocks from the church, on one of the steep side streets that climbed toward the high ground west of Concord. I found a space on the sloping parked-up street, set the emergency brake, and followed a group of young people up to a small two-story house. Mexican men in jackets stood on the porch smoking and drinking, and light and shadows and conversation spilled from the doors and windows of the house onto the snow. I slipped into the living room and found wall-to-wall people. Betty had already changed into jeans and a flannel shirt, and her cousins were teasing her about being a tomboy. Someone handed me a can of beer, and someone else told me to throw my coat in the bedroom. Betty got busy, and I talked to people I'd met at the dance. I felt at home. Betty's cousins drank beer and laughed a lot, and I ended up sitting on the kitchen counter talking sports with a couple of them while people bustled in and out getting more beer and bags of chips.

From the counter I could see an angle of the front hall, and as the kitchen talk turned to that afternoon's installment of *ABC's Wide World of Sports*, I saw Betty walk Ramón, the tall boy she'd danced with first, to the front door. He hadn't changed clothes, and at the party he'd seemed stiff and bored in his dress shirt and slacks. He had on a long camel-colored coat, and I watched him with Betty at the door, the two of them alone in an eddy of the party. She said something, and he crooked a forefinger under her chin and tilted her face up and kissed her. I felt a flash of angry confusion. The kiss lasted a long moment, then Betty shook her head. She rested her hand on Ramón's chest, red nails showing against the camel-colored wool, and talked animatedly, looking up into his face while he nodded at what she said. Then he let himself out, and before Betty turned around I shifted my attention back to her cousins.

"So, who's this friend of Betty's, this Ramón?" I asked when I got the chance.

They looked at each other, and one snorted. "Fuck," he said. "Ramón. He's high. He goes to the University of Chicago."

Later, once the party thinned out a bit, we all danced to the Stones in the living room. The floor shook and the dancers jostled one another and during slow songs Betty danced close to me.

When most of the adults had gone, she took my hand and led me down to the basement rec room and a couch by the pool table. She put Fleetwood Mac's *Rumours* on the stereo, then climbed onto my lap, straddling me while we kissed to the funky beat and bluesy vocals of "Second Hand News." Betty's long hair shadowed us both, her mouth was quick and eager, and the rec room was warm and lit by the stereo panel. Above us, joists creaked. A few people were still upstairs, moving around and talking. They seemed far away. Betty and I shifted against each other, and I untucked her shirt and touched the soft skin where her hips curved into her waist. When I pushed her bra up off her breasts, Betty made a small noise. Her nipples were erect under my thumbs. But a few minutes later, when I started fumbling with the button on her jeans, she put a hand over mine. "That's enough," she said. She stood, pulled the bra back into place, and tucked in her shirt. "Let's play pool."

"What the hell?" I said. I liked pool, but not at two in the morning with a girl I'd had on the couch a minute ago. I took a deep breath.

"Don't you like me on my feet?" Betty said. There was a quick edge to her voice.

"You're beautiful anywhere," I said. I planned to skunk her and get her back on the couch. The old man had taught me the game at the Half Time Rec, when I could barely reach the table. But Betty's cousins heard the clack of pool balls and came down, and Betty played with one side of her face screwed up, her tongue poking out of the corner of her mouth. She beat me two games out of three.

"Damn, girl," I said, as I put our cues back into the rack on the wall.

She tossed a cube of chalk and caught it. "I don't like to lose."

I left Betty's cousins' house so late it was early, my head full of Betty's scent and her skin and lips. It had gotten colder, and walking downhill to Mom's Plymouth I shivered in my overcoat and slacks. My dress shoes slipped on the pavement. The street was quiet, and there were pickup trucks in the yards of the small houses. Across Concord Street I could see the lights of Holman Field and out beyond that the black curve of the river.

After the quinceañera, Betty's parents let us start seeing each other. They were already in their fifties—she was a late child— and their West Seventh bungalow was a very traditional Mexican home, every surface crowded with family photos and knickknacks and colorful plaster saints. There was a shrine to Our Lady of Guadalupe, the same turquoise shawl and gold stars on her shoulders. There was a shrine to Betty's oldest brother, a Marine killed in the street fighting at Hue during the Tet Offensive. Betty was two when Gabriel died, but she claimed a memory of him: a man in a green uniform drinking beer with her father at the kitchen table. She had toddled in and sat at his feet, playing with the laces on his shiny black boots until her father swept her into his lap. Many of the photos on the living and dining room walls were black-and-whites of young Mexican men in US military uniforms dating back to World War II. "What a lousy way to be a part of this country," Betty said. "I'll work for my people like Hank does." There were pictures, too, of Betty's aunts and uncles when they were younger, including Hank in a Central High football jersey. He'd played tight end and been the hope of his family, and his eyes held the arrogance and fear of a young man expected to go places.

The centerpiece of one wall was a pair of framed prints of Jesus and Mary, heads tilted toward one another, chins and eyes upcast, intricate sacred hearts exposed on their chests. Betty and I stood looking at those prints one night after a date. Her father was working the night shift at Ford, and her mother had fed us

Mexican sweet bread and coffee, told us to be careful, and gone to bed.

"Jesus," I said.

"What?" Betty stood in front of me, resting against my chest. I had my arms around her shoulders.

"We had statues like that in the hallways in grade school," I said. "In first grade, I thought holy people had their hearts outside their bodies, like dead animals in the street."

Betty stiffened. "I think they're beautiful," she said. "I love the little cross on top, and the way the roses loop around. I used to imagine my heart that way, a home for my soul."

"I used to want to be a priest," I said.

"Why?"

"Sex used to scare me." That was true, and easier than talking about my family.

Betty twisted in my arms. "It still scare you?"

"Nope," I said.

"Me either." We started kissing and lurched a little into the sideboard, and all of the holy medals and candleholders and china saints rattled.

I'd dated some before Betty, but she was edgier than any girl I'd been with, and I found it alarming and attractive. For a month that winter, sidelined from basketball with a badly sprained ankle, I'd go to her house after school. Betty's parents both worked and her dad had moved to the swing shift, so between his leaving and Betty's mother coming home, we could squeeze in a couple hours of heaven on the living-room couch. Naked except for a taped ankle, I jumped whenever a car drove past, but Betty, the mechanic's daughter, laughed at me, swearing she could recognize the sound of her mom's car turning off of West Seventh a block away. That winter I was driving a 1960s Dodge van the old man had bought with the never-realized idea of going into business for himself as a handyman. Betty and I would make out until just before her mom was due home. Then I'd run out to the van and, still tingling from the warmth of Betty's naked breasts against my chest, try to get the damned thing to start. It was even money it wouldn't, and I'd flip up the cover of the engine compartment that sat between the driver's and passenger's seats, unscrew the air filter and prime the carburetor from a gas can I kept behind the seat, then jiggle the wiring harness on the back panel of the compartment, all with shaking hands. The slant-six engine would finally turn over, and as I backed out of the drive, always expecting to see Betty's mother pulling in behind me, I'd wave at Betty, watching out the lace sheers of the front window with a comforter clutched around her shoulders.

One snowy February day, after we'd done all we would let ourselves do, we dressed and sat in the breakfast nook in the kitchen. It overlooked the backyard, where the ground underneath Mrs. García's bird feeder always attracted a big flock of pigeons to feed on the sunflower seeds spilled by cardinals and chickadees. We were talking, holding hands across the table, when suddenly the pigeons lifted into the air as one and wheeled low over the chainlink fence at the edge of the yard. There was a *whump!* of brown feathers, and a hawk sat in the foot-deep snow, the pointed tip of a pigeon wing sticking out from beneath it. The hawk squatted for a while with glazed eyes, slowly shifting its legs like a man trying to keep his feet warm, then it hopped up onto the crust of the snow and began tearing at the pigeon, its hooked beak occasionally lifting the body half out of the hollow it had driven into the snow. After a few minutes, the snow and the hawk's brown-barred white chest were speckled with red, and feathers and bits of fluff blew about in the dusk. Betty moved over beside me. I put my arm around her, but she was absorbed by the scene in the yard. When a whorl of gray down that radiated from a crimson center floated up and settled on the hawk's back, she stood and busied herself putting her hair into a ponytail. "Fucking pigeons," she said.

"I love you," I said, and carried her back to the sofa.

We dated all that school year, and by summer we were fighting about birth control: I wanted to use the rhythm method, while Betty called that Vatican roulette and insisted on rubbers. Whatever I'd said, sex still scared me. In junior high, a couple of heavyset, middle-aged women from Birthright had visited our classroom, armed with films that proved birth control was both a sin and unreliable and that premarital sex led directly to the murder of unborn children. Our school nuns told us sexuality was a gift from God for married couples. As we prepared for Confirmation they told us boys the Holy Spirit would make us soldiers of God, that if we were disciplined and strong, we'd be worthy of a girl dressed in blue and pure as the Virgin Mary. At the end of eighth grade, I had watched Susan Reading, the nuns' favorite, crowned at a school Mass celebrating Mary, the Queen of May. Susan stood on the altar in a long, butter-yellow dress with a garland of daisies in her hair, and I dreamed that night of a virgin bride. Now, I worried that intercourse with Betty would leave her soiled in my eyes. But I couldn't tell her that, and so we argued.

Since grade school, I'd worked every other Saturday morning answering the phone in the rectory office, and sometimes Father Phil would stop in—back from an early-morning trip to the lake in a fishing hat and vest, or with a handful of papers for me to file, or with a parishioner in tow—and talk to me about the priesthood. We were friends, sort of: I'd served Mass for him since grade school, and back then we'd talked about the priesthood afterward while he hung his vestments and I sealed the plastic baggie of unconsecrated Hosts and carefully rinsed the chalice and cruets and made sure the markers were in place for the readings at noon Mass. Phil was the sort of priest a boy from a family like mine could imagine becoming. He was a short, round man with jug ears and a whiskeyed face, and if he pulled you aside about something he meant business. His priesthood was the priesthood of the men's club: he'd been a chaplain in Korea and drank at the VFW with other veterans, he bowled in the Veterans Administration league with my grandfather, and he fished and tied his own flies with fingers that were thick and calloused and surprisingly nimble. When I told him I was afraid I didn't think about God enough to be a priest, he waved a hand. "Priests don't think about God any more than your average Joe," he said. "Being a parish priest is about doing God's work. You can leave contemplation of the Almighty to the monks at Saint John's."

Because of Phil, I was part of the parish youth group. We visited nursing homes and the VA hospital, where Granddad had just retired as a veterans benefits counselor, and where he still took me for an occasional lunch and to buy dress shirts at a discount in the hospital canteen from his friend Jack Crow. Once a month I lectored at Mass and afterward drove around with a lay minister, bringing Communion to shut-ins.

Late one Saturday afternoon I went to confession. Father Phil had met Betty, and I was sure he knew my voice and shadow in the confessional just as well as I knew the smell of his heavy aftershave and the curve of his big nose through the carved wooden screen. When my eyes adjusted, I could make out his bald head and the fringe of gray hair, but he kept to the fiction of anonymity. After I'd made my confession, I saw him rub at one eyebrow with a knuckle. Then he spoke in a low voice: "When a young woman loves a young man, she wants to show her love. And then it's up to the man to be strong for both of them. Remember, if you're seen leaving her house at all hours, it's her reputation that'll suffer. It would be best if you dated around, but I suppose you won't do that. Sometimes exercise helps." He paused, maybe embarrassed at the tumble of advice he'd given, and then finished with "Say three Our Fathers, go to Mass every morning this month, and come back in two weeks."

I said my penance and went to Mass and prayed for strength, but when I was with Betty, sin and reputation and the future paled again and again before the immediacy of her body, our desire. Then on Saturday mornings, warm with the memory of how the night before Betty had drawn in her stomach as I slid my hand down the front of her jeans, I would file papers while Phil talked to me about the priesthood and answer him by asking if he'd caught any fish that morning, or how he thought the grade-school football team would do in the CYO league next fall.

In July, Betty went on a long car trip with her parents to visit her father's family in Pueblo, Colorado, the Texas panhandle, and Topeka, Kansas. She sent postcards of mountains, cactus, the world's longest grain elevator. This last, from Kansas, said: *I love you. I miss you. I hate Kansas, but I'm getting tan.* That Saturday at the rectory, I found myself avoiding Father Phil. The next evening, when Betty came home, we drove slowly down Summit, hanging our elbows out the windows of the Plymouth, looking at the rich people's houses and remembering the night we'd gotten together. Betty picked out a favorite house on each block.

At the end of Summit, I parked in the overlook lot. We took a blanket from the trunk and walked a block south, to where a wooded ravine cut through the bluff down to the Mississippi. As soon as we stepped from the sidewalk into the woods, we were in a new world: a green chaos of trees, the trickle of water over a mossy stone lip and its insistent spatter on rock, a steep path slick with clay and stone. Halfway down we were breathing hard, knuckles caked with clay where we'd slipped and caught ourselves, the occasional hum of a car on Mississippi River Boulevard a distant reminder of a place we'd left.

"Bet no one's down here tonight," Betty said. There was a patch of sand beach at the bottom of the ravine, a hollow in the bulge of the bluff with the ashes of a bonfire in front of it, charred driftwood and beer cans, a half-buried wine bottle. Kids came down here to party and scratch their names into the soft sandstone, but Betty was right: we had it to ourselves. We spread the blanket in the hollow and sat looking out on the river. The trees on the Minneapolis bank were thick and unbroken. In the channel, a buoy tilted with the current. It was a dry summer, and the water was low, and you could see the gravel shelving out under the ripples for a long way. The shadows of minnows flickered over the gravel. Betty and I hadn't seen each other for three weeks, and we sat there feeling the summer heat coming off our bodies. Betty's brown limbs were lean and dark in the night. I reached for her, and we rolled together on the blanket, pushing off each other's clothes. She'd tanned in a bikini every day of the trip, leaving white triangles over her breasts and belly.

The rumble of a jet rising from the airport broke the still sounds of our breathing and the river. Betty reached across me and fumbled for her cutoffs. "I found rubbers in the room my uncle from Colorado stays in when he visits *Abuelita.*"

"They only work half the time," I said.

"Bullshit," Betty said. "Those numbers they gave us in Catholic school are propaganda. Ramón didn't mind—" She stopped and stared at me, and I felt the way I had when, drunk after a skating party that winter, she'd dared me into racing across an unfamiliar lake in the dark. I remembered the slice of our skates, the way the wind forced tears from our eyes as we squinted ahead for the blackness that would be open water, the feeling of uncontrolled speed.

"You and Ramón?" Swallows darted over the river from the cliff face behind us.

Betty shrugged one shoulder. "We hung out last summer. His family has a lake house, and me and his sister went there weekends to tan and water-ski."

"I thought he was boring."

"He is. But he can ski."

"And fuck?"

"So? I wanted to try it. It wasn't that big a deal."

"It must have been quite a summer."

"It was." Betty in this mood could not be shamed. She tore open the wrapper, wiggled the milky latex circle at me.

I took it. I wanted this summer to be even better.

5

THAT WINTER, BETTY STAYED SATURDAY NIGHTS with her grandmother on the West Side. We weren't supposed to see each other those nights, but I would cross the river about ten, and Betty and I would crawl into the backseat of Mom's car with a blanket from the trunk, fumbling under heavy winter clothes until after midnight, the lovemaking better for the cramped quarters and the cold. Then her grandmother, worried by our late nights in the car, told her we could go upstairs, but to be careful.

Abuelita came from a different world, from turn-of-the-century Mexico. She had still been a little girl when revolution drove her family from its ranch; Betty told me her grandmother remembered lanterns, wagons, and muffled voices, carefully packed heirlooms that were stolen at the border. In America, in reduced circumstances, she married at sixteen and had a dozen children. She never learned English, living entirely in the Spanish-speaking world of Saint Paul's Lower West Side, doing all of her shopping on Concord Street. When she talked with Betty at her kitchen table before bed, she included me by occasionally wagging a finger in my direction and laughing. The staircase in her house was tall and narrow, and she slept in the front room downstairs.

Upstairs, Betty and I made love. Sometimes we dozed afterward—I had no set time to be home—and sometimes I would wake and sit by the lace-curtained window, parting the curtains slightly to look out over the chain-link fences and alleyways of the snowy neighborhood, where Christmas lights were left up until March for the cheer they brought in the long winter, red and green and blue against the snow.

Saint Paul white nights. A foot of snow on the ground, a blanket of low clouds, the world between bathed in milky light. Nights bright enough for trees to throw shadows. The snow on garage roofs lay in long folds arranged by the wind. On the houses, bare shingles marked thin spots in the insulation. There was a gray fox hunting the backyards of the West Side that winter, taking cats and rabbits; the neighbors said that it had likely come into town along the river. I spotted it from the bedroom window one night, flowing over a low fence like a ghost that left footprints in the fresh snow. Behind me, Betty lay under the quilt, hair spread about her face. All was still save for the metallic tapping of a radiator and the wind that made itself known more as a rising and falling pressure in the ears than a sound. The house breathed slow and deep, drafts moving about the window sashes and frames; cold from the window glass washed my face, rested a chill hand on my chest. Betty snored lightly. I tipped the chair against the radiator and, with a teenager's false nostalgia, dreamed warm dreams of someday buying this house for Betty, of our children in the sunlit backyard struggling to do pull-ups on the clothesline poles or running to show us four-leaf clovers they'd found.

That basketball season Central won the city-league title and I split playing time between guard and small forward. Hank came to every game. He and I played one-on-one occasionally in Betty's parents' driveway, Hank playing dad-ball, using his butt to back me up under the basket and his height to shoot and catch rebounds until the ball went in. He was quick for a big man, cutting the angles on the court, blocking me from the basket, and I always lost to him.

He threw a party for Betty and me after Central's season ended. It was the first time I'd been at his house. He lived in a rambling one-story rancher on Mississippi River Boulevard, above Hidden Falls Park. The wide picture window in his living room looked out over a long, sloping, winter-browned lawn to the Mississippi River gorge and the old stone of Fort Snelling. The party was a kegger, and Hank pretty much stayed out of the way after making sure we knew not to bother the neighbors. Hank's daughter Tina flirted with me all night. She wasn't as smart as Betty, but she favored lots of makeup and low-cut shirts with push-up bras, and she was pretty hard to ignore. Around midnight, Betty tired of this and pulled me outside for a talk. I protested that I'd done my best to stay away from Tina, and Betty and I ended up in my car. We were making love when someone knocked on the fogged-up driver's side window. "Go away," I said. The knock came again louder, the heavy thuds of the meaty side of a man's fist. I cracked the window.

"Get out," Hank said.

We scurried into our clothes, and Betty followed me from the backseat, smoothing the front of her shirt.

"Inside," Hank said to Betty. She was spending the night with Tina.

"Uncle Hank——" she said, holding on to my arm.

"I just want to talk to him," Hank said. "You go inside now."

After Betty left, Hank reached into the backseat and picked up the wine bottle nested in the blanket there. He sniffed it, frowned, and took a sip. "Jesus, kid," he said. "My niece should be drinking better."

I laughed weakly. Hank leaned on the car, scratched his neck. "I have a dozen brothers and sisters in this town," he said. "Cousins. In-laws. Last family reunion, we had over three hundred people. So I move to Wonder Bread Highland Park for the room and the view"—his hand swept out, taking in the darkness of the gorge, the lights at the fort—"and, of course, I've got people coming and going all the time. Then I introduce myself to one of my new neighbors, and the first thing he says is: 'So how many families are living in that house, anyway?' Beautiful autumn day, sky so blue you could fall into it forever, and I stand there thinking about using his head for a posthole digger. But that's what they'd expect, see? I always tell my kids: You have to dress better than the *gringos,* or they'll call you a dirty Mexican. You have to be smarter, more polite. So I smile with my big white teeth, and I say, 'I'm blessed with ten fine children.' The next weekend, I invite him over for barbecue."

"That's some story," I said, not quite following.

"I'm not done." Hank leaned his face down into mine. "The point is, I don't need you in a parked car in front of my house with my niece after I've thrown a party for you." He brought his big hand up and slapped me on the cheek, just hard enough to sting. "Understand?"

"Yes sir," I said. "I'm sorry, sir."

Hank nodded slowly. "I believe you are." He poured the rest of the wine out onto the street. "Go on home now. And don't get stopped."

He lumbered up his long drive, whistling and flipping the wine bottle in the air. I leaned my head back on the roof of the car. High clouds brushed the stars. It was a soft winter night with the smell of stirring soil in the air that tells you spring's coming.

A month later, Betty told me she was pregnant. We were alone at her parents' house on a day off from school that we'd looked forward to as a chance to make love in her bed. Thin spring sunlight filled the house, and when I went to use the bathroom I glanced into Betty's room at the high cottage bed with its white eyelet comforter and frilled pillows and stuffed animals, and I was angry that we could not be entwined in all that light and warmth. Instead, we sat in the breakfast nook at the back of the kitchen talking in circles, always coming back to the one fact that wouldn't change.

After a while, we went into the living room and argued on the couch. Betty said something about "looking into options" that I wouldn't hear. Before her parents came home from work, she kissed me good-bye at the front door, a distant embrace.

The rest of the week we talked around the pregnancy on the phone. Betty cried quietly, and I paced the length of the cord, brought up short in every direction. I was useless in school, distracted at track. There'd been an April snowstorm, but the team practiced despite the weather, our thighs aching from the effort of running in snow, lungs burning from the cold. I threw up one night after practice, retching on all fours beside a shrunken, exhaust-blackened drift of snow near my car on Marshall Avenue while my friends laughed and lobbed snowballs at me. None of them knew that my life, which had just opened up with baseball and history scholarships to the College of Saint Thomas, was constricting around Betty's womb. Finally, on Saturday morning, listening for Mom's step on the stairs, I called Birthright and talked urgently in a low voice. The volunteer told me that my girlfriend needed to call, that we would want to come in. She said I was doing the right thing, sticking by my girlfriend and our baby. God had a plan He would reveal to us in time.

That night, in the car on the way to a Mexican wedding dance at the state fairgrounds, I told Betty about Birthright—that I was ready to do the honorable thing.

"I am not going to those people." Betty bit off the words, and I felt her close into herself on the other side of the car, saw her small, thin hand tighten on the door handle, as if she meant to leap from the car at the next stoplight.

We danced all evening, clinging to each other during the slow ones without talking. After the last set, we sat alone at the corner of a long table, drinking warm beer out of plastic cups. The band was packing up. A few scattered groups of people remained in the hall, talking in low, end-of-the-evening voices. We were soaked with sweat, and the emptying hall was suddenly cold.

Hank wandered by, looking for his coat. His pinstriped vest was open, his tie loosened, and sweat stained the chest and armpits of his burgundy button-down shirt. "You two still here?" he said. But when he saw our faces, he swung his leg over a chair and sat down on it backwards, arms crossed on the metal backrest. "What's going on?"

"I'm pregnant," Betty said.

"Jesus," I said, "that made it real."

Hank gave me a hard look, then turned on Betty. "Goddamn, I thought you were smarter than this."

"Hank." Betty's voice was pleading in a way I'd never heard.

"My sister didn't raise you to act like a whore," Hank said.

Betty's head jerked back, and I started to my feet. "How many kids did you mean to have?" I snapped at Hank.

He faced me full on and half rose himself, his face dark with anger. "Sit down," he said. "I'm gonna forget you said that."

Betty began crying, twisting her purse strap. "Please, James—"

I forced myself to sit. "Look, I'm graduating." I said, suddenly desperate to fix things for them both. "My old man'll get me a union job."

Hank ignored me. "What are you going to do?" he said to Betty. "Look at me."

The lenses of her glasses were splashed with tears. "I want to be a lawyer."

"I'll put you through law school," I said quickly. Neither of them heard.

"I'll tell you what you do," Hank said. "You get an abortion. I'll pay."

"I've got the money," I said. I didn't want Betty getting an abortion.

"My niece's honor is out of your hands." Hank flicked me a glance, then said to Betty, "This is one helluva thing you've gotten yourself into."

I tried again to argue that I could support Betty and a baby, but my words trailed off under Hank's cold gaze. Betty stared at her hands in her lap.

"Maybe we should talk to a priest," I said, playing my last card.

Hank laughed aloud at that. "Like who? Father Shannon?"

"Father Phil," I said. "He's been friends with my family for years."

Hank rested a hand on his thigh and squinted at me in a way that made my stupidity clear. "And what's he gonna do?" he asked. "Last I heard, there aren't any special dispensations to end a pregnancy."

Beside Hank, Betty started to say something, then shook her head. "Please," she said. "I can't stand to think about it anymore tonight."

In the end, Hank walked with us out to Mom's Plymouth. There were only a few vehicles left in the lot. It was a blustery Minnesota spring night, a wind from Canada spitting snow, and we all stood there shivering and rubbing our arms. "You make a decision, Betty," Hank said. "Fast. Or this time next year there won't be any dances." Betty nodded, face pale around her red lipstick in the glare of the streetlight. At that moment, I hated the stickiness of her lips, the way women packaged their sexuality and used it. Hank put a hand on my shoulder. "I respect what you're going through, son."

I jerked away from him.

It started to sleet; ice crystals flickered in the streetlamp's halo. Hank left us and walked across the lot to his truck, hunched and stumbling into the weather.

It was then that I went to my mother, telling her about Betty at the kitchen table one morning when no one else was home. She took the news without blinking.

"Her uncle's right, honey," Mom said.

"I thought you liked her." I had expected to set a plan in motion, something that would be fittingly hard—like Betty and I living here with the baby while I worked two jobs to support them and put her through school, a penance that would allow me to step up and be a man, to be strong for both of us. Mom's matter-of-fact answer made all my plans into an adolescent wish, like Jacky thinking his first car would be the burnt-orange Corvette on the showroom floor of the Midway Chevy dealership. Mom liked Betty. I remembered my parents taking us to a football game at Hamline the past fall and after the game all of us leaving the little stadium and walking home through the leaf-bright neighborhoods, how Betty had walked ahead with the old man, chatting away because he didn't scare her at all, her long blue-black hair shimmering against the back of her jean jacket, and the deep autumn blue of the sky, and how Mom, walking beside me, had taken my arm for a moment and said, "She's a keeper."

"I thought you liked Betty," I said again when Mom didn't answer.

"It has nothing to do with that," Mom said.

"But Dad was only a year older when you—"

"You're different than your father." Mom picked up a deck of cards from the table, squared them absently in one hand. "It doesn't make you better or worse, but this isn't right for you two."

"I can," I said. "I could." At my age, the old man had made a family work. Maybe it wasn't a perfect family, but he'd done what he needed to do, supported a wife and three kids.

Mom drew on her cigarette, looked out the window. "If I had it to do over—" She stopped and shook her head, her voice and eyes gone elsewhere.

"Anne?" I'd known for years that my parents had to get married, but that they'd considered other options back in 1962 had never crossed my mind.

"She wasn't Anne then."

"Oh." I felt as if there wasn't enough air in the room and gripped the table, spots dancing before my eyes. It was my first adult knowledge of just how bad my parents' marriage might be. "Oh," I said again.

The Monday after I graduated from high school, Hank and Betty and I met at Hank's cramped storefront office on Concord Street. HANK RAMIREZ, ATTORNEY-AT-LAW, the window proclaimed in big block capitals. And below: IMMIGRATION, NATURALIZATION, WORKMAN'S COMP. Inside, every surface was littered with legal papers with Hank's name at the top. There were metal shelves filled with law books that leaned against each other at different angles, and there were casebooks and three-ring binders stacked on top of filing cabinets and weighing down piles of loose paper. It was after five, and Hank closed the Venetian blinds and locked the door behind us. We sat around his desk, and he leaned forward and looked back and forth between Betty and me. His right hand drew boxes with a pen on a yellow legal pad.

"We have an appointment in Chicago Saturday morning," Hank said.

"Chicago?" I said.

"That's how it's done," Betty said.

"We won't run into anybody she knows," Hank said.

"I see." With the blinds closed, the only light came from Hank's green-shaded desk lamp. I frowned at the beaded light glancing off its gold pull chain.

"Something the matter?" Hank said.

"When do we leave?" I said. I wanted to reach for Betty's hand, but didn't.

"You're not going," Hank said.

Betty cast him a glance.

"I told your parents it was a cultural weekend." Hank spread his hands, then closed them. "Museums, the symphony, *A Chorus Line*. I didn't tell them he would be along."

"You didn't tell them lots of things," I said.

Hank rocked back in his upholstered desk chair and gazed at me. He folded his hands on his belly.

"What do you want?" I appealed to Betty.

She pressed her lips together. "Do what Hank says."

I sank down in my chair and regarded my tennis shoes. Part of me was relieved to be spared from this trip. But then I thought of Betty alone with a strange doctor under harsh white lights, his hands impersonal and calculating. I drew in a breath.

"It's settled then," Hank said. He stood and closed a law book that was open on his desk, shuffled a stack of papers.

Betty looked at me.

"If that's what you want," I said. My body suddenly felt untethered, as if I might rise to the tiled ceiling.

They left Thursday, and Hank's oldest daughter, Linda, went with them. For two nights, Linda and Betty heard Hank pace all night in the connecting room. Betty had the abortion Saturday morning. They came home Sunday. Betty called that evening to let me know she was home and that everything had gone well. She told me that Friday, Hank had taken them to the Field Museum.

"I can't believe you," I said.

"He was trying to keep my mind off things." Betty's voice snapped in my ear, brittle over the phone. "It wasn't like he was throwing me a birthday party."

"Bad choice of words," I said, regretting my own as soon as they were out of my mouth.

"Hunh." Betty sounded as if I'd slugged her in the gut.

Then she said, "You should've been with me. Hank said he understood, but I don't." There was a click on the other end of the line. I sat in a kitchen chair I'd pulled under the stairs by the phone, staring at the handset without seeing it, listening to the dial tone. Goddamn Hank—he'd gotten his way and still managed to make it my fault for not being there. I started to dial Betty's number, then I slammed the phone down and went up to my room.

I let a week pass before I called back. Betty's mother answered and told me that Betty had left town for the summer to work at a camp for inner-city kids that Hank helped organize up on the North Shore. "Didn't she tell you?" She offered me the camp number and promised to let Betty know I'd called. But the people at the camp said they couldn't find Betty, and when I tried her at home again toward the end of summer, Mrs. García was short with me, her voice tight. She knows, I thought: Betty told her. If that were true, the two of them would never tell Betty's father; it would be a secret kept between the women and Hank Ramirez.

In mid-August, Jacky and I were warming up before the last game of a weekend American Legion tournament when Jacky pointed down the third-base line. "Hey, ain't that that big Mexican umpire you know?"

Sure enough, Hank was lounging against the fence in his umpiring blues, watching us. We'd drawn him for the game. I started over, but he walked away quickly and joined a group of people standing around at the next diamond. I turned back to Jacky and shrugged. Jacky didn't know about Betty, just that we'd broken up. "What'd you expect?" Jacky said. "You dropped his niece. Those Mexicans are touchy about family." He threw me a rope and I caught it in the palm of my glove, stinging my hand. I pulled the hand out and shook it, and Jacky laughed.

In the top of the first, Hank, running down the line to cover a play at first, gave the call to the runner. I was pretty sure the ball had smacked my glove in time, but I'd had my eyes on the ball and not the runner's foot, so I kept my mouth shut. In the stands, the old man had a different opinion. "Horseshit call, Ump."

"Shut up, Dressler," someone in the crowd yelled.

I batted third in our half of the inning. "Hi, Hank," I said cheerfully, digging in, determined to draw a response. He stared as if he didn't know me. The first pitch was off the corner of the plate. "Strrr-ike!"

I glanced back to meet the same blank stare. "Eat me," I muttered, but low enough that Hank could ignore it.

On full count, Hank called me out on another ball, this one just below the knees.

I slung my bat against the chain-link fence in front of our bench. "Helluva strike zone, Blue."

Jacky, batting seventh, got the same treatment the next inning.

Every close call went against us. Jacky, not one to take things quietly, got ejected after a disputed steal in the sixth. All the while, the old man howled from the stands, raining obscenity and Bible verse in equal parts: "Vengeance is mine, saith the Lord! Blue, you blind fucker."

In the eighth, Hank bumped me when I got in his face after another called third strike. When I walked back to the dugout, I looked up and saw Dad's eyes had gone gray and worried.

After the game, Jacky and I were walking through the parking lot, caps pushed back on our foreheads, when we spotted the old man trundling along ahead of us on his way to the car. Then Hank stepped out from beside a van and said something to our father, who stopped short, swiveling his head, his shoulders and gut following. The old man looked small and misshapen next to Hank, and I sprinted across the lot, my spikes biting rutted dirt. "Hank," I yelled, but my father shoved me aside. "Stay out of it."

When my father looked at me, Hank swung from his blind side, a roundhouse that caught the old man in the ear and dropped him to one knee. Dad would have finished a man then, but Hank hesitated, and Dad drove to his feet, wrapped his arms around Hank's waist, and hung on. It took Hank a moment to wrestle loose, and by then my father had his legs back. They went at it, and I backed away, flinching at the sounds two big men make beating the hell out of each other. Other men came running and formed a loose ring, but no one stepped in and tried to stop it. A few of them probably wanted to see my father get his. And it looked like he might. Hank was a brawler, had worked as a meatpacker to put himself through law school, and the old man gave ground before his size and reach. "C'mon, Dad," Jacky pleaded beside me. But I was silent, watching like I'd been taught with boxing, and I saw that my father ducked and wove like a fox, his head tucked down between his big shoulders, and that none of Hank's blows was hurting him. When Hank tried to wrestle, my father hit him and slipped away. I knew then how it would end, and I left the circle of men and walked down the parking lot toward our car.

I was almost there when I heard Hank call out in Spanish. I looked back. The old man had got him on the ground and was kicking him, and Hank was trying to crawl under his own truck to get away from my father. I made myself watch. My father stepped in with short vicious kicks, his full weight behind them, until a bunch of the other fathers closed in and pulled him off. The men gathered in a knot about my father, then he was pushed into the open, stumbling and half running to catch his balance. He started back toward a half-dozen men, then thought better of it. "Fuck all of you," I heard him yell, and he came striding down the parking lot, arms swinging like hawsers, Jacky running to keep up. Far away, I could see Hank face down on the ground, one hand clutching at the step of his pickup. My stomach rose, and I steadied myself against the trunk of our car. My father stopped in front of me. "Why didn't you stand by me, son?"

I shrugged.

Dad glanced back to where the other men bent over Hank. "You know that big spic?"

"Fuck you," I said.

He backhanded me across the face. "There's for you."

I shook it off and went and climbed into the backseat of the car. Jacky followed, slipping into the front, turning with his elbow on top of the seat. "You okay, Jimmy?" Outside the old man was kicking in his own fender. Finally, he got into the driver's seat. He stared straight ahead while he started the car. "I'm a hothead," he said. "There's no percentage messing with me."

Dad drove us out of the lot, passing down a lane of cars near where the men had gotten Hank to his feet. I saw someone ease Hank into a car, and then, standing nearby and staring at our car, I saw Betty. I didn't know where she'd come from—whether I'd missed her in the crowded stands or if she'd arrived late, come to meet Hank. Or to find me. Then Dad had to slow for another car and before I knew it I was out of the backseat, brakes and curses behind me, and then I was in the midst of a crowd, men milling about and Betty screaming, "You leave my family alone!" Someone punched me in the ribs and rough hands shoved me back toward our car and my father was shouting and swinging his fists and then we were all in the car and moving again. "Dad," I said, leaning forward. "Shut up," he said. There was a bruise on my cheekbone and the taste of blood in my mouth. There were sirens in the distance. We turned out of the lot, the old man stepping hard on the gas, and I looked at the banged-up toolbox on the floor behind the driver's seat. My father had kept a .38 in there ever since he was beaten at the Gossip. I imagined taking the gun from the toolbox as he drove and putting it to his head. Pulling the trigger. I imagined his bloody head against the window, the car swerving into the oncoming traffic.

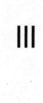

6

WHEN BETTY TOLD ME ABOUT HER SEPARATION that Sunday afternoon years later, I called Jacky. He was the street department's union
rep, which meant he and Betty caucused together for DFL labor
candidates. "Oh yeah," he said. "She had an affair with some big-
wig, and it blew up on her."

"Think you might've mentioned that?" I said. "I walked right
into it."

"I wanted to spare Betty you getting all priesty on her," Jacky
said.

"Christ, Jacky—"

"The Lord's Name," Jacky said.

I took a deep breath. The wall already had one hole in it. "All
I'm saying is I could have talked to her earlier if I'd known."

"If Betty needed a priest," Jacky said, "they aren't hard to
find in this town." I couldn't argue with that. My brother is pretty
smart about people, and he was saying what we both knew: Betty
García did not want my advice.

I got off the phone with Jacky and patched the wall where I'd
punched it, sweeping up plaster from the floor by the baseboard.
I hung the calendar back over the patch until I could paint. My
right hand was swollen and red and sore. In the cabinet above the
sink, where Dad had used to keep his liquor, I found a dusty bottle
of Maker's Mark. Uncapped it.

"Damned if they ain't a whiskey priest into my liquor!"

I juggled the bottle, splashing a little on my shirtfront. The old man was at the back door, nose pressed to the screen. He was grinning, a Saint Paul Saints ball cap perched atop his curly gray hair, season tickets in his hand. "Just bought these offa Nordyke. Helluva deal. Figured you and me and Jacky could use 'em this summer."

This was typical of the old man's enthusiasms, to decide to go to a ball game and then buy season tickets. He let himself in, and I poured the bourbon into shot glasses he'd left behind when he moved out. He hadn't taken much with him: his tools, his clothes, his bowling ball.

"Jacky coming?" I slid the bottle back onto the shelf.

"Just you and me this aft." He smacked his lips over the bourbon. "I figure Jacky's got his face buried in Mary Beth's muff right about now."

I slammed the cabinet door harder than I meant to. It slowly swung back open.

"Used to be a priest would've concerned himself about a couple fornicating before their wedding day," the old man continued, his fist balled around the shot glass. "Now you got everyone holding hands during the Our Father like a bunch of pansies."

Fornication had never bothered my father, and it wasn't likely he'd been to Mass lately. But the idea of some earnest young parishioner reaching for the old man's hand during the Lord's Prayer made me grin. "I do my best to discourage that sort of thing," I said. "I'm all for the hard line. Bring back the stake for sinners like you."

He set down the shot. "Give me a head start on the hellfire," he said. The old man took pleasure in the idea of damnation.

"So, we going to this ball game or not?" I said.

I hadn't seen the Saints since the Northern League was resurrected the year before. The ballpark was full, Municipal Stadium in the Midway spruced up with new paint and planters of red and white petunias on the wall under the grandstand. Dad bought us Grain Belts and brats, then we ignored our tickets and found seats behind the plate, where we had a good view of the pitching. It was a cloudless afternoon, cool enough that the sun felt good on my neck. A Canadian National freight rattled by the left-field fence, the crowd chanting *train, train*. Someone from Ax Man Surplus wandered through the stands in a black executioner's hood, selling toenail clippers for a quarter, and a barber with a red-and-white pole set up on one of the grandstand walkways gave quick haircuts. Nearby, Sister Rosalind, a nun who'd found a calling in therapeutic massage, had a chair set up and was kneading a biker's thick shoulders. All the typical minor-league oddities. Dad pointed to a sign on the outfield fence that read *Real Grass and Real Beer.* "Fuck the Twinkies, huh?" he said.

I'd gotten a glass of ice water at the concession stand and had my hand stuck in it. The old man noticed this. "What'd you do to your hand?"

"Punched a wall."

"That's smart."

"I guess I'm feeling a little antsy," I said. I was in the mood to talk, but Dad tugged the bill of his cap down over his eyes, dug a pencil stub out of his pocket, and began scoring the game. I walked over to say hi to Rosalind, whom I'd met in seminary. She was in her sixties, a small woman with thick glasses, apple cheeks, and strong hands. She'd taken up massage in the early seventies and nearly been driven out of her order before the other sisters figured out that her healing work didn't include happy endings. Now she ran Sister Rosalind's School of Massage, and she'd talked to one of my seminary classes about following God's call wherever it led. She didn't remember me, and I introduced myself, then paid for a massage. I climbed onto the chair, leaned my face into the cradle, and closed my eyes and listened to the announcer. Rosalind worked at my neck and shoulders. She ran her thumbs along the edges of the shoulder blades, found a knot of muscle, hooked the tip of her thumb into it and held a steady pressure. I felt the muscle soften under her thumb, let go.

When I stood, Rosalind shook a finger at me. "Father," she said, "always listen to God."

Back in the stands, the old man scowled. "What the fuck was that?"

"Massage," I said.

"From a nun?"

"You oughta try it. Help you relax."

"I'm not the one punching walls," he said. He took a swig of beer, swiped a forearm over his mouth. "Massage was more—" he searched for the word "—*localized* when I was young. Yeah, little hot oil, sweet thing, five bucks extra for—"

"Forget it," I said.

He shook his head sadly. "Boy, you've always been a bit backward."

I rested my elbows on the back of the aluminum bench, pushed my cap up, and let the sun warm my face while I watched the game. In the top of the fifth, with the first Fargo-Moorhead batter working the count to full, Dad, who'd been quiet for an inning or two, said, "You could play for these guys."

I glanced at him. "What are you talking about?"

"I know a guy knows Mike Veeck—you suck, Ump!—could get you a tryout."

I'd done well enough in Division III college ball for Dad to convince himself I had a shot at the pros. "I'd never hit this pitching, Dad. You know that."

Dad flipped his cigarette pack out of the sleeve of his T-shirt. He leaned forward with his elbows on his knees. I thought the conversation was over.

"Sure you could," he said, "if you got your head out of the clouds."

"Thanks for the faith," I said. "But you're nuts."

"Just watch the damn game."

By the seventh, the old man was ready to talk again. With the visiting manager out to the mound for a conference, he leaned into me. "Nordyke and I have the usual deal going," he said.

I nodded. Bob Nordyke, Dad's supervisor in the maintenance shop at one of the office buildings downtown, bought run-down houses to renovate and resell, then kept Dad on the clock while the old man worked on them. He paid less than the going rate, but Dad was getting his wages on top of it, so they both came out ahead. If anyone asked after the old man, Bob would say he'd sent him out to Menards for supplies.

The PA announcer began narrating an imagined conversation on the mound. "Say there, ya think ya can get this next fella out? Nup? Me either. Better give me the ball. Remember, win or lose, we hafta go back to Fargo."

"So, I'm figuring, you're at loose ends, why not help me on this job? I charge Bob the usual, we get done in half the time, and you keep what he pays me. Pretty good deal, huh?"

Fargo's middle reliever was warming up now, and the announcer dropped into a weak, breathy voice. "Gotta get the ball to the plate. Oof!"

"Why's it a good deal for you?" I asked.

"Look, you want it or not?" the old man snapped. He waved at a vendor. "Grain Belt here!" The vendor poured us two cups, shook his head at the tip Dad offered. "Put it in the collection plate." Dad turned to watch him climb the steps. "Man likes his work," he said.

So that was what this was all about, the baseball game, the whole afternoon. I'd walked away from my job, and you just didn't do that in my father's eyes. Working with him was dicey—I calculated the odds of someone, probably me, getting brained with a two-by-four—but I needed money for the summer. "I'll take it," I said.

After the game, Dad got on 94 and headed for the suburbs. "Visit your grandfather," he said, by way of explanation.

"How's he doing?"

"Like shit. I'd've left him die at home if I'd known."

"They treat him okay, don't they?"

"They treat him fine." His knuckles whitened on the wheel. I let it alone.

The last time I'd seen Granddad had been just before New Year's, when he was still in his home down on Sargent Avenue. In front of the house, an empty tomato cage stuck out of the snow by the steps, a dried brown stalk caught in the wire. I rang the doorbell and waited, thinking of summers past, when Granddad brought tomatoes to the neighborhood widows, leaving a small paper bag full of ripe fruits on someone's porch every time he worked in the yard. I rang the bell again and heard a gruff "Come in!" The old man had warned me that Granddad wasn't looking after himself, but I opened the front door to find him sitting on the sofa, freshly shaved and wearing slacks and a new cardigan. He looked like he'd been waiting, excited to see his grandson the priest. "There's Hamm's and cheddar in the fridge," he said. "Why don't you bring it on out."

In the kitchen, I sniffed at half-empty jugs of milk and orange juice and found they'd gone off. There was some curled, discolored lunch meat in the vegetable drawer and the cheese had a few spots of mold. The freezer was full of TV dinners and the cupboards were bare except for a fifth of Vat 69 Gold. Notes printed with a thick marker in Granddad's shaky hand were taped to the refrigerator and the front of the stove: "Make sure Freezer door closed" and "Exercise!" and "Turn off oven." I cut the bad parts off the cheese, found some crackers that weren't too stale, and rinsed dust out of pilsner glasses. Back in the living room, Granddad sat smoking a cigar, the air rich with tobacco. When he tapped the cigar in the ashtray stand at his left hand, his lips worked around his teeth. There was a scab on his forehead, which I connected to the whiskey in the cupboard. After we'd talked awhile, he began scooting along the sofa. I was puzzled until I noticed his walker at the other end. He saw my look and gave me an appeasing smile. When he stumped off with the walker toward the bathroom, he bent over the aluminum frame. He'd thinned to the point that I could see his shoulder blades working under the cardigan as he shuffled away.

My grandfather had always been a husky little man, walking with a soldier's bearing through Gram's death and the indignities of old age. He'd been an infantry sergeant in World War II, landing at Utah Beach with the 79th Division a week after D-Day. In Normandy, with his squad pinned down during the assault on Cherbourg, he won a Bronze Star for running across an open hillside under machine-gun fire to get a wounded radioman under cover and call in artillery. Three days later, he got the Purple Heart and a trip home when shrapnel from a mortar shell severed the artery in his right shoulder. He told me how he found himself sitting on the ground, blood in his eyes, blood all over. How his right arm was numb and he felt along it with his left hand until he found the spurting artery, and how he saved his own life by sticking his thumb in the wound. He came home to Saint Paul in 1945 from a hospital camp in Missouri to his wife and the two-year-old son he'd never seen. Granddad was thirty-one then. He might have tried college on the GI Bill, but he chose to take a job with the Veterans Administration and place his hopes and ambitions in my father. Too bad. Dad married his pregnant girlfriend at nineteen, did a stint in the Marines that didn't quite land him in Vietnam, went to trade school, and boozed and brawled his way through Saint Paul.

That last time I'd visited Granddad, a devout man in spite of the whiskey, I realized, sitting there in my black suit and Roman collar, that he saw me as the redemption of my father. But the quick stir of pride only brought up shame to think of my father that way.

Before I left, I took Granddad to the grocery, where he had a long conversation with the cashier and called the bag boy by name. When we returned to his house, he spent forever getting the front door open, stooping over his walker, peering at the lock, trying to fumble the wrong key into the slot. When I reached to help, he batted my hand away. "I've got it." "It's the wrong key." "I know that!" I rested on the cold wrought-iron rail beside him, like my sister waiting patiently while one of her children struggled into a T-shirt.

Later that day, I found Dad sitting at the bar in Charlie's Aldine. I clambered onto the stool beside him and ordered a Jameson on ice from Charlie. A curling team at a nearby table was discussing a Fort Road steak house. "They ruined the ambience," I heard someone say, "when they took down the Christmas lights."

Charlie slid my drink across the bar. "On the house, Father."

Dad raised his eyebrows. "Oughta get myself a black suit."

"Yeah, that'd work," I said. Then: "Granddad shouldn't be living alone anymore."

"The hell you say," the old man said. "What do you know?" But in the end, he had to agree, and Granddad was in a nursing home by February. Now, watching the old man tailgate cars on 94, I was sure he blamed me for noticing Granddad's failing body.

The nursing home, next door to a little park with a water tower in it, was one story, laid out like an H. A priest sees the inside of a lot of such places, and this one smelled better than most. Still, it was there under all the disinfectant, that sour note of shit and decay. I crossed myself reflexively, adding a silent prayer for the people who worked here and for the relief of the suffering. The old man was ahead of me in the hall, his neck hunkered down into his shoulders and his gait stiffened like he was getting ready for a fight.

Granddad's room was the last on the wing. He nodded in a wheelchair facing the wall, shoulders collapsed, like any smoker with emphysema I'd brought Communion to in a hospital or nursing home. A wheeled oxygen machine thrummed on the floor beside the wheelchair, its clear tube contrasting with a yellowed catheter tube that ran into a flowered cotton pouch.

I touched his shoulder. He raised his head, looked at me with clouded blue eyes.

"It's James," I said. "Your grandson."

"My grandson's a priest."

Dad smirked but kept his mouth shut.

"I don't have the uniform on tonight, Granddad." I squeezed his shoulder while I talked—nothing there but bone. It's hard to eat when you can't breathe. Granddad's face brightened at the touch, and I massaged the fragile skin of his back.

After a minute, Granddad dropped his chin and stared at the call button he gripped in one shaking hand. "Get me in my chair," he said.

Behind me, Dad cleared his throat. "Best wait for the nurse."

I looked to the call light, but it was already on. "He'll be more comfortable," I said. I'd helped with plenty of transfers on nursing-home visits—hated priests who used the collar as an excuse to just watch. I wheeled Granddad so he faced his recliner, set the brakes, and pried the call button from his hand, which remained clawlike, clutching air. I unhooked the catheter pouch from the back of the wheelchair and dropped it on the floor out of the way, careful not to pull on the tube. "Goddamn you," Granddad said. When I moved the oxygen machine and lifted the tube off over his head, his eyes widened. "We'll have that back in a jiffy," I said, patting his wasted forearm. I lifted his feet off the chair's footrests. His ankles were swollen.

I stepped to one side and outlined the transfer for Dad, then bent to Granddad. "Let's dance," I said, mimicking the cheerful nurses of the River County Rest Home, part of my weekly rounds for the past two years.

Granddad lifted his arms. I hooked my hand under the left one. Dad, watching me, did the same with the right. We pulled Granddad to his feet. He lurched forward. "Shit!" he said.

I kneed the wheelchair out of my way. Dad hesitated. "Walk him," I said. I couldn't keep the frustration out of my voice. How many times had the old man watched this?

Dad got moving. Granddad's slippers scuffed over the floor.

"That tube. It's pulling. Mother of God!"

I glanced down at the catheter pouch. There was still slack in the line. "Keep going."

We eased Granddad into his chair. "Well, that's taken care of," I said, clapping my hands together.

Granddad glared up at my father. "That little nurse Renee does better'n you."

Dad stood there, face reddening. "It was a good transfer," I said, busying myself with looping the oxygen tube back over Granddad's ears.

"My ass," Granddad said.

Dad walked over and sat on the bed. It was just high enough for his feet to dangle.

Granddad was breathing hard. "Give me the thing," he rasped.

I picked up the call button. "We're here, Granddad."

"Give me the thing!"

When I handed it to him, he resumed his clutching. I sat on the edge of the wheelchair and looked around the room. Granddad's sick-call crucifix hung on the wall by the door; its hollow back would contain an instruction sheet for last rites, a small bottle of holy water, and two candles. Beside the crucifix was a bulletin board with month-old birthday cards pinned up on it—candy-colored balloons and cartoon dogs—Mom's doing, I was sure. The television sat on an antique chest that had been banged up by the wheelchair. On top of the TV were a framed picture of me, taken at ordination in my brand-new chasuble, and one of Gram in a striped shirt, her gray hair styled short. She had pulled off youthful fashions and hairstyles all her life—no piled-up blue hair for her. The table beside Granddad was jammed with his *Saint Joseph Sunday Missal* and a ruby-beaded rosary that had been my grandmother's, another vial of holy water, boxes of latex gloves and Kleenex, nail clippers, two plastic cups half full of water, a phone, and a couple of paperbacks—Hemingway's *The Snows of Kilimanjaro* and Dinesen's *Out of Africa*, the edition with Robert Redford and Meryl Streep on the cover. Granddad had always been a reader; I got it from him.

His eyes had gone cloudy again. I leaned close. "Granddad?" The eyes focused and he smiled. "How you doing, Granddad?" He kept smiling, didn't say anything. I picked up one knobby hand in both of mine, began rubbing the splotched, papery skin with my thumbs, slow circles. "Anything good on TV?"

"They got a show on Channel 4," he said. "It's on all the time."

"What show's that?"

"It's a show."

"Yeah. You reading about Africa these days?"

"Can't keep my mind on it."

"How 'bout I read a little to you?" I picked up the Dinesen. There was no bookmark, so I started at the beginning. "I had a farm in Africa. . . ." After a little while, Granddad laid his head back against the recliner, and the hand with the call button stopped shaking. Dad got up and fiddled with the coins and combs on the built-in dresser, patting his hair in the mirror. He'd slip out of the room soon. He had no interest in reading outside of the Bible, the sports page, and the comics.

"In the highlands you woke up in the morning and thought: Here I am, where I ought to be—"

"He's asleep. What the hell you keep reading for?"

"He hears it," I said. Granddad's thin lips curved in a slight smile. I doubted he could follow the story, but maybe he enjoyed the rhythms of Dinesen's prose. Besides the war, Granddad hadn't traveled much except for visits to his sister in Wisconsin's North Woods and to my grandmother's family in Duluth. Did some corner of his mind regret that he'd never seen the Ngong Hills and Kilimanjaro? Or was he back in Cherbourg?

A nurse came in. "Do you need something?"

The call light was still on. "No, we just got him in his chair."

"Sorry. It takes a while to get everyone settled after dinner."

"Takes time, I'd imagine," I said, to make up for my father's harsh laugh.

"It does." She checked the catheter bag, unclipped it from its tube, and went into the bathroom. When she came out, I handed the book to Dad. "Read to him," I said.

"I'm not reading that book."

I followed the nurse out into the hall. Behind me, I heard Granddad's cracked voice: "Words, they always scared Little Joe."

"I'm his grandson," I said to the nurse, whose name tag read *Renee*. "Father Jim Dressler." I identified myself out of habit, and her eyes searched the hollow of my throat where the Roman collar ought to have been. She had light brown eyes, a splash of freckles over her nose, and a nurse's strong, smooth arms. I guessed she would give me straight answers. "How's he doing?" I asked.

She brushed at a strand of sandy hair. "He's got emphysema," she said, "and congestive heart failure. His kidneys are bad. He has his good days. Last week he had all the nurses in there, telling them how to bowl. This week. . . ." She shrugged, then said: "He was happier when he first got here. He was still on his feet, could roll his neighbor to dinner in her wheelchair. He joined the residents' council right away. He'd assign people little jobs, then say to me, 'You've got to keep these people busy.'" She smiled at this.

"That's my grandfather," I said. He'd worked as a benefits counselor for the Veterans Administration, Gram driving him to work in their car every day, across the Ford Parkway bridge to the VA hospital complex at Fort Snelling. He prided himself on negotiating red tape and helping vets get the full benefits of the GI Bill. Before he retired, dinner-table talk at my grandparents' house turned around the small victories Otto had won at work that day, the bureaucrats he'd straightened out. Gram was an admiring audience, encouraging him as though she hadn't heard a hundred similar stories. My father, if he were there, would roll his eyes and shift in his chair.

"Your grandfather's a very helpful man," the nurse said. "It's hard watching that taken from someone." She left me and walked down the hall, a big-shouldered woman in sneakers and scrubs.

I turned back to the room, heard my father say, "What do you keep looking at me for?"

And Granddad: "Why's he here?"

Dad leaned toward him as I peeked around the edge of the door. "Is that what you think? I'd tell you if you were dying."

Granddad's half-open eyes were cast in his direction without any particular focus to them. He pursed his lips, then stared at the ceiling.

Out of Africa was shut beside Dad on the bed. I picked it up and started where I'd left off. "The hill country itself, when you get into it, is tremendously big—"

Granddad made a gulping sound. His eyes were wide open. He planted his elbows on the armrests, strained against them with no result. "Help me sit up."

I stepped over the oxygen tube and call-button cord to get behind the chair and grip him under the arms. The chair top was greasy, littered with flaked skin. He slid up easily against the leather.

"Jacky's having his wedding videotaped, Granddad," I said, settling back into the wheelchair, "so we can watch it together after." I reached for the book. Granddad struggled to lean forward, then brought the call button up in front of his face and began punching at it with both thumbs. "Shit, shit, shit." Then he bellowed: "Nurse!" He had good lungs for a man dying of emphysema.

"Is there something I can do, Granddad?"

He was trying to push himself up in the chair again. He held still a moment, panting. "I need the nurse!" I heard the old man leave the room.

There was a little crust at the corner of Granddad's mouth. I wet a Kleenex in one of the water cups and went to wipe it.

"I need the nurse, damn it!"

"I'll see if I can find her." Out in the hall, Renee hurried my way, trailing an aide. I saw Dad turn the corner by the nurses' station.

"Bathroom time," Renee said. "You might want to say good night."

"Nurse! Help! Get me on the thundermug!"

I shut my eyes for an instant, then followed the aide into the room. Renee had gone into the bathroom for the portable toilet stand. The aide, a thin, unkempt man of about fifty, with a drooping, nicotine-stained mustache, stood to Granddad's side, looking down on him. I thought of my grandfather being young and strong, running across that open hillside, helmet clasped to his head, machine-gun bullets clipping the June flowers of Normandy. I leaned over and squeezed the bone of his shoulder, speaking quickly. "I'll be back later in the week, Granddad."

His eyes were fixed on the bathroom door. "Nurse!"

. . .

Out front, the old man was finishing a cigarette. I closed the gray, Alzheimer's-secure inner door behind me and glared at his back for a moment through the wire-mesh glass of the outer doors. He dropped the cigarette, ground it out, started to reach for another, then stopped and rubbed at his temples with the blunt fingers of both hands. I stepped out, rapped him on the arm with my knuckles. "Let's go."

I was halfway around the car to the passenger's door when I heard the old man's growl behind me. "Put him in a home. Great idea, boy."

I let myself into the car. The old man stood there a moment, his face hidden by the roof. When he went around to his side and got in, he said, "You may be doing a funeral instead of my boy's wedding." Then he was silent. We rode like that back into town, the old man fiddling with the volume on the Twins game. He kept a decent distance behind other cars this time as he steered through the snarl downtown where 94 met 35E. Hrbek was batting in the second. A big, good-time guy. When I was a little boy in a Twins cap, Granddad told me that whenever Harmon Killebrew hit a home run his teammates bought him a beer. "Kill a brew, get it? Haw-haw!"

"I hate this," Dad said softly.

The highway hummed beneath us. Hrbek struck out. I waited for my father to say more, and by the time I realized he wasn't going to, it was too late for me to say anything.

As he eased off the highway onto the Dale Street exit, Dad grunted, "I'll pick you up at seven tomorrow." And a minute later: "I'll drop you at home. I'm going to the Gossip."

7

THE OLD MAN STUCK HIS HEAD in my bedroom door about half past six the next morning. I was still groggy, digging a sweatshirt out of my chest of drawers.

"Try knocking," I said.

"Try getting your ass out of bed." He was unshaven, with purple bags under his eyes and a cut beneath the right one.

"You look like shit."

"Roy Doolin looks worse."

I imagined the bar at the Gossip. The old man grown suddenly silent, fingering his shot glass. Mr. Doolin missing the warning signs, because he was drunk himself, because he was Roy Doolin, a hard guy in his own right. Dad would have worked up Roy's sense of grievance about the way the line was run at the Ford plant. He would have egged Roy on while Roy complained about his foreman, his wife, his life. And then, out of left field: "Doolin, you're breaking my heart. I never imagined you'd be such a weepy cunt." There would have been a moment while that sunk in past the haze of a half-dozen boilermakers, and then Roy's fist would've shot out, his Knights of Columbus ring catching Dad beneath the eye, laying open the skin. Quicker than the old man expected, but not much, because my father knows when a man like Roy will swing before Roy does.

The old man poked me in the chest, just above the Saint Thomas logo on my sweatshirt. "All that dough for a fancy education, and now what? You're ripping drywall with a shit heel."

"You got that right." I stepped around him and the laundry pile in the middle of the hall. On the stairs, I called over my shoulder. "But it didn't cost you a dime."

"Church shoulda paid you for that." In the old man's eyes, I'd been a fool to trade thousands of dollars for an education in chastity and obedience.

Dad's Buick was out front with one wheel on the curb. "We'll get the breakfast special at the Florida," he said, once we'd gotten in the car. I buckled up and found a place for my feet in the litter of fast-food bags and drink cups on the floor. Dad drove down to Thomas and took a left. The Florida Tavern was on the East Side and anyone else would have gotten on 94, but the old man never used the highway except to go to the suburbs to see Granddad. He liked driving his big four-door Buick through Saint Paul's backstreets at about twenty-five miles an hour, letting traffic build behind him, leaning forward, hands crossed on top of the wheel; the car, badly in need of an alignment, occasionally wandering across the centerline.

I settled into the spongy bench seat and rolled down the window to the morning air. There was no hurrying the old man, and anyway, he knew the backstreets well enough he could get pretty much anywhere in the city in under half an hour. It had rained last night and the air was wet, and I hung my elbow out the window and watched Frogtown roll by: tired houses with a strip of front yard behind chain-link fences; squat Hmong men in worn button-front shirts and slacks climbing into cars parked along the curbs to go to work; a fleshy black woman in a tan suit with a matching scarf helping three children into a minivan. The old man had taken both hands off the wheel and was steering with his knee while he lit a cigarette. "Hirschmann's is a nigger bar now," he said, a little after we'd passed Hirschmann's Liquors.

"Yeah?" I said. When I was at Saint Thomas, I'd argued with the old man about his vocabulary. Bob Nordyke, his boss and best friend, was black, and Dad didn't use the N-word around him, but that was as far as his sensitivity went.

"Yeah. Turned the last couple of years. For a while, you could still go in there during the day, but now it's just shadows and eyes and teeth." Dad was watching me out of the corner of his eye, aiming to get a rise. We drove by Saint Agnes church and school, a few teachers' cars in the lot already, then the long, low cinder-block building that housed B.T. Bombers, a sort of boxing club/community center run by a retired cop.

The truth of the matter, which I could have explained to neither the old man nor my former professors, was that I wasn't sure I had the right to be self-righteous. Dad still drank at Hirschmann's if he was with Bob, and he was more at ease there than I ever would have been.

"Well, you've got plenty of other bars, don't you?" I said.

"Sure," Dad said. He clicked on the AM radio, searching through static for a station that worked. "Shame about Hirschmann's, though."

"Everyone's got to have someplace to drink," I said.

"Well, you're right about that."

When Thomas dead-ended at Marion, Dad turned right. We crossed University, the white marble dome of the Capitol visible to the east, and passed the loading docks back of Sears, where Dad sometimes unloaded semis for extra cash at Christmas when I was a kid. The Cathedral of Saint Paul sat before us, big as a Monument Valley butte looming over downtown.

"So how's your boss?" Dad nodded at the Cathedral.

"The archbishop? I don't hear much from him."

"Thought you might rub elbows occasionally." The old man was probing again, looking for a place to dig.

"I'm just a parish priest, Dad."

"Not even that, now." He was leaning forward, both hands on top of the wheel, talking around his cigarette.

"You're right." I jammed my feet up on the dash. "I'm just a shit heel ripping drywall."

"That's my boy." Dad settled back and reached up to rub his neck with one thick hand. I hoped he was buying breakfast.

We were on Kellogg now, downtown Saint Paul spread out before us, the buildings nowhere near as tall or spectacular as those of Minneapolis and crowded into a bowl-shaped valley that dropped them beneath the rest of the city. The lowlands were the first place settled here, Saint Paul then a pair of steamboat landings known as Pig's Eye after a one-eyed French-Canadian trapper who ran a saloon in a river-bluff cave. It took the settlement's first priest to suggest that *Saint Paul* might be a name more in line with civic ambition. I pictured Pig's Eye Parrant, the trapper, looking a great deal like the old man, less an eye.

Dad sped up to about thirty, and we swung along Kellogg where it swept between the Mississippi and downtown: on one side lampposts and sidewalks overlooking the river and the Wabasha and Robert Street bridges, on the other a cliff face of stone and brick buildings broken by side streets. We passed West Publishing and the main post office and the Depot Bar where the postal workers drank, then climbed the long Third Street bridge to Dayton's Bluff, the old man humming to himself, then muttering "fuck off" to an impatient driver who honked and pulled by on our left. My mother had been born below this bridge in the Connemara Patch, an Irish shantytown in the wide Phalen Creek valley, cleared during urban renewal in the fifties. Off to the right, where the valley opened to the river, I glimpsed a barge nosing downstream where the Mississippi curved around the Lower West Side; then we were on top of Dayton's Bluff, making the straight run across the East Side, past the Bee Hive Bar and Parkway Little League fields and Harding High football field, out almost to White Bear Avenue, where the Florida Tavern sat in a grassy lot tucked away on a dead end.

The Florida had a palm tree painted on the door and a dead ficus in a pot at one end of the bar—nods to the tropical. Legally it was open at eight, but anytime after seven a knock on the door would get a guy just off the night shift in for the breakfast special, which included one complimentary beer. Dad and I shared the bar with two haggard men who'd skipped the food part of the special. The bartender looked like he'd slept on the pool table, and the cook, to judge from the pots banging in the back, had had a short night. Dad ordered his eggs over easy and a beer with tomato juice. I gave Dad my beer, ordered black coffee, and tried to brighten the surroundings with eggs sunny-side up. While I spooned the yolks over two slices of burnt toast and added bacon on top, Dad said: "Know how to tell if you're in Saint Paul or Minneapolis?"

I'd heard this before. "How?" I said.

"If the place looks fifty years old cuz some faggot designer made it over to be retro, you're in Minneapolis. If it hasn't been cleaned in fifty years, you're in Saint Paul." He gestured at the bar's unswept concrete floor, the torn vinyl booths.

"Looks like they saved a lot of money here," I said. Saint Paul is sometimes called the last eastern city, and I thought that right: Minneapolis is forward thinking and Saint Paul settled in subtle ways that mark the line between East and West every bit as clearly as the Mississippi.

When we finished breakfast, the old man went to the bathroom, then headed for the door. So I was buying—part of the job, no doubt. Union dues. I slid off my stool and walked down to where the bartender sat on the beer cooler, drinking coffee. "I'll take the check," I said. He ignored me, calling after my father: "See you, Joe." The old man lifted a hand, waved without looking back, and went out the door. I caught up with him in the parking lot.

"They feed you for your personality?" I said.

Dad leaned an elbow on the roof of the car. "I do some work there," he said. He paused and grinned. "I'm diversified." It had been that way since I was a kid. Once he came home with a paper bag full of steaks he'd "gotten a good deal on at the Gossip," which Mom had refused to prepare. "The Gossip?" she said. "Those came out of the Rainbow meat department in the front of some-one's pants." And the old man, puzzled: "For Christ's sake, what's it matter, Maura? You're gonna cook 'em, ain't ya?" He'd ended up frying them one at a time himself, standing in front of the stove and whistling, every night at midnight when he came home from the bars. Sometimes, then, the old man would put Jacky and me— never Anne—in the backseat of the car while he made his early evening rounds, driving from one bar to another, drinking beer and whiskey and playing the occasional game of pool, conducting small business transactions. He might buy a gold ring of dubious origin and quality, or a Radarange oven that had fallen off a truck; he might collect money someone owed him for a pool game or a handyman job; he might pay a bar tab or arrange to look at a tavern owner's plumbing problem. He could build cabinetry and repair just about anything. Depending on the evening and what he had to do in a place, Dad would leave Jacky and me in the backseat of the car, playing with the little plastic cocktail swords he brought out of bars for us, or he would bring us in and set us up with Cokes, leave us perched on bar stools. I remember him leaned over a pool table in smoky light like a movie, or on his back under a bar sink, his toolbox beside him and a pipe wrench in hand. I remember arguments, and a few terrifying fights. I saw him hit men with an open hand, his fist, a pool cue. I saw him threaten a man with a hammer. Before I was ten, I'd been, it seemed, in every bar in Saint Paul: on University Johnny's, where they'd cash your payroll check at a barred window, John's Tap, Christensen's Saloon, the Trend, the Gossip; in Midway and Frogtown Charlie's

Aldine and the Victorian and Hirschmann's; on the East Side the Bee Hive, the Mounds Park Lounge, the Florida; and downtown the Gopher, where the waitresses asked *what the fuck you want?* and served coney dogs; and Alary's, the cop bar, its ceiling hung with damaged cop-car doors sent by departments across the country. Bars in West Seventh, bars in the North End. Bars on Rice Street. Bars on Arcade. More bars than I can remember. The cops knew my father. So did the criminals. In a bigger city he might have been mobbed up, but in Saint Paul he was just a guy getting by, as he put it. "How you doin', Joe?" "Gettin' by."

Almost two hours after he'd picked me up, Dad drove us into the west end of Frogtown and parked in front of a four-square, next to a Vasko roll-off container full of garbage. "Spent all last week cleaning out the fucking place," he said. "Like usual, you managed to miss the nasty part of the job."

"You should've asked."

"Gaahhh," the old man said, brushing aside the logic with a wave of his hand. He led the way up the walk, snapping his key ring off his belt to search for the porch key. Inside, I saw that Bob Nordyke had made another good investment. The oak floors needed to be redone, but the woodwork was fine, and there was a built-in buffet at the back of the dining room. I walked around the front rooms, examining the buffet and the piano window and the six beveled-glass panes set in the front door, where I tapped a forefinger at a single bubble trapped a century ago.

I whistled. "Bob scored on this one."

"No shit," the old man said. "He'll sell it to some do-gooder wants to live in a colorful neighborhood."

Upstairs, the floors were maple and the woodwork was painted. Dad ran a hand down a doorjamb and bent to study a spot where the paint had chipped off near the strike plate. He grunted. "Maple.

Too bad they painted it." Half of the windows upstairs were painted shut, and most of the sash ropes throughout the house were broken. Dad had propped open a few windows with paint paddles so we had some air.

Windows were the day's job. The old man worked in the basement, sanding and repainting the second-floor sashes and stops as I brought them down. Upstairs, I used a putty knife to break paint seals and pry off the stops, then replaced sash cords and sanded and waxed the jambs. When I was a child, my father let me help him on our house, giving me some easy, repetitive task or asking me to reach something in a tight spot. When I was older, he taught me plumbing and wiring, even how to work with gas pipes. He was different when he worked like this: a house made him patient. He moved with care and precision, a kind of love for wood and glass and stucco.

At midmorning, Dad went out and came back with Wonder Bread, cold cuts, a foot-long box of Velveeta, and a vat of mustard. There was a gallon glass jug of sun tea in the fridge. I poured the tea while Dad spread mustard on the bread and layered on the processed cheese and meat. "Horse-cock sandwiches," he said affectionately, which took the joy right out of bologna.

We ate lunch on the front steps. Above the roof of the house across the street, you could see the bell tower of Saint Agnes with its green copper onion. Next door, a petite Hmong woman swept her sidewalk. The old man nodded in her direction. "That one's probably got six kids already. Some young buck grabbed her out front of her parents' house one day in high school, and she started pushing them out. They're practically cavemen. I've cleaned up rentals where they pissed in the sink."

I swallowed a bite of bologna, noticed the way the woman's black ponytail fanned slightly on her back as she swayed in rhythm with her broom. "I worked with some Hmong in seminary," I said. "It's a sad story: get screwed by the CIA in Vietnam and end up in the icy north, next door to a dumb German redneck like you."

Dad looked hurt. "Jesus, don't be so touchy. I'd piss in the sink myself, but your mother always left it full of dishes."

"When's everyone getting into town?" I asked.

"Next Thursday or Friday. The rehearsal dinner's at the Lex."

"Too bad Granddad won't be there."

Dad grunted. Before the nursing home, my grandfather was in the habit of holding forth beneath the gilt-framed paintings in the Lexington's walnut-paneled bar. He'd proposed to my grandmother there when it was a glitzy new cocktail lounge in the 1940s, and, when I was a kid, you still could find him there most Sundays—Wednesday nights, too, after the Rosary society at Saint Luke's. If you were patient enough to sit and drink Cokes, you might be rewarded by one of his war stories: how his squad called him *Boss* and warned him away on a moonless night in England when the enlisted men waited by the camp latrine to blacken the eyes of their sergeants; how if a German tank trapped a GI in his foxhole it would park there and let the exhaust get him; how a Texan nobody thought was much good carried their captain out of a field after a machine gun had shot off the captain's legs. How the same Texan later asked the captain for his good field boots.

"I keep thinking," Dad said, studying the knuckles of one hand, "we could get him out in his chair with a nurse for the wedding. But I don't reckon that's going to happen."

"Nope," I said. My father, despite his comment last night about a funeral Mass, didn't know how sick Granddad really was.

"You'll give him last rites?" Dad asked, as if catching the drift of my thoughts.

"We call it Anointing of the Sick now," I said. "But it doesn't fool anyone."

"Why would you want to?" Dad pulled himself to his feet, then bent and rubbed his knees before going back into the house. A moment later, I heard him hammering at a window stop.

My sister had phoned Sunday and made me promise to come over after work, but Dad drove to his place. "We'll have a bite and get a drink," he said. He rented a one-bedroom apartment above a superette across Front Avenue from Calvary Cemetery. A wooden stair, unpainted and grayed by the weather, climbed up the outside of the frame building under a Canada Dry sign. Dad got his mail and let us into the stairs through a chain-link gate. At the top, he opened the door without a key. The inside knob had a screw driven in beside the lock button so it couldn't be punched.

Dad tossed the mail on the counter and went into the toilet, leaving the door open behind him, sure sign of a single man. It can be a problem for priests, parishioners having a tendency to wander into the living areas of the rectory if they're looking for you. While the old man pissed, I glanced at the mail (past-due bills, a letter from a law office) and then went into the front room. There was a broken-down couch against one wall, a TV on a chest opposite that. A table and two chairs by the front windows. All the furniture was pressed wood with scarred veneer. The table and chairs wobbled. I stood at the window, watching the occasional car go by on Front. The neighborhood, built originally for millwrights and gandy dancers, had small houses squeezed onto tiny lots between the tracks and the graveyard. I felt claustrophobic.

The most startling aspect of the breakup of my parents' marriage had been the old man's offhand approach to it. One day two years ago, so Mom told it, she noticed Dad's clothes were missing. "Where's your clothes?" she asked at the dinner table that night.

"I got a place," he said.

"Oh," Mom said. She picked up his plate, then walked into the kitchen and scraped corned beef and sauerkraut into the garbage.

"The hell you doing?"

"If you don't live here, you don't eat here."

Their marriage was no worse at that time than at any other: Dad spent his evenings in bars, came and went when he wanted—usually showing for dinner—and slept on the living-room couch in front of the TV. Mom would turn off the morning show when she came down to fix breakfast. In the family's memory, Dad had never slept in the marriage bed; the room upstairs was always "Mom's room" in our minds and conversations. Dad clearly regarded it as hostile territory. He might have been right. "Girls," Mom used to say, waving a coffee spoon at Anne and her teenage friends, "some people say marriage is a fifty-fifty proposition. But you remember, it's sixty-forty at best. And make sure you get the sixty." If the old man was present, he'd chime in at that point: "'Course, you can call it fifty-fifty and flip a coin now and then."

The toilet flushed. I heard Dad rummage around in the kitchen, opening the fridge, then he came into the front room with a Red's Savoy carryout box and two cans of beer dangling in a six-pack collar. He turned the TV to golf on ESPN, then parked on the couch with the pizza beside him. "Goddamn, now this is a boring game." He gestured with his beer can. "Look at this shit. Whack! Goddamn camera swings up and looks at the sky. And the fricking announcers whispering, like anyone could hear 'em—"

"Watch something else."

"Don't tell me what to do."

"So watch the golf." I popped the tab on the remaining beer and opened the box to find half a pizza and a stubbed-out cigarette. "Nicotine supreme, huh?"

"What?" A bus had pulled up at the stop outside, its rumble filling the small apartment. One of the front windows vibrated in its frame.

I raised my voice. "Ever get tired of the bus?"

"You kidding? I got smokes and TV dinners right downstairs. They never run out."

"You got a girlfriend?" I asked. His second marriage had been over before I knew it existed. I'd never seen so much as a picture of the woman. Jacky, who'd been one of the witnesses at the wedding, said she was youngish and blonde, attractive enough in a cheap way. He said she and the old man had come into the courthouse looking like moony teenagers and gone out fighting.

Dad snorted. "I get about as much action as you do, Padre." He scratched his ear. "Ah, what the hell. Women are good for two things: fucking and making coffee. For that, they want to run your life. I got a Mr. Coffee on the counter."

After we finished the cold pizza, Dad said, "I'll run you home." We went down to the car. Dad drove slowly along Front, then pulled to the curb in front of the Half Time Rec.

"I've got to get to Anne's," I reminded him.

"I promised you a drink," the old man said. He opened the door and put a foot on the ground, then glanced back. I hadn't taken my seat belt off. "Relax, boy," he said. "Won't hurt your sister to cool her heels for once." He got out and disappeared inside the bar. I climbed out, too, pausing on the sidewalk to look down Front in the direction of home—it was walkable, and the just-leafed-out saplings along the street were waving in a fresh breeze—then I shrugged and went into the darkness and smoke. Dad was already sitting at the bar with a cigarette going. I took a stool beside him.

"Hi, Joe." The bartender set Dad up with house whiskey and a Leinenkugel. The old man put a crisp fifty on the bar, and I winced. "Guinness and a shot of Jameson," I said, figuring we'd get through the fifty faster that way. When the bartender put the pint in front of me, Dad tilted his head at it and then stuck his forefinger in the foam, like Mom's house cat examining a glass of water. "Aren't you fancy?" he said, licking his finger. "Where'd you come from—your mom have a yuppie on the side?"

"Weren't any yuppies then," I said. "Good looks and brains just skipped a generation. Cheers." I tapped his shot glass with my own.

The old man appeared to be studying his reflection in a mirrored rum sign behind the bar. I glanced at him—the pitted nose and blotchy skin, the gray cast of whiskers over his cheeks. He launched into one of his favorite anecdotes: "So, your mother and me start seeing each other, and one day she looks me right in the eye and says, 'Joseph Dressler, if you ever lay a hand upon me in violence, that day I'll take the children and myself, and you'll never see us again.' And I scratch my chin, and I say, 'Hell, Maura, we don't have children, we ain't married, we ain't even fucked yet.' And she looks me right in the eye, and she says, 'We will.'" Dad lifted his glass to the mirror. "Here's to family."

"Here's to family," I repeated, absently thumbing a cross into the foam on the Guinness with the same motion I used to apply the ashes on Ash Wednesday.

"You ever think about purgatory?" Dad said.

"Mmm."

"I do." He shook the forefinger that had been in my Guinness. "'Cuz someday, the old man up there's gonna look at me and say, 'Joe, you're a fuckup, but for all that you didn't do half bad.' Then he'll give me about ten thousand years in purgatory, and we'll call it even."

"Hmm."

The bartender moved to the far end of the bar and began washing glasses.

"Then there's heaven," Dad said. "Could be boring—no fight-ing or fucking. But God must've worked that angle. Can't have a hard case like me roamin' around wrestling angels. Heaven'll be like sitting around after eating a big dinner, or sleeping off a fine fuck: you settle back, and you think, 'Life's good.' Or maybe, 'Afterlife's good.'" He lifted his Leinenkugel and belched.

"The problem"—he paused, searching for one—"with priests"—another pause, then his eyes brightened—"is you're all obsessed with sex. Your vices ain't in balance. We all got vices; it's vanity to think you can overcome 'em." He waved his empty beer glass at the bartender, who came within earshot to pull him another draft. Dad leaned forward and captured his wrist. "Henry, ya know how to get a Catholic girl pregnant?—Dress her as an altar boy! Haw-haw!" It was an old joke. Henry shook his head and went back to the other end of the bar. Dad went on. "You ever watch Father Crankshaft"—it was Cruikshank, Father Phil's associate—"at a funeral? Sumbitch can't wait to get to the food. He don't give a shit what he says about the deceased." He paused, considered his whiskey, and then set it down on the bar. "So tell me true, Father," he said, "how often does a priest really get laid? There must be a market for it."

I knocked over my beer. The old man amused himself by spin-ning his stool back and forth while I reached a bar rag from be-hind the counter to wipe up the spill. Henry came down without comment and pulled another Guinness, then went away again. I settled back with the fresh beer. "You know, you're right about appetite," I said. "Aquinas ranked the seven deadly vices by how likely they are to give you a taste for more sin."

Dad stared at me for a moment, then rolled his eyes. "You think too much," he said.

Even though it was late by the time Dad got me home, I decided to drive up to Roseville to visit Anne. From Snelling, I could see the lights of a Saints game, and I almost went to catch the last in-nings; I shifted into the right lane for the Energy Park exit, then back, cutting off a pickup truck. The driver honked and flipped me off as he swerved past. I was reluctant to see my sister. This spring, after hearing about my upcoming leave, she'd written me long, con-cerned letters that I didn't answer. When I drove up to the house, her husband, Daryl, was out in the drive working on his car in the dusk. It was a self-perpetuating hobby: Daryl tinkered with the car constantly when the weather was warm, ensuring that it ran rough all summer. Come winter, he'd give up and take it in for a tune-up.

"She's in the kitchen," Daryl said from under the hood. I threaded my way through the garage, past the family minivan shoehorned in among Daryl's Craftsman tool cart, table saw, band saw, grinder, drill press, leafblower and snowblower and rid-ing mower—enough machinery for a small construction site—and rapped on the screen door.

Anne looked up from bottle-feeding her youngest, and I let myself in. My sister had our father's eyes and coloring, although her blonde curls came from a curling iron. After five kids she was a solid, strong woman. She stood, baby on one hip, and gave me a hug with her free arm, pecking me on the cheek. "I've been ex-pecting you since seven." She sniffed. "You've been drinking."

"I couldn't get away from Dad."

She was instantly sympathetic. "How is the old monster?"

"Life's catching up on him."

"Nothing he doesn't deserve." As a child, Anne had adored the old man, but when she hit adolescence, she moved into Mom's camp and stayed there. Mom worked that, of course, but it didn't help that Dad could roll his eyes and whine well enough to put any teen-age girl to shame. When Anne went through her hippie phase, the old man rode her unmercifully: "Eww, let's go watch a sunset," he'd say. I still remember some clueless longhair, one of Anne's earnest boyfriends, presenting himself in beads and a brocade shirt, and the old man looking him up and down balefully from the couch before saying, "So, Maharishi, when's enlightenment coming?"

"Anyway," I said, "I'm working on a house with him."

Anne frowned. "I knew it. You're leaving the Church."

I sighed. "I'm not even leaving the priesthood. I'm taking a break—a teaching position at Saint John's."

"Why would you want to do that?"

"It's a long story."

"Try me."

"I don't want to go into it tonight. What I was trying to get at is I've got classes to prep this summer, and the old man suddenly wants to be my buddy. You know how he is."

Anne bit her lip. She still wanted to talk about the Church. Then her oldest son, Daryl Jr., almost a teenager, wandered in to raid the cupboards. "Hey, Uncle James," he said. I feinted a punch and roughed his hair. Lean like his father, he had the makings of a good outfielder. And the appetite. He left with a half bag of cookies and a quart of milk. Anne shook her head. "He's like you and Jacky, always in the fridge."

My sister went straight from hippie to devout Catholic homemaker. In junior college, she met Daryl on a retreat sponsored by their Newman Center. They cut their hair and had five kids, ranging from Daryl Jr. to Kelsey, the baby in Anne's arms. Daryl Sr. worked for General Mills, and Anne took care of their split-level ranch, where she stenciled Jersey cows in the kitchen and baby ducks in the nursery. She had a vegetable garden out back, in the midst of which stood a white, peak-roofed shrine to the Virgin Mary. Ceramic deer and rabbits grazed about Mary's feet or looked up adoringly. Anne worked hard to have a happy home.

"Congratulate me," Anne said brightly, turning from the sink. "I'm having a baby. You're the first to know, after Daryl and Mom."

"Congratulations," I said, thinking they didn't have enough money as it was. I wrapped an arm around her shoulders and squeezed her against me. "My sister. Looks like the family line's not in danger." That was something to be grateful for: midnights in my rectory when the certainty of old age with no family of my own sometimes struck hard, there was comfort in knowing I'd always have plenty of nephews and nieces. Anne was a saint when it came to making me feel welcome at family gatherings and holidays, but I tried not to overdo my presence—entertaining his wife's priest brother didn't sit well with Daryl, who never seemed to know what to say to me.

Anne set the formula bottle on the counter, pushing aside dinner plates waiting for the dishwasher, and skipped around the kitchen, waltzing the baby in the air. "We're having a baby," she sang to Kelsey.

"You know," I said, turning on my heel to follow her circuit of the room, "a lot of clergy don't agree with the Church on birth control. A damned good Saint Paul bishop resigned over *Humanae Vitae.*" The bishop, James Shannon, a rising star in the late 1960s, had resigned after Pope Paul issued the encyclical. Shannon was a legend in the archdiocese: an inspiration to some priests, a tragedy to others.

Anne stopped dancing. "I didn't ask the bishop about birth control," she said.

I felt like a jerk. I brushed her cheek by way of making up for it, then put my hand under her chin and lifted her face. There was no sign of the black eye Daryl had given her this winter, the one I wasn't supposed to know about.

In January, I had slid open the confessional panel and heard a familiar voice: "Bless me, Father, for I have sinned."

"Mom?" I bent and peered through the metal grill. There she was, with her head bowed and her hands clasped in front of her face. "What are you doing here?"

"Daryl gave Anne a black eye," she said.

"You drove an hour to tell me this in confession?"

"So you can't tell your father and brother."

"It doesn't work that way. It has to be your own sins."

Silence. Then: "Don't tell them."

"I'll kick his ass myself," I said, wondering what a waiting peni-tent would make of that.

"She won't leave him. You'll only make things worse."

I sighed. "So what do you want me to do?"

"Talk to Daryl."

"Mom, if I talk to Daryl, his next conversation's going to be in the emergency room."

"I thought you were my helpful one."

"I'm a priest, not Jesus." In the silence that followed, I pressed a fist against my mouth. "Look," I said, "I want to talk to Anne."

"Don't," Mom said. "She's ashamed."

That stopped me. In the silence, I heard her pick up her purse. "Stay," I said. "I'll buy you dinner."

"I need to get back," she said, then added: "Your grandfather's going into a home." Light cut into the confessional, and I listened to her footsteps down the aisle, fainter and fainter.

Anne's eyes narrowed. "Is something the matter?"

I let go of her chin. Outside, a wrench clinked on concrete. Daryl was still working on his car. "Do you do much with Jacky and Mary Beth?" I asked.

"Maybe when they have kids. They're still drinking in bars and clubbing."

Anne moved a basket of laundry waiting to be folded and sat me down with coffee and the last piece of streusel cake from a grocery-store bakery box. "Sorry I didn't have time to bake some-thing," she said.

"Do you remember Bob Nordyke's cabin?" I said, searching for small talk.

Anne squinted as if digging through a box of old photographs and party invitations. "Oh, I know," she said, nodding. "Our last family vacation ever. Dad kept us out fishing all day, and you threw up in the middle of the night. The next day, we were sunburned and squalling, and Mom and Dad were hungover and had a terrible fight."

Daryl came in and filled a plastic *Star Wars* cup (Darth Vader almost completely worn away with age) from the kitchen tap. He leaned against the counter, gulped the water down, and stood holding the cup, looking back and forth between Anne and me. He had hazel eyes and a wispy blond mustache I thought he'd be better off without.

I watched him talk with Anne. Sometime this last January, maybe in this very kitchen, maybe in front of my nieces and nephews, this man had hit my sister in the face. How had he hit her? How would you hit a woman, a wife? I looked at them standing close to one another. They were bantering about some wool blanket Daryl had put in the dryer and shrunk to the size of a washcloth, and I felt foolish again, stewing about a situation that was, I hoped, long over with.

"You want a beer?" Daryl opened the refrigerator.

Anne's mouth tightened. "He's been out with Dad," she said. "He doesn't need another beer."

"It's 3.2," Daryl said. "It's like water."

"So give him water," Anne said.

"I'll take a glass of water," I said. I held a cup under the tap. "Anne's never stopped being my big sister."

Daryl, on his way back outside, turned in the doorway and smiled at his wife. "You gotta love her for that."

Anne and I visited until we were interrupted by the sound of running feet in the other half of the house, followed by a crash, then hollering. Anne smiled and said, "That'll be the twins' bed-time. Don't be a stranger."

On the way down the drive, I stuck my head under the hood with Daryl. He was adjusting the carburetor jets with a long, thin-bladed screwdriver in the glare of a trouble light.

"How's it going?" I said.

"Think I got it figured out." The unshaded bulb above us threw the hard shadow of his hatchet nose across one cheek. "What I need to do to fix this car," he said, "is take off the radiator cap."

"Huh?" I said, playing along.

"Yup. And then drive a new car under that radiator cap." A tired joke, but Daryl grinned as if to say he knew the joke was old and he was a shitty mechanic and he didn't care. Anne, I realized, had picked him for this: his understanding of his own faults so like our father's, the charm that made us all forgive far too much.

8

HERE IS HOW I REMEMBER Bob Nordyke's cabin. Late one spring
when we kids were little, Dad took the family there for the weekend.
The cabin was on some tributary of the Saint Croix in Wisconsin.
Dad showed us how to fish for crawdads in a muddy little creek
that emptied into the bigger stream, tying a length of fishing line
around a hunk of liver: we'd toss it in the water and pull it back
almost immediately with six or seven crawdads hanging onto it,
which we dumped into a bait bucket. We were on a broken pier
of concrete that extended halfway across the creek, the concrete
warm in the sun. Anne and I fished for a while, then ran back and
forth on the pier screaming. Dad sat on an overturned bucket,
smoking, watching Jacky, who caught crawdads by feeling around
under the rocks at the water's edge, then jerking his hand out
when a crawdad latched on, flipping the crawdad onto the pier.
He laughed every time this happened, and Dad laughed along
with him. Then Anne gave a cry and pointed at the opposite bank,
which was tall and shadowed by cottonwoods. I stopped imitating
a diving airplane to follow her finger, and a rippling movement in
the shadows resolved itself into hundreds of crawdads emerging
from holes in the steep bank and tumbling into the water. "Lookit,"
Anne said. "I'll be damned," our father said, moving to stand beside us. Jacky crouched froglike on a broken slab of concrete at the
water's edge, his right hand stirring the water absently. We stood as
if in a tableau, Anne's arm frozen in a point, Jacky's head cocked

like a curious dog's. Dad took his cigarette from his mouth, an uncharacteristic open smile on his face. Then I shook myself out of it and glanced around at the others, still standing as if locked in time while I was free to look and remember.

What I remember is a happy family, that afternoon and night. We purged the crawdads in saltwater, washed them again in fresh, and boiled them for dinner. Around the fire pit in front of the cabin, Dad split a can of Grain Belt among us children, and Mom let us make a mess of ourselves and everything within reach. The three of us sat in a line on a log, seasoned with dirt and crawdad juices. Mom and Dad—thinner then—crowded into a chaise lounge across the fire from us, Mom snuggled under his arm, the chair's aluminum frame and frayed nylon webbing creaking every time they shifted their weight. They smoked and drank whiskey with their beer and told stories in slurred voices about their grandparents and great aunts and uncles, and the stories about people and times I didn't know weren't as interesting as the warmth and mystery in my parents' voices as they told them. The night and the stories went on so long that I began to imagine I saw the palings of first light in the eastern sky. But when Mom herded us into the cabin to be scrubbed off and go to bed on the big mattress in the loft, I got a look at her watch and it was only eleven. This did not disappoint me; if the first few hours of the night were so deep and full of treasure, I could imagine the whole night as a vast, cavernous entity with countless secrets and delights that would reveal themselves as I grew older.

I sometimes wonder if the lives of happy families are made up of a series of moments like our family's evening at Bob Nordyke's cabin. For the rest of us, happiness comes from what we manage to forget. What I had managed to forget was vomiting at three a.m., a gutful of crawdads coming up in noisy violence after I'd spent a sleepless, fearful night trying to keep my sickness to myself. The cabin's dim lamps seemed to blaze at that hour, lighting Mom's white, weary face and, in the background, Dad's unshaven, red-eyed disgust. The vicious fight the next morning began with the old man accusing Mom of not cooking the shellfish long enough and Mom yelling back that the old man was an idiot, that everyone would be sick in that case, that he'd kept us out in the sun too long. After that, there was the long ride back to the Cities, we children holding still in frightened silence in the backseat.

I also remember this:

An hour after Mom put us all to bed, I came out of a restless early sleep to hear strange sounds in the cabin below the loft, shufflings and gruntings, low cries from my mother. A bear must be down there, I thought, and, steeling my courage, I had begun to sidle across the striped mattress when Anne's hand on my wrist stopped me. She put a finger to her lips. We lay on our sides facing each other and listened while the sounds below reached a certain pitch, then faded with a last, muffled profanity from our father. I saw that Anne understood what was happening, but when I started to ask, she rolled with her back to me and punched up her pillow in a way that let me know she was going to sleep and I'd bother her at my own risk. I couldn't sleep after that. My stomach began to rumble, and the country, which everyone always spoke of as peaceful and quiet, wasn't that way at all. Once I was awake with everyone else asleep, the night sounds from outside came into my consciousness and wouldn't go away: crickets and bullfrogs, katydids and tree frogs, the night louder than it ever was in the city. I became fearful that something from the river might creep into our cabin, and that I, alone among my family, would be awake and aware of the doom stealing upon us. It was during that long night, curled around my aching stomach, sweating under the sheet with only my nose sticking out while I prayed the Our Father over and over, that I first apprehended nature as a frightening, insistent process that I was a part of, powerless to stop or shut out.

IV

9

I COULDN'T HIT THE CURVE.

I learned at the College of Saint Thomas that good breaking balls were beyond me. But they were also beyond most Division III pitchers, so I started at first base by the time I was an upperclassman, occasionally sitting against lefties. The old man came to every home game. If I didn't start, he'd throw a consoling arm around my shoulders afterward and shake his head. "I've got a lot of enemies in this town," he would intone darkly.

My junior season ended with an away game on a muggy May afternoon. It turned into a pitching duel with the only score coming when we managed a run in the sixth, putting together a walk, stolen base, bunt, and sacrifice fly.

In the bottom of the ninth, after two quick outs, our closer gave up a triple. The next batter was a left-hander who'd hit a hard grounder my way in the seventh. I wiped a sleeve across my forehead, settled my cap over my eyes. Came up on my toes, ready and relaxed. The pitcher hung a curve, and the batter slapped what should have been a Texas leaguer into right. I turned, thinking extra innings, and saw Mick Shankland coming in fast. He was a fleet outfielder from Rochester, a Mayo doctor's son with a razor mind and a big-league arm. He caught the ball at his shoestrings and rifled it home. It went over the catcher's head. It also went over the backstop, the stands, the trees behind the stands, and the equipment shed behind the trees behind the stands. We found it after the game on a practice field.

The crowd applauded, causing Mick to pause in the middle of stomping on his glove. "Hey Mick," I shouted. "It's okay. It was the third out."

'He tipped his cap to the stands. "That last one always sneaks up on me."

Back in Saint Paul, a bunch of us went to O'Gara's for beer. Mick and I grabbed a table to ourselves and resumed a long-standing discussion. He was a senior in Saint John Vianney, the undergraduate seminary at Saint Thomas, and wanted me to follow him to the graduate seminary across the street. I was majoring in history and minoring in literature, but Mick believed I had a vocation. He saw that I was active in the campus church as a lector and Communion server. What he didn't know was that I was working hard for my soul, which I believed had an extra burden upon it.

"You're clearly not preparing for any other career," Mick said. He poked a finger at me. "And that's because you know in your heart." He thumped his chest. "Right here, bud."

"So my old man and some hick from Rochester don't like my major," I said, but Mick's attention had shifted to a hip Macalester coed in black tights and a checked miniskirt who was looking for a table with a group of friends. He leaned back in his chair, dropping one arm from the table to dangle in a way that emphasized his long, lean muscles, the Popeye forearm that could drive a baseball four hundred feet. He gave the girl a skilled once-over, lingering just long enough on her tight canary-yellow top to toe the line between appreciation and lechery, then met her green eyes with a rakish grin. She turned her back on him and flounced away, but she gave her butt an extra swing as she did it, then landed at a nearby table, which she and her friends settled around with much laughter and flipping of hair, a nervous flock ready to spring into the air again.

"You know, you're not the most convincing candidate for the priesthood," I said.

"I'm making an informed decision," Mick said. "It ain't the fifties." This was true, to a point. High-school seminaries were largely gone; men entered seminary as undergraduates and graduate students or as a mid-life career change. Still, if undergraduate seminarians sometimes dated, the practice was discouraged, and few played the field as enthusiastically as Mick. Even among a bunch of randy ballplayers, he had a reputation as a cocksman.

"I don't see it happening," I said.

Mick leaned forward, rolling his shoulders for the benefit of the Macalester girls. In a little while, he would pick up his chair carelessly in one paw, swing it across the aisle to an opening at their table, and drop onto it as if he belonged there. And just like that, he would belong there. Later, he'd let slip that he was going to become a priest, a gambit that worked especially well with the liberal Macalester women, who immediately rolled back on their heels to save him from the clutches of repressive Mother Church.

Mick was punching at me with his finger again. "This isn't about me, it's about you. You're smart, devout, a perfect candidate." I shook my head and went to the bar for another beer, figuring that when I got back Mick would be busy with the girl in the checked miniskirt.

Right idea, wrong girl. When I turned around with my beer, Mick stood leaning up against the wall with one hand, his arm framing a black-haired girl in a dark blue top with khakis belted at her tiny waist. She was looking up at him and talking animatedly, quick eyes sparkling behind her glasses.

I walked over without thinking.

"Betty," I said. I hadn't seen her in three years.

Her eyes snapped to mine. Mick looked startled. "Well—" he said.

"James." Betty frowned.

"Betty." I needed to come up with something else to say.

Mick scratched his head, looked back and forth between us.

"Sorry," I said. "Mick, this is Betty, my high-school girlfriend."

Mick gave her his smoothest smile. "Didn't know Dressler had so much taste."

Betty's eyes remained locked on mine.

"I'm out of here," Mick said.

As Mick walked away, Betty gave him an exaggerated once-over, taking in the sprinter's ass and the stevedore's shoulders. "Who's Casanova?"

"He's going to be a priest," I said.

"What a shame." She stuck her tongue out, and I was sorry for about a million things.

"How's Hank?" I asked, getting to one of them.

"Same as ever."

I guessed we weren't going to talk about the fight.

Betty went on. "You know he lost Hank Jr.? He was shot to death on the West Side a few weeks after you graduated. It was a gang thing. And drugs." Betty looked down, as if embarrassed someone in her family had died that way.

So Hank had been grieving a son at that game. How had I missed the news? "Jesus, I'm sorry," I said. "Why didn't you tell me?"

Someone pushed between us. Betty looked annoyed. "I thought it would make it real," she said.

"I'm sorry," I managed again, letting it go. I pictured Hank Jr. tossing a football back and forth with Betty at a Labor Day picnic at Lake Phalen, gunmetal gray water shining through the trees in the background. He'd looked like Hank had as a young man: tall, with long legs and a confident, easy stride. He'd been Betty's favorite cousin, had treated her like a kid sister when he already had a handful. On impulse, I touched the tip of my forefinger to the shadowed hollow of Betty's throat, where her top tied at the neck. A familiar electricity leaped between us. Betty blushed.

"How'd you get in here?" I said, wanting to carry her safely past Hank Jr.'s death.

"Linda's ID." She grinned then, the familiar lopsided one. "Us Mexican girls all look alike." Someone else stumbled into us. "Is there any place out of the way here?" Betty said.

I led her into a quiet side room where we shared a two-topper. I didn't know what to say, so I told her this room had been Charles Schulz's father's barbershop and little Charlie had lived in an apartment upstairs. There was a building in *A Charlie Brown Christmas* that looked like my brownstone, just west of O'Gara's on Selby. When I'd pointed this out to the old man the past Christmas, he'd grumped from the couch: "You pay too much for that apartment. Damn strip hasn't been funny since the talking dog took it over."

Betty laughed at that and fished a Marlboro out of her purse. She was one of those people who could smoke a cigarette on a night out and leave it at that. She reached for an ashtray. "How is your father?"

"Same as ever," I said. "It's easier being out of the house. And your folks?"

"The same, too," she said. "They still think I'm in college to find a husband."

I remembered Mr. García toasting us at a family gathering: "*Salud,* to my daughter and her *novio.*" And Betty: "Dad, he's not my *novio.* I'm going to law school."

"Sure, Hank." Mr. García and the men with him had laughed.

Betty and I talked until O'Gara's closed, a negotiation broken by only a few awkward silences. She smoked and drummed her nails on the tabletop. I popped my knuckles and shifted my feet. She gave me a ride home, pulling to the curb in front of my apartment. "Why don't you live on campus?"

"Ever try to study around a bunch of ballplayers?"

She laughed, we leaned toward each other, and I took her hand. She smelled of tobacco and rum and a perfume that sent me straight back to high school.

"Hot day for May," I said.

"Kiss me," Betty said.

A few minutes later, gearshift digging into my side, I asked her upstairs.

"That wouldn't be a good idea."

I drew back, the sting of the abortion fresh again. Betty's manicured nails grazed my cheek. "It's all right," she said.

She clicked over the ignition far enough to turn on the radio. It was the same station she tuned in on our first real date after her quinceañera, when we parked by the river, the girders of the old High Bridge drawing geometric shapes in the air above us. "Let's listen to jazz," she'd said then, "it's sexy." Her mother set strict curfews in those days, but Betty talked her into extra time for malts at the Saint Clair Broiler, and we left movies early. "What if your mom asks how it ends?" I worried the first time we did this. "They get back together," Betty said. "Don't you pay attention in English? Boy meets girl, boy loses girl, boy gets girl back." One night, when we got home ten minutes late, flushed and giggling, Mrs. García quizzed her about the end of a movie and Betty killed off the entire cast of *Ordinary People,* daring her mother to doubt her, eyes dancing with mine all the while. It had been that Betty who raced ahead of me across an icy lake in the dark, that Betty who'd wiggled a condom at me one evening along the Mississippi.

The Betty in the car with me on Selby had a different edge, guarded even after a couple rum and Cokes. It made me wonder how I had changed, but only for a moment, because so much was the same: the way she leaned back suddenly from a kiss with an easy half-smile to loose the bow at her throat with a slow flourish, the way she wriggled into my arms in the cramped car, the way she made me feel as if any good thing could happen.

We sat out front a long time, talking and kissing, watching groups of Macalester students straggle by on their way home from O'Gara's, their voices loud and full of slurred profundities. Then Betty asked to use the bathroom, and we went inside. On the landing in front of my studio apartment, I apologized. "It's a mess," I said. "Been busy studying." Old term papers, dirty clothes, and paperbacks from my lit classes hid most of the carpet. Mick once had toed a sweatshirt and said, "Geez, Dressler, you oughta wash and fold your floor."

Betty arched an eyebrow. "Looks like your room in high school. You didn't study a lot then." She punched me in the shoulder and went into the bathroom.

She came out trailing fresh perfume and circled through the room: the kitchen along one wall, the breakfast nook by the window, the desk and bookshelves, the futon sofa that made into a bed.

"I don't see any pictures of girlfriends turned face down," she said.

"I date around," I said. "You?"

Betty shrugged, looked at me from under her bangs. "I've been seeing Ramón," she said, "off and on. It's tough because he's in grad school out East."

I started to say something jealous, but caught myself. Betty had been right in the car: this wasn't a good idea. We were both smart enough to see that, but we were also college kids and having had a few drinks in a bar and come to a room alone together made us feel adult and made high school seem long ago.

The tie at Betty's throat was still undone. I reached for it, found instead her ear, her cheekbone, the fine hair at her temple. I leaned over and bit her trapezius, loveliest of muscles. I murmured praises into her shoulder. In a moment we were on the futon couch.

"C'mon," Betty said, when we came up for air. "Do you have lots of pure-hearted Saint Thomas girls up here? Or just one special one?" She caught her long hair in one hand and flipped it over her shoulder.

"I really do study a lot," I said. There'd been girls, one or two each school year, but I didn't get too close to any of them, and I was careful about birth control. I was popular on campus, an honors student and an athlete. Mornings strolling by Aquinas Hall with a knapsack slung over one shoulder, afternoons on the ball field clowning for the girls in the stands, evenings at O'Gara's telling one of my father's bad jokes over burgers and beer, I was one of the guys. Nights alone, I brooded over the dense histories of Minnesota and the Church that I would write my honors thesis on. The life of the mind and the asceticism of priests struck me more and more as noble self-sufficiencies. I liked the confident way the undergraduate seminarians in my classes carried themselves, the quiet, considered answers they gave to difficult questions. Mick, though I wouldn't give him the satisfaction of admitting it, had me half-convinced.

Then Betty undid the top buttons of my shirt and played a game with her fingernails where my shoulder muscles met my neck. We tumbled about on the overstuffed futon, and she started a tickle fight that ended with her straddling my hips, laughing, hair falling over us both like a black silk sheet.

Betty pinioned my wrists to the couch. "Gotcha," she breathed.

I swung my feet to the floor and reversed our positions. Betty struggled to hold me, then fell back on the futon giggling. "Oh!" she said. Her face was open. Then serious: "What happened to us?"

I sat back on my calves, worked my jaw. Our wrestling match had left me scented with her perfume. Why did she have to ask?

She sat up and kissed my chest, fingertips absently tracing a tendon in my forearm. Even in high school, Betty had been ambitious, liked sex best after I'd hit a home run or won a scholarship. She'd known her own mind at a young age, and I'd always liked her for that. Could I blame her for not letting a baby get in the way of our lives? Shouldn't I be grateful? I no longer thought abortion an absolute wrong. Even at Saint Thomas I'd come to see that life rarely offered clear choices between good and evil acts, but rather wrenching decisions between bad and worse outcomes, made without knowing which would be bad and which worse. In grade school, though, the women from Birthright had done their work well. Their words and the images of their films still resonated inside me.

Betty ran her hand inside my collar, pulled out the Saint James medal my grandfather had given me for First Communion. She bent her face to it, tracing with her thumbnail the book the saint held, the little sword at his side. "This medal," she said, "always got caught in my hair."

I lifted the medal from her fingers and slipped it inside my shirt. "I wish you hadn't had the abortion," I said.

Betty's head jerked up, then she lurched to her feet. When I stood and reached for her arm, she backed up against the window.

"Don't touch me," she snapped. "God damn you."

I slammed the heel of my hand into the window frame by Betty's head. She threw up her arms to protect her face and got the futon between us, stumbling over a pair of running shoes I'd left in the middle of the floor and catching herself on the futon. "Shit!" she said. For a moment neither of us moved, then I bent and picked up her purse from the floor by the futon and held it out to her. Betty's hands were trembling on the back of the futon. Her breath came in short, ragged bursts. She weighed all of a hundred pounds. She eyed the purse.

"Don't go," I said.

Betty looked up at me, eyes black and unblinking. Her face was pale, flushed red in splotches. The only sound in the room was the alarm clock ticking on the windowsill. She took the purse from my hand. "Give me a minute," she said, and went into the bathroom. I heard the door lock behind her.

I got two beers out of the refrigerator, opened one, and leaned against the counter and drank it while I waited. My heart was beating fast, and I felt a little ill. A few minutes passed before Betty came out of the bathroom. She'd done her face, erased the signs of our make-out session. I handed her a beer.

"I need a cigarette," she said.

I reached into a cabinet and got down a cracked saucer for an ashtray. We sat on either side of my small kitchen table. I tried to think of something to say, but couldn't. I felt as small and abashed as a child.

Betty lit up, let out a stream of smoke. "That scared me."

"Me too," I said. I studied my hand, the heel red and smarting.

"I shouldn't have said that," Betty said.

"That you were scared?"

"No," Betty said. "The *God damn you* part. Your good Catholic soul." She smiled and tapped ashes on the saucer. Her hands were steadier.

"What about yours?" I said. I looked at our reflections in the kitchen window and the blackness beyond.

Betty gave me a tired half-smile. "It's sad," she said. "But it's done."

I wasn't sure whether she was talking about us or the abortion, but I nodded, feeling an unexpected release from the past. "Yeah," I said, "it's all done." Betty was resting her chin on her hand, watching me. "Don't you ever get tired of being right?" I asked her.

Betty picked up her lighter from the table. She thumbed the wheel and studied the flame before letting it go out. "I don't think I'm right all the time," she said, her eyes still fixed on the spot where the flame had been.

We stayed at the table after that and talked and sipped beer through the wee hours of the morning, catching up now with no agenda between us. Betty was getting through the University of Minnesota in three years and had already been accepted to study law at William Mitchell. I had a 4.0 at Saint Thomas and no definite plans. We talked about Hank Jr.'s death, Betty saying her cousin had had a hard time living up to Hank's expectations. We didn't talk about my father kicking Hank while Hank tried to drag himself under his truck. And we didn't talk about the abortion. When Betty stubbed out her last cigarette and I walked her out to her car, we kissed once, and I stood in the street and watched her taillights down Selby to Fairview, where her signal came on and she turned right and was gone. Then I went back upstairs and dumped her cigarette butts into the garbage and rinsed off the cracked saucer and put it back in the cupboard.

That's how Betty García and I became friends. After that evening we lost touch for a while, but later I would be at her wedding—not to Ramón, but to Ethan, another law student at William Mitchell—and at the baptism of their son. Five years from that night, in May of 1990, I would attend her law-school graduation, and she my ordination.

10

AT SAINT THOMAS, JOINING THE PRIESTHOOD was honorable in the same way that joining the Marines had been in my father's place and time. The autumn of my senior year, Mick came down the street from the seminary every Friday to meet me for coffee in the student union. He carried himself more gravely now—perhaps it was the prayer book—and he no longer flirted with the Saint Thomas girls, though sometimes I caught him eyeing one thoughtfully. He asked about Betty, and I told him how we'd gone our separate ways. When Mick described the seminary, it sounded like a place I wanted to be, a place where largeness of spirit and good manners were taught, where a honed mind was valued as much as sports and knowing how to hold your liquor or tell an off-color joke. It was a locker room full of knowledge and power. I recognized the team colors, the black and white of God's own all-stars.

Priests were neither strange nor distant to me. Father Phil had bowled with my grandfather for as long as I could remember; I had brought him cocktails on my grandparents' patio when they entertained the nuns and priests. I'd gone to Catholic grade school, been proud of the cross of ashes I wore on my forehead among the neighborhood public-school kids on Ash Wednesdays. Shortly before I met Betty, I had attended a vocational weekend at the Benedictine monastery in Collegeville. Now I saw that the weekend at the monastery had been like the barest sip of Communion wine; it lingered sweetly in my memory, promising purpose and grace.

I began to go into the Chapel of Saint Thomas Aquinas between classes. I would kneel in the back, sometimes in solitude, sometimes while a custodian ran a sweeper or a choir practiced near the altar. I prayed and tried to clarify and open my heart to God's will, to discern whether He were calling me to the priesthood. Afterward, apparently without answer but doing my best to trust that there would be one, I would step back out onto the quad, where my friends played Frisbee and pretty girls walked in twos and threes, backpacks slung from one shoulder, skirts fluttering about their knees. Yet a certainty must have begun to grow in me, and one day I was aware of it.

"I could be a priest," I said to Mick on a Friday in November.

In college, I continued to volunteer at our parish office, as I'd done since grade school. When I was younger, Father Phil had been jovial and easygoing with all the altar boys but never close to any of us. Now we became friends, and my last winter at Saint Thomas, I began asking him carefully worded questions about whether a theoretical young man with a vocation would be better off joining a religious order like the Benedictines or going to the Saint Paul Seminary and becoming a diocesan priest. He argued the diocesan route, saying there was nothing better than to be a priest guiding and guarding a parish flock. Then he invited me ice fishing at a lake north of the Cities where the priests of the archdiocese had a fishing camp.

Mid-morning on the appointed Friday, Phil eased his Olds slowly across snow-covered ice to a hut hammered together out of plywood and two-by-fours. It was an overcast day, the sun a dull nickel behind the clouds, blowing snow stinging our faces when we emerged from the car. Our breath steamed in the cold air. Phil patted the front of his coveralls and glanced around the snow-shrouded lake. The trees on the shoreline were gray shapes in a white mist. "Hard-water fishing," Phil said. "Nothing beats it." He opened the trunk and began setting gear on the ice.

"It's great out here," I said.

Phil straightened from the trunk and winked. "Everyone loves walking on water."

Inside, the shack felt more intimate than a confessional, creaking in the wind in the middle of the lake. Phil got a Coleman lantern going for warmth and opened a hole with an ice auger. "Welcome to the Chapel of Saint Andrew," he said. Then he showed me how to set up one of the short ice-fishing rods he'd brought, making each step a little ritual, and said a prayer to Andrew the Apostle, patron saint of fishermen. Phil and his buddies had built the hut years ago. There was a crucifix on one wall, and opposite that, a painted icon of the saint, complete with both a curved fish and the X-shaped cross he was martyred on. We settled into camp chairs, Phil sitting with his elbows on his knees, jigging his line occasionally and smoking Pall Malls, a squad of dead soldiers gathering in the snow at his feet. Between smokes, he drank from a hip flask that stuck out of the chest pocket of his coveralls. His whiskey nose and jug ears were bright red in the cold, and his thick-fingered hands rested on his knees like baseball mitts. We sat in silence, and by turns I watched my breath rise in front of Saint Andrew like smoke from a censer and used my boot to toe snow into the slushy hole that wasn't producing any bites. I planned to ask Phil to sponsor my seminary application, but was hesitant to bring it up—it was a big step. I could already imagine Phil's proud grin, and Granddad's when he heard the news.

I made a game of it. I would ask Father Phil about the application when he finished that cigarette. I would ask when we caught a fish. I would ask when he broke into the coffee. The cold had worked its fingers into the seams of my insulated coveralls and my toes were going numb. I shifted in my camp chair. Phil snuffed out a cigarette and, rolling forward in his bulky coveralls, reached for the gray-green metal Thermos that tilted in the snow by his left foot. The flask fell out of his pocket and bobbed in the black water, a big silver ice cube. "Shit," Phil said. I fished it out with the ice skimmer.

Steam rose from the Thermos. Phil let it warm his face, then filled the cup and added some whiskey from his flask before passing it over. I took a gulp, relishing the double bite of Maxwell House and Jameson. Phil had lectured me on Irish whiskey: Jameson, dark and sweet, was what good Catholics drank; Bushmills, light and dry, was for Protestants. I turned the cup between my hands, sloshing coffee.

"I'd like to apply to seminary," I said.

Phil's red-rimmed blue eyes were sharp in the close air of the hut. "Yeah-uh," he said, pulling at his lower lip. "I could see that coming. Church needs good men. You're bright, a fine athlete. You'd go far. Play golf?"

"No, sir."

"Learn. Take you further than fishing. Fishing's good too, though." He seemed worried that he'd slighted fishing. "Nothing wrong with fishing."

At that, Phil's line jerked. "See," he said. He set the hook and began reeling in line hand over leather-gloved hand—he was using a homemade jigging rod without a reel. Every so often he stopped to play the fish before taking in another turn or two. I kept silent. Phil bent over the line as if listening for news. "Swims like a northern," he grunted. "Big one." I moved the lantern and knelt by the hole. By the time Phil eased the speckled head and underslung jaw out of the water, he was panting a bit. "Watch the teeth," he said. I leaned forward and made a grab for the pike just as Phil shifted for a better angle, and we knocked heads. I slipped and kicked the ice auger into the wall, but got the fish by the gills.

Phil's face was redder than usual. "You've got a hard head."

"Thick skull," I said. Then I asked the question that had kept bugging me, the one all my remaining worries gathered around. "Does it get lonely?" The fish struggled in my grip.

"What?" Phil muttered, working at the Russian spoon lodged in the corner of the pike's jaw. He jerked a finger away from the teeth.

"Not having a wife and kids," I said. "Being a priest." The pike was one long muscle. Its tail whapped against my knee.

Phil freed the hook and dropped his line back into the hole. "Greatest job in the world." He took off his black wool stocking cap and rubbed his bald head. He gazed at me shrewdly. "Got a hobby?"

"Huh?" I knocked the pike's skull against a two-by-four, cracked open the door, and tossed the fish out on the ice.

"Get a hobby."

I gave Phil a blank look. He had a red splotch on his forehead where we'd collided, and I took off a glove to finger a lump just above my hairline.

"Keep your hands busy, boy. Fishing works, though a lot do well with gardening, and I know one good man who's a fine model railroadist." He shook a cigarette from his pack, held it unlighted. "Good men are harder to find than you might think. Remember that, too."

I'd taken the first step, and it turned out to have been onto an escalator. Phil, who still bowled with Granddad in the Veterans Administration league, called my grandparents. The old man got wind of it, probably through Gram, and threw a fit—*no son of mine's gonna be a goddamn bead juggler.* Granddad responded by putting four years' worth of tuition, room, and board into a savings account in my name. He also presented me with a brand-new leatherbound set of Butler's *Lives of the Saints.*

I was grateful for the gifts, but the *Lives of the Saints* was a weighty one. My grandfather attended Saint Thomas on a partial scholarship in the fall of 1932, the first in his family to go to college. It's easy enough to imagine him on the first day of class, a late summer day with the leaves of the young cottonwoods on Summit Avenue shimmering like water in the cool sunlight. He would have taken the Grand Avenue trolley in slacks and a dress shirt ironed and starched by his mother, and he might have paused on the grassy median in the middle of Summit, tugged at his tie and squared his shoulders, before crossing the westbound lane and entering campus proper through a stone archway. His blue eyes would have brimmed with anticipation and goodwill. He had always been the nuns' favorite, his mother's golden-haired boy, and so it was easy for Otto to love the world and to believe it loved him back, even in the middle of the Depression.

But Otto had been in the vocational track at Central High, and he was unprepared for Saint Thomas. He lost his scholarship when he flunked chemistry, and, for good measure, theology. The last was a particular insult, as if someone had said he had not loved God enough. "I told that professor," he would say in his cups at the Lexington, "that I knew the *Lives of the Saints* better than he did." When he said this I could see him disdainfully slapping his failed exam onto a wooden desk at the front of a high-windowed, ill-heated hall, then stumbling out into a late afternoon and through the long December shadows of bare trees on brown lawns.

In the years following, Granddad married and went to war. When he came home, he scraped and saved to send my father to college. After my father failed him, Otto chose me to fill with a vision of college life he'd cribbed from F. Scott Fitzgerald. My grandfather's attitude toward Fitzgerald was proprietary—"just another Saint Paul drunk"—and he believed that the Princeton of *This Side of Paradise* waited on every college campus: football games on drowsy autumn afternoons, freshmen in beanies, drinking clubs and pranks and young men with long woolen coats and elegant scarves spending late nights in diners hashing out the great issues of the day. And if Saint Thomas were not exactly Princeton, I was happy there and content to know that I had given my grandfather an image of his grandson strolling across the green quadrangles that lay amid the school's handsome Mankato-stone halls.

Now I would give him another gift, a priest in the family. When he heard the news, Otto put on his hat and marched into the Saint Patrick's Guild store at Randolph and Snelling, where he purchased their most expensive set of *Lives of the Saints*. He liked the Lord just fine.

When I was accepted into the seminary, there was a family celebration dinner in the bar at the Lexington with my parents and grandparents, Father Phil, and myself. Jacky didn't show, and Anne and Daryl couldn't get a babysitter and decided not to come with the kids.

Granddad flirted with the big-haired waitress who took our drink orders. "Donna—what a lovely name! I'll have a martini." House Scotch for Gram, beer for the old man, sherry for Mom. The waitress moved along the table, bent near, perfumed hair about her face. I ordered a Jameson on the rocks for myself and one for Phil.

The drinks came. Dad lifted his beer glass toward me, but Granddad spoke first, martini held high. "To my grandson, who'll make a fine priest." Dad lowered his face to his beer, but Granddad went on, speaking around the cigar he was drawing to life. "It's not the first time this joint has been the launching pad for a noble endeavor. I proposed to the lovely Alexandra here. She and the Lex are both as glorious now as they were then."

"It wears a little thin, given time," Gram said dryly.

Granddad's smile stiffened. "Alexandra's always had aspirations to match her name," he said. "When I got home from the war, broke and with a bum arm, she proudly shows me a chest full of monogrammed Gorham silver. She'd been buying two pieces every month with my sergeant's pay. And I said, 'We'll set a fine table if we have anything to eat, Alex.'"

Gram didn't answer. She dipped a fresh cigarette toward Father Phil, who dutifully lit it for her with his chrome Zippo. Dad's beer was gone already, and he signaled for another, then rested his elbow on the table and smoked and watched the goings-on in the rest of the bar. When the beer came he perked up and said something I couldn't hear. The waitress laughed, and her hair and chest shook. Mom leaned over and put a hand on Dad's forearm while she ordered a second sherry, then blew cigarette smoke at the ceiling and pretended to study the murky oil painting on the wall over my grandparents' heads.

Phil glanced around the table with some alarm as the family disappeared in clouds of blue smoke and it appeared no one was going to speak again. It wasn't unusual for family dinner conversations to founder—we often covered lapping waves of silence with the clink of silverware and the business of eating. Phil was an old friend of Granddad's and must have known by now what to expect from us; still, I searched for something to say, something to prompt a war story from Granddad or Saint Luke's bridge-club gossip from Gram, or even an off-color joke from the old man. But I was as tongue-tied as the rest of them, family alchemy turning every glint of conversation to lead and sending it straight to the bottom.

The bottom was deep. In the late thirties, my grandfather, then a hurly-burly little rogue with a quick tongue and quicker fists, had settled into steady employment working nights for the state printing office, where he met Alexandra Mueller, an ambitious young woman just moved down from Duluth. She was German, too, but Lutheran and a teetotaler, both of which Otto figured could be remedied. To her, he was an entertaining kind of trouble, a bundle of energy with a cigar clamped in its teeth. He had friends in Saint Paul nightlife left over from Prohibition, when he tended bar for a Saint Paul gangster in the Green Lantern, a notorious speakeasy. He claimed to have served a martini to John Dillinger and rolled dice for drinks with Creepy Karpis—"the politest killer you ever met," Otto liked to say. He squired Alexandra to American Association hockey games, hustling off the trolley on the way to place bets with his bookie. He took her drinking and dancing at Jerry's Nite Club at University and Snelling or the Covered Wagon downtown, where they danced to the music of the Cow Hands. He courted her with extravagant bouquets from Johnson's on Grand. She converted to Catholicism, took up Scotch, cigarettes, and bowling.

In an old photograph taken in some nightspot, they stand out in the center of a group of their friends, a pair of dandies dressed in better clothes than they can afford. Otto wears a suit with wide lapels and what looks like a pearl tie tack and stands smiling over Alexandra's shoulder. She sits at a table, a stone marten around her neck, a broad-brimmed hat cocked low over one eye. There's a telephone on the table and a little lamp with menus standing on either side of it.

"We had big-city eyes in those days," Gram said to me once, musing over the picture on a rainy October afternoon. She claimed they had plans to go east, to Chicago at least, with a Great Lake to match the one she'd grown up on. Or New York, even, where the skyscrapers blinked like starry northern nights. The war got in the way. Otto brought home a bad arm and worse dreams. He drank more, but martinis no longer made him want to waltz her around every dance hall in town. Alexandra unjustly blamed the drinking on Gerry Donovan and Will Reilly, Irish raconteurs Otto had buddied around with since boyhood, and she drove a wedge between Otto and his friends. Otto took a job with the Veterans Administration, respectable and well-enough paid, but with little hope for advancement. And Alexandra found herself at home, raising a difficult child in a small house not far enough from her in-laws. In the early 1950s, when Otto turned down a VA offer to transfer to Washington, Alexandra saw too clearly the outlines of her life. So she did her best to erase them with Manhattans at the bridge table and exotic cocktails with colorful umbrellas at the supper clubs they frequented.

And my father grew up an only child in a house full of the scent of furniture polish and Ajax, where the rising and falling pitch of a vacuum cleaner's motor as it was swept back and forth was a constant background to grim German silences. Otto dreamed of football stardom and college for him, so Joe fled to the streets and alleys of Midway, where he drank and smoked and fought his way off the Saint Agnes High team, and then sealed the deal by impregnating, in Otto's never-forgotten nor forgiven phrase, "that black-Irish trollop," my mother.

Tonight at the Lexington, Otto wore a checked jacket with a Knights of Columbus lapel pin, and Alexandra a blue silk dress with a necklace that had a gold pendant made to resemble a tiny, hand-painted Japanese fan. My father sat at the end of the table in a rumpled sport shirt with his shoulders rotated away from his father. Mom sat silently watching Alexandra advise Father Phil about his sister's sciatica. Granddad brooded over his martini, mouth turned down, talking, it seemed, to himself.

The waitress came back and handed out menus. Granddad lifted his chin and said, "Doll, would you bring an old gentleman another martini? A little lighter on the vermouth?"

Gram looked at him with distaste. "Otto—" she warned, but martinis made him hard of hearing.

Then everyone was clamoring for another round of drinks. I went for beer, knowing that to weather the evening in this company I'd have to pace myself. Talk turned to the merits of the Lexington's chicken potpie and walleye and who was going to have what and would they share a bite? When the waitress came back, Phil ordered the surf-n-turf, Gram the orange roughy, and Granddad the porterhouse.

"How do you want that?" the waitress asked.

"How's that, dear?" Granddad said, cupping an ear. His voice was slightly slurred.

"She wants to know how you want your steak, Otto," Gram said loudly, then coughed and brought a napkin to her lips.

"I heard her!" Granddad glared at the waitress. "Bloody!"

I swirled my beer and thought about what a great idea it had been to have a family celebration dinner. Mom had tried to talk me into it and, when that failed, mentioned it to Granddad, knowing he'd insist.

"C'mon, Josephine," Granddad boomed, when my father ordered a turkey sandwich, "it's on me. He'll have the porterhouse," he said to the waitress, who looked down at her order pad and wiggled her pen in the air.

"I'll have the goddamn turkey." Dad snapped at the waitress as though she were the one insisting on steak. Then aside to Granddad, but too loudly, the old man said: "Wallet burning a hole in your pocket? The Church'll take care of that."

Phil flushed, and I closed my eyes. When I opened them, Granddad was sitting ramrod-straight, face frozen, staring ahead with his lips pursed. Mom ordered chicken potpie and more sherry, I ordered walleye, and Phil gestured desperately with his empty whiskey glass.

The waitress hurried away, light shimmering on her black hose, skirt hugging her round bottom. More beer came, and a warm fuzzy feeling started to creep up the back of my brain. I'm not missing a thing, I thought, watching Gram and Granddad and the old man and Mom study their drinks and their fingernails, the bar paintings, other diners, anything but each other. Let the waitresses of the world bring me walleye and whiskies forever. I would never have to decide when to call, or remember an anniversary, or choose whether to share my feelings or just shut up.

The waitress arrived with our entrées, then came back a few minutes later to ask if everything was all right. She patted Father Phil's shoulder, and he beamed and ordered another whiskey. When she brought it, she gestured at the bar and said, "This one's on Neil." A stout man with sandy eyebrows that I recognized from campaign advertisements came over and shook hands around the table, ending with Phil. "Always a pleasure, Father," he said, then turned to the rest of us and waved a hand at the restaurant. "Best place in town for a heart attack: there's always two or three priests to pave your way to the Hereafter."

Phil chuckled. "It might take two or three for an old pol like you. I'm coming by next week to put the arm on you for new jerseys for the grade-school football team. Nothing fancy—we don't need names on the back, just a little blue and gold piping for the greater glory of God."

Neil slapped him on the back. "Pleasure doing business," he said, and moved on to another table.

When dinner was over, there were coffee and cigarettes all around. My parents shifted in their chairs and cast their eyes toward the door, and Dad lit one cigarette after another for himself and Mom, but they were tangled in the net of Granddad's relentless hospitality. Three martinis to the wind, Otto leaned forward and chatted happily, patting the table for emphasis, reaching out with long arms as though to draw them in. Phil and Alexandra had their heads together, and I was left alone, momentarily forgotten.

The crowd thinned, and the conversations around and among us fell off. Then the lights came up a little, and we all looked at each other with the stunned confusion of a long evening and too much food and drink. Granddad paid, and everyone moved for the door. I lingered long enough to leave an extra bill on the table. My grandfather still lived in the era of the ten-percent tip, and even if I were no longer to be a man of the world, I wanted to be a good priest in the world, generous and cosmopolitan.

Outside it had rained. The air smelled of mud and budding leaves, and the pavement reflected the lights of the traffic. Phil was at the corner, hunched in his black windbreaker waiting to cross Grand, and my parents were hurrying away. I'd driven my grandparents in Mom's rusty Plymouth that she'd given me for college, and we were parked in the alley lot behind the restaurant. My grandparents walked with the slow, uncertain steps of old people who've had too much to drink and can't see well at night anyway, so I took Gram's arm and cut my own stride in half. We shuffled back to the car, and I held the back door for Gram while Granddad climbed stiffly into the passenger's side front, though not before clapping a hard hand on my shoulder and saying, "You make me proud." Ducking my head at the unexpected praise, I stumbled over the parking block and made my way around the front of the car with a hand on the hood. In the driver's seat in the dark, I fumbled the key into the ignition, then felt the Plymouth's tired V8 turn over. I navigated along Grand at five miles below the speed limit, enjoying the respite driving made after the restaurant. Beside me, Granddad chanted in a soft sing-song: *the cavalry, artillery, and the corps of engineers, could never lick the infantry in a hundred million years,* then segued into "The Caissons Go Rolling Along." At *shout out your numbers loud and strong,* I made a left on Syndicate to Sargent and the bigger house Otto had bought Alexandra once Joe was on his own. He'd made some money on stocks by then, but my father claimed Granddad had always had money salted away and that they'd lived an unnecessarily tight life when he was a boy. That some of that money had been the college fund he'd never used didn't occur to him. I parked in front of the house and helped Gram up the steps to the door. The yard made a little hill up from the sidewalk, and Granddad had put in plantings to save mowing his steep lawn. He insisted I come in and offered a nightcap.

I asked for a Coke, tossed my purple Tommies letterman's jacket on the sofa, and sat down. Gram put Bunny Berigan on the console stereo and went into the kitchen to mix drinks for herself and Granddad. Some small thing had happened, and they weren't speaking again. Granddad handed off my Coke and tromped his way upstairs, where I could hear him fumbling around, drawers and doors opening and closing.

Playing upstairs in this house as a ten-year-old, I had found a white cardboard box in Granddad's dresser. Inside was a slender black-leather case, hinged at the top, and inside that, resting on gold satin, were military medals: the Combat Infantryman's Badge with its long rifle on blue background, campaign ribbons, the Purple Heart, the Bronze Star. This last had my grandfather's name inscribed in the back. Beneath the leather case were folded newspaper clippings from the war, a perpetual novena booklet, dog tags that clinked on their chain when I lifted them, and strange coins with kings and crowns and coats of arms. I sat on the bed and examined the coins and dog tags until Granddad's heavy tread downstairs made me afraid to be caught with them. I folded everything away and carefully replaced the cardboard box in his sock drawer. At home, I had a box of Army men of mixed sizes and vintages, and from them I chose a dark green soldier who stood with his head bent to sight down the barrel of a long rifle. That soldier was me, and when Jacky and I played war—always the European campaign, with the Battle of the Bulge being our favorite—I was a marksman, shot straight and true.

Granddad stumped back downstairs. He'd changed into his pajamas, a well-worn flannel robe, creased leather slippers. He went to the marble-topped antique commode by the front window, shook a cigarette out of Gram's pack there and busied himself with lighting it. He turned back to me. "Proud of you," he said. It seemed necessary tonight that he say it often. "Want you to have this." He fumbled for something in the pocket of the robe. What would it be? One of his medals, the dog tags?

Gram came and stood swaying in the door of the kitchen, blinking, holding a glass of Scotch on the rocks, quietly disapproving. I rested my head against the back of the sofa, waiting.

Granddad's hand floated in front of my face, his rosary looped from his fingers, the crucifix face down in his palm. He leaned toward me and let it drop, and I jerked upright and caught the crucifix as it swung, the rosary hanging for an instant on the crooked last joint of his forefinger.

I'd seen my grandfather's rosary often enough, but I examined it now under the light of the lamp on the end table. On the back of the crucifix was the sacred heart of Jesus, surrounded by thorns. The metal figurine on the front was tarnished, worn in places so it looked like bones showing through: ulna and radius, ribs and tibia. Jesus' face had been rubbed away with time. The cross was metal inlaid with cracked black wood, and the beads were hand-worked of rose paste, some chipped, some worn smooth, each a little varied from the others, dark reddish-brown with a hint of translucence to them. I saw all of the details with the clarity that comes at the exhausted end of a long day.

Gram turned back into the kitchen. Granddad stood still, peering at me. His blue eyes glinted, and he dragged on his cigarette. "I had a First Communion medal once," he said at last, letting go of a mouthful of smoke. "Your father traded it for cigarettes in grade school."

"I'll take care of it," I said. "It's beautiful."

He patted me roughly on the head and stumbled toward the stairs. I was his beloved grandchild.

"Granddad—"

He turned and shushed me, shaking his head with his finger to his lips. "It's past the witching hour," he said, "time for all good boys to go to bed."

A few minutes after he went upstairs, Gram brought a lowball glass from the kitchen and handed it to me. "Take this up to him," she said. I found Granddad at prayer, kneeling at his bedside with his shoulders drawn up and his head bowed. He didn't like to be disturbed, so I left the drink on his nightstand.

Downstairs, Gram was sitting in the armchair by the stereo, her feet on the ottoman. Her eyes were shut and her hands rested in her lap. On the lamp table beside her, there was a cigarette going in an ashtray. Her Scotch gleamed in the lamplight. I sat in the upholstered rocker on the other side of the table and listened to Bunny Berigan sing about how he couldn't get started loving someone. When the needle hit the end of the side and the tonearm clicked back into place, I reached over to stub out Gram's cigarette and found her awake and watching me. She smiled, but said nothing. My grandmother would chat with anyone at a cocktail party, but one-on-one she was like Mom and hid behind platitudes—*it's no hill for a stepper, tomorrow's another day,* or, if you lost something, *pray to Saint Anthony, then stand in the middle of the room and look.*

Only once did I get past her surface, on a Christmas Eve at the house on Sargent. The family was in the living room, waiting to open presents until Gram finished the dinner dishes. But when she came out of the kitchen, carrying a drink and trailed by Granddad, she went upstairs without a word. Granddad put on a Christmas album, then sat down in his recliner, and no one said anything. I was thirteen, but I was the one who got up to the tune of "The Little Drummer Boy" and went upstairs. Gram was sitting very erect at her dressing table, looking into the mirror. Her Scotch and water stood untouched at one hand; she held a cigarette in the other. While I stood in the doorway and watched her, she tapped it in an ashtray. I went into the room and sat on the bed. She was a small woman—I had passed her in height the year before—and she looked frail in front of the mirror. When she spoke, it was to the mirror. "We always had Christmas with your grandfather's parents," she said. "Duluth was too far away. The weather was too bad. Now my parents are dead." I was frightened. She had opened a door into adult life, where mistakes were permanent. Gram squared her shoulders. "Nothing to be done about it," she said. She took a long inhale from her cigarette, then stubbed it out. "You go on downstairs, Jimmy. I'll be down in a few minutes." She opened a jar of makeup and started to dab at her face. It was a brief moment, one that opened and closed and was gone so completely that neither of us would ever bring it up. After Gram died at the end of my first year in seminary, I realized how much silence had lain between us, that I really didn't know her at all.

But the night of my celebration dinner, in the living room of the house on Sargent, I wanted to know something about her: what it was like growing up in Duluth during the Depression, why she thought "buck up and button your lip" was a good answer to any sorrow, why she and Granddad had only the one child.

"Do you think I'm making a mistake?" I asked.

"You know your own mind," Gram said. If I pushed her, her eyes would become vacant and she would pretend not to hear. Maybe she didn't hear at those moments.

I finished my Coke. "What happened between Dad and Grand-dad?" I asked offhandedly, putting my hands on the chair arms to push myself up.

Gram surprised me with a real answer. "Your grandfather's very Catholic. The world always disappoints him in the end."

I sat back but lost her to a coughing fit. She went into the kitchen for water. When she didn't come back, I followed and found her standing at the sink, holding onto the water glass. She was breathing deliberately, puffing her cheeks out when she exhaled, drawing her head and shoulders back when she inhaled. I waited to make sure she was okay, then kissed her on the top of the head and let myself out.

I didn't drive straight home, but stayed on Lexington and turned down Front, going past the Half Time Rec and the apartment that would one day be my father's, and parking on a side street across from Calvary Cemetery. After waiting in the shadows while a police cruiser prowled by, I stepped over the chain across the cemetery driveway and followed the road uphill toward the circle where John Ireland, Saint Paul's legendary archbishop, is buried alongside his fellow prelates and row upon row of priests and nuns. Fifty yards short of Ireland's hilltop grave, I crossed the wet lawn to the Dressler family plot. A strong breeze tossed the trees, making shadows leap and start among the graves.

On Memorial Day trips here, my grandfather would tell family stories while he cut the turf away from grave markers with the blade of his World War II bayonet. Often my great-aunt and godmother Marie Therese would come over from Wisconsin for Memorial Day weekend and the trip to the graveyard, and ever since I was a child she had whispered cautionary tales in balance against my grandfather's romances.

For almost as long as there has been a Saint Paul, my family has been a part of it. Otto's great-grandfather, Theodor Wiemann, was a pillar of nineteenth-century Saint Paul's prosperous German merchant class. He was fashionable and wealthy, and his monument, in the center of the plot, is a Gothic fright that sits on the hillside at a slight angle, as though it might fall on its face; the stone is castellated about the top and chemically blackened around the edges to look old, the height of Victorian fashion. There's an unremarkable German verse celebrating Theodor carved into the base. Marie Therese claims he shattered an expensive cut-glass wine decanter, brought from Westphalia, the November day in 1880 that his beloved daughter Anna married Michael Dressler, an immigrant cigarmaker.

The wedding made the society column of the Saint Paul *Volkszeitung*, with the Mass celebrated in Assumption, the city's first German-Catholic parish. The church is still there, the witch hats of its twin steeples a downtown landmark, but Michael Dressler didn't fare nearly so well. In 1887, he confirmed his father-in-law's doubts by cracking his skull in a drunken tumble from a sleigh at the second-ever Saint Paul Winter Carnival.

Michael's son, my great-grandfather Karl, grew up to work as an accountant for the Great Northern Railroad. Karl fathered Marie Therese and my grandfather and two other children, twin girls who died in the Spanish flu epidemic of 1918. They weren't the only losses of the war years. Otto's birth in 1914 came at the last great moment of German culture in Saint Paul. By the time he reached the age of reason, the affluent, separatist German community he'd been born into had been erased by the prejudices of the Great War, which even established families like the brewery-owning Hamms and lumber-baron Weyerhausers were unable to overcome. German beer gardens closed, and the Germania Life Insurance Building lost its statue of Germania. Germans remained the city's largest ethnic group, but one that hid its very nature.

Otto was raised in an Irish city, hearing stories from his father of how the Germans had been persecuted, especially by Archbishop Ireland, an Americanist who opposed German national parishes like Assumption and fought the influence of the Benedictines at Saint John's. A national temperance leader, Ireland disapproved of the German brewing industry and fired one of Karl's cousins, a stonemason on the Cathedral of Saint Paul, when he caught the man with a bottle of beer in his lunch. Ireland had a hard time with the Germans. When he spoke at parishes, he was in the habit of asking his audience to stand and take the temperance pledge. At Assumption, the parishioners folded their arms and stared at him in stony silence.

Still, it wasn't John Ireland's fault that the Dressler fortunes declined. The men of my family have always loved strong drink and a good fight. After Prohibition was repealed, young Marie Therese would watch her mother Claudia, a long-suffering German woman, go to the Great Northern offices on payday to collect Karl's wages and pay the bills before Karl spent the money on buckets of beer at the Grandham Tavern. Marie Therese would watch a drunken Karl curse her brother Otto for his Irish friends and expensive clothes. The Dresslers attended Mass at Saint Agnes, the then-German parish in Frogtown, long after Karl built his family a better house near Irish Saint Luke's.

In January 1946, Karl spent a bitterly cold weekend on a binge, then suffered a stroke Monday morning as he boarded a streetcar for work. He fell backward down the steps and was carried home between a pair of policemen. He spent the last two years of his life in an upstairs bedroom, knowing only to ring the bell on his bedside table when he wanted something. Since Karl wanted health and another drink, the bell rang often.

Otto, home from the war, was enlisted to help nurse his father. One night, or so Marie Therese tells it, Claudia was out at the Rosary society, and Otto sat at the kitchen table, drinking and brooding over a fight with Alexandra, only half-aware of a faint ringing. And if it is true that Claudia came home to find her son asleep with his head cradled on his forearms and a whiskey at hand, while upstairs her husband lay dead on the floor beside the bed, holding his bell, and if it is also true that Claudia forgave her son, then Otto was not so generous. After all, he never forgave his own troubled son for bringing home my pregnant peroxide-blonde mother.

The story of my family's failed promise is in some ways the story of the erased German Saint Paul; though, since Germans pride themselves on being able to hold their beer, the fatal prat-falls belong to us alone. But tonight a Dressler was climbing again, picking his way uphill from Theodor Wiemann's leaning monument and the sod-obscured gravestones of Michael and Karl Dressler, away from the intemperance and violence of my own father. At the top of the hill, four slabs of granite mark the graves of the early bishops and archbishops of Saint Paul: the French-born Joseph Cretin and the Irishmen Thomas Grace, John Ireland, and Austin Dowling. Ireland built the Cathedral of Saint Paul, and from his grave its floodlit copper dome is visible beyond the bell tower of Saint Agnes. I stood there in the wind, made a bit dizzy by the movement of the low clouds rushing past the distant green dome and the exhilarating sense of my own aspirations, and I thought grandly that this time a Dressler had done it, that given time I would scale the very Cathedral itself.

11

I WAS HALFWAY THROUGH SEMINARY when Anne's oldest son received his First Communion. We had a family gathering afterward. Mom hadn't cleaned, and we walked in after Mass to find the house jammed with junk: stacks of the *Pioneer Press* and *Reader's Digest* in the living room, sewing patterns scattered over the dining-room table, ashtrays full of cigarette butts everywhere. The floral pattern of the couch was muddied by swirls of cat hair. Anne and I cast despairing glances at one another. "I'll neaten up," I said. "I'll help Mom get the food ready," Anne said. Granddad paused in the door with exaggerated disapproval—Alexandra, dead a year now, had never let their house sink into such a state. I guided him to a chair in the corner, started clearing the couch of newspapers. Anne told Daryl Sr. to watch the kids and went into the kitchen. The old man got a beer for himself and a drink for Granddad, then switched on a baseball game and settled on the couch, rolling onto his side and reaching for a crumpled pack of cigarettes on the coffee table.

"Sit up," I snapped. "You've got company. Some of them might like a place to sit."

The old man regarded me for a minute like someone he was about to start a bar fight with, then sat up. "Whose wife are you?" he said.

"It wouldn't hurt you to help out around the house a little," Granddad piped up from his corner. "Your mother didn't raise you to live like this." He had a cigarette going, and the ashtray beside him was spilling over, so I took it to the kitchen to empty. Mom and Anne were loading the kitchen table with food: a spiral-cut ham, a blue plastic bowl of potato salad, ambrosia salad made with marshmallows and sour cream and pieces of canned fruit.

Jacky and Mary Beth, coming in last, paused in the hall, looked at the disorder and the amount of work that needed to be done, and headed for Jacky's old room off the back of the kitchen. Mary Beth—who at that time was just Jacky's latest girl—steered him along the wall with her hands on his shoulders, making putter-ing noises that sounded like a motorboat. She was an inch taller than Jacky in flats. Slender and long-limbed, she had sloe eyes and brown-black hair that billowed about her shoulders and face. She was the granddaughter of Otto's long-lost friend Gerry Donovan, who'd sired a large and successful family. She was the outlaw of that family at the moment because of her wild ways, which in-cluded not only pool halls, cigarettes, and motorcycle boots, but also a real motorcycle (though here her family's money was evi-dent: it was a BMW).

Then there was Jacky, another of her wild ways. He didn't mind being with a woman taller than he was, but he wouldn't ride on the back of her motorcycle and was saving up for one of his own. I thought he'd better hurry. I had the strong feeling that—like my high-school track buddy Nick Hawthorne of the Tudor house on Summit, who'd gone through a cocaine phase then settled in Phoenix with an engineering degree—Mary Beth was going to come through her wild period just fine and live up to her family's expectations. I hoped against all odds that she'd take my brother with her. Jacky had just started working for the city, driving a dump truck in the summer and a snowplow in the winter. It was a union job, and he made good money and claimed to enjoy the work, but he drank too much and got into too many fights. Even the old man was trying to tone him down: "Don't think you're bad," he would say when Jacky turned up with a black eye or fat lip. "I seen bad, and you ain't it."

Jacky and Mary Beth disappeared into his room, and Anne shooed me away from the stove so she could put a green-bean casserole in the oven. She straightened and rapped me on the arm with a wooden spoon. "Quit mooning over your brother's girl-friend," she hissed.

"Jealous?" I said. She and Mom spent their time gossiping about how Mary Beth had only a part-time job but could afford to wear designer leathers when she rode her motorcycle.

I wiped out the ashtray with a wet paper towel and took it back to Granddad. As soon as Anne's back was turned, Daryl Sr. disappeared outside to tinker with his car. Chrissie, who was five, was trying to watch the twins, Kevin and Katy. They were old enough to toddle about, and she wasn't getting any help from Daryl Jr., who was racing laps from the entry hall through the kitchen and living room and dining room.

When Junior made a pit stop to shove his sister into a stack of newspapers I'd just piled out of the way under a window, Grand-dad took the chance to lean forward and seize him by an arm. He pulled the boy across the floor and shook him. "You sit on the couch and stop running around like a wild Indian." My grandfather was rough without meaning to be—his sudden slaps on the back still jarred my teeth. To top it off, Junior was scared to death of my father, so when he looked over and found the old man grinning at him from the couch, he burst into tears.

Anne was lugging Mom's sewing machine out of the dining room toward the stairs, and she stopped and frowned. Granddad caught her look and drawled: "You let these kids run your life, girly."

Junior sniffled into the lapel of his little boy's sport coat. Anne eyed Granddad, and I hoped she wouldn't let him goad her into a fight. Dad had set him up with a glass of bourbon, which tended to make him mean. Dad was peering around Anne to watch the game, and when he said mildly, "You make a better door than a window," she shrugged, hefted the machine, and headed for the stairs. "You're on your own, kid," she said to Junior over her shoulder.

Granddad gave Junior a two-fingered shove in the back to propel him over to the old man. Junior pulled up short, dried his nose, and marched like a little soldier out the front door. Mom's current cat, which had been hiding from Junior behind the TV stand, made a dash for the basement. A short while later I glanced out and saw Junior handing wrenches to his father.

I finished neatening up the dinner table, then followed the cat's example and ducked into Jacky's room while Mom was busy with Chrissie, who'd brought the twins into the kitchen. Jacky's high-school stereo and furniture were still back there, and Jacky and Mary Beth had Bad Company on the turntable. He was sitting on the bed against the wall with his legs out straight before him so his feet and ankles dangled in the air, and Mary Beth lay on her back with her head in his lap and her long legs arranged gracefully on the bedspread. Jacky was stroking her hair when I walked in. "Knock-knock," he said.

I closed the door behind me. "You oughta lock this."

"No shit," Jacky said.

"Hi, Father," Mary Beth said.

"I'm not a priest yet." I settled into the orange vinyl swivel chair by Jacky's stereo stand and glanced at his record collection.

Mary Beth leaned up on an elbow so her hair cascaded like a model's over Jacky's knee. Mary Beth was stunning, and she knew it. She was always striking poses.

"So how do you like seminary?" she said.

She asked this every time I saw her, and I always gave the same answer. "Even better than I thought."

"But what is it you like about it?" Mary Beth pressed this time. She was sitting up beside Jacky now. She rested her chin on one hand and blinked at me. When I didn't answer right away, she said, "I'm waiting."

She had the kind of open smile that made whomever she was looking at the center of the world, and I'd've taken a shot at explaining Jesuit theology to hold her attention.

"When I was little," I said, "I used to watch Granddad kneel at his bedside to pray. He reads the *Lives of the Saints* and believes in every martyrdom and miracle. God's immanent in his world in a medieval, metaphysical way that's mostly lost to the modern world. There's still a sense of that wonder to be found in the priesthood." I leaned back, satisfied with my Latinate eloquence. The orange vinyl of the chair squeaked under my butt.

Mary Beth cocked an eyebrow. "That's it? A medieval mind?"

What she wanted was the sort of clichéd epiphany I'd seen college buddies write into med-school applications: the good doctor who'd saved a dear one, the heartfelt desire to do the same. I could say that the priesthood was one of the few callings that mattered in more than a material sense, that I'd spent last summer assisting the chaplain at the Veterans Administration hospital and learned I could comfort the sick and calm the distressed and angry, talents I credited to my stormy home life. I could cite the influence of Granddad and Father Phil, and, finally, I could tell her about the Mass: how it had always been the anchor of my week, safe harbor from my tempestuous home, and that I, like so many seminarians and priests, loved it. But even then it would be hard to say aloud that my love was deep and physical, that woven into my mind since my earliest memories was the unexpectedly sensual fabric of Catholicism, made up of rosary beads and silver crucifixes, the weight of altar robes on my shoulders, incense and candlelight, the red and blue cloth markers in my grandparents' black leather missals and the old-paper smell of the gilt-edged pages, the ritual rhythms of the Mass, the hymns of the Christmas season that promised more reason to the world than we could see.

"Let's talk about your future," I said to Mary Beth. "Business school maybe?" She took classes part-time at Saint Kate's and worked in a clothing store at the mall. She had dressed like an elegant cowgirl for Junior's First Communion—suede boots, denim skirt, silver concha belt, and a peasant blouse.

"You're trying to change the subject."

"No way." I grinned. "Face it, Mary Beth, you're as conventional as I am. Your future lies in a wealthy husband and a tasteful boutique in Highland Village. Dump Jacky as soon as possible."

Mary Beth laughed. "Dump Jacky, huh?" She punched him in the shoulder. "Hear that? You better be good."

Anne opened the door in the midst of this. She came in and closed it behind her, folded her hands behind her back and rested against the door. "Blessed peace and quiet," she said. "Bad Company and my brothers."

"Bad Company's quiet?" I said.

"You don't have kids." She pulled her hair back, twisted it in a loose bun. "Dinner's ready."

What followed happened with slapstick timing: I stepped toward the door, Mary Beth swung her feet off the bed, and I caught one of those pricey suede boots square in the groin, clutched at myself, and fell over.

Jacky burst out laughing.

Mary Beth snapped "This isn't funny!" and dropped to her knees beside me.

"Ah, what the hell," Jacky managed, "he's gonna be a priest."

I rolled onto my back, took an experimental breath. Mary Beth hadn't done that much damage. She was bent close, the very image of concern. Seeing Jacky's face beyond her shoulder, I couldn't help starting to chuckle myself.

"Let's go," Anne said, helping Mary Beth to her feet. "You didn't kick him hard enough."

Jacky and I found ourselves alone in the room. I sat up. Jacky was still snickering and wiping his eyes. "Sorry," he said.

"Nothing funnier than someone else getting kicked in the nuts," I said.

"Getting? You volunteered."

"Dinner!" Mom yelled.

The table was set. Mom had put up a little card table in the living room for Anne's kids. Daryl Sr. came in, buttoning the dress shirt he'd taken off to work on his car, and sat under the dining-room arch where he could easily slip into the living room to keep the kids under control.

The adults crowded around the dining-room table. Mary Beth wouldn't look at me. Mom asked me to say grace, and I bowed my head and prayed: *Bless us, O Lord, and these Thy gifts, which we are about to receive from Thy bounty. Through Christ our Lord. Amen.*

Mom beamed when I was done. "A real priest in our family," she said. "Father James Otto Dressler." She looked to Granddad for approval, and he nodded.

"Mary Beth kicked James in the balls," Jacky said. "Pass the potatoes, please."

Mary Beth's face was nearly in her green beans.

"Hell," Dad said, "remember *Butch Cassidy and the Sundance Kid*? Best kick in the balls I ever saw in a movie."

"The worst one," Granddad chimed in, hands still folded under his chin, "was third grade on the playground of that kindergarten on the way home from Assumption. Under a hundred-year-old elm that's gone now. Skinny Red Peterson says 'Wanna fight?' I said 'Sure' and he stepped up and let me have it. I had no idea what was coming. He told me later he'd just heard of it and wanted to see if it worked. It worked all right."

"Jacky racked himself once," I said, forking a slab of ham. Jacky reddened, and Mary Beth's head popped up from the green beans. "It's true," I said. "We were watching a Twins game in high school, a bunch of us in Friesen's basement, and John Castino got a big hit. Jacky was hollering and flailing around when all of a sudden he goes white and creeps off into a corner."

"Could we please change the subject?" Mom said.

Mary Beth caught Anne's glare and swallowed a smile. "Yeah, it's Junior's First Communion," she said.

"This is polite company," Anne said.

Dad pretended to look around. "Where?"

"How 'bout those Twins?" Jacky said.

Over dinner, Granddad launched into stories about Prohibition, when Saint Paul, a commercial city that did a thriving trade in speakeasies and brothels, was a haven for gangsters. Under the O'Connor system, named after a corrupt police chief, the cops left the bad guys alone in return for bribes and good behavior within the city limits. In fact, detectives were known to give tourists like Ma Barker and her boys a call if Hoover's G-men were on their way. The result was that, by 1932, when Granddad was eighteen and drinking in speakeasies like the Hollyhocks and the Green Lantern, banks all over the Upper Midwest were getting knocked over, while none at all were robbed in Saint Paul.

"I'm with Gerry Donovan in the Hollyhocks, Jack Peifer's place out in Highland Park," Granddad said. He nodded at Mary Beth. "Your grandfather. The joint is full of rumrunners and pimps, newsmen and senators. Maybe even bank robbers. I'm throwing dice for the next round when Gerry, who thinks he's king of the world once he's had a few, spins around on his stool, leans back on the bar, and says, *I can take any man in this room!* You better believe I got him out of there fast."

Mary Beth's eyes grew soft. "I never get to hear stories like that about him."

This got the old man going—like the rest of us, he loved attention from Mary Beth—and he traded stories with Granddad that grew bawdier and funnier until everyone was laughing, even Anne's children, who were drawn into the room and ran in circles around the table making jokes of their own that made no sense.

After dinner, I played a card game with the twins, making up the rules as I went along so they were sure to win. I went into the kitchen once to get a paper towel to clean up a spill, and Mom was at the sink doing dishes. The old man stood behind her, his arms wrapped around her waist, and they both swayed slightly to some shared and unsung melody. Daryl Sr. was out in the backyard with Junior and Chrissie, and later the old man went outside to join them while Anne helped Mom finish the kitchen. Granddad snored on the couch. I took the twins outside to avoid disturbing him, and they ran around for a while, then Anne put them down for a nap on a blanket on the living-room floor. I got a bottle of pop from the fridge and stood in the back door sipping it. I was watching my father show Junior how to stay in front of a grounder when Jacky tapped me on the shoulder. "Time for Mary Beth and me to go," he said. "We'll run you home."

12

JACKY AND MARY BETH AND I SQUEEZED into the front seat of his car. Her long thigh pressed against mine, and I thought resolutely of other things. At the house, when I was out back with Anne's twins, I had sat on the limestone planter tossing a Wiffle ball to Kevin, who wanted to learn to play catch. In the yard, Daryl Sr. pushed Chrissie on our rusted swing set and the old man chased Junior about, growling and waving his arms like a monster. Kevin stood before me, hands outstretched. He was at the stage where he had the hands-out part right, but not the catching part. I would lob the Wiffle ball, it would bounce off his chest, and he would look puzzled for an instant, then join Katy in the chase after the ball. Next year, he would be catching and throwing.

"You two going to get married?" I asked Jacky and Mary Beth, trying to put my brother on the spot. We were cruising down Summit, Jacky speeding and slowing against the stately pace of the other traffic.

They looked at each other in mock alarm.

"Right now, I like having the wide world before me," Mary Beth said.

Jacky snorted. "She thinks she's going to ride off into the sunset on that bike and live by the ocean in California."

Mary Beth tilted her head onto his shoulder. "I'll live in a tree house and sell designer clothing—mostly animal prints—in a little boutique, like James said. But no rich husband. Instead, I'll be an eccentric middle-aged lady who takes wildly inappropriate younger lovers. And I'll have a pet mountain lion to devour those that displease me. Jacky—" she brought her hand up to rough his hair— "I'll let visit once in a while to show my tragically hip friends a fossil from the ancient Midwest."

"Where d'you get this shit?" Jacky said. He pulled into the seminary lot. My spiritual director, Father Friedel, was pacing the sidewalk in front of the residences, reading from his breviary. I saw him stare at Mary Beth, and he approached me with a tentative smile as I watched Jacky's car turn back out onto Summit.

"And who were those beautiful young people you've been privileged to spend the afternoon with, Mr. Dressler?"

I was trying to figure out how Mary Beth's odd gears possibly meshed with my conventional little brother, and I didn't hear him for a moment.

"Mr. Dressler?"

"Uh, that's my brother and his girl."

He laid a thin hand on my shoulder. I squelched an urge to brush it off. Friedel was a worrier about sins large and small, nicknamed "Father Fritter" by the seminarians. He was a throwback to the fifties, or maybe a glimpse of the future—one of the reactionaries starting to creep back onto seminary faculties twenty-some years after Vatican II. Either way you looked at it, I didn't much care for him.

"Even if a particular woman doesn't become an occasion for temptation," Friedel said, "their company can give scandal among parishioners."

"I'll keep that in mind, Father," I said, and went inside. *Give scandal.* It was a popular phrase among priests, a great fear—and, I sometimes suspected, a great hope.

It had been two years since Father Phil advised me on celibacy and fishing and Granddad gave me his rosary and the College of

Saint Thomas gave me a history degree with honors. I lived now in Grace Residence, one of three tall, boxcar-shaped dorms financed at the turn of the century by James J. Hill, the Empire Builder of the Great Northern Railroad and a Scotch-Irish Protestant. During the Civil War, Hill had fallen in love with a Catholic waitress named Mary Mehegan. The early French priests of Saint Paul, faced with a mixed marriage, took note of Hill's economic prospects and immediately sent young Mary to a Milwaukee convent to be groomed for her society wedding. Ecumenism paid off with an uneasy alliance between Hill and Archbishop John Ireland that's still visible at the east end of Summit Avenue, where Hill's mansion sits across the street from Ireland's cathedral, and at the west end, where Ireland built his seminary in the 1890s with a half-million dollars of Hill's money.

Ireland believed seminarians needed fresh air and room to study, so the seminary was housed in several separate buildings— exposing young men to the moral air of Minnesota winters—and the residence halls provided each student with a private bedroom and study. Mick, no less cynical after three years of seminary, said that by favoring private rooms over shared quarters, the seminary's designers had also chosen masturbation over sodomy. He came up with this theory the day one of the faculty told us that pre-Vatican II seminaries dealt with masturbation by having emergency confession before morning Mass so that long lines of seminarians could cleanse their souls of what was then called *the solitary sin*. Today, I guessed some of my fellow seminarians practiced the solitary sin about as casually as so many lay Catholics practiced birth control, but I was serious about chastity in all its forms, and Ireland's architectural philosophy was a mixed blessing: the daily traipse through the cold and snow in the long winter was good, the privacy sometimes difficult. I was in my mid-twenties, in the bloom of health, and there were erotic possibilities everywhere—Mary Beth, co-eds from Saint Thomas sunbathing on the lawn, and even, given enough frustration and imagination, the boarding-school sections of *Jane Eyre*, which sat innocently enough on my bookshelf.

This afternoon was proving to be one of the difficult ones.

I'd taken leave of Father Friedel and come up to my rooms. The residence halls, with their lead plumbing and groaning radiators, were luxurious only by turn-of-the-century standards, but I had a great view. The seminary was built on a rise above the Mississippi River bluffs, and my rooms were under the hall's roof. I stood at the dormer window, watching a thunderstorm come in over Minneapolis. Below, I caught an occasional glimpse of Friedel's black suit as he paced on the sidewalk. The sky had turned heavy and green. I could see the leaves of the trees in the ravine below the hall frozen in the still air. The ravine was the very same one Betty García and I had followed down to the river the night we'd first made love. It started northwest of Grace Hall and curved slightly south through the seminary grounds before running west, where it was bridged by Mississippi River Boulevard and dropped through the river bluffs. On the seminary side of the bridge, a muddy path through overhanging trees and brush was set with the Stations of the Cross, which public-school kids, spurred by the Latin inscriptions at the base of each concrete cross—*Condemnatio, Jesus Assumptio, Jesus Primus*—believed to be the grave markers of a mass murder. At the ravine's head was a grotto to the Blessed Virgin, in which we seminarians held devotions every spring and fall, and which young Saint Thomas couples used for rites less devoted to virginity.

I started studying—Augustine's *The City of God*—but kept getting up and going to the window to watch the sky. The storm, all moist air and energy roiling out of Montana and the Dakotas, rose over downtown Minneapolis, the anvil tops of the front slit with lightning. When a few big drops of rain started to fall, a couple hurried out of the ravine, hand in hand. From my elevated view, I imagined disarrayed clothes, flushed faces, smeared lipstick. *The City of God* disappeared. My radio was playing jazz interspersed with the crackle of the oncoming storm.

Smoky clubs, girls in black tights, warm rain on midnight streets. Suddenly, I wanted the girl in the ravine, Betty, and the sorority girl I'd seen jogging on Summit yesterday. All of them at once. I prayed to Augustine, who had struggled—*make me chaste, Lord, but not just yet* (not yet!)—and then I wanted Mary Beth and her concha belt, Susan Reading in a garland of daisies, Mitzi Barnard in her cashmere sweater. I wanted grass stains, the smell of the river on a warm day, a first kiss.

I wanted the waitress from the Lexington, and every girl or woman who'd ever smiled back or ridden on a Ferris wheel. I wanted the world. I prayed to Thomas Aquinas, who with angelic help had driven a temptress from his room. No angel appeared, and I was suddenly sure that if one did, she would look great in a diaphanous white robe that hinted of heavenly curves.

If all else fails, remove yourself from the occasion of temptation. I pulled on a raincoat and went to the chapel. On the way out, I nodded at Father Friedel, who'd taken shelter in the hall's entryway and was watching the storm with a delighted smile. The weather met me at the door, and I pounded through hard rain, kicking up mud. When I got to the chapel, I found it empty and silent, the solid sandstone walls muting the sounds of the storm.

The front passed over, and the steady wash of rain against stained glass replaced thunder and lightning. I knelt and for the first time in years remembered my boyhood knee condition, how it had caused me such agony when I knelt on the marble steps of the altar to serve Mass that I had squeezed back tears and consoled myself by offering the pain to Jesus. I wished I had something like it to offer now. I rested my chin on clasped hands and prayed while I studied the apse's mural: Jesus after His resurrection appearing to the apostles on the shore of the Sea of Tiberias. Decades ago, Archbishop Dowling had chosen this scene from John 21 to inspire seminarians with the idea of feeding God's people as Jesus had asked the apostles to do that day. *Amen, amen, I say to thee, When thou wast young, thou didst gird thyself and walk where thou wouldst. But when thou art old, thou wilt stretch forth thy hands, and another will gird thee and lead thee where thou wouldst not.*

In a couple of years, by the grace of God, I would be girded in the stole and chasuble of a priest. Someday, I would give First Communion to Jacky's children. I prayed to be worthy, then added the Act of Firm Purpose that my grandfather had taught me for after confession: *Give me a change of heart, O Jesus, Thou who hast sacrificed Thyself for love of me! Make known to my spirit the excellence of Thy sacred humiliations. Let me begin today, illumined by Thy light, to destroy this part of the natural man which lives in me in its entirety, the obstacle that constantly keeps me from Thy love.*

Sometimes prayer works. I went from the chapel to dinner with friends in the refectory, then returned to my rooms and Augustine and *The City of God.* That evening I was at peace; Augustine and *The City of God* made perfect sense.

Late that night, when I went to the bathroom at the end of the hall to use the toilet, I found Mick at the sink, washing his face and hands. He smiled and whistled into the sink when I asked if he'd been studying late, and as I stood at the urinal I caught a faint whiff of a perfume that was popular with the Saint Thomas girls that year.

13

AT MY ORDINATION in the Cathedral of Saint Paul, I knelt with a handful of classmates before the archbishop while the priests of the archdiocese filed past, laying their hands briefly on our heads in blessing. The procession took a while, slowed by the aged and infirm, some men helped to and from the altar by seminarians drafted for that purpose, one pulling a wheeled oxygen tank. Among the younger priests, many were from Africa, Central and South America, Ireland. Scattered among them was the occasional first- or second-year man I knew from seminary. John Ireland had founded his seminary so that he wouldn't have to depend on foreign-born priests; a century later we were back where he'd started.

But it was a day for celebration, not doubt. Mick, a year past his own ordination, appeared in front of me and grinned and winked. A little while later, Phil rested his thick-fingered hands on my head. In a sudden motherly gesture, he brushed at a piece of lint on my shoulder, then leaned down to whisper, "I'm proud of you, boy." He smelled reassuringly of cologne and cigarettes, and I let my senses fill with the ritual—pew upon pew of white-albed priests, some faces bored, some joyous, at least one asleep; tinkling bells, a crystal cruet ringing the gold rim of a chalice, the rise and fall of the celebrants' voices, the echo of the congregation; the organ, the choir, the hymns; the intoxicating scent of the incense that drifted in a haze through the nave; the bit of infinity caught and made tangible by the Cathedral dome. I murmured my vows and pledged obedience to the archbishop, my hands in his.

The Cathedral was crowded with family and friends of the ordinands, people from our home parishes and the teaching parishes where we'd trained, and Catholics from all over who wanted to celebrate a new generation of priests. After Mass, my classmates and I were sent to various corners of the building to receive congratulations. I shook hands with well-wishers in front of the statue of Saint Luke, startled to find myself on the other side of the familiar custom of a priest greeting his parishioners. My family waited, then rushed forward in a group through a gap in the milling people. Mom hugged me and said, "I'll be out front with your father"—the old man had disappeared as soon as Mass ended. I visited with Anne and her family, and Marie Therese, my great-aunt and godmother, who had traveled from northern Wisconsin. Then Granddad said that he wished Alexandra could be here, corrected himself to say that he was sure she was present in spirit, and went to the Chapel of the Blessed Virgin, where I knew he would kneel before the statue of Saint Anne and light votives for his wife and his mother. After Marie Therese had gone to wait in the pews at the back of the nave, Jacky shook my hand, then dropped it and fidgeted for a moment. I could tell he wanted to make a joke and was silenced by Saint Luke looming over my shoulder. Betty García, there with her husband, a tall and hale and extraordinarily handsome lawyer, stepped into the moment to hug me, her body pressing mine, and I thought that such occasional embraces would define the boundaries of the rest of my life.

When all was done, Phil and Mick joined me, and we pushed out through the heavy wooden doors together, three men in black suits and Roman collars, and found my family waiting among the knots of other families at the top of the broad steps that overlooked downtown. My father stood apart, leaning against the stone balustrade, smoking, dwarfed beneath the massive face of the Cathedral. His suit jacket pulled across the shoulders, and his neck bulged above his collar. I left Phil and Mick with my family to organize cars to the Lexington, and trotted over, a kid's lightness to my feet.

"How you doing, old man?" I said.

He dropped his cigarette. "Hello, Father," he said, offering a hand. My father's hands look pudgy, but his fingers are blocky and strong, and the nails are never clean. When I took his hand solemnly, he snorted and said, "We'll see how you do."

V

14

FOUR YEARS AFTER ORDINATION, renovating a house with the old man, I didn't bring up how I'd done. And Dad either wasn't curious or had decided to let me alone for a change. We spent the rest of the week working upstairs. After we finished the windows, I prepped for painting while Dad did electrical work, rewiring a couple of receptacles that weren't working, adding an exhaust fan in the bath, taking down bedroom fixtures and buying ceiling fans to put up once the painting was done. Midweek, Erma Nordyke, Bob's wife, came over with a book of paint chips and walked around the house humming to herself and holding various combinations against the walls and trim.

Dad slid up beside her in the front bedroom. "You're not gonna get fancy on me?"

Erma, a husky, light-brown woman about twice the size of her husband, turned her handsome face away from looking out the window at the porch roof and smiled at the old man. "No, Joe, I just want to make sure you don't paint everything off-white. We'll put a couple of nice pastels here in the upstairs bedrooms, make it all summery and happy, and something muted downstairs that'll go with the woodwork."

"Yuppify the place," the old man grumped.

"It sells," Erma said. "Are you coming for dinner Saturday? Bring Jimmy if he wants." She looked me up and down. "Goodness you've grown. I can just picture you up in front of that church."

"Well, it has been about twenty years," I said. When I was a kid, our family grilled out with the Nordykes a few times each summer. Bob and Erma had a new house out near Pig's Eye Lake, and four children around the age of us Dressler kids. In the warm weather, the Nordykes had picnics in their large yard, which backed onto woods now long gone to development. My brother and sister and I and the Nordyke children and their friends would spend the afternoons playing cowboys and Indians and war and capture the flag in the woods, while the adults drank beer and smoked cigarettes and grilled walleye filets, the fish fresh caught by Bob on trips up to his cabin. It sounded as if the old man still ate with Bob and Erma at least semi-regularly, and I was happy he was getting the occasional home-cooked meal. "I wish I could," I said to Erma, "but Jacky's drafted me to move a few carloads of shower gifts."

"What are you doing home?" Erma said.

"He's on vacation," Dad said before I could answer. "And come this fall, he's going to be a professor up at Saint John's. They need good priests in the classroom."

"Well, congratulations," Erma said. She gave me a hug, enfolding me in her heavy arms, and after she went downstairs I looked at Dad and raised my eyebrows.

He shrugged one shoulder. "It's true, isn't it?"

Friday Dad and I finished the upstairs painting—as Erma promised, the rooms ended up sunny and happy—and then cleared out of the second floor, moving drop cloths, tools, putty knives, and the stepladder to the living room, and washing out brushes and rollers in the basement laundry sink. It was late by the time we stepped out the front door. Dad treated me to a hamburger, and then—as usual, without asking my plans—drove to the Gossip Inn.

I'd managed to avoid the place for years. Dad parked in the alley lot and led the way through a gray metal door, down a dim, uninviting hallway, past the bathrooms, and into the bar. The Gossip was long and narrow and smelled of urine and ashes and stale beer. There was a line of stools at the bar and a row of booths against the wall. The grated window at the front looked out on University Avenue, and, tonight being warm, the front door was propped open so the room was filled with the rush and halt of traffic. The old man sat at the bar and talked with the bartender about men I didn't know and troubles I didn't care about, so I swiveled to look out the front door and sipped a beer. Across the street, I could see a slice of used-car lot and the flutter of red, white, and blue pennants strung between light poles. Teenaged Asian girls and boys, dressed up for Friday night on the town, came and went at the Vietnamese take-out place next door. A shambling, gray-bearded black man in a stained army coat wandered in and asked the black couple at the end of the bar for bus change, but was refused with a shrug and upturned palms. Later, a thickset Indian accosted a young Vietnamese man in restaurant black-and-whites just outside the door. "Where you from?" "Saint Paul." "No, I mean—" "Vietnam, all right?" "You kicked America's ass." "Be nice." "Naw, us Native Americans admire you. You're warriors." The conversation drifted down the sidewalk and faded, the Vietnamese talking over his shoulder as he edged away. It was a slow night in the Gossip—the only customers besides Dad and me were the couple near the door, who looked like their marriage had been made in a bottle.

After an hour or so, I was ready to go and about to interrupt Dad and the bartender when I saw both of them glance toward the back hallway with expressions bordering between hostility and alarm. As I swung my stool that way, three young black men with puffy Raiders and Seahawks jackets worn open over jerseys and low-slung jeans sauntered up and stood at the bar on the other side of my father. They were in their late teens, kids really, not one of them old enough to drink. The gangly leader, who was working a lollipop around in his mouth, smoothed a hundred-dollar bill out on the bar. "Got change?" he said to the bartender.

Poker-faced, the bartender shook his head. "Not tonight. Sorry." He didn't look happy. My father eyed the three thoughtfully, cutting his eyes from their hands to their coats, from one to the next. The stout kid on the right stared back flatly, too confident, one hand running the zipper of his jacket up and down. The number double-zero showed on a blue mesh jersey. Then I saw the crosshatched metal butt of a handgun. My stomach turned over.

"Get a drink?" the leader said, pushing the bill forward again. The lollipop clicked against his teeth. The smallest kid walked to the front door and leaned against the frame with his arms folded, then shut the door. The couple at the end of the bar stopped their conversation.

The bartender shook his head. "You got ID? I still don't have change." He had a lined, wasted red face, and he was aging right in front of my eyes. Lollipop widened his eyes at him, crunched the sucker.

Then we all heard the back door. A moment later, two men came out of the hallway and up to the bar. They were involved in some discussion, and the older and smaller of the two, a Ford cap pushed back on his forehead, hiked a foot up on the rail, still talking over his shoulder to the other man. I recognized Roy Doolin and his oldest son, Roy Jr., a bricklayer. "Give me a shot of rye," Roy Sr. said, turning to the bartender. No one moved. Roy straightened from the bar and seemed to realize the situation for the first time— my father, the out-of-place black youths. Dad didn't take his eyes off of the three kids. Calculation hung in the air, then Lollipop jerked his head toward the front door and the other two followed him out.

Everyone breathed. "Never seen it so dark in here," Roy said, as the bartender slid him his drink.

I glanced at the black couple at the end of the bar. They hadn't heard, but Dad caught my expression. "Don't get on your high horse, boy," he said. "That bunch was trouble. Didn't matter what shade they came in."

I felt obliged to defend what I hadn't said. "Why's it get mentioned then?"

The bartender stared, and the old man shrugged. Roy Sr. took a toothpick from his mouth and shoved his face in mine. It was a lean face, and Roy was a small man, but all wire and muscle. "Are you a nigger lover, son?" he asked in a dry voice. I looked from him to grinning Roy Jr., bigger than his father, with a brutal body, and then dropped my eyes.

The old man picked up his cigarette between thumb and forefinger and took a drag. He spun his barstool slowly toward the Doolins and drawled, "Seems like just yesterday I kicked your ass, Roy," as casually as if he were asking who was pitching for the Twins. I felt like I'd walked into the middle of a Western, the staged lines and choreographed moves before a bar fight. Roy Jr. was close behind his father, and he took off his gold watch and put it in his pocket and rolled up the cuffs of his shirt. His forearms were corded with muscle, and looking at them made my ribs ache. *In a fight*, the old man liked to say, *always bet on the man who works with his hands*. I wanted to point out to everyone, since they seemed to have forgotten, that I was a priest—and a peacemaker. Instead, I stood beside my father's stool.

And then Roy Sr. stepped back. "Let's leave it go for tonight, Joe." He picked up his shot of rye, and he and Roy Jr. walked away and took a booth.

I felt dizzy. Everything from the moment the three young gangsters had walked in the back door had moved as if it were on rails. Then my father had an arm around my shoulder and squeezed me briefly against him before turning back to his beer.

Saturday morning I woke up with a finger in my ear. Mom was sitting on the edge of my bed. "Bicycle Irish," I muttered, another of the old man's jokes. *There's three kinds of Irish: lace-curtain, shanty, and bicycle. Bicycle? Yeah. A pain in the ass.* I rolled over, tried to pull the blanket over my head. Mom stopped me. "Get up, lazybones," she said. "We're going to see your grandfather. He's better in the morning. Your coffee's on the dresser."

When she left, I pulled myself upright against the headboard, fumbled for the coffee mug, and waited for the caffeine to hit. After the black kids, after Roy and Roy Jr., Dad and I had a few beers at the bar, sitting in companionable silence until I ordered Jameson on the rocks and he said, "They don't have fancy priest whiskey here, boy." I'd ended up drinking Cutty Sark, and this morning I had a big head.

I put on my black shirt and trousers and collar for Granddad, then went downstairs, where Mom had a bowl of oatmeal waiting. "You drive," she said when I finished, handing me the keys to her car. She had a maroon '82 Cougar now, a Detroit car that had bloated from sporty early models to a boxy family sedan. I'd unlocked the garage door when Mom remembered she'd left her purse in the house, and I gave her the keys and looked around the backyard. Last fall's leaves were still down, the yard muddy, spring grass struggling against the sodden leaves. The oak in the middle of the yard had always made grass back here a chancy proposition, except for a sunny spot by the garage, which Mom had used for vegetables. Now it was full of last year's weeds. I went into the garage and hit the opener. Nothing happened. I checked to see if the cord was plugged in, and Mom came through the door carrying her purse.

"Your father's been promising all winter to fix it," she said. "All winter I've been getting out in that icy alley, all hours of the day and night, to open that door. It's a wonder I haven't broken my neck. Or been mugged, the way this neighborhood's going."

"Why doesn't Samuel fix it?"

"Samuel's not doing your father's work."

I yanked open the garage door, hard enough that it rocked back and forth on its rollers. "Somebody needs to fix it," I said. "Shit, I'll call the garage-door people." My family could stew forever over who should do something. And my head still hurt.

We got on the highway at Dale and took 94 East through downtown, then out past the Sun Ray shopping center and 3M campus. On the passenger's side, Mom smoked cigarettes, a rich flare of tobacco and then the harsh cut of nicotine every time she lit up. Neither of us said anything until I pulled off the exit for the nursing home.

"It's not as fancy as some of the places we looked at," Mom said, "but the staff seemed friendly, and it's got nice light. We did our best."

I headed north, looking for the water tower that stood across from the home. I could never remember the name of the side street.

"Here," Mom said.

I took a right. "It's nice, as these things go," I agreed. "No one's happy in one of those places. There's no kidding yourself anymore once you land there." Mom and Dad had made a good choice, considering they were divorced, couldn't get it together over a garage door, and were doing a job no one wants to do. "It's a really good home," I said, pulling up in front.

Mom got out of the car and turned away from the home, across the street toward the park with the water tower, lighting one more cigarette. "You go in," she said. "I'll be along."

At the front door, I paused to watch her wander around the park, a busty, overweight blonde in jeans, a Vikings sweatshirt, and sneakers. The park was nothing more than a flat square of grass with a swing set and teeter-totter in one corner and a high chain-link fence around the base of the water tower to discourage adventurous children. Mom sat down on the teeter-totter, stretched her legs out along the wooden plank, tugged at a bra strap, and smoked. She seemed to be considering the suburban neighborhood around her, the small ranch houses and saplings and quiet green lawns, the brick-edged flower beds under front picture windows. A flag fluttered and snapped from a flagpole.

Inside and down the hall, I found Granddad in his recliner, fast asleep. The oxygen machine thrummed quietly, and I sat in his wheelchair and considered whether a bird feeder outside his window would give him any entertainment. Of course, someone would have to keep it filled. Maybe if I bought the seed, one of the nurses—no, they had enough to do. If I stayed—I should come out more often anyway. Nothing as depressing as an empty bird feeder.

Granddad's eyes were open now, cloudy blue. He regarded me without removing his chin from his chest, and I got the sense he didn't know me.

"It's James," I said. "Jimmy. Your grandson."

"You're a priest," he said.

"Yes," I said.

"Turn on the TV. The Twins're on."

"Not until this afternoon."

"Turn on the TV."

I swung the wheelchair around, reached up and hit the power, then flipped the channels. Granddad stopped me at 4, some cartoon. The sound was loud, and I muted it with the remote.

"What's cartoons doing on Sunday?" Granddad said.

"It's Saturday."

"What're you doing here? You bring me Communion?"

I grimaced and swung the chair back toward Granddad. "No Communion, Otto," I said. "It's James, your grandson. I'm visiting."

"How's that church of yours?"

He meant Saint Hieronymus. "It's fine, Granddad. Doing great." The half-truth bothered me enough that I trotted out another one. "I'm thinking of taking a break from parish work."

"Why the hell would you do that?"

I rocked the wheelchair back and forth. "I need to be sure of what I want." That sounded weak.

"Shit," Granddad said, "when I was young we didn't worry about what we wanted to do, we worried about what we had to do."

I smiled. "I'll bet in a lot of ways it made life simpler. We've got too many choices."

"I don't," Granddad said. He pushed himself up a little in his recliner. Then, "Hello, Maura," as Mom walked into the room.

She left her purse on the bed and walked over to the window, stopping to pat his cheek along the way. "Don't they ever water this?" She shook his potted petunia, and brown petals fell. Then she crossed back to the bulletin board by the door and started taking down birthday cards, pulling out the push pins and then stabbing them back into the board. "We'll put these in your dresser," she said.

"Leave them up," I said. "They add some color."

Mom paused, then tossed the cards in my lap.

I got up and began putting them back, playing with arrangements so the cartoon characters on the fronts seemed to interact with each other. I was trying to come up with a plot line, running from "Happy Birthday" to "Sorry I Forgot."

Behind me, Mom said, "How's the food here these days, Otto? You eating well? The inner man satisfied?"

"Food's good," said Otto, who wasn't eating well. "They got the White House cook."

I stuck the last card back on the board and turned to Mom. "White House cook?"

She shrugged. "The corporation that runs this place says they have a former White House chef designing their menus."

I sat back down in the wheelchair, and we were all silent for a while, watching cartoons. A half an hour passed, and the shows changed. Then: "He should've kept it in his pants," Granddad said. Paula Jones had filed her lawsuit against Clinton two weeks before.

Mom stared at Otto, then laughed. "Talk about your presidential poles," she said. "Slick Willie!"

Granddad's mouth tightened.

"I'm a crude woman." Mom agreed with his silence, smiling. "More than good enough for your son, though."

For a moment, the cartoons on TV flickered soundlessly in the corner of my eye, all movement and bright primary colors. Then I looked at Granddad. His eyes had gone clear and cold. When I saw his teeth grit and his lips pull back, the expression that of Clint Eastwood about to bite off a line, I clapped my hands together loudly, jumped up from the wheelchair, and said, "Well, it's been a good visit. Granddad, do you need anything the next time I come out?"

Otto gave me a puzzled, sad look as his mind tried to catch up with the room going from fighting to farewell. "Communion," he said.

"I'll remember," I said, patting his shoulder. "Enjoy the Twins this afternoon." Mom kissed him on the forehead and picked up her purse, and we walked down the hall together.

"Presidential poles?" I said to her. "Slick Willie?" My grandfather, rough edges aside, had his older generation's aversion to sex talk. He'd once told me he'd never heard the term *motherfucker* before he went into the Army. "Those Southern boys used it," he said. "I thought it was the filthiest word I'd ever heard."

Mom shrugged. "It just came out."

"What the hell you come out here for if you're going to fight?"

I'd stopped to ask it, but she plowed ahead. "I just can't help it."

On the way home, I realized Mom was crying quietly, and I didn't know what for. She and Granddad weren't close; neither of them had ever quite forgotten the *black-Irish trollop* remark. Maybe that was why she was crying—lost husband, lost in-laws, lost chances.

Keeping my attention on the traffic, I reached over and patted her knee, caught her surprised look out of the corner of my eye.

"What was that for?" she said.

"Nothing," I said. "Just saying hi."

"Divorce or not, a marriage never really ends," Mom said. "They oughta tell kids that."

"You caught a break," Jacky said that evening when I finished telling him the story about the night before at the Gossip. We were sitting on the porch of Mary Beth's house. "Those kids—they could have taken everyone back in the walk-in and shot you, left you stacked with the beer kegs. No one would have heard. Dad and Roy knew that."

"So they nearly beat each other up out of relief? With me in the middle?" I left unsaid that the old man had set me up and then come to my defense.

"Makes sense to me."

I'd spent the last twelve years in a private college, a seminary, and a little town up north. I'd forgotten that kind of sense.

Jacky checked his watch. "Jesus, how late can a hen party go?"

We were waiting for Anne to call from the wedding shower for help with the presents. The shower had been postponed a couple of weeks before when the hostess, a friend of the Donovan aunts, was hospitalized for her gall bladder.

"They still haven't shut up about this being bad form," Jacky said, meaning the shower was too close to the wedding. Being a groom had gifted him with a surprising fund of previously unguessed-at knowledge. "Speaking of which," he went on, "you coming to my bachelor party Thursday? We're hitting the titty bars in Minneapolis."

"No thanks," I said. Jacky refused to get why his brother couldn't come to his bachelor party. I crossed an ankle over my knee, tugged up my sock. "I can see the headline now: *Priest Defrocked after Stripper Scandal.*"

Jacky started to argue, but the phone rang. "That'll be Anne," I said.

The shower was in Little Canada. When Jacky pulled into the drive, Mary Beth's Honda Prelude was already full, and women were pushing boxes and bags into the back of Anne's station wagon. "Looks like most of the work is done," I said.

As we walked by the Prelude and wagon, Jacky peered into each at clear vinyl zipper bags full of plush bath towels and hand towels, comforters and comforter covers, cotton sheets for summer and plaid flannel for winter, napkins and tablecloths that coordinated with the dinnerware on the wedding registry. It looked as if several malls had been looted. Then there were the appliances.

"You're going to have to rewire the kitchen," I said, picking up a large Cuisinart box to examine its labor-saving features.

Jacky had opened a small box he'd found on the tailgate of the station wagon and was frowning at what I recognized as a metal espresso pot. He looked from it to a coffeemaker that apparently ground fresh beans and brewed coffee at a preset time in the morning. "My life just got a whole lot more complicated."

"I hear it happens with marriage."

"Not complicated," Mary Beth said behind us, holding open a shopping bag scented with bath gifts. "Pleasant—in small ways men never dream of left to themselves—and all you have to do is carry a few boxes."

"All I want is a cold beer at the end of the day," Jacky said.

"And now we have pilsner glasses." Mary Beth said happily, glancing in the back of the wagon. "Somewhere."

"Sounds like a good deal to me," I said. Jacky looked doubtful, but he took the shopping bag from Mary Beth and slid it across the backseat.

"Careful," Mary Beth said, and led Jacky by the arm up to the house to introduce him to the woman who'd thrown the shower.

I crawled into the wagon's cargo area to rearrange a couple precariously balanced items, then backed out to find my sister and Betty García standing in the drive with more packages.

"Look who's here," Anne said.

"Hey, Betty," I said. "You look nice." She had on a brightly flowered dress with a white knit sweater open over it, and her hair was pulled back in a French braid, but I saw the remnants of circles under her eyes and frown lines around her mouth that I didn't remember. "How was the shower?" I said to my sister.

Anne gestured at the full cars. "I don't think Mary Beth will ever have to buy another tablecloth," she said. "This is what comes of a lot of aunts and good friends."

"This is our brother who lived in a rented room with one pot he never washed?" I said.

Anne laughed and went up to the house, leaving me with Betty, who'd been busying herself with a coffee-table book on the Arts and Crafts movement.

"Good book?" I said.

Betty clapped it shut and wrinkled her nose. "People should stick with the registry," she said. "I was hoping I'd run into you."

"Really?" I said.

She set the book on top of a hibachi. "I'm sorry I was so abrupt on the phone," she said. "I'd just had a rough conversation with Ethan. You were one call too many."

I fiddled with the loose luggage rack on the roof of Anne's car, half aware of women walking around us with more packages. I couldn't think of a thing to say. Then I flexed my right hand, the knuckles still stiff from when I'd punched the wall Sunday, and said, "It was a rough day for me, too. I put my hand through a wall."

Betty raised her eyebrows, remembering, no doubt, the time in college I'd slammed the same hand into a window frame next to her head.

"Anyway," she said, "I'm sorry." She turned abruptly and walked up to the house, her sandals clacking on the concrete. Jacky passed her on the front walk and came over to me.

"How's Betty?"

"She'll be all right."

Betty was on her way back down the walk, purse on her shoulder, car keys jangling.

Jacky started toward the house. "I'm saving you a dance at the wedding, Beautiful," he said to Betty as they passed. Betty gave him a broad smile, and I remembered the night we got together, how she'd said Jacky cracked her up. My brother the charmer.

Betty stopped for a one-armed hug and a peck on the cheek. "Take care," she said. When she pulled back, I noticed again the shadows under her eyes.

"We should at least have coffee," I said.

Betty stepped back, tapped her fingernail against the car window. "If I say no, are you going to put your hand through this?"

I shook my head.

"Too bad. It might have been entertaining."

"Give me a break."

Betty cocked her head at me. "I don't think so."

"C'mon," I said. "I'll go light on the priest stuff."

"Okay," Betty said. She bit a thumbnail. "Meet me at the office after work Wednesday. We can go someplace downtown."

The office was Hank's firm. He'd made her a partner. "Why don't we pick a time and meet at a coffee shop?" I said.

"Still scared of Hank?"

"I'll see you at five."

When Betty had gone, I turned toward the house and found Anne leaning against the fender of the wagon. "Where'd you come from?" I said.

"Congratulations, little brother, you managed to not carry a single package." She chucked me on the shoulder. "C'mon. I'll give you a ride and put you to work at Mary Beth's."

By the time we finished unloading, Mary Beth's small living room was filled with goods for the kitchen, bath, and table. A goose-down comforter in a zipper bag perched atop Jacky's prized Bang & Olufsen turntable. My brother wrapped his arm around his fiancée's waist and pulled her against him. "Didn't we already move in once?"

"You can build an addition," she said.

"Great," Jacky said.

"I know a priest who's handy," I said.

"Get Dad to help," Anne said. "Welcome Mary B. to the family."

"For better or worse," Jacky said.

Anne surprised me by coming in at Mom's house. "Mom's at Samuel's," I said.

"I know," she said. "And Daryl's got the kids up at his folks' in Bemidji. I'm staying here tonight—I don't like being in the house alone."

I raised an eyebrow. "My big sister?"

We were in the kitchen. Anne rummaged around in the refrigerator and came up with a jar of salsa, half-empty and crusted around the rim. She sniffed it, then poured it into a cereal bowl. "See if you can find some chips."

I found a stale bag and then an unopened one in a high cupboard. Meanwhile, Anne had uncapped a Coke for herself and a beer for me and was sitting at the table. I opened the chips. Anne rested her chin on her hand. "You know, I lived here until I married Daryl. Then we had kids. I'll sleep better knowing you're across the hall. But you tell anyone I was scared, I'll kick your ass."

"Gotcha," I said. "Anyhow, time was I used to get spooked alone in my rectory."

"You never told me exactly why you're on leave," Anne said.

I dropped a chip on the floor, picked it up and checked for cat hair, then dipped it in salsa. "Two-second rule. What do you think of Samuel?"

"He tries hard," Anne said, "but I don't like him." She tilted her Coke back, then set it down. "You're not answering my question."

"It's a long story," I said. "And it's late." I started to slide my chair back.

Anne stopped me with a hand on my forearm. "Please?" she said. "We never get the chance to visit, just us." When I nodded, she stood and started looking through the cupboards, talking over her shoulder. "We've got the house to ourselves and a party-size bag of chips no one will miss. When we were teenagers, this would've been the occasion for a late-movie marathon. Now I want to know what brought you home." She sat down again with a pack of Mom's Winstons, an ashtray, and a book of matches. "And I am going to have half a cigarette."

"Little stimulation for the baby?"

Anne drew out one cigarette, then flipped the pack onto the kitchen counter, where it spun to rest against the toaster. "I have five healthy children," she said. "They're not fragile, and they're not overly frightened of the world. You and I survived a lot worse." She lit up, crossed her eyes over the glowing tip of the cigarette. "I've got all night," she said.

VI

15

TWO YEARS AFTER ORDINATION, I stood on a gravel drive under a blue June sky, admiring the eighty-foot spruce at one red-bricked corner of Saint Hieronymus Church in Pretty Prairie, Minnesota. That it was now my church and my parish was just beginning to sink in, although I'd received the call from the Chancery three weeks before. Looking at the arched stained-glass window above the church doors, I quelled a quick uprising of pride, reminding myself that so soon out of seminary the promotion was more a reflection of the shortage of priests than a compliment to my pastoral promise. Mick had been given a parish in this same county a few months earlier, and we'd traded cynicisms over the phone. My predecessor was retiring at the age of eighty, moving down to the Cities to live with his sister and her husband; Mick's had run off with his housekeeper and a retirement account skimmed from the collection plate.

"Where do you want this, Father?" Nels, the groundskeeper, called from the back stoop of the rectory. He was holding a beat-up black Everlast heavy bag wrestled from the passenger's seat of my Chevy. The bag was about his size and considerably younger. I trotted over and took it, then said, "Would you grab that box marked *Sports Stuff*? It all goes in the basement." He followed me in. The basement was cool and musty, with seepage at the base of rough-cut limestone walls. I dumped the punching bag on the workbench, worried about the wet floor. A drainage problem, maybe gutters. I'd had a look around already, and I guessed the church and rectory were suffering from about thirty years of neglect. I almost welcomed the disrepair; I was confident with a hammer and screwdriver. I was less sure about running a parish, although I'd been pretty much on my own the past two years, working for an alcoholic pastor in one of the older, poorer Minneapolis suburbs. It turned out I had a knack for bookkeeping, and it was as much administrative ability as anything else that got me promoted.

"Good equipment, yup," Nels said. He'd put the *Sports Stuff* box beside the heavy bag and was delving into it, extracting my basketball, baseball mitts and boxing gloves, the leather jump rope, the red speed bag, holding each up in the glare of the bare bulb above the work bench. I looked around for a spot to hang the punching bags, taking in the undercarriage of the house, conduits and pipes, the floor joists shimmed to eliminate character squeaks, the long I-beam running front to back.

"My old man was a Gold Gloves champion," I said to the ceiling. I'd taken the boxing equipment out of the garage without asking. Dad would never miss it. He'd just left Mom, and at the moment no one in the family knew where he was.

I fingered Granddad's rosary in my pocket and walked around the basement. The water heater was an ancient thirty-gallon Montgomery Ward model on its last legs—I'd heard the sacrifice rod knocking after I washed my hands earlier. I squatted in front of the Hydrotherm boiler and brushed caked dirt off the face of the temperature and water pressure gauge, which wasn't working.

I heard Father Phil's words from six years ago. *Keep your hands busy, boy.* Well, there would be no lack of busy work.

"How long was Father Canby here?" I said to Nels, who hovered behind me.

"Forty, forty-five years. He was a good man."

"Sounds like it," I said. At the very least, Canby had staying power. Replacing him would be tough. There was the other half of Phil's advice: *Good men are harder to find than you might think.*

The unloading didn't take long, a young priest having few belongings. There was a second carful of books and winter clothes to bring up from the Cities on another day. Nels thumped around upstairs, carrying in my suitcases, the last of the load. I was hanging tools on the pegboard above the workbench when I heard a motor idling in the drive. The first parishioner come to vet the new pastor? I went upstairs and out the back door.

"Dressler!" It was Mick in a T-shirt and shorts, burly as ever, smoking a cigar and standing in front of the rusting Ford Ranger pickup he'd driven in seminary. He set his cigar on the hood and loped over, catching me up in a bear hug.

We walked around the grounds and then explored the church, which was nearly a century old, with spare decoration that made clear the parish had never been wealthy. Mick briefed me on what he'd heard from Canby about the parish situation, passing on the names of a few particular parishioners I could count on—a scheduling problem had caused me to miss meeting the man myself. Later, Mick got a ball glove from behind the seat of his truck, and we played catch on the sunny lawn between the rectory and church, stretching out our arms for a few minutes, the ball orbiting the blue sky, then rocketing into a waiting glove with a *pop*! There were the smells of fresh-cut grass and oiled leather, the sun on my forehead, the sting of a well-thrown ball. It was a weekday afternoon, and the town's streets were quiet enough that you could hear traffic on the interstate just to the west. I wasn't officially here until tomorrow, when I had a day of meetings lined up with the parish's volunteer staff: the music and youth directors and the heads of the parish council and the liturgy committee. Playing catch, I did my best to keep my mind off the fact that soon I would be stepping into a supervisory role with people who'd been staff at Saint Hieronymus since I was a kid.

"It's not so bad," Mick said after the catch, as we sat and talked in the cold shade of the back stoop. "You tell 'em you're not here to make any sudden changes, that you know they've got ways of doing things they've worked out over time, and that you want to learn from them. Over the next six months or a year, you may decide you want to replace someone, and if you feel that way, likely they do, too. Half the time, volunteer staff remove themselves before you have to do anything. Things work out."

Mick's laissez-faire attitude toward parish administration, given his scant experience at it, was surprisingly comforting, partly because it was the approach I'd worked out for myself. But what he said next wasn't so reassuring: "You'll want to keep an eye on the youth director, make sure he's not fucking the children. He'll be eyeing you for the same thing. That's not going to be a problem here, though, because this guy at Saint H. has been in place for fifteen years. Someone would've talked by now. Once the congregation sees you're not taking the boys on camping trips, or having private meetings at the rectory with the high-school girls, they'll trust you, too."

"It's that bad?" I said. The shadows of leaves shifted across the stoop.

"Everyone's aware of it," Mick said. "No one thinks it could happen in their parish, but they're watching us all the same." He shrugged. A neighbor turned his car down the dirt alleyway that ran behind the church grounds, slowed to peer at us, then waved. Mick and I waved back.

"Great," I said. I'd already developed protective habits during my two years as an assistant pastor: I never met with a young person alone or behind closed doors. It wasn't difficult. But it was unsettling to know people would be watching me with that in mind. Guilt by association. Guilt by profession.

Mick clapped me on the shoulder. "Comes with the job," he said. "Your job is to live here. You're active. You join the KCs, the Chamber of Commerce. You become part of the town." He picked up his ball glove, then told me the county had an amateur baseball league, the Farm-Industrial League. He was batting cleanup for the Blue River Raiders, and the Pretty Prairie Pioneers could use an infielder.

"The who?"

"Pretty Prairie Pioneers. Try saying that three times fast. Dave Stanfield, owns the garage over yonder"—he waved in the direction of the block-long business district—"manages 'em. Pitches, too. Not much velocity, but he can get a breaking ball over the plate. You oughta go talk to him, first thing."

"Think he'd want a priest playing first base?"

"He's Methodist, but his infield's a sieve. And I'm leading the league in home runs—convinced everyone the clergy can hit."

I shook my head. "I'm going to be plenty busy."

Mick moved to the lawn and started doing hurdler's stretches: "Word of advice," he said, turning his head sideways while he tried to touch an ear to his knee: "Clear the time—it'll be good for your mental health."

"So what's Blue River like?" I asked.

"Come on over. I'll show you my place."

And so my first day in Pretty Prairie, I got in the Chevy compact I'd bought used after ordination and followed the bouncing tailgate of Mick's truck out of town, past the grain elevator and along the railroad tracks. It was a trip I was to make many times over the next two years. My parish was in farm country of the sort you'd expect to find in Iowa, corn and bean fields edged by small hills and stands of mixed hardwood and pine. The road ran south, past prosperous farms whose barns had foundations of brick or stone, their roof-lines and nearby silos echoing the lines of small-town churches and steeples—the institutions of the countryside—past the occasional abandoned silo with a tree peeking out the top, past barns that were a slow collapse of weathered gray or red boards. After ten minutes, the route turned southeast, onto a curving two-lane that paralleled the Saint Croix River valley for twenty miles or so before dropping steeply into it just short of the town of Blue River, where Mick was stationed. It was a good thirty miles between our parishes, and when Mick climbed out of his truck that first day, I chided him for not warning me how far it was. He grunted that I'd get used to it, long country drives being the price of priestly companionship up here.

Mick's church was a white-steepled limestone building that looked Protestant until you noticed the Saint Christopher statue over the front door. Like the rest of the town, the church was built on the steep slope of the valley side, the Saint Croix far below, sparkling through the trees. The town stretched along the valley, a pleasant region of small hotels, restaurants with nautical themes, state-park campgrounds, bait shops, and rambling shacks where you could rent bicycles and canoes. A couple of blocks down the main street from Saint Christopher's was the Outpost, a storefront bar and restaurant with Guinness on tap and country bands on the weekend. Mick told me Pam Dempsey, the owner, was a tiny, hard-edged ex-Catholic who let priests drink for half price, and so the Outpost had become a Sunday rendezvous, a hedge against loneliness when congregations and housekeepers went home to lazy afternoons and family dinners. The county priests would drift in after their last Masses to spend the afternoon sitting at the bar, a line of men in black watching sports on TV.

After a communal dinner at the round table in the front window, the group would adjourn for an evening of nickel-dime-quarter poker if there were enough players to make a good table—there were always absences, priests responding to crises or dinner invitations. The county's other young priest, Danny Linz, had named the gathering the Sunday Afternoon Cards, Recreation, et Dram Club, then listed formation of the SACRED Club as a pastoral accomplishment in his annual report to the Chancery; the sort of sophomoric joke that, like seminary pranks, gets retold among priests as evidence of rebellion and daring.

The poker was usually at Saint Simon's, southwest of Blue River in the prosperous lake town of Piney Woods. From Blue River, the highway wound its way back up out of the river valley, then ran to Piney Woods through good fishing and hunting country, a landscape of small, shimmering lakes and marshes waving cattails, the road lined with bait shops and boat and snowmobile and hot-tub and antique dealers. Saint Simon's had a palatial brick rectory, the home of Father George Martin. With Linz as his assistant, he ran the biggest parish in the county. The two of them were Benedictines, and it was an open secret that the Chancery badly wanted Saint Simon's back under diocesan control. But there was no way to move George Martin, who was beloved in Piney Woods. George also ran the poker game, a Sunday-night institution among River County priests. Mick made sure I understood that my standing here depended as much on regular attendance and correct play as on anything I did in my parish.

My first Sunday, after eleven o'clock Mass and a parish welcome luncheon, I drove to Blue River—Mick was right, the drive already felt shorter—and knocked on Mick's door. We strolled down the main street, crowded with antique hunters and day-trippers up from the Cities, both lanes full of honking, braking vehicles pulling huge powerboats or the occasional slender sailboat, trucks with canoes and sailboards tied to camper covers, rusty Detroit four-doors with inner tubes bungeed to their roofs.

"Hopping place," I said, while we waited to cross the street. A car with a trio of mountain bikes arrayed in a roof rack slowed for us. Mick gave the girl driving a cheerful wave, and, as she and two outdoorsy-looking friends waved back and laughed, we threaded our way through the traffic in the opposite lane, backed up from the stoplight at the corner.

Mick stepped up onto the sidewalk in front of the Outpost. "It's a lot quieter in the winter." He held the door. "Pam likes priests at the bar—reminds the tourists to behave."

Despite high front windows and the sunny day, the Outpost was cool and dim. Two priests were already sitting at the far end of the bar, where a good-sized TV hung from the ceiling. Mick introduced me as *Jim*. I went by *Father Jim* with parishioners; *Father James* sounded too formal to me. Bill Snow, a dour, balding man with a protruding lower lip, was knocking out a stubby black pipe as we came up. The other priest was Harold Lamplighter, a gray, square-headed man in his seventies with a deep smoker's cough. Mick joined them, pulling a cigar and cutter from his chest pocket, and Snow and Lamplighter proceeded to get to know me through the oblique process of commenting on the Twins-White Sox game on the television.

"Think Hrbek's worth three million, Dressler?"

"Hear you played for Saint Thomas, Dressler."

"Nobody does a Miller Lite commercial like Madden."

"Who'd you have for Liturgy, Dressler?"

"They're making pastors young these days, aren't they, Harold?"

"That split-finger fastball ruins a lot of good arms."

"You've got a pair and an ace, Dressler. Keep the ace for a kicker, or draw three?"

George Martin and Danny Linz arrived from Piney Woods in the middle of this inquisition and immediately lit up—George an unfiltered Camel, and Danny a long-stemmed churchwarden pipe. Linz was a slender, terribly earnest redhead, and I noticed Bill Snow regarding his elegant pipe with disdain.

Mick was laughing at my own expression. "You might as well take up smoking in this crowd, Dressler. You're not going to keep those pretty pink lungs long."

I gave him a rueful smile. "I'll take my addiction secondhand. Cheaper."

"I don't miss Gaetti," Snow commented as the camera panned around the infield between pitches and stopped on the Twins' new third baseman. "Getting religion hurt his hitting, and he became tiresome."

"All these right-wingers finding God," Lamplighter muttered, "as if He's ever been lost."

"For some, He has been," Danny Linz said quietly.

"Born again." Lamplighter snorted. "Once was enough for me."

"Diana," Mick called, "would you fire me up a cheeseburger?"

The blonde barmaid wandered down the bar to us, drying a beer stein. "You want onions with that?"

"Just the usual quart of grease. I might have to counsel a lost soul this afternoon."

She gave the rim of the stein a last swipe of towel and set it upside down under the bar, then aimed a slow smile at me. "Anything for you, stranger?"

After she'd gone back to the kitchen with our orders, Mick nudged me. "Diana—goddess of the hunt," he said, raising both eyebrows. "Hear she's a dead shot with a deer rifle. She could bag me." He pitched his voice low enough that the others couldn't hear.

"It's nice to know you haven't changed," I said.

Mick waved a dismissive hand. "Don't worry, Dressler. She's been hooked up with the county newsman forever. Stonecutter's an ass, but I kinda like him."

The poker game started at seven thirty that evening, after the Twins had lost and we'd all had dinner at the Outpost and then driven over to Piney Woods. The Saint Simon's rectory was on a hill overlooking Piney Woods Lake. We played at an oak trestle table in George's dining room, which was at the back of the house, with wide windows giving a panorama of the lake. The house threw a shadow over the hillside. On the water, a last sailboat leaned east with the evening breeze and skimmed for home. "Nickel-dime-quarter," George said for my benefit as he shuffled a fresh deck of cards. "Nickel ante. Dealer's choice, though we frown on the excessive use of wild cards. Harold," he nodded at Lamplighter, "will let you know if you transgress. Liquor and glasses are to be found on the sideboard. Don't take the Lord's name in vain. First jack deals."

During the evening's cards, I got to know my fellow priests' tics and prejudices. Snow and Lamplighter were old-line Catholic leftists: liberal on social policy, conservative on sex. When I mentioned the fall elections, Lamplighter coughed and said: "I'd vote Republican over abortion, if they weren't against labor and any other kind of social progress. Since Johnson, the Democrats have taken the moral stand on civil rights and even—" he paused, considered, and took the plunge—"on gays."

Snow, hunched over the table so low that the bowl of his pipe clicked against a stack of blue chips as he talked, squinted at his friend. "Didn't know you were a fan of gay rights, Harold. You running a lavender rectory up in Bell's Crossing all these years without telling me?" His mouth twitched at the corners. "Tsk, tsk. I thought we were close."

Lamplighter leveled a forefinger at him. "Don't be a comedian. The point is, the only reason the GOP still exists is it's played the race card since the sixties, and now it's starting to play the same ugly game with homosexuals."

Danny Linz fiddled with his cards. He leaned forward and placed a dime in the pot, then glanced at his hand and added another. "Twenty cents. I don't think you can reduce the entire Republican platform to bigotry."

"Damn it," Lamplighter growled, leathery face reddening while his forefinger swiveled to cover Linz. "What I said was that enough knuckle-draggers vote Republican over coloreds and faggotry to tip a lot of elections. I fold." He slapped his cards face down on the table.

"Even abortion's tricky," I said, not thinking.

Snow turned on me, all traces of humor gone. "It's murder," he said. "What do you find tricky about that, Dressler?"

I felt myself flush. I knew better than to bring up the A-word. I answered as best I could, meeting Snow's angry glare: "Saying it's not debatable takes the Church out of the debate, when it's clear people of good conscience can disagree."

Everyone but Mick stared. I lowered my head and put a quarter in the pot and drew out a nickel. "Call."

Lamplighter stood and frowned. "Someone needs to stand for the moral absolute."

Mick tossed his cards into the middle of the table and tipped his chair back. "Fold. How's that square with what you said about gays?" he asked, his tone one of mild curiosity.

Lamplighter regarded him over the tops of his glasses. "I was talking about the Church's stand. A priest can disagree privately, but he's vowed to keep ranks with his bishop and through him the Pope." He stepped away from the table. "Anyone besides me want another beer?"

Everyone made a visible effort to relax. Snow, whose own face was red, nodded at Lamplighter and spoke to me: "Don't get him going, Jim. George forgot to tell you we try to avoid politics for the sake of Harold's blood pressure."

Lamplighter came back from the kitchen and handed beers around—Rhinelander Bock, a cheap Wisconsin brand George bought for five dollars a case.

Mick flipped the cap off his beer with a church key and said, "Let me get this straight, Harold. A priest can disagree privately, so long as he keeps public face? So I could sleep with my housekeeper, like Sprenger,"—he named his predecessor at Saint Christopher's—"if I kept it quiet?" He gave the table his most disarming smile.

"Great," Linz said. "Another topic we try to avoid."

I laughed, but Harold paused in pulling his chair out from the table. "Shankland," he said in a tight voice, "you didn't know Mike Sprenger. Keep your mouth shut about him."

"Sure, Harold." Mick's easy grin faded.

"Could we play cards here?" said George Martin, who so far had limited his opinions to the Gopher hockey team's prospects and the finer points of wing shooting and fly tying. "I'll see your twenty cents and raise you a quarter."

Linz called, and I folded. "Let's see 'em," Linz said.

"Two pair, aces over tens." George spread his cards on the table.

Linz grinned and laid down three sevens. "There's a moral absolute for you. A trinity beats two pair every time." He gathered in the pot.

"I'm just happy we kept it in the parish," George said.

Late in the evening, a couple priests from the next county west rolled in: Gavin Mullowney, who looked like an Irish politician straight out of central casting, and Michael Draper, a tall, angular man with a Fu Manchu mustache. They'd been drinking, and when they saw we had a full table, they sat on the couch and kept up a steady stream of wisecracks, mostly at Linz's expense. Mick and I looked at each other, unsure of our place, but none of the other priests, including Linz, said anything. When the deal passed to Linz, Mullowney said: "How about a hand of *Chase the Queen,* Linzie? Your favorite."

Linz, whose back was to the couch, turned in his chair. "The name's Linz," he said to Mullowney. "And I like five-card stud. You oughta try it—it's a no-bullshit game."

Mullowney widened his eyes. "I'm just suggesting," he said. "Linz."

Linz turned back to the table. His ears were red, and after a couple hands in which no one said anything except to bet, he made a production of yawning and stretching, then cashed out and went upstairs. Draper rose without a word and took his seat.

George counted out ten dollars in chips, frowning as he shoved the stacks across the table. Finally he said: "That wasn't kind, gentlemen."

Still on the couch, Mullowney lit a cigarette and crossed an ankle over his knee, smiling genially. "You have to admit he's not much of a card player, George."

George turned in his chair to face Mullowney. The creases in his face deepened. "You're laughing at me. *Country George*—well, I know about Linz's problem. But he's a young man trying to find his way. I don't need the two of you riding him. It's the last time I'll say it." He tapped his cigarette in an ashtray and bent his face to his cards.

Mullowney looked abashed. "I'm sorry, George. It won't happen again, will it?"

When the game broke up, George dropped chips into cedar cigar boxes and Snow carried Rhinelander Bock empties into the kitchen. Mullowney and Draper went out the door into the night, boisterous, and a chorus of "Danny Boy" drifted back to the house from the driveway. Lamplighter and Snow were close behind. I was following Mick out the door when George laid a hand on my forearm. I stopped. George had what Mick called a country face—hound-dog eyes and a downcast mouth that caved in between a pointy chin and a beak of a nose. It was a shrewd face, but not unkind. "Orthodoxy's the best bet at this table," he said, and turned back into the house.

I caught up with Mick at his truck.

"Thanks for getting me off the spot in there," I said, my voice hidden from the others under the shrill of locusts.

Mick opened his door, then turned to me, unexpectedly serious. "You've got to learn to play the game better, Dressler," he said.

"Poker?"

"Priesthood."

"I don't see it as a game," I said.

Mick got into the driver's seat, then leaned an elbow out the window. "At the end of the day, it's a career, same as any other," he said. "Don't mistake it for something else."

He drove away, following the other priests into the road and leaving me standing on the gravel drive in front of Saint Simon's. The wet, late-night air coming off the lake chilled me, and I shivered, watching the brakelights and taillights of the other priests' cars flash and fade.

16

MY FIRST COUPLE WEEKS IN THE PARISH, I spent busy days meeting the staff and reviewing finances and bills and parish programs. The evenings were taken up visiting prominent parishioners. My predecessor, Canby, had been a careful steward of parish money, but his age had begun to tell by the end, and there were book-keeping mistakes to be straightened out. The staff was strong and for the most part liked each other. The liturgy committee were an innovative bunch, which was good because when it came to cre-ative ways to celebrate the Mass I didn't have much imagination. The music director was competent enough for a Catholic parish, though he'd never have made it with the Episcopalians, and the youth director a solid family man. The head of the parish coun-cil made clear he was taking a wait-and-see attitude with me, but when I explained the problems with Canby's bookkeeping, he gave me the name of a parishioner who was an accountant, and she agreed to do a one-time reconciliation of the books.

Once I established myself with the staff and the books were bal-anced, I went out to a ball game or two. There were four teams in the local league: Blue River and Pretty Prairie plus the Piney Woods Indians and Bell's Crossing Harvesters. They played on high-school fields—dirt infields and tussocky outfields—and drew a handful of spectators: buddies and girlfriends, wives and kids. A couple of the wives ran an enterprising concession stand that consisted of a card table, a charcoal grill, and a cooler full of beer and pop. It was typical amateur baseball: games Saturday afternoons and Tuesday evenings, with the Tuesday games shortened to seven innings. Teams had about fifteen players, a good pitcher who pitched Saturdays, and an adequate second pitcher. The good pitchers threw fastballs in the seventies and got their breaking balls over the plate most of the time. The backup pitchers had less heat and less control, and the fielding ranged from spectacular to slapstick.

Before trying out, I drove over to Blue River, where Mick hit grounders to me in an empty lot near his church, and we went to the batting cages and fed money into the pitching machines. When I'd improved as much as I was going to against a machine, I walked into Dave Stanfield's garage one Friday afternoon to introduce myself. There were four bays, all busy, and there was a red-white-and-blue NRA eagle sticker on the office door. Stanfield was a squat, wide-shouldered man with a handlebar mustache and wire-framed bifocals that matched his silver hair. He wore grease-stained coveralls with *Stanfield's Super Service* sewn over one chest pocket and *Dave* over the other.

"I'm not Catholic," he said, "but I'll work on your car, if that's what you want."

"I want to play baseball," I said.

"This ain't a church league."

"From what I've seen, it isn't much more," I said.

He tapped his pen against an invoice on the counter, studied me. "We've got a game tomorrow. Batting practice at noon. Come then, and we'll see what you've got."

The next day, Stanfield told the team I was the new priest in town and trying out for team chaplain. Like Mick had said, he had control, a good curve, and a mediocre fastball. I was still rusty, but I waited for the fastball or the occasional hanging curve and was lucky enough to rocket a few around the outfield. Once I put a hard liner back over the mound, and it ricocheted off Stanfield's up-flung forearm, straight into the air. The first baseman caught it. Stanfield held his arm and grimaced. "Damned hard hit for a pop fly," he said. After he'd seen enough, he called the team together for a vote, then walked over. "You pay for your own uniform and bats, and we've got a kitty for umpires and lights," he said. "How's your fielding?"

The summer passed in a blur. I got up before dawn most mornings to say my office, beginning the day with matins and lauds, a habit I'd started in seminary. So much prayerfulness had aroused suspicion among my classmates and the seminary faculty—as Phil said, contemplation has always been the role of the religious orders, a monastic schedule not fitting parish life. Out in the world, though, I found that when the dailiness of my job—the meetings, bills, and reports—became overwhelming, observing the liturgical hours and seasons was a good reminder that I was moving in God's time and at His behest. It was also said to make celibacy easier, measuring out a life in moments, each directed to the service of God.

When the weather was good, and sometimes when it was bad, I said my morning prayers while walking the border of the bean field behind my rectory. I would stroll away from the house beneath paling stars toward the first brush of color in the eastern sky, and maybe, as I skirted the edge of the woods on the field's far side, spot the gray humped shadow of a raccoon scuttling into the underbrush or hear the sudden thud of hooves as a deer retreated deeper into the trees. When I made the last turn, toward the Saint Hieronymus steeple, I'd close my breviary and number the tasks that needed to be done that day: counting the collection plate, doing the books, arranging repairs and improvements, writing reports to the Chancery. A rural parish is a business run on a frayed shoestring. My congregation was small and aging—last rites and burials more common than marriages, the confessional more necessary than the baptismal font—and that meant a small collection. I envied the parishes in the Cities where a priest could afford a support staff to take up the slack. Up here, my paid staff consisted of three part-time positions: secretary, housekeeper, and groundskeeper. I had to budget even for urgent needs like a new roof for the sanctuary, and I did what I could on my own, starting with nailing up new gutters on the rectory.

The old man agreed to come up one Friday in the fall to help with the gutters. That morning, when I turned the corner of the bean field, I saw him and Granddad leaning against the fender of Otto's Park Avenue, smoking cigarettes and watching my seven a.m. Mass regulars, all middle-aged working people and retirees, drifting into the church.

"I didn't know you were coming," I said to Granddad when I got close. He'd lost weight, I thought then, but he looked hale enough. He wore a houndstooth vest and matching hat. Dad was in his usual working duds. His short-lived second marriage had happened over the summer, the new wife come and gone before most of the family were aware of her. I was curious, but I wasn't going to bring it up in front of Granddad.

Otto dropped his cigarette on the blacktop and crushed it under the polished toe of one shoe. "Wanted to hear my grandson say Mass." He coughed into his hand and nodded at Dad: "This heathen won't attend, though."

Dad was leaning against the car door, arms folded over his belly. "Not since Phil refused me Communion," he said. "I'll have a look at the gutters while you get the mumbo-jumbo out of the way."

"Jesus!" Otto said. "Christmas-and-Easter Catholic, divorced— your generation wants everything its own way." He thrust his face into Dad's.

Dad stuck out his lower lip at his father. "I just wanted Communion. Phil had no call to refuse. I'll lay odds the good Father here won't serve me either."

"Pigheaded," Otto said. Elderly Mrs. Dombrowski, passing on the far side of the car, stopped and stared. I smiled at her, and she put her head down and shuffled toward the church.

"I didn't know the Eucharist meant so much to you," I said to Dad. "But you're right. I can't give you Communion. That's my job."

"He just wants something to fight about," Otto said.

"Now where the hell did I get that?" the old man said to the bean field.

"I've got a Mass to say." I pulled the sacristy key out of my pocket. "You two sort yourselves out. There's coffee on in the kitchen if anybody wants it."

At Mass, Granddad sat in the front pew, eyes shining. He took Communion with his hands clasped and chin lifted, proud as a little kid. When Mass let out, we found the old man whistling, with a ladder up against the side of the rectory and half of the old gutters already on the ground.

I went inside to change, and when I came downstairs I found Granddad in the entry hall, talking to a bulky bleached-blonde woman with the shoulders of a linebacker. She turned bloodshot eyes to me. "Help me, Father. My man says he's gonna kill me. He's got a gun." Her breath smelled like a distillery.

"Why don't you come into the kitchen and sit down," I said. While Granddad got her a cup of black coffee, I called the county sheriff. She kept talking about her boyfriend and his gun, but the story didn't make much sense. Dad came in, and he and Otto stood in the dining room, glancing in the doorway occasionally. My housekeeper, Mrs. Gunther, who never failed to let me know what

Father Canby would have done in any given situation, showed up in the middle of this one and pulled me aside.

"That Theresa Panser's no good," she said. "Father Canby wouldn't have wasted his time."

"Well, here's the sheriff," I said, saved by a knock at the back door. "So we're not wasting time either, are we?"

The county sheriff, Matt Miller, was a Saint Hieronymus parishioner. When he saw Theresa, he sighed and pulled up a chair across from her. Mrs. Gunther started a vacuum in the living room. I herded Dad and Otto outdoors, where Dad and I went to work while Otto supervised from the picnic table. After a while, Sheriff Miller drove away. After another while, he came back, went into the house, and came out with Theresa. They stood by his car and talked for a moment, then she began gesturing and arguing, and finally she turned with an exaggerated shrug and put her hands behind her back. "Go ahead," she said. Miller handcuffed her, then eased her into the back of the patrol car.

I walked over. Miller paused with one foot on the doorsill of the cruiser. "She's got a pretty fair left hook," he said. "Her boyfriend's pressing charges over two black eyes and a broken nose. Tim Harley."

I must've looked puzzled because Miller went on. "Frank Harley's son," he said, naming a member of the parish council.

"Frank never mentioned him," I said.

Miller climbed into his car. "He wouldn't have."

Dad came up beside me as Miller drove away. "How's the shepherd business?" he said.

17

COLD WEATHER CAME, heralded by hundreds of migrating hawks that soared down the North Shore of Lake Superior, passed over Duluth, then followed the Saint Croix valley south. Mick would pause while we threw a football in the Saint Christopher parking lot and name passing silhouettes in the sky: marsh hawk, redtail, sharp-shinned; Cooper's, kestrel, merlin. He had an outdoorsman's eye, had grown up hunting deer and turkey in the countryside around Rochester with his doctor father. Now he and George Martin were planning a pheasant-hunting trip to North Dakota, and he commented on how quickly the leaves had gone: "Gonna be a rough one."

With Mick watching the October sky warily, a city boy like me might expect the rural winter to be a long, cold night of the soul. And it was. When it came, many of my parishioners disappeared, snowbirds joining the flocks of Airstreams and Gulfstreams, Coachmen, Southwinds, and Winnebagos migrating to Florida and Arizona. At the same time, icy country roads and the poor heater in my used car made visiting my fellow priests less appetizing. I was busy as ever during the day, but spent too many evenings alone at home, watching sports on TV or reading and thinking about the community life I presided over but wasn't yet a part of—the First Communion classes, the baptisms where I appeared long enough at the family gatherings afterward to have a bite to eat and exchange pleasantries with the proud parents, the once-a-year visits to parishioners to bless their homes. Mick sometimes complained about the attentions of the faithful—"I'm never wearing my collar on a plane again," he said after spending a flight to a liturgical conference in DC trapped between the exit door and a Catholic dowager; "I almost went out that exit"—but that winter I found myself wanting more of my flock's company.

Mom came up sometimes for dinner, bringing me hot dishes and groceries and clothes that I could wear with my clerical blacks: good dress shoes and belts, undershirts, black cardigans. She kept me up on the family: Anne wanted to have one more child; Daryl thought he might soon see a promotion at General Mills; Jacky and Mary Beth had split, no, wait, they were back together. Mom didn't know where the old man was living—he was no doubt dodging subpoenas and bill collectors, she said—but he called now and again to berate her in the middle of the night. He hadn't been paying his alimony, and she was seeing a lawyer about it. My family, it seemed, spun in the same exhausting circles, and dinners with Mom left me as empty as the wine bottle on the kitchen counter the next morning.

Stumbling up to a cold bed late at night, saying my evening prayers, I longed for a woman for the first time in years. In bed, listening to the night sounds of the house, I would imagine a light footstep, remember the way a college girlfriend's bangs had fallen over one eye as she turned back the sheets, another's smile in the morning. Maybe one of those women, one of the Saint Thomas girls I might have married had I chosen a different life, was up tonight, right now, at a bar with friends or out dancing with her husband. I, on the other hand, was alone in the way only a priest could be, vowed to God.

Desire—for sex, for companionship—hadn't bothered me since seminary. I broached it with Mick one night as we drove back from an evening in the Cities, snow blowing across the highway in the headlights of his truck. We'd gone down to watch college basketball, a holiday tournament, with one of our former Saint Thomas baseball teammates. But Steve had two sons playing on the floor of the family room and a wife so solicitous of the presence of priests in her house that she kept unwittingly interrupting the game. At last, with the kids in the sack and the best game of the evening ahead of us, Steve clicked off the television. "Sorry, guys," he said, "gotta work early. Why don't you come down some weekend when I have a little more time?" Mick and I glanced at each other. "Uh, we work weekends," Mick said, and Steve had laughed. "Yeah, I guess you do."

"That didn't go so well," I said in the truck, speaking over the rattle of the heater fan cranked on high.

Mick shrugged. "Something bothering you, Dressler?"

"Remember those late-night seminary conversations? Half a dozen guys sitting in the lounge bullshitting, having a go at solving the spiritual problems of the ages? What happened to all that?" In the window beside me, I could see the faint reflection of the dashboard lights against the snowy fields outside. "You and I trade practical ideas on the phone a couple times a week, and at poker everyone bitches about the Chancery or talks about whose parishioner serves the best cut of steak."

"What's your point?" Mick hunched over the wheel to peer along the headlight beams. We had conversations like this: I talked and Mick asked obtuse questions, drawing me along. He played poker the same way: the bluff, the blank stare, the occasional sudden raise.

"I knew there wouldn't be women," I said. "I didn't know there wouldn't be anybody. Hell, all I see is the human side of my parishioners, but God forbid they should ever see mine. Days at the office I'm too busy to think, and come evening there's nothing to do but think." It all came out in a rush. I'd said more than I meant to.

"Looks like something you're gonna have to work through." Mick braked at a paper bag blowing across the road, and when the back of the truck began to fishtail on the snow-slick pavement, he lifted his foot and counter-steered. If he had any doubts, he wasn't letting on. I pulled my stocking cap down tight over my ears and settled against the door, watching the rearview mirror, where the white line on the side of the road unreeled into the dark behind us.

In early January, I gave a guest lecture on the history of the archdiocese to an eighth-grade class at Our Lady of the Snows, the Catholic grade school the county's parishes ran in common. Afterward, the first-year teacher, a young woman named Mary McGlothlin, brought me to the lounge for coffee. She told me she'd taken a master's in history, writing a thesis on rural Irish Catholics in the Upper Midwest, including a chapter on Archbishop Ireland's ill-starred attempt to settle the poor of Connemara on real estate he owned along James Hill's Great Northern railroad lines. From the East, Mary had come here to do her master's at Marquette, but then discovered she had no stomach for academia and ended up in River County because of connections she'd made while researching her thesis.

"So, how's living in rural Minnesota compare to studying it?" I asked.

She laughed. She had swirls of black hair and an upturned lilt of a nose. "I can give you a good idea of that from the first day of school last fall. I was seeing my students out to their parents' cars when I noticed a line of pickup trucks parked across the street." She set down her coffee, indicated the main drag of Bell's Crossing, visible out the dust-coated windows of the teachers' lounge. "In each pickup, a young or not-so-young man in a feed cap and overalls, watching the front of the school. Weird, huh?

One of the other first-year teachers asked the principal about it. Guess what?"

I shrugged and smiled over my Styrofoam cup. "House husbands?"

She smiled back. "Hardly. They were checking out the new crop of teachers. Annual ritual. Single women are a rarity here." She stirred more powdered creamer into her coffee. Her smile turned rueful, and her black eyelashes fluttered. "Sometimes it can get lonely."

"I know," I said, and with that innocuous comment, it came to both of us that we had been following the well-marked path of any two young people discovering a mutual attraction. We averted our eyes from one another, and I squelched an urge to apologize.

In the next instant, we both stood. I extended my hand. "I enjoyed teaching your class, Miss McGlothlin."

She took it formally. "It was a fine lecture, Father. I'm sure my students learned a lot."

That winter, when I couldn't sleep, I'd occasionally get into my car and drive south on 35 the hour to Saint Paul. When 35 split into East and West, I'd stay on 35E, passing exits on the long downhill into the city—Larpenteur, Maryland, Pennsylvania, University—until the downtown lights suddenly emerged from the glare of highway vapor lamps, the buildings rising like low constellations, corners marked with red warning lights for planes, the Bremer Tower with its blue-and-white logo, the neon First National Bank sign. Once I got off the highway, it didn't matter if the downtown streets were deserted, I was in the city and could feel its restless energy in my stomach.

I drove all over the city on those nights: through downtown, where the lights left on in the big buildings only made them look all the emptier, where a janitor ran a vacuum in a lighted skyway, where Mickey's Diner was a bright thrum of people and cars; then south over one of the downtown bridges and into the West Side, or southwest on West Seventh past Mancini's Char House and the old Schmidt's brewery with its castle tower, and eventually into Highland Park, turning off just short of where Highway 5 leaped the river into Minneapolis and Northwest airliners descended on invisible lines to the airport, back along the river on Shepard Road, or north up Mississippi River Boulevard, first past the Ford plant, then following curves between the wide lawns of the big darkened houses on the right and the bare trees of the river gorge, turning east on Summit at the seminary and passing Saint Thomas and Macalester College, crossing Snelling and Lexington and Dale, the houses getting bigger and older as you went—Fitzgerald's museum of architectural failures—until, where the University Club perched at the top of the Ramsey Street hill, Summit curved northeast and I came to the Hill Mansion and the Cathedral and drove John Ireland Boulevard toward the Capitol—perfect geography for a street named after a cleric with Ireland's political ambitions—and then west again down University, past all of the Asian restaurants and supermarkets shuttered in the middle of the night, and the run-down shopping centers with two cop cars at an angle in the middle of the lot, and the all-night fast-food joints and the tattoo parlors; past the city bus pulling away from a stop, its lighted windows, its one black man sitting alone in the back.

Eventually, I'd turn north on Snelling and back east one final time on Thomas, brushing my family's neighborhood, the familiar side streets—Asbury, Simpson, Pascal, and Albert; Syndicate, Griggs, and Dunlap; Oxford, Chatsworth, Milton, and Victoria. I could have turned into the neighborhood anytime, found a light on, found Jacky watching the late movie in Mary Beth's living room, found Mom sitting in the kitchen drinking sherry and playing solitaire, but I never did. It wasn't exactly company I wanted those nights I drove to Saint Paul, but movement. I wore my priest's clothes and collar, as if I were Superman, as if I might be called to the rescue. Once I swore I passed my father's car going the other way at three a.m. on Maryland Avenue. Sometimes I saw his car parked in front of a bar, but I never stopped.

Still, when I look back on that time, those moments of dissatisfaction—the late-night longing, the sudden confession of uncertainty to Mick, the brief flirtation with Mary McGlothlin, the long nighttime drives to Saint Paul—were fleeting. By and large, I was satisfied with my life. The older priests who played poker at George Martin's table were practical, moderate men whose camaraderie was that of an Army barracks. By upbringing and inclination, Mick and I fit in better with them than we did with many of our contemporaries, who, liberal or conservative, tended toward a softer, more feminine style of priesthood. And so the longer I was in River County, the more I came to see my assignment there as a form of grace.

One morning in deep winter, I was awakened at three a.m. from a bad dream: I'd been a child again, alone in the halls of my Catholic grade school, and the eyes of the statues with the sacred hearts outside their bodies were alive and terrible. The bell rang, but no one came out of the classrooms to find me. Then the bell turned into the phone; it was the River County Rest Home calling for last rites for a former Saint Hieronymus parishioner.

I pulled on my black slacks and shirt over pajamas, found my kit for the annointing, got into my coat and muffler, and stepped out into the bitter cold. It was long after moonset, the snow cover catching just enough light to make the night ghostly. A current of snow blew around my ankles, across the bare pavement and patches of ice in the parking lot, swirling between the rectory and church. Besides the rasp of the wind and the brittle rustle of evergreen needles in the sub-zero air, there was no sound. In the garage, my Chevy's engine groaned and groaned and turned over, and I took the county two-lane south toward Bell's Crossing, hunched behind the wheel against the cold. The old snow in the fields had settled and crusted in the furrows, and ridges of frozen earth broke through.

At the nursing home, the dying woman gripped the rails of her bed. "Her name's Alice Remboldt. She doesn't have any family," the nurse whispered, then left me at the door of the bare, dim-lit room. Alice Remboldt's eyes rolled toward me, and her breath came in short gasps. I took her hand while I delivered the sacrament, and in the midst of it I was aware of a great relief coming into the room. When I finished, her breathing slowed and her eyes closed. I got a cup of coffee from the nurse's station and sat with the dying woman while a clock ticked toward dawn. Long before first light, the first sounds of morning just beginning in the halls, her breath caught in her throat and stopped. I said a prayer for the dead, then talked to the nurse, making sure arrangements were in place with an undertaker.

On the drive home, barbed-wire fences stretched and glittered with ice in my headlights, and I was suddenly and unexpectedly glad to have a calling that could draw me shivering forth into such bleak beauty. Later, while I drowsily intoned early Mass to a handful of weekday regulars, the rising sun lit the east windows of the church.

In March, I won the parish NCAA tournament pool, picking North Carolina over Michigan in the final, then donated my winnings to the roofing fund and made a joke about Blue Devils in the next Sunday's homily.

By then, besides the other priests, my closest friend in River County was Diana, the bartender at the Outpost. Raised in Blue

River, she had dated Roger Stonecutter, the county newspaper-man, for years, so she was a "safe" woman. We had long conversations over the bar, especially when I figured out Diana was smarter about sports than most of the men I knew. She played fast-pitch women's softball in the summer and was a regular in the bleachers at Farm-Industrial League games, sitting and drinking beer with her girlfriends or keeping Stonecutter company while he scored the game.

That winter, Diana and I got in the habit of watching college basketball together at the Outpost. Then, during the Final Four, with Kansas losing to North Carolina while sleet spattered against the front windows of the bar, she said, "Roy Williams' teams are disciplined and well prepared, but he's not good at adjusting if his game plan isn't working."

"No way. Look at his winning percentage."

"Look at his tournament record."

I narrowed my eyes.

"Gotcha thinking, didn't I?" She picked up my beer and took a drink, and when she set it down we became aware of a man at the other end of the bar. He was staring at us—at the blonde bar-maid sipping from the priest's beer, at the way their hands almost touched when she set it back on the bar.

"Oops," I said.

"Yeah," Diana said, squinching up one eye.

And maybe it was only that the tournament ended two nights later, but Diana and I quit watching games together and I began going to the Outpost only in the company of other priests.

Then spring arrived. The snow melted and the Saint Hieronymus neighborhood emerged, people blinking in the sun-light and exchanging gardening tips while they oiled lawn mow-ers and raised ladders to paint houses, one side each summer, and passed advice and tools across chain-link fences. I renewed acquaintances with neighbors who'd been only bundled figures shoveling their driveways for the past six months—Mom says Minnesotans get along so well because we don't have to see each other for a good part of the year—then dug out my purple-and-white Pioneers uniform and prepared to start my second year as pastor of Saint Hieronymus.

18

ONE JULY AFTERNOON, I WAS SITTING in the Pioneers' dugout—
a chain-link fence around an aluminum bench—changing from
spikes to street shoes after we'd beaten the Harvesters under a
green sky that promised thunderstorms, when Frank Harley came
and rested his chin on the top rail of the fence. I knew Frank better now than I had the previous fall, when Theresa Panser was
arrested for beating up his youngest son.

"Looks like a gully washer," Frank said.

"Sure does."

"Crops can use it. Verna wants you to come for dinner tonight.
After Mass?"

"It'll be about six-thirty, seven."

"That'll do."

The Harleys were a retired farm couple. They'd sold their land to
a large commercial operation and moved into a neat brick house
on a side street in town. Frank was a tough-minded member of
the parish council whose quiet opinions carried a lot of weight,
and Verna regularly brought me pies—rhubarb as the first sign of
Minnesota's late spring, blueberry in July, cherry in late summer,
apple all fall, and, of course, pumpkin at Thanksgiving—their
crusts a wonder, delicate and flaky, never too wet or too dry. A
bulletin board in her kitchen sported a collection of blue ribbons
she'd won at the state fair.

The Harleys had a daughter who was a doctor in North Carolina, a son who was an agriculture professor at the University of Minnesota, and another son who was a mid-level executive with 3M. Then there was Timothy, not so much the black sheep as the runt. He'd never left Pretty Prairie. A few years back, when he'd been mixed up in a burglary ring, Sheriff Miller arrested him with great reluctance, knowing he'd be sent to Stillwater and knowing what would happen to him there. Tim was out on parole now, working at the town convenience store. He'd taken up with Theresa Panser and moved into her trailer, which sat on a dirt lot in the shadow of the grain elevator. As I'd learned, Theresa was a hard case, and every once in a while they'd fight and she'd throw Tim out, often as not giving him a few bruises to remember her by. He'd show up at Mass with his parents then, a slight, scared-looking man in his late twenties, with a shock of dirty-blond hair hiding his eyes. Even there he was separate, a thin figure at the end of the pew, a distinct space between his shoulder and his mother's. If Frank and Verna paused afterward to visit with someone, Tim would wait for them by their car, smoking a cigarette and managing to look furtive doing it.

I arrived at the Harleys' just after six thirty and just in front of the storm. While it thundered and lightninged outside, we ate at a round farmhouse table they'd moved with them, the table too bulky and heavy for the new kitchen. Frank stumped around in worn overalls and farm boots, as much too big for the house as the table was for the kitchen. He had a farmer's iron handshake and the appetite of a man who'd done outdoor labor all his life. Verna ate well, too, and the platter of pork chops and bowls of corn and mashed potatoes were passed three times. I kept up to be polite, and when Verna put a quarter of a blueberry pie on my plate after dinner, I sighed. Frank had been keeping an ear on the progress of the storm by an AM radio crackling on top of the fridge. Now he leaned back from the table and patted his belly. "I've got a favor to ask," he said, "and I'm not sure exactly what I'm asking for."

I cocked an eyebrow at his hesitation. "Well, ask," I said, "and we'll figure it out."

Rain drove against the window behind him. "Verna and I want you to talk to Timmy," he said. "We just have a feeling you ought to." Tim Harley was back with his woman for the time being.

"That's enough to start," I said. "I'll drop by and see where we go from there." If there was one thing I'd figured out since becoming a priest, it was that most people wanted to talk. You just had to give them the chance.

"Tim never was very strong," Frank went on. "But prison ruined him. He was a pretty fair high-school shortstop, though, and I guess it might help if he could play some baseball again."

I glanced at a pantry shelf, where a baseball trophy—a batter in his crouch—stood curiously among mixing bowls and bottles of vegetable oil and five-pound bags of Gold Medal flour. "We'll see," I said.

Finding Tim Harley wasn't easy. He'd quit the convenience store in some dispute, and there was no phone listing for Theresa. The Harleys didn't have the number either, and Verna thought maybe the phone was cut off. Finally, I stopped by the trailer on a Saturday morning and rapped on the warped metal screen door, which sounded like a cheap snare drum. There was country music inside, but no answer. I knocked again. The door opened, and Theresa stared at me with that mixture of hostility and fear that marks the most desperately poor and uneducated.

"What you want?"

"I'd like to speak with Tim." The sweet scent of marijuana drifted from the trailer.

"He's asleep."

"Would you ask him to call me? Father Jim at Saint Hieronymus."
I involuntarily touched my collar.

She snorted. "I know who you are."

I didn't expect Tim Harley to call, so I kept an eye out around town,
planning to make another stop at the trailer in a week or two. I had
no idea what I'd say, but if Frank wanted me to have a talk with
his lost son, I planned to do just that. On the other hand, I wasn't
going to ask Tim to play ball. Dave Stanfield would never go for
it, and the other players would be angry if we imposed a man like
Tim on them. But that was a moot point because I couldn't find
Tim—even in a small town, the hours and company he kept made
it unlikely we'd cross paths, and I was plenty busy with the people at Saint Hieronymous who actively sought a priest's counsel.
There'd been a run of crisis and tragedy: a pregnant valedictorian,
a retiree hit by a car in the crosswalk downtown, a young father
drowned in wheat at the grain elevator. For several weeks in a row,
I'd skipped the Sunday gatherings at the Outpost and the poker
game afterward while I performed triage in my parish. George
had called to be sure I hadn't lost my taste for cards.

Then my life got busier. One Saturday morning after a Farm-
Industrial League game in Bell's Crossing, I walked out to the
parking lot and found Diana, who'd been playing softball for the
Outpost's team on the adjacent field and couldn't get her car to
turn over. The starter was shot, and after she called AAA, I offered her a ride. In my small car, I was uncomfortably aware of
the way she kept flipping her long honey-blonde hair while she
chatted about getting good grades in community college account-
ing and how she was thinking of moving to the Cities after she got
her associate's degree. "I made mistakes in high school," she said.
"Typical country kid—drugs, sex, and rock'n'roll." She laughed
and shifted her knees toward me.

"What's Roger up to these days?" I asked. Stonecutter was the one-man staff of the county's weekly newspaper. He and Diana had been an item long before I arrived in Pretty Prairie.

"We split," she said. "It wasn't going anywhere."

Diana had an apartment overlooking Blue River's main drag, reached by a set of steps from the alley. I parked in her spot, and she rested a hand on my knee. She had large hands for a woman, with strong, graceful fingers and ruddy skin that stood out against the white fabric and purple pinstripes of my baseball uniform. "Thanks," she said. Then: "I really enjoy talking with you."

I moved her hand back to her knee, sure now that she liked relationships that couldn't go anywhere. She touched the zirconium earring that sparkled in her ear. "Why don't you come up for a cup of coffee?" she asked. "I baked this morning, and if I eat a whole coffee cake, it'll go straight to my thighs."

I shook my head.

"C'mon," she said, and bounced out of the car and up the steps. Her softball uniform was light blue and clung to the long muscles of her flanks. It didn't look as if her thighs were in any danger, but I shut off the engine and followed her up the stairs anyway and then over a short boardwalk across the tar-and-gravel roof to the door. While she unlocked it, I tried to deny the meaning in my shaking knees.

Diana held the door. "I'll get the coffee ready," she said. "Cream?"

In an emptying countryside, barmaids apparently could afford gorgeous apartments. Diana had a rambling place that had been gerrymandered in above a couple of businesses and finished with French doors and a bay window. The living room was large and filled with Victorian furniture that must have been worth a fortune. I wondered aloud about this, and Diana said from the kitchen that it came from the estate of a maiden aunt,

who'd left Diana her furnishings and given her money to the
Church.

"Do you go to Saint Christopher's?" I asked.

"When I go. Father Mick tells funny stories in his homilies, but
with a point, if you know what I mean."

"He's good," I agreed. There were parlor chairs and a matching sofa with mahogany frames and upholstery in tufted brocades
and jacquards. An oval mirror with worn silvering hanging by a
doorway must once have reflected elderly Catholic ladies playing
cutthroat bridge. Against one wall were a glass-fronted secretary
and a marble-topped table. An incongruous back corner was occupied by a deer rifle and women's-sized field boots on a mat. I
went into a hallway and found the bathroom, then, on my way
back to the living room, glanced in another door and saw the un-
made foot of a brass bed and a star-patterned quilt folded on a
cedar chest.

"I really need to get back to the office," I said.

"What?" Diana came out of the kitchen with a tray crowded
with Victorian silver and china, including dessert plates with generous slices of cinnamon coffee cake. She set it down on an inex-
pensive coffee table that clashed with the antiques.

I took one end of the sofa, the other choice being a very cozy
love seat. Diana plopped herself at the opposite end and clapped her
hands on her thighs. "There. I hope you like the coffee cake." The
sky-blue softball uniform set off her tan, and I wanted very much
to touch her upper arms, where the sky and her skin came together.

"Tell me about the maiden aunt," I said.

"She lived to be almost a hundred and divided her money
among every Catholic charity in the state, a few hundred dollars
here, a few hundred there." Diana leaned forward and poured
cream into one cup of coffee. The movement wafted healthy scents
of green grass and infield dirt my way.

I fingered the carved grape cluster in the back of the sofa and said something clever about wood finishes.

Diana tapped a grape with a manicured nail. "Roger says the Victorians clamped down so hard on sex that it oozed out of their pores into everything they did."

I choked on a bite of coffee cake. "He did, did he?"

"The cake's too dry," Diana said, patting me on the back.

"No, no. It's plenty moist." I reached for the coffee.

"Are you sure?" Diana said.

"Love to have your recipe," I said. "Give it to my housekeeper. Did the Outpost win today?"

Diana was sitting beside me now. "We sure did," she said. "The paper says you and Father Mick are fighting for the batting lead. Roger said something funny about hard-hitting priests in his sports column this week."

"I haven't seen it yet," I said. Her knee pressed against my thigh.

"Hard-hitting priests," Diana repeated. She smiled. "Don't they box in the movies?"

"I box," I said. "But only with the punching bags in my basement. They don't hit back." I leaned forward to refill my coffee, shifting my leg away from hers. "Where'd you learn to hunt?" I asked.

"My father wanted a son and got four daughters," Diana said. "I've always loved the outdoors." She walked to the bay window as she was saying this, then stretched. The sky outlined her figure in light. I imagined her sighting a deer rifle, Artemis with a gun, and I followed her to the window, Actaeon after his hounds. It had been eight years since I'd been alone with a woman. Diana went on: "When you study the terrain to learn where game will be, you become more intimate with it than any backpacker ever dreamed."

There was a view across the green river valley, the steeples of the Wisconsin town on the opposite side mostly lost in the trees. Diana turned toward me, starting to laugh at herself. I brought my hands up and feathered my fingers over the backs of her arms, tested her taut biceps with my thumbs. Her face changed in a good way. Her eyes, gray in the Outpost, were blue in the sunlight, matching her uniform. She rested a hand behind my neck and pulled my mouth down to hers. Her lips were firm, and her body against mine was both a familiar memory and the most amazing new thing in the world.

My baseball cap fell off. I stepped back. "I've really got to go." I fumbled my car keys from my pocket, dropped them, and kicked them under the radiator. Diana giggled nervously, and I felt my face redden as I knelt to retrieve them and the cap. I worried that Roger Stonecutter still had a key to this apartment. That someone on the street might have seen us in the window. That I liked what had just happened.

"I'm so sorry," Diana said above me, then she made a sort of choked noise.

I stood up. "You didn't take a vow of chastity," I said. I had though, and I remembered an evening at the teaching parish where I'd been posted during seminary. A priest from a religious order who was a dinner guest at our rectory had been called to a nursing home to give last rites, and my pastor sent me along to observe. The dying man's middle-aged son and the son's younger wife were present, and when the sacrament had been given, the son mentioned that he and the wife had just flown in from Memphis. Father Dominic brightened and said he'd spent most of his career there, then started talking across the dying man's bed about Beale Street blues joints and Graceland and Sun Records and the ducks at the Peabody. I moved to the doorway, and I could see Dominic run his eyes up and down the young wife's body as he talked, and

I saw the husband see this, saw his moment of sorrow and confusion before he put a hand on his wife's shoulder and said, "I guess you'd better go now, Father. We need this time with Dad." During our drive back to the rectory, Dominic chattered about Memphis Tigers basketball, how he'd hated giving up his season tickets when he was transferred to Minnesota. Now, I wondered if the start of that man's graceless and lonely road had looked anything like this.

"You didn't take a vow of chastity," I found myself repeating to Diana.

"Roger's a good man," she said, as if searching for solid ground. "He called the other night. He wants to try to work things out. We have a lot of time invested."

I answered in my most dispassionate pastoral voice. "Sometimes we have to leave a relationship to grow, but other times, with the right person, the growth can take place together." This was the kind of aphoristic advice a priest often gave, and I was never sure whether it was wise or cowardly. Right now, I just hoped it would get me out the door with our dignity intact.

Diana leaned up and kissed me on the cheek. "You're good too, Jim," she said. "Stay and talk with me."

My cheek burned where her lips had touched. "We'll talk at the Outpost," I said. "Grab a quiet corner."

"I'm sorry," she said again, as if she couldn't say it often enough.

I found the doorknob and let myself out onto the roof. Sun shimmered off the tar and gravel. A summer's day was heating up, and I had no idea what to do with it. On my way back to Pretty Prairie, I stopped at an overlook where I sat on a rock wall above the blue Saint Croix. I prayed my office for a while, then got caught up in watching a hawk ride a thermal into the clear sky. Mick would have been able to identify it.

19

ONCE WHEN I WAS A CHILD AT THE LAUNDROMAT with my mother, I stuck my forefinger into a wringer, just to see what would happen. The rollers were soft rubber, and Mom hit the off switch right away, so when I stopped hollering all I had were a bruised finger and the memory of the sudden grab of the rollers, the way the machine pulled and pounded and shuddered at my hand. The funny part was that, even though I was a child, the mechanical bent I'd inherited from my father had forewarned me what would happen, and I'd watched with puzzled curiosity as I stuck the finger in anyway.

The moment when I'd touched the smooth backs of Diana's arms was like that. I should have known better, I did it anyway, and it wouldn't be easy to back out.

And, like at the laundromat, the first person I went to was my mother. I told her about Diana after dinner at my rectory, but only after making sure Mrs. Gunther had finished with the kitchen and was gone for the evening, not eavesdropping behind the kitchen door, where I'd caught her in the past.

The confession didn't go quite as I'd expected. Mom lit a cigarette. "I can't say I'm surprised, sweetie," she said.

"You're not?"

"A man needs his release."

"Mom!"

"Well, all I'm saying——"

I got up and went into the kitchen and poured Mom a glass of the sherry I kept for her, then myself a Scotch on the rocks, some of which I downed at the kitchen counter. "Here," I said, fortified and back in the dining room, handing the sherry to Mom. "We didn't have that talk when I was twelve, let's not have it now. Have you heard anything from Dad?"

She was laughing at me. "Maybe you ought to talk to another priest," she said. "What about your friend what's-his-name? The big, handsome lunk?"

"Mick," I said. "I'm not sure he'd be much of a resource."

I wondered how Mick was managing celibacy. He could cause a stir just walking into a parish kitchen full of matrons baking lemon pie for a fund-raiser. "Mmmm, smells good in here, ladies," he'd say as we strolled into citrus-scented bakery heat, and in an instant he would be surrounded by fluttery homemakers and twittering blue-haired church ladies. I was sure he had at least one lapse in seminary, but we'd never talked about it.

We had dinner at the Outpost that Thursday. Mick's idea, and I accepted his invitation like a penance, intending to punish myself with Diana's presence. But the Outpost was crowded that night and Diana was busy enough behind the bar that our brief kiss Saturday morning felt more imagined than remembered. I wished it were imagined—I, of all people, should have understood the cost of being unfaithful. I'd heard the confessions of adulterers, and I knew that the guilt and ugliness they felt was nothing that the TV screens of their imaginations had prepared them for. Now that same guilt and ugliness was inside me. I tried to work myself up to telling Mick what had happened, but instead talked of everything else: fund-raisers (lemon pie was a good one), the Farm Industrial League (our teams were tied for the lead), and Tim Harley (I still couldn't find him).

Late in the evening, Mick left with a parishioner who asked for counseling, and I sat at the bar until last call. Then I helped Diana close, putting up chairs and making chitchat while she wiped down the bar and tables. I was trying to think up a way to talk about Saturday morning when she turned out the last lights. "Walking after Midnight" was on the jukebox, the silver herringbone necklace at her throat glimmered in the faint shine the streetlight cast through the front windows, and I compounded my sin by making out with her in one of the back booths. It ended the same way our first kiss had, with blushing apologies and expressions of never again.

Driving home, smelling of Diana's perfume, I could imagine the old man saying gleefully that I had round heels. In our evening bull sessions at seminary, guys had constantly joked about women—*Did you see the Saint Kate's track squad this afternoon? Spandex is a tool of the devil, I'm sure of it*—but no one ever admitted to genuine doubt. In theory, the charism for celibacy is separate from the calling to be a priest, but in practice, with small seminary classes and not enough priests, nobody looked too closely at whether one man truly had the gift to be celibate or another man might be gay. Mick, for all his undergraduate reputation as a ladies' man, had sailed through at the top of his class, and it was impossible to spend five minutes with Danny Linz and not know he was gay. But there weren't any classes offered on celibacy, and, as with abortion, we mirrored the Church's absolute stance and didn't talk about it.

Still, I needed to discuss Diana with somebody, and within a few days I was on the doorstep of the Saint Germain rectory in a northern suburb of Saint Paul. I had an appointment with my confessor, Father Harry, who answered the door on the second knock, beer in hand, and led me into his office. I could hear a cooking show on the TV in the kitchen. Harry set aside his beer and sat down behind his desk, and I settled in across from him. There was a golf trophy on the desk, a Cross pen set that looked unused, and a calendar from an insurance company with entries in Harry's sloppy cursive. On one corner, a trailing houseplant spilled from a colorful planter shaped like a circus car driven by a clown, thriving despite a lack of natural light and attention.

"Haven't seen you in a while," Harry said, a reference to my infrequent confessions.

"I've got a big one this time," I said.

Harry sighed and looped his purple stole about his neck, then swiveled his chair a little away from me and put his hand up beside his face.

I told him about Diana.

He tilted back and clasped his hands behind his neck, looking up at the tiled ceiling of the office. "It happens," he said. "Celibacy's a process, much as we'd like to pretend it's a finished product." But before I could ask him what his experience had been with the process, he rested his forearms on the veneer of the desk and asked, "What are you going to do about this woman?"

I was silent.

Harry didn't waste time. I'd chosen him as my confessor because, unlike myself, he was not prone to overanalyzing matters of the soul. "Tell you what," he said: "I'm not giving you absolution yet. You're looking to clear your conscience so you can drag this affair out, end up in bed with this woman. Seen it before." He lifted his stole off, folded it, and tucked it in a drawer. "What you need now is sensible talk. Let's go out to dinner. I'll buy."

We ate at an Indian restaurant in a strip mall near Harry's church, the meal washed down liberally with Bass beer. Harry ordered a sampler platter and narrated a tour of Indian dishes and spices, discoursing on the British Empire and how the India Pale Ale brought out the flavors, and then talking about women and priests. In French-speaking Africa, where he'd done mission work, the *priest's woman* was a common thing. "Every village had one." He shrugged. "That's the French for you. Here, it'll destroy your spirit, if not your career."

We had a booth for two against the wall. In the middle of the room, tables had been pushed together for a family group that was Indian except for a stout, pink-necked Scandinavian, who had one arm loosely draped over the round shoulders of his Indian wife. Halfway through the meal, she lifted a blond baby boy—a perfect little Viking made by some odd splash in the gene pool—from the high chair next to her and passed him into his father's arms. At the far end of the table, an older Indian man watched the goings-on with a prideful curve to his prim mouth.

"My grandfather goes to confession every Saturday," I said to Harry. "Has for as long as I can remember." I dipped a samosa in tamarind sauce, then went on: "I take hearing confession as seriously as any of my duties. And when I give absolution, I feel I've given a gift from God that ought to be beyond my power to bestow. But lately, I have a hard time asking it for myself."

Harry spooned rice onto his plate. "You're a young man, still discerning who you are." He tapped the air with a forefinger. "When you know that, confession comes easier."

"Okay," I said, not understanding. "But when I confessed to you about Diana, it wasn't because I wanted an intermediary with God, but because I thought you'd give me some advice."

"You sound like a Protestant." Harry turned a bite of tandoori chicken on his fork. "Reason alone fails us every time. We're a Church of mysteries: three persons in one God, the divine and the human joined in Christ, the bread and wine becoming His body and blood. Wisdom comes from communion with the divine."

We finished our beers, and Harry picked up the bill. At the table in the center of the room, the Viking baby had been passed along to the Indian patriarch. The old man held the infant in his lap, head cradled in one arm, and took a bottle of formula from the mother. He bent his face to the baby's, cooing and widening his eyes until the child gurgled with laughter and waved its hands about.

I took back roads home, hanging an arm out the window and listening to the country chorus of insects and frogs, a now-familiar rendition of the same concert that had so unnerved me as a child at Bob Nordyke's cabin. It was a stifling July night, muggy enough for a monsoon. I tugged at my collar, chafing my neck in the humidity.

Harry had given me a last bit of advice: "After ordination, the first time you realize women are still interesting—and interested— is tough. Then it comes and goes. Celibacy is like a marriage: there are times when a couple is absolutely in love, and then there are the rocky periods in between. How you handle the rocks is the measure of your vocation."

My measure: I knew what I was doing when I took my vows, and I had no excuses. We were playing at Blue River tomorrow. If Diana wasn't at the game, I would go to the Outpost, take her aside, say what needed to be said. I would stay away from the Outpost after that, if that was what it took to remain true. I would not slip up again, not even a little. I would be a good priest.

I drove into Pretty Prairie after midnight, full of resolution, British ale, and curried lamb. I was ready for the sack, but as I slowed and drew nearer to the center of town, I saw a half-dozen sheriff's and highway patrol cars in front of the convenience store, which was all lit up when it should have been closed. I turned the corner to my rectory and garaged the car, then walked the block back to the highway, letting the night air clear my head.

"What's going on?" I asked Sheriff Miller. He was in his sixties, a spare man with liver spots and bifocals. In his customary spot halfway back in the pews at Saint Hieronymus Sunday mornings, he looked more like a retired clerk than a cop, but he was an effective sheriff. After thirty-some years on the job, he was able to head off most trouble in River County's handful of small towns before it happened. But not all of it.

"Tim Harley shot a private detective in the butt, and we're trying to find him," Miller said.

"The detective or Tim?"

"Tim. The detective's over there. Standing." Miller had a horse-toothed grin.

In front of the store, a dumpy, middle-aged man in a threadbare brown polyester suit stood with his foot on a parking block, gesturing to a pair of state troopers and Roger Stonecutter, who had his reporter's notebook open. The private eye kept wincing and shifting his stance.

"Looks uncomfortable," I said to Miller. "What happened?"

"It's ugly all around." Miller looked unhappy. "Tim'll go back to Stillwater."

Insects buzzed around the parking-lot lights. Every so often a June bug would hit one of the lights with a snap and drop to the pavement. Chub Williams, the store manager, came out carrying Styrofoam cups in a box lid. He offered coffee to the group in front of the store, then sauntered over to Miller and me. Stonecutter closed his notebook and put it in his breast pocket. He moved a little apart from everyone else, holding the coffee at his lips, looking over the rim at the three of us. It was almost as if he was sizing me up.

"Poor Tim," Chub said. "Dumb little shit. Sorry, Father."

I took a cup of black coffee. "The Harleys know?" I asked. Across the lot, Stonecutter finished his coffee and dropped the cup on the pavement, then stepped on it. The small parking lot felt crowded. Kissing a woman who'd been involved with the county newspaperman wasn't the smartest thing I'd ever done.

"They're out of town," Miller said.

"What happened?" I asked again.

Chub looked at Miller, who ran a hand over his tarnished silver hair. "Tim bought a used car from the dealership in Bell's Crossing and then stopped making payments. The dealer hired a private eye to repossess." Miller nodded in the direction of the man in brown polyester. "In the course of things, he took up with Tim's girlfriend on the sly. Today Tim was supposed to work a double shift,"—Chub had apparently rehired him—"but the guy who usually works evenings changed his plans and showed up. Tim walks home and finds our man over there in bed with his woman. Puts a .22 slug in his tail as he exits the trailer carrying his pants."

"What a lousy little comedy," I said. Stonecutter was talking to the private eye again.

"Lousy's right," Miller said. "Tim's disappeared, along with a shotgun."

Roger Stonecutter walked toward us across the lot.

"I'll get out of your way," I said to Miller. "I'll be at home. Call if you need me."

Stonecutter overheard. "I'll give you a ride," he said. "We haven't met."

There was no graceful way out of it. Stonecutter owned a 1970s Pontiac with cracked vinyl bench seats and safety belts that didn't work. When he saw me fiddling with mine, he leaned over and said in a low voice: "Seat-belt laws are where this country started to go wrong." I couldn't tell if he was joking.

The car lurched out of the lot, bouncing on bad springs. Stonecutter had a downturned mouth framed by a close-trimmed beard with some gray in it. He was a good deal older than Diana. It was rumored he came from money and used it to subsidize his paper. He certainly ran his weekly with a harder edge than most small-town papers: he didn't mind pissing off advertisers. There was belligerence, but also calculated intelligence, to the way he slouched in the driver's seat with a hand draped over the steering wheel and talked out of the corner of his mouth while he scanned the shadows of people's yards. "Doubt he's out and about," he said. "Plenty of places to hide in this county. Plenty to hide." Diana had told me he lived in the only apartment building in River County that had a security door. He cruised a zigzag route through town, taking corners abruptly. "Maybe Elm Street," he muttered.

After a sudden right slid me across the vinyl seat and practically into his lap, I hooked an arm through the shoulder belt dangling by my head. "I'd really like to get home," I said.

His head swiveled slowly, and he stared at me until I expected we would run off the road. "I'm sorry," he said. "I get distracted. New priest is always newsworthy." He pinched his bearded chin. "I hoped we might get to know one another. The Fourth Estate and the First."

"I read your story on the Indian County scandal," I said. He'd won a state press award the past winter for breaking a story on illegal wiretapping by the neighboring county's prosecutor and sheriff, who'd been doing a favor for a small-town mayor whose wife was having an affair. The Twin Cities papers had been running stories about the allegations for months without being able to find anything solid. Supposedly Stonecutter had procured confessions from each of the three principals in one evening of inspired phone calling. "How'd you get people to come clean like that?" I asked.

He shrugged. "People have a guilty conscience, they want to talk. I'm a sympathetic ear."

I laughed. "Until next week's paper comes out."

"Even then," he said. "People are relieved to confess their sins to the community. You ought to understand that."

"I was just talking about it with another priest," I said. Stonecutter was an interesting mix of smarts and brusqueness. We could be friends, I thought. Then the Indian spices made them-selves known in my stomach. I farted.

Stonecutter gave a short bark that passed for a laugh. "Can't escape the body, can we, Father? I like to call it the *scatological imperative.*"

I relaxed, forgetting Diana for the moment. "Take me home, Roger. Tim's not out here, and I need some sleep tonight."

He turned down Meadow Street to Saint Hieronymus. "Here you go. I've been in the back of church a couple of times. Your homilies aren't bad, but they go on about a minute long. Edit yourself—take it from an old newshound."

"Thanks." I opened the car door. "I'll call next time I need a cabbie with an opinion."

Stonecutter barked again. "I may decide to like you after all."

I let that one go.

Inside, I checked the answering machine, then went upstairs and sprawled on top of the sheets in my boxers, a little humid air moving from the open bedroom windows. A week or two every summer up here was like this, sticky enough to wish for an air conditioner. An insect buzzed against the window screen. I tossed and turned, said my night office, thought about Diana. Meeting Stonecutter put a sharp edge on my broken vows. Eventually, I drowsed, waking late in the morning with just enough time for breakfast and the drive to Blue River for our noon ball game.

When the phone rang, I was upstairs buttoning my Pioneers uniform, hoping my stomach would settle down. Who knew Father Harry had such a taste for spices?

"Father, it's Miller. Tim Harley's holed up at the old Hockensmith place. Out County E, about a mile. You can't miss it. He wants to talk to a priest."

Fumbling at buttons with numb fingers, I changed uniforms and drove out to the abandoned farmstead, slowing at the sight of a dozen pickups parked alongside the county road. Farmers leaned on hoods and gathered in twos and threes along the barbed-wire fence on the other side of the ditch. I should have known this would be a public event. I pulled up to the gate, where a state trooper bent to my window and waved me on to the cluster of police vehicles halfway up the drive.

The troopers from the night before were there, and Chub Williams stood with Miller near Chub's new Ford F-150. I was relieved to see no sign of the detective or Tim Harley's woman.

Miller was beside me as soon as I climbed out of the car, mopping sweat from his mottled forehead with a white handkerchief. "Tim's threatening to kill himself. He wants to talk to a priest." He nodded toward the abandoned farmhouse: gray planks stained with rust around the nails, black windows covered with sagging screens. "The state boys have a SWAT team on its way with a negotiator, but we don't have time to wait. I'll find you a vest—if you're willing." His voice was quiet and confident, and made it seem as if I could stroll up the drive, chat with Tim Harley, and walk back out with him like old buddies out to shoot dove. Maybe I could carry Tim's shotgun.

"His family?" I asked.

"Frank and Verna are trying to get a flight from North Carolina. The brother at 3M is on his way—I think. He sounded pretty disgusted on the phone. The other one's at the university, and we can't find him."

I crouched behind a highway patrol cruiser and stripped off my black shirt while a patrolman who was about my size got out of his uniform shirt and bulletproof vest. While I put on the vest and started to dress, Roger Stonecutter clicked off a roll of film on autowind. I paused with my shirt half-buttoned to say something, but Miller stepped up and said the priest wasn't a floor show. I snorted. Stonecutter let his camera dangle from his neck. "Any thoughts, Father?"

"Why don't you interview Tim Harley?" I said.

Miller stooped beside me while I fixed my collar.

"You okay? You don't have to do this."

I nodded, not trusting my voice. Miller went on: "Talk to him from the porch. He's most dangerous to himself at this point. Stay out of the house—we don't want a hostage situation."

"I'm not going in that house," I said.

It was a long walk up the drive with the weight of the vest under my shirt and all those eyes on my back. And one set of eyes ahead somewhere. I started to sweat, hitched up the hidden vest. Halfway to the house, my knees threatened to buckle, and I broke stride for a moment. I realized I was mortified at the possibility of dying in front of a crowd, and wondered how that could possibly make any difference. But my heart thumped in my throat like a frog kicking.

In the dirt in front of the crooked porch steps, I hesitated, then took a breath and stepped forward. "Tim," I called.

The front door squeaked a little. "Hi, Father."

"Meet me at the window," I said, nodding to my left where a flutter of ragged curtains told me the sash was up behind the rusted screen. Without waiting for an answer, I crossed the creaky porch and knelt by the window, tearing my trousers and knee on a nail head that had worked its way up out of a board. Blood traced a ticklish line down my shin, and I rubbed my leg and tried to recall my last tetanus shot.

When I looked up, Tim Harley had appeared on the other side of the screen. He still had on his lime-and-blue polyester uniform, and when he raised an arm to shove the window open a little wider, the smell from his sweat-soaked armpit made me wish I'd never heard of him. He knelt on the other side of the screen, mirroring me, holding the shotgun by the barrel with his right hand, the butt resting on the floor.

"Hi, Father."

"Hi, Tim."

"I shot a man last night, Father."

"He's all right."

"I'd've killed him if I could've found my shotgun right off."

"Are you sorry?"

"I guess I am."

"Is this a confession?"

Silence.

I said the words of absolution. Out here they lacked gravity, foam floating on the sea. Beyond the end of the porch, the leaves of a sapling elm stirred slightly in the stifling air.

More silence.

"You'll need to come out of there, Tim."

"In prison, a guy like me, he has to take up with a stronger man." He shifted inside the screen, studied something in a corner of the room I couldn't see. I watched a spotted beetle crawl past my nose on the screen. I didn't want to hear this. Tim went on. "After a while, I got to feeling like I was sort of in love. I confess that."

I pushed a hand over my forehead, rubbing sweat up into my hair, then spoke evenly: "God gave you the ability to do what you needed to survive. God doesn't see that as a sin."

"I think He does," Tim said. "And I'm not going back to prison."

"Maybe you won't have to," I said. "A judge can be pretty forgiving of a fellow who finds another man in bed with his woman."

"System don't work that way for me," Tim said. "I'm going to shoot myself, and I want to confess that."

I bought a minute by shifting knees. "I can't absolve you in advance."

"I'll go to hell, then."

My stomach spasmed, and I doubled over.

"You okay, Father?" Tim said.

He had his face pressed against the screen. I could tell my own face was white. "Spicy dinner last night," I managed, feeling foolish.

Tim nodded sympathetically. "I always liked Thai, down in the Cities with my brothers. But it makes you pay."

The spasm passed, and I straightened. "Your family loves you. They're good people."

"They're better off shut of me."

I argued with him then for fifteen minutes, twenty, half an hour. I argued harder than I'd argued anything before, drew on every bit of counseling training and practice I'd had, but I was a dog turning in circles on an ever-shortening chain. Tim had a long list of grievances, starting with his mother beating him with a leather strap when he was a child. I couldn't picture Verna Harley doing that, but I nodded with as much sympathy as I could muster. Tim's life had sunk, one bad decision at a time, to the point where his next decision was to live or die, and my job on the porch quickly shrank to the single focus of getting him to say yes to the next moment. And the next.

The day heated up and sweat ran down between my shoulder blades. We paused our conversation when a black van pulled into the drive. The SWAT team tumbled out in flak jackets and helmets and disappeared behind the van. After that, I figured there were sharpshooters behind me. My train of thought wasn't helped by that, or by the way now and again Tim Harley absentmindedly let the barrels of the shotgun lean toward the window. I kept waiting for a SWAT negotiator to break in on a bullhorn, but it didn't happen: I learned later he'd spent a few critical minutes getting briefed by Miller. Every little while a wave of pain rose from my guts, and I froze and gripped the window frame until it passed. Tim was concerned, and I tried to work that angle without success. In the end, we were both soaked with sweat, stinking, frustrated. When I ran so short of arguments that I offered to put him on the Pioneers—"We need you at short"—it made us both chuckle. Tim cut it off.

"Let's go, Father."

"You'll walk down the drive with me?"

"In a minute."

"Really?"

"Honest Injun." He brushed at the hair on his forehead and looked about five years old.

"Bless you, son." I relaxed and made the sign of the cross in front of the rusted screen. It was the first time I'd ever called anyone *son*.

For an answer, Tim blew me a kiss, then rested the butt of the shotgun on the floor and lowered his mouth over the barrel.

Maybe I could have punched through the screen, made a grab for the gun, but my limbs and stomach were suddenly filled with wet sand. I was looking Tim Harley in the eyes when he pulled the trigger and blasted his brains and skull and bits of scalp with dirty blond hair all over the walls and ceiling of the room. One eye disappeared from its socket as if it had been jerked by a string.

My body twisted away from the blast on its own, and I ended up sitting with my back against the siding of the house. The police cars and uniforms in the yard were a red-blue blur. The thump of the shotgun and the heavy thud of the body hitting the floor were still echoing when the sulfur and iron stench of gunpowder and blood washed over me. I saw the eye go away again and vomited into my own lap.

There were TV cameras there by the end. Film at six. It even made the networks, I'm told. I never saw it.

Roger Stonecutter ran a three-picture spread across the top of the *River County Tribune* front page. I was in all of them: crouched behind the cop car putting on the bulletproof vest, kneeling on the porch with Tim Harley's face a ghost image behind the screen, sitting against the house as the cops stormed up. If you look closely enough, you can see the vomit. The wire services picked up the photos.

At home, reporters pounded on the door. I didn't answer, and eventually they stopped. I pulled the blinds and sat at the kitchen table in the dimness, drinking whiskey. The window shades moved a bit with the breeze, sending bars of light across the kitchen floor.

I left a message on the Harleys' answering machine and called Mom to warn the family I'd made the TV news. When I heard Mick's truck in the drive, I let him in the back door. He was wearing his ball uniform. "There's a TV truck across the street," he said. "I heard you'd been shot, but Miller steered me over here." Someone rapped on the back door. I shook my head. Mick walked over and opened the door, filling the gap with his broad body. "He's not here," he growled. "I'm watching the house. I'm a center fielder, who are you?"

I avoided the media. Tim Harley deserved privacy in death, and I didn't want to be made out a hero for having tried to save him. A priest friend who taught journalism at Saint Thomas managed to get in touch the first night: "Disappear. Don't answer the phone, don't return calls. After a day or two, they'll be on to the next big tragedy."

I took the advice and stayed with Mick for a few days. George Martin covered my weekday Masses. The parish secretary called if any real business came up, and I was available for parishioners who wanted to talk about Tim Harley. Mick and I attended Tim's funeral Mass, said by doddering Father Canby, who'd baptized Tim. We went in suits and ties and the few reporters there didn't notice me, except for Roger Stonecutter, who slid up next to me in the mix afterward: "Anything to say, Jim?" "No way." "Sorry. It's my job." The sidewalk was crowded with friends of Frank and Verna and their more successful children.

There was a funeral luncheon in the church basement. Mick waited in his truck while I ducked in to give my condolences. Frank and Verna drew me aside.

"I tried to talk to Tim," I said. "I didn't find him in time."

They looked confused, and I realized they were thinking of Tim and me at the farmhouse. "I mean, you'd asked me to talk to him earlier," I said.

"One conversation's not going to change what's been coming for years," Frank said. "We're just grateful for you going up on that porch."

Verna stood behind Frank while he talked. The day before at Saint Simon's, I'd confided to George what Tim Harley had said about being knocked around by his mother, and how I hadn't believed him. The other Harley children had turned out fine, healthy and well balanced as far as I could tell. We were by the kennel run on the south side of George's garage, and his three pointers came out of their shed and wriggled against the chain-link. George crouched to scratch the animals through the fencing. "Don Canby would have told you different," he said, then squinted up at me from his dogs. "Don't look so surprised, Jim. Haven't you ever seen a bitch kill the runt?"

"I wish I could have done more," I said to Frank and Verna.

"What did Tim say to you on that porch?" Verna asked. It was the first thing she'd said.

I considered all the possible answers to that question before patting her on the arm. "He said he loved you both."

In Blue River, Mick and I got a quiet booth in the Outpost. Diana brought us Guinness, standing there awkwardly after she set the pints down. Then she asked, "How was the funeral?"

I shrugged. Mick gave her his charming smile. "An exercise in putting the best face on tragedy. Necessary and painful."

Diana looked to me, and I avoided her eyes. It was the first time I'd thought of her since Saturday when the phone rang and it was Sheriff Miller. Our brief dalliance, my resolution to end things, all had been swept from my mind by Tim Harley's death. I hesitated to call it grace.

Diana went away with our lunch orders. Mick followed her up to the bar to remind her he didn't want pickles, and they talked for a couple of minutes. When he came back, he said: "This sorta shit's gonna happen. You did everything you knew how."

"You would've found him." I was that close to telling him about Diana.

Mick ruffled his straw-colored hair. "God didn't use Tim Harley to punish you for some failing," he said.

Mick was right, of course: it was ego to think that somehow I could have saved Tim Harley. Mick was sharp that way. He didn't know exactly what was bothering me, but he knew how my mind worked. In that respect, he was a good priest.

My last evening staying at Mick's, we sat out on the screened-in porch at the back of the rectory. Below us, the woods were thick with summer, and the only sign of the river was the occasional muffled noise of a powerboat. Mick set up his small wooden chess-board on a table between us and went to fetch drinks. He was keeping house for himself; the priest he'd succeeded had run off with the old housekeeper, and Mick seemed in no hurry to hire a replacement.

Maybe he'd observed the situation at my rectory. Before arriving at Saint Hieronymus, I'd managed one phone conversation with Father Canby, who briefed me on the parish staff and ended by mentioning that the housekeeper came in weekdays and I'd be responsible for my own meals on the weekends. "Good luck," he said before hanging up, and I assumed he was referring to my new pastorate or maybe my cooking. Then I met Mrs. Gunther, who intimated on my first day that good Father Canby had been a saint and she expected the ruin of the parish, if not the entire two-thousand-year-old edifice of the Church, on my watch. My rectory, in all practical ways, belonged to her. On the one hand, she kept the icebox stocked with homemade ice cream. On the other, she regularly went through my drawers, and she made it clear that every snared dust bunny and overcooked vegetable were sacrifices for the sake of the Church and "poor Mr. Gunther, who can't lift a hand for himself." The only relief was that poor Mr. Gunther was an invalid who needed a lot of care. I was solicitous of his health, fearing that he might die. Or get better. I'd thought of letting Mrs. Gunther go—a lot of priests nowadays didn't have housekeepers; a lot of priests, in fact, rented their own apartments rather than live in a rectory—but I couldn't very well fire a woman with a sick husband and thirty years of service to the parish. Gunther would outlast me at Saint Hieronymus, and evenings when she clattered a plate of dry meat and mushy vegetables onto the dinner table, I reminded myself of the old seminary joke that the pecking order in a typical parish was housekeeper, pastor, pastor's dog, assistant pastor. I needed to get a dog.

Mick came down the short flight of steps onto the porch and set a Scotch and water on a coaster in front of me, then settled in across the board. He tuned in a classical station from the Cities on the porch radio, then hummed along with Beethoven as we played. A dozen moves into the game, I was on the defensive. I could usually beat Mick, but now my mind was all over the place. "I didn't think he'd do it in front of me," I said.

Mick didn't answer, occupying himself with capturing a rook I'd left exposed. We'd been over Tim Harley enough. "I hired a housekeeper," Mick said.

"Who?" I started calculating moves, but I'd lost too many pieces to have any hope of coming back.

"Diana from the Outpost," Mick said. "Just part-time."

20

I CAUGHT DIANA ONE QUIET NIGHT at the Outpost, and leaned over the bar when there was no one within earshot. "I hear you're going to work at Saint Christopher's," I said casually.

Diana kept washing glasses in the sink under the bar. "It's a little extra money," she said.

"Mick'll be a good boss," I said. "He's easygoing for a priest." Where was I going with this?

Diana glanced at me, squirted more soap into the sink. "Yup."

"I was planning to talk to you the day Tim Harley shot himself," I said. That sounded bad, as if I was trying to let myself off the hook for a number of things at once.

"I can't imagine why, Father," she said, holding a beer glass to the light, then scrubbing at the ghost of a lipstick print on the rim.

"Shit," I said. Then: "I'm sorry."

Diana straightened from the sink and stood squarely in front of me, her eyes a flat gray. "I always knew you were a priest."

And so Diana started working part-time as Mick's housekeeper, arriving at the rectory just before noon to prepare lunch. She spent afternoons cleaning, then cooked Mick's dinner before leaving for class or her job at the Outpost. She kept her apartment—there was no way a priest could have a live-in housekeeper who was so young and attractive.

When fall came, Mick hosted poker some weeks, it being easier to wander down the street from the Outpost than drive over to Piney Woods. And there was Diana to mix drinks and make hors d'oeuvres. One night we were shorthanded, Snow and Lamplighter being at a retreat, and George tapped Diana on the forearm as she handed him a beer. "Diana," he said, "it's an article of faith with me that the cards are better with at least five players. Would you like to learn the game? Tuition's cheap."

Diana smiled. "Sure, George," she said.

Mick had been shuffling for his deal, and now he pushed out the empty chair on his right with his foot. "Guess we'll have to get our own beer tonight." He finished shuffling and set the cards in front of her. "First lesson: you cut toward the dealer."

Diana proved to be a quick study at poker, and soon enough she was a regular player whenever the game was at Mick's. The other priests, even Linz, acted like boys around her, vying for attention. Her husky voice and lustrous hair, the splash of color over her cheeks and in her blouses, the occasional breath of perfume under cigar smoke, enlivened Sunday evenings.

Then one Sunday when the game was in Piney Woods, she and Mick showed up at George's front door, side by side. That night, while the others joked with her, George sat at his usual spot at the head of the table, a small, round-shouldered man with his cards cupped under that beak of a nose, and watched Diana and Mick, the sorrowful creases in his face deepening. Diana caught George's look once, and her laugh faltered, then she laughed all the more loudly and reached her purse from the back of a chair to get out a breath mint. I occupied myself with the cashew bowl or ordered my chips into neat blue, red, and white stacks.

The next week, I went down to the lake for dinner with George and Linz. After dinner, George asked me to help him bring in a load of firewood and we went out to the woodshed together. Geese honked above us, hidden in low clouds.

"What do you make of Mick's new housekeeper?" George asked, filling my arms with logs.

I answered with difficulty, since I was holding the top of the load in place with my chin. "She makes me wish you'd run off with Mrs. Gunther."

George laughed. If he was the dean of the county's priests, Mrs. Gunther was the queen of its housekeepers, and her unpleasantness was legendary. He examined a last piece of birch, then dropped it in my arms, and I thought I'd steered the conversation away from Mick and Diana until he said, "I've known Diana since she was a little girl. I'm mighty fond of her, but I shouldn't have asked her to join the game."

I woke very early one morning soon after that on Mick's living room couch, having drunk too much to drive home while losing at poker the night before. Harold Lamplighter had offered me a ride, but it was miles out of his way and would have left me without a car, so I shook my boozy head and wrapped myself in an afghan on the sofa. In the morning, I was a collection of unpleasantness: back stiff from the sofa, tongue a cotton ball, brain rattling in my skull, and topping it all a bad conscience for having let myself drink too much whiskey. It was a family weakness, and I ought to have known better. I stumbled upstairs to see if Mick wanted breakfast.

His door was shut. I was about to knock when I heard Diana murmuring urgently that she needed to leave, then a light laugh and grunt from Mick. I slipped back downstairs and let myself out of the rectory into the cold mist rising from the river. As I drove out of the downtown, I glanced in my rearview mirror and saw Diana making her way down the sidewalk, head down and hugging herself against the morning chill, her blonde hair loosely tangled and pale against her back.

Not long after that morning, I was in Piney Woods for another Saturday dinner at the Saint Simon's rectory. George had the best cook in the county, and he ate every night with silver and china inherited from his sainted mother. He and Danny Linz were pleasant company; Linz had a good mind for the Liturgy, and I enjoyed going over my liturgy committee's suggestions with him.

At dinner that night, George said out of nowhere, "So, how about Harold?"

"What about him?" I said. Linz put down his fork.

George looked surprised. "Why, he's got cancer," he said. He saw that I didn't know, and his voice took on the slightly eager tone that tempts us all when passing on bad news. "Lung cancer. Advanced. I told Mick a few days ago."

I hadn't been to Mick's since the morning I heard Diana in his room, but the day after getting the news about Harold I drove to Blue River after eleven o'clock Mass. My last Sunday Mass was an hour earlier than Mick's—the difference between a farm parish and a resort parish—and he was still standing in front of church saying good-bye to people when I parked on the side street. I sat on the hood of my car with my jacket pulled up around my throat and watched him laughing and joking with his parishioners, a popular, athletic man who appeared to put his whole heart into his parish, yet had enough left over for a woman on the side. He was widely regarded as a man who was going places in the archdiocese, and I wanted to know how he squared it all.

The last family left the church, parents hanging onto a bouncy little boy with a crew cut and a Gopher hockey sweatshirt and a wobbly-kneed little girl in a tartan coat and tights. Mick waved good-bye and ambled over. I hopped off the hood. We shook hands. "Our choir director just found out she's being laid off from the processing plant," he said. "I've got to stop over. I'll be back in time for the Packers game. Go on in and relax; Diana's making lunch."

When I got to the rectory, I stuck my head in the kitchen and said, "Hi, I'll be staying for lunch," and retreated to the TV in the downstairs rec room. A few minutes later, I heard Diana's firm step on the stairs. "I thought you might like a beer, Father."

She brought it in and set it on a coaster beside me, then stood in front of the chair, shifting back and forth. "So," she said.

"You and Mick," I said.

She looked at her feet. "He misses you," she said.

"You told him?"

"He guessed."

I knew the moment. The first week Diana had sat in on the game, I'd made some comment about her cards—I no longer remembered what it was—and Mick had looked up from his own hand, cut his eyes from Diana to me, and nodded. I was fortunate the other priests weren't so sharp. Then again, they weren't playing the same game as Mick and Diana and I.

She kicked a foot against the floor. "I never would have imagined myself doing anything like this," she said. "But Mick takes everything in stride."

I stood up. "I have to go," I said. I didn't want to see Mick just then. At the foot of the stairs, I paused. Diana was still standing in the middle of the room. "One thing I know about Mick," I said. "He'll never leave the priesthood."

"Father," she said, "this is none of your business."

A week later, I got a letter from Diana. She'd heard about Harold's cancer and was sorry. She was sorry, too, for what had happened between us. She talked about growing up in Blue River and her difficult teenage years and how her faith had helped her get through them intact. She said that sometimes she confused the intimacy she felt for the Church with its priests, and that she was paying for that now. She hoped I could forgive her and myself and even Mick. The letter was smart and well written and heartfelt, and I stuck it in the bottom of my sock drawer with a few other letters from family and close friends from college and seminary. Some nights before bed I took it out and reread it. Then, after a few weeks, I rubber-banded it together with the others and left it alone.

21

WHEN THE WEATHER TURNED COLD for good, I exchanged the rectory screens for the storms kept in the garage rafters (someday, perhaps, I'd budget for new combination windows) and taped up plastic to keep out drafts.

The same day I weatherproofed the windows, I was up on an extension ladder scooping handfuls of mucky leaves out of the gutters when a voice below startled me.

"The work of the world's never done, is it Father?"

I looked down to find Stonecutter in a plaid hunting cap, the earflaps tied up over the crown. I plucked a sapling out of the gutter and let it flutter down. "How you doing, Roger?"

"Better than Father Harold. Damned shame about the cancer." He flipped open his reporter's notebook. "Does the archdiocese have contingency plans to cover his parish if he's incapacitated?"

"He's not."

"He will be."

"George Martin's your man for questions like that."

He leaned against the siding, lowered his notebook. "George is a company man."

"What makes you think I'm not?"

"Oh, c'mon Jim, you and I have a lot in common."

"Name one thing."

"Diana."

"You going to print that?"

"It's not news."

"Why are you still here?" I dropped a handful of watery leaves and twigs in his general direction.

Stonecutter stepped back, and the mess plopped at his feet. "I'd like to be friends."

I rested on the ladder. "If I could stay off the record."

He closed his notebook. "Deal," he said. "In fact, I'll let you in on some dirt." He slid his notebook into the pocket of his wool jacket, then took off his cap and wiped his brow. He put the cap back on, folded his arms, and eyed me while he spoke. "You know Father Sprenger?"

"Mick's predecessor. Ran off with his housekeeper."

He smiled, set the hook. "Not exactly. Sprenger was Diana's daddy."

I shook my head. "She's got three sisters."

"And doesn't look like a one of them." He rested a hand on the ladder. "Come on down," he said. "Let me wet my whistle, and I'll tell you a story."

He had me. I went inside and got a six-pack of beer because the story sounded like a long one, and we sat on the back steps together.

"Understand," Roger said, "I was a great admirer of Sprenger. Still am. He was the priest in Blue River for twenty-five years, and a good one. A little immature, like most of you—"

"Go on," I said.

"—but he had that childlike generosity that goes with it. He lived for two things: his parish and his mother. She was a widow, he was an only child, and they doted on each other. When he was first stationed in Blue River, she came up every Sunday to cook dinner for him. One Sunday—and mind you, this was years ago, when I was a college intern and Sprenger a few years out of seminary—anyway, I was at the paper pasting up ads when I heard

on the scanner that there'd been a bad accident out on the interstate. I got there just behind the highway patrol. Guy on his way
back to the Cities pulling a cabin cruiser had crossed the median
and hit a car head-on. Would've killed both of the drivers anyway,
but the boat shot forward and made a fucking mess of them. The
cops were just running the plates for IDs when Sprenger showed
up. Poor sap. Blue River isn't anywhere close to the interstate, but
he'd gotten word and rushed over to give last rites if need be. Of
course, it was his mother in the car." He drained half his beer.
"Who was it said the world's a slaughterhouse?"

"Yeah," I said.

"About the same time, Sprenger was counseling Diana's mother
for marital problems. Textbook case. They both needed comfort,
and Diana's what came of it. Sprenger was a wreck. Never unfaithful to his vows again."

"He ran off with his housekeeper."

Stonecutter swallowed beer, shook his head. "Nuh-uh. Diana's
born, and Sprenger loves the little girl. You saw the two of them
together and you knew—only people can blind themselves to just
about anything. But Sprenger's housekeeper tumbled to the situation. Blackmailed him. Small-time. Just enough to make her shitty
life a little easier. Sprenger skimmed the collection plate for years,
then he slipped up—on purpose I think—and when the parish council got suspicious, they both split town. People thought
they were together, but that was never the case. She disappeared.
Sprenger works at a halfway house in Minneapolis. He's got a little
one-room apartment on Portland Avenue. You saw him on the
street, you'd take him for one of the people he tries to help."

I made a connection. "Does George Martin know about this?"
I said.

Roger chuckled. "George was a close friend of Sprenger's. He's
always kept an eye out for Diana. He's her godfather." He let that

sink in, then went on: "We were together a long time before your friend Mick came along. Her mother's in an institution. And Diana believes her father—the deer hunter, not Sprenger—wouldn't love her if he knew. Your charming buddy's taking advantage of a very vulnerable and confused young woman."

"And you didn't?" I lifted my beer and found the bottle full. I took a long pull at it, then pressed the cold bottom of the bottle against the tense muscles of one shoulder. "You're—what?— twenty years older and never asked her to marry you."

Stonecutter uncapped another beer. "Not true. I asked, and she ran. Her mother's nuts, her father's no prize. She's codependent as all hell."

"But you love her."

Stonecutter looked to be sure I wasn't making fun of him. Then he gave his mirthless laugh. "I never said I didn't have problems." He stood, brushing off the seat of his slacks. "She's probably always had a thing for priests. Women are attracted to men like their fathers." He reached down, took a third beer, and shoved it in his coat pocket. "But she'll come back. Shankland's a company man, too." He started to walk away.

"I'm sorry about Diana," I called after him.

Stonecutter turned, taking his cap off and holding it in both hands. "You did what any man would do. Less than most would have done."

"Well, that's still a problem, isn't it?"

"I'm not so sure it is, Father." Stonecutter shoved his cap on his head and disappeared around the corner of the rectory.

I considered the rest of the beer, then climbed back up the ladder to the gutters.

Mick brought Diana with him the evening all of us gathered at George's rectory to watch the sixth game of the '93 World Series.

She served beer and salsa, then settled onto the couch a cushion away from Mick. Everyone was ecstatic when Paul Molitor, a former star at Cretin Catholic in Saint Paul, was named MVP after Joe Carter won the Series for Toronto with a walk-off home run in the bottom of the ninth. It was the third year in a row a Saint Paul boy had been MVP, Jack Morris having led the Twins over Atlanta in 1991, and Dave Winfield doing the same for Toronto over Atlanta last year.

After George turned the television off, I put on my jacket against the October chill and took a glass of Scotch down to the shore. At the end of the creaky, sagging dock, I stood listening to the soft slap of waves behind me, the scent of pine in the air, lake a darkened mirror, stars white points in a sky cold and void. Across an arm of the lake, where a single window was lit at the back of a house, shadows moved. There would be the warmth of a woman's body, languid undressings. The distance made it easy to romanticize. I turned the glass in both hands. The dry resin of alcohol stung the cold air. I savored the anticipation, then sniffed at the whiskey. George had uncorked a bottle of cask-strength Scotch. It smelled of sherry and peat smoke, and when I drank it burned all the way down. The light across the way went out, and I floated in darkness, unmoored, swaying on the dock, made queasy by the barely sensed movement of water beneath me. I caught the first scent of winter in the air, then heard myself softly singing the opening lines of "O Little Town of Bethlehem" and saw as if from above the desert village, starlit sand and houses. I saw it as I'd seen it in my child's mind, standing sleepily beside my brother and sister at midnight Mass, the nave of Saint Luke's dim and candlelit. We were with our grandparents on Christmas Eve. Alexandra's hand rested on my shoulder; the sleeve of her fur coat tickled the back of my neck. On the other side of Anne and Jacky, Otto stood with his chest out, eyes on God's crucified son, singing loudly and a little off-key.

Footsteps on the dock, then Mick stood beside me. Wound up, unfurled his arm. Far out in the lake there was a splash. "What you doing out here, bub?" he said, slurring the words.

The midnight church, the desert village, slipped from my mind.

The snip of Mick's cigar cutter was followed by the orange flare of a match, then the sounds of Mick drawing to life one of the good Dominican cigars he preferred. I breathed deep, caught the narcotic hit of nicotine. For just a moment, out on the dock in the night with Mick beside me, the compass of my vocation shrank to a point like the faint North Star, which disappeared if you looked directly at it.

"Why'd you become a priest?" I asked.

Mick answered, not knowing I'd been talking to myself. "Remember how sure priests seemed when you were a boy? I'm a doctor's son. When Dad fetched up against his limits, he called the priest." He chuckled. "I can prove the limits of science, but not God." He threw a heavy arm around my shoulders. "You?"

"I love the Mass," I said, trying to grasp the midnight memory again. "In a world of preachers and politicians, it's the last place we're allowed mystery."

"Flowery. Especially considering we're some of the preachers."

"I'm not doing a very good job of explaining myself."

Mick lurched sideways, threatening to spill us both into the lake. He squeezed my shoulder, and I was aware of how big he was. He sat down, worked off his shoes and socks and pushed his trousers up around his knees, then dangled his feet in the lake. He swished them around, bent over his knees to watch his feet trail in the dark water. "Try it. Clears your mind."

Sitting cross-legged beside him, I shook my head.

"Suit yourself." He brought his cigar up and drew on it, the reflection of the coal glowing among the stars wavering in the water. "You think I'm doing a bad thing." He lifted his feet, rubbed them with both hands. They were pale as fish against the gray wood of the dock.

I sat quiet, trying to sort it out through the blanket of peat smoke the Scotch had thrown over my mind. I wanted to warn him about Sprenger and Diana and Roger Stonecutter, and how George was on to it all, but I didn't know where to start. Mick had been drinking, too, and he misunderstood my silence.

"Everyone needs something to get through the night," he said. "You're every bit the hypocrite that I am, Dressler, and I love you anyway. Don't forget it."

I was angry at him for comparing us. "Three guys are pissing off a bridge," I said. "First guy says, *Water's cold tonight.* Second guy says, *Deep, too.* Third guy thinks a minute, says, *Nice sand bottom, though.*"

Mick snorted. "So?"

"I'm not as big a dick as you." I stood.

"Wait." He grabbed my wrist. I twisted loose and started up the dock, hearing him clamber to his feet behind me.

"You think you're better than me, don't you, Dressler?" His voice was angry. I faced his slope-shouldered form at the end of the dock. He went on. "But you know you're just jealous."

I was on the verge of going back to punch him. "You go to hell," I said. When I stepped off the dock onto the lawn, I kicked a dead pine bough, which tumbled with a dry rustle off the sod and onto the white rim of sand below. At the end of the dock, Mick sat down again, and I heard his feet plunk back into the water.

22

THE SATURDAY BEFORE THANKSGIVING, Saint John's hosted Coe
College in the first round of the NCAA Division III football playoffs.
The Johnnies had gone undefeated that year, beating second-place
MIAC rival Saint Thomas 69-13 the same day we'd watched the last
game of the World Series. Saint Thomas went up to Collegeville tied
for the conference lead, and the game cost Mick and me a case of
beer and an inordinate amount of ribbing from George Martin and
Danny Linz, the good Benedictines. Maybe that was why George
sounded hesitant when he called to see whether I'd like to go to the
playoff game. "Thought we might invite Mick, too," he said. Then,
after a pause: "Unless you can think of someone else."

I couldn't tell from his voice whether he knew about the tension between Mick and me, but I said, "Why don't I invite my
grandfather?"

Otto was only a few months short of the nursing home by
then, but in November he was still getting around. I went down
the afternoon before the game, and he took me to dinner at the
Lexington. Afterward, when I turned from the coat closet by the
front door of his house, he was standing in the kitchen doorway,
holding up an unopened fifth of Johnny Walker Red.

"This is that good Scotch you like?" he said.

"It's good Scotch," I said. In fact, it was the good Scotch he
liked. I felt a tightening in my stomach.

"I might just go for a beer," I suggested, "or a glass of water."

"Water's for washing." Granddad turned unsteadily into the kitchen, and the bottle thudded on the table. "On the rocks?"

"On the rocks." I was doing the mental math of my family, balancing the two martinis Otto had at dinner plus Scotch on one side of an equation, and on the other dinner and black coffee. I could deal with the meanness that might come, but now Otto fell when he drank. Usually he popped right back up, but five years ago he'd gashed his forehead on the raised hearth of the fireplace at Aunt Marie and Uncle Paul's house in Wisconsin.

In the kitchen, Otto topped off lowball glasses with Scotch. When he set the bottle down, I casually picked it up and slid it into the high cupboard over the sink, where he had kept his liquor before it became hard for him to reach. He looked at me sharply. "Don't want to tempt myself too much," I said.

He grunted, went into the living room, and found a John Wayne Western on cable. I sat at the opposite end of the couch and swirled the ice in my glass.

"What happened to that boy who blew his head off?" Granddad said.

It took me a minute to figure out he was talking about Tim Harley.

"He's buried, Granddad."

"I know that. What happened to him?"

The question puzzled me. On the TV, Indians had surrounded a wagon train.

"Never understood suicide," Granddad said. "God gives you a life—it isn't yours to end."

"He had a lot of problems," I began, which was a long way from saying Tim Harley hadn't wanted to spend a few more years being raped in prison.

Granddad snorted. "Problems! The Depression was a problem. The war was a problem."

"Everyone has a threshold," I said. "It's hard to judge someone else's."

"Shit," Granddad said. Then: "How many Indians can you get with one bullet?"

With every shot fired from the beleaguered wagon train, a half-dozen Indians and horses plowed into the ground. "They were men in those days," I said, and Otto laughed.

When the battle ended and the wagons uncircled and headed west, I glanced over at Granddad. He was asleep, head tilted back, mouth open. The Scotch glass sat on the coffee table, water from condensation pooling around it, staining the wood. Otto's hand hung over the arm of the couch, a cigarette held loosely between two fingers, smoke curling up from the long ash at its end. As I watched, an inch of ash curved, then dropped to the carpet.

"Granddad!"

He jolted awake, then looked from my face to his right hand. He took a drag on the cigarette and stubbed it out in the ashtray on the coffee table. "I don't smoke in bed."

"This sofa goes up and it won't matter," I said.

"You kids always worry about what might happen." His mouth set.

I went into the kitchen and got a dishrag, wiped up the water around the Scotch glass, and set the glass on a coaster. I shook a finger at my grandfather. "Gram would be furious at me if I didn't get on you about this."

That mollified him. "Don't want to get Alexandra mad," he said, then chuckled. "If she pays you a visit, tell her she'd better have a bridge game lined up in Heaven."

"I don't think she's paying any visits, Granddad."

His face fell. "She wouldn't like me sitting around this damn house staring at the walls all day. It's no good when you get old, Jimmy."

"Better than the alternative, right?"

"Used to be." He pushed himself up from the couch, taking the Scotch glass. John Wayne rode off into the sunset, and I followed Granddad into the kitchen. He stood at the sink, rinsing out the glass. "I'm going to bed," he said. "Guest bed's made up."

I was in the living room collecting my glass when I heard a thump from the stairs. When I got to the foot, Granddad was sprawled out halfway up. He'd fallen forward, catching himself on his forearms, and now he looked like a supplicant stretched out in prayer. I hurried up the steps.

"You all right?"

"Short fall when you're going up. Slept here the other night."

"At least they're carpeted." I squeezed between Otto and the paneled wall and got him under the arms. We lurched upright and made our way up the stairs, one step at a time. His skin had a dry, unwashed smell about it. When we reached the top, I steered him toward his room.

"You can let go now," he said, but then stood in the hall as if he'd forgotten where he was going. "Your grandmother kept herself together, even when she'd had a few. Quiet and observant. Sometimes I can still feel her, sitting in that chair by the TV."

"It must be hard," I said.

"Keep thinking I'll catch her smoking a cigarette out of the corner of my eye, but she's never there."

"I'm sorry," I said.

"Just an empty house and time."

He stepped slowly forward into his room and sat on the edge of the bed, staring at his shoes. Gram's ruby-beaded rosary was on the nightstand, along with a ceramic basset hound, its head and tail pointed to the sky. The tail was meant to hold a man's rings, and in the middle of the dog's back there was a basket where Granddad kept spare change.

I knelt at Granddad's feet and untied the thin laces of his wingtips.

Granddad laughed. "You gonna wash my feet next?"

I gripped the back of his left ankle, worked his shoe off, then peeled off the thin dress sock underneath. "'Bout right for a priest, isn't it?" I said. I'd worn my Roman collar, knowing Granddad would appreciate the service it brought us at the Lexington. He lifted his other foot, and I got that shoe and sock off as well, then sat back. "We'll leave about eight," I said. "Plenty of time for breakfast at George's and the trip over to Saint John's."

"You dress warm tomorrow," he said.

"Yes, Boss," I said, to please him.

"I tell you my platoon used to call me *Boss*? One night in England, just before D-Day, when we knew we were going soon, some of the boys came to me and said, 'Boss, you use the enlisted latrine tonight. Don't ask, just do it.' Next morning, the other officers and noncoms had broken noses and two black eyes. Some of the GI's had laid for 'em, settled some scores that night. But not me."

"It's a good story," I said.

"They called me *Boss*. I looked after them and they looked after me."

I kissed him on the forehead and turned out the light. "See you in the morning."

The next morning, Granddad sat at the kitchen table with a cup of coffee and a cigarette, beaming at the roller-coaster flight of a couple of chickadees coming and going from the bird feeder in the side yard. I helped myself to coffee. Otto wore a pair of thinly woven slacks and a dress shirt with a cardigan.

"You're going to freeze in that," I said.

He leaned forward to pull up the leg of his trousers, revealing long underwear. "Want to be dressed right if there's Mass after."

"I don't think anyone's going to be looking at your clothes."

Otto shrugged and dumped what was left of his coffee in the sink. He went to the front closet and came back in a long overcoat and a billed cap with earflaps. Around his neck was the purple-and-white Saint Thomas scarf I'd given him for Christmas my freshman year of college.

"Wrong colors," I said. "George may leave you by the road."

"Those monks have a rule about hospitality," he said. "I'll be okay."

We parked by the back door of the Saint Simon's rectory on the stroke of nine, the church bells ringing as Otto opened the passenger's door of his Park Avenue and climbed stiffly out. Through the kitchen window, we could see George bustling around. The kitchen was painted yellow with white cabinets, and brightly lit on this gray morning.

"Right on the lake," Otto said. He lit a cigarette and stopped on the steps.

"You can come in," I said. "George smokes."

But Otto turned up his collar and walked to the edge of the parking lot nearest the lake.

I let myself in. George was already in the middle of cooking steak and had just started the eggs. He was always punctual and expected everyone else to be. He turned a steak with a quick flip of his spatula. "Your grandfather coming in?"

"He's getting some air." In the dining room, Danny Linz was setting the trestle table with George's mother's china and silver. He was wearing a cardinal-red Johnnies sweatshirt and a pair of red-and-white-striped snowmobile pants.

"Jesus, Linz, you look like a fruit," I said.

Linz grinned. "I look like a football fan."

Otto came in, pulled out a kitchen chair, and launched directly into a monologue, telling George things we all knew about John Gagliardi, the Johnnies' coach: he'd won his three-hundredth game that season, he was one of the winningest college coaches ever, and he did it with an unorthodox style—no scholarships, no blocking dummies, no full-contact scrimmages. I leaned in the kitchen doorway.

"He's quite a character," Granddad was saying. "You watch him on the sidelines. Team might be driving for a touchdown, and he'll be off at the far end of the bench, staring at the sky."

"George," I said, "this is my grandfather, Otto Dressler."

"Has his team lay on the grass and stare at the sky during practice, calls it the Have-a-Nice-Day Drill," Otto said.

"Breakfast's ready," George said.

"But I'll tell you, he goes out on that field to give those refs a piece of his mind, and they listen to him. Yessirree." Otto switched to a sing-song: "Come to the table, you who are able!"

In the dining room, Linz arranged a last place setting. "Your grandfather's not shy."

"He doesn't get out much lately." I glanced out the picture window: the sky was overcast and there were small waves on the lake—a bit of wind that would make it a cold day to be sitting in a football stadium.

Over breakfast, George brought up Bill Langer, a colorful mid-century North Dakota politician. "The Dakota Maverick!" Granddad said. "Wild Bill. He might've been a Republican, but he wasn't a son of a bitch. Cared about farmers and wanted health care for everyone. Isolationist and corrupt as hell. When the court ordered him out of office, he holed up in the governor's mansion and declared martial law. Came out of jail and was a senator for three terms, died in office. He was a character!"

"I remember when he died," George said. "I was a senior at Shanley."

"Now Sid Cichy was a coach," Granddad said, pausing in the middle of cutting his steak. "Won ninety percent of his games over thirty years. That little Catholic high school from Fargo beat the biggest public schools in Minnesota and North Dakota year after year—and Cichy didn't bring in ringers like a lot of Catholic schools. Hardly any of his boys even played at the college level. But they won fifty-nine games in a row. The Deacons."

"I was a pulling guard for Cichy," George said.

"Pulling guards!" Granddad said, setting down his fork.

Danny and I fidgeted, but George caught my eye and winked. Throughout breakfast, he fussed over Otto like a mother; it was a side of George I'd never seen.

We took George's Town Car to Collegeville: up 35E to North Branch, then across to Saint Cloud on 95. The ride through the brown countryside was silent and smooth, and Linz and I dozed in the backseat. I could half hear George and Granddad discussing Park Avenues and Town Cars, and the drone of their voices in the warm car reminded me of late-night rides home when I was a little kid, everything in the adults' hands. I woke up once and saw a few flakes of snow settling against the windshield, but when we got to Collegeville the snow had stopped.

The game had already started, and while I was buying hot dogs and hot chocolate at the concession, a call went against the Johnnies. The crowd booed and a man in the stands yelled at the refs. The red-cheeked Saint John's student serving me shook his head. "Just as long as they're not rude to the visiting team," he said. I raised my eyebrows. Beside me, Granddad nodded approvingly. "Rule of Benedict," he said. "What did I tell you?"

The Saint John's field was set in a natural bowl, so you came in at the top of the stands. We found seats at the forty-yard line, sitting in the top row so Granddad didn't have to do any climbing. I kept an eye out for George and Danny, who were parking the car. As soon as we sat down, the wind made itself evident, but when George showed up he was carrying a couple of stadium blankets. He draped one over Otto's shoulders and pulled the ends over his knees, then swung the other one around himself like a shawl and settled down next to Granddad. Linz hunched next to me. "Blankets!" he said. "Do you have to be over fifty to think of blankets?"

Saint John's had won its games by an average of over fifty points that season, but their quarterback had an off day and they struggled until Coe's backup punter shanked a punt late in the third quarter. The Johnnies got the ball on the Coe 36, and after a big gain on a reverse, went ahead for good with a touchdown from the 5.

The stadium was small enough that we were right on top of the action. The stands were shadowed by pines on the home side and backed by wooded hills on the other, bare except for a few oaks holding their leaves. A handful of people watched the game from folding chairs in the grove of pines on a hillock behind the home stands. If the sun had been out, it would have been a perfect day for football. But the wind kept finding its way into my parka, and the cold settled into my knees and thighs, and I was glad when the final seconds ticked off.

We decided to skip Mass. Linz walked up to the Great Hall to buy bread from the monks, and Granddad and I waited in the shelter of the concession building while George got the car.

"So is this Linz queer?" Granddad said conversationally as soon as we were alone.

"He's a priest," I said. I looked toward the center of campus, where Linz had disappeared. The ten-story-high bell banner of

Saint John's modern concrete church dominated the view. Behind it you could see the honeycombed stained-glass front wall.

"In high school, I had a bachelor history teacher who paid me to grade exams at his house," Granddad said. "While I sat at the dining-room table, he'd play piano in the other room."

"Ever make a pass?" I said, stomping my feet a little to get blood back into the toes.

"Just played that piano," Granddad said. He hitched the stadium blanket tighter around his shoulders. "Couldn't have been very satisfying."

"Here comes Danny," I said.

Linz ambled down the hill from the Great Hall, his arms wrapped around a shopping bag filled with Johnnie bread. He hauled out one of the big loaves. "You could beat someone to death with this."

"You two going to eat all of that?" Otto asked.

"We'll freeze it," Linz said. He handed the loaf to Otto. "You take one, Mr. Dressler."

The ride back to Piney Woods was quiet, everyone tired and out of things to say after spending the day together. From the backseat, I could see George fighting sleep behind the wheel. I nudged Danny, and the two of us managed a little conversation. The light was going by the time we got to Piney Woods, and I drove Granddad back to the Cities.

"What do you want to do for dinner?" I asked when we got off the highway.

Otto was sunken against the passenger's side door. "Not hungry," he said. He'd tried to light a cigarette earlier, but given up when he couldn't get the lighter going.

"We'll feel better," I said. "I'll drop you off and run out for burgers."

"White Castle," Otto said.

We went to the drive-through, but when we got to the house on Sargent, Dad was in the kitchen, with steaks seasoned and in the pan, ready to cook. "Figured you'd be tired," he said when we walked in. "Good game?" He was in jeans and a clean sport shirt, and he had on Otto's grilling apron, which had LORD, GIVE ME A BASTARD THAT CAN COOK printed on the front.

Granddad gave the old man a gray look. "I always dreamed you'd play for the Johnnies," he said. "You could've been on the line when they won the national championship in '63."

Dad lit the burner under the steaks. He smiled. "Never been a team player." He reached for his beer on the counter.

"Married a whore instead," Granddad said. Then to me: "Mix us up some hot toddies."

Dad's hand hesitated over his beer, then he picked it up and took a sip. "Don't talk about Jimmy's mother that way," he said softly.

Granddad tossed the White Castle bag on the table and shuffled into the living room, unbuttoning his coat.

"He's tired," I said to Dad.

"Fuck him." Dad took off the apron and draped it over the back of a chair.

I boiled water, then mixed in lemon juice and honey and some cheap bourbon I found in Otto's cabinet, approximating the portions. Dad drank his beer and stood every once in a while to turn the steaks.

Granddad shuffled upstairs and came down in his slippers and an old bathrobe. The three of us sat at the kitchen table and ate a largely silent dinner of steaks with Johnnie bread and butter on the side. At one point, Otto nodded appreciatively at Dad. "Well, I guess the Lord did give me a bastard who could cook."

After dinner, I went down to the basement to get a new bulb for the ceiling fixture. When I came back up, Dad had gone.

Granddad sat at the table finishing his drink while I stood on a chair and changed the bulb.

"Why are you so mean to him?" I asked, screwing the glass cover back on.

Otto snorted. "That boy's been looking for a fight since he was two," he said. "I'm just ornery enough to give it to him."

"Why do you suppose that was?"

"It just was," Granddad said.

I went into the living room and turned on the TV. Granddad sat at the other end of the couch, pulling one of the afghans Gram had knitted around himself. "Good game," he said. "But it tired me out." A few minutes later, he was sound asleep.

I went into the small office in the front of the house that Dad had built long ago for Otto and Alexandra by converting half of the three-season porch into a room. It was lined with bookshelves, and Otto had a reading chair in there, along with a desk. Gram had read mysteries from the library, turning over three or four a week, but Otto favored history and literature and politics. He had a nicely bound if unread set of *Great Books* on a bottom shelf, but there was also a set of *Compton's Encyclopedias* that I'd used plenty as a kid. The rest of the shelves held a mix of tattered paperbacks and worn hardcovers with chipped dust jackets: *The Wit and Wisdom of John F. Kennedy,* Charles Reich's *The Greening of America, The Saturday Evening Post Sports Stories,* edited by Red Smith, *In Cold Blood, The Thurber Carnival,* Bill Mauldin's *Up Front,* an illustrated Constance Garnett translation of *Anna Karenina,* even a set of early *Doonesburys.* It was the mixed reading of an active but untrained mind, up on current events through the 1970s. Otto still subscribed to a selection of middlebrow magazines—*Newsweek, National Geographic, Smithsonian, American Heritage*—that now piled up unread on the office's window shelf.

This was the first place I'd been aware of books; there weren't any in our house, and Otto used to encourage me to go through whatever I wanted. On a cold day, he'd set me up with a blanket in his leather reading chair and bring me a glass of milk and a cup of the chocolate chips Alexandra kept hidden away to use for baking. "Shh!" he'd say, and pull the door closed behind him when he went into the living room to watch TV.

Tonight, I picked up *The Saturday Evening Post Sports Stories* and reread "The Gravy Game," about a small-college football program pulling an upset against an upper-division powerhouse in what's supposed to be the bigger school's season-opening warmup. It wasn't bad for what it was. Then I went upstairs and went to sleep in the guest bed. I had nine and eleven a.m. Masses in the winter, and when I got up and left the house at seven, Granddad was fast asleep in his room, curled on his side with the spare pillow hugged against his chest.

23

HAROLD LAMPLIGHTER WASN'T DOING WELL. He had a lung removed, followed by rounds of radiation and chemo that made
his mane of gray hair fall out and wore away at his square body.
The other priests took turns covering his Masses, and Danny Linz
ran the parish while Harold spent more and more time at the
University of Minnesota cancer center in the Cities.

One day that December, I went down to visit and arrived just as
a respiratory therapist was getting ready to put a tube into Harold's
remaining lung to suck out the sludge he was drowning in. I went
out to a sunny waiting room overlooking the Mississippi and was
sitting there with my nose in a magazine when I became aware that
I was being watched. I looked up to find an eight- or nine-year-
old boy who was nothing but translucent skin and a bony skull,
bald and ugly as a baby bird. He wore a thick flannel robe that
looked too heavy for his frail limbs. The robe had a long belt at the
waist, and one end of the belt was tied around a plastic bowling
pin, which the child was twirling with his right hand. "This is my
mischief-maker," he said.

"I see." I nodded solemnly because he made the pronounce-
ment with great gravity. "What do you do with it?"

"I make mischief." He walked unsteadily, like a very weary
man, to the window. He let the pin drop by his side and crossed his
arms on the window ledge. "In spring, Davy Crockett's going to

come, and we're going to take a canoe all the way down the river. It'll be warm again, and we'll have a big adventure."

A nurse beckoned from the direction of Harold's room. "I'm sure you will," I said. I closed my magazine and stood. I could see the river, dark water running between sparkling white banks of snow. The boy rested his head on his arms. I made the sign of the cross over him and said a prayer as I walked down the hall.

Harold looked exhausted, sunken into his pillow, arms resting lifelessly atop the blanket. A monitor was taped to one forefinger and an IV dripped into an arm. One forearm was nothing but a large purple bruise, and there were bandages over the veins on the insides of his elbows. There was a scattering of get-well cards under the window, from across the state, Winona to Crookston, and as far away as Rome.

"Harold?" I said.

"That tube's awful," he said. "I'll die before I let them do that again."

I pulled up a chair and warmed one of his hands in both of mine while I told him about the boy, the mischief-maker, and Davy Crockett.

He moved his eyes to watch me while his head remained on the pillow. "It's my experience," he said, "that we all want to believe we've made some kind of mark on the world and that there's someone out there who gives a damn."

In the new year, Harold returned home to a hospital bed in his living room. Linz stayed at Holy Sacrament to look after him with the help of a hospice nurse.

I took to driving down to Bell's Crossing, fifteen miles south of Pretty Prairie, to visit. Harold liked the company, and I missed

Mick. We hadn't talked except across the poker table since the night on the dock.

Evenings when Harold felt strong, we'd sit at his oilcloth-covered kitchen table. His rectory was bare of any decoration, unrelievedly masculine, and one night he commented on it. "A housekeeper's touch isn't enough." He dug at an ear with his little finger. "I wish I could have married. I never wanted to be anything but a priest, but it needn't have been so lonely." His eyes glistened, and I studied a farm-implement calendar held to the refrigerator with a Dinner Bell Cafe magnet. "I'm sorry," he said. "It's all this medication. Makes me weepy."

I patted his ropey-veined hand, attempted a joke. "You ought to have Linz decorate."

Harold chuckled. "No good. George says he got the only gay curate with no taste in the whole archdiocese."

I was going to let it go at that, but then I thought that if Harold wanted to talk about his life at its end, I ought not to avoid it. "You never strayed?"

Harold shook his head. He wore a sweat-stained khaki fishing hat now that he'd lost his hair. "I was shy, not that good-looking. It's not as if it took any great moral fiber." He pushed to his feet and walked to the counter. His legs and arms were like sticks attached loosely to the diminished square of his torso.

Harold opened a drawer with some effort and lifted out an ashtray and a red-and-white pack of Marlboros. He set them on the counter and stared at them a moment, supporting himself with the palms of his hands. Then he shook his head and came back to the table, leaving the drawer open and the cigarettes and ashtray out. "I want a cigarette worse than anything in the world," he said. "But the coughing. . . ." He scratched his thin chest. "Ah, shit," he said. "It's just cigarettes. Remember what

I said about wanting to believe you'd made a difference? And that there was reason to give a damn about that difference?" He caught his breath with difficulty. "I believe both those things. That makes me luckier than most."

Perhaps my faith wasn't as strong as Harold's. About the time he began seriously dying, I began to be afraid. At first it was only in the basement, unease creeping up my back to crouch on my shoulders while I took a turn at the punching bag or folded laundry or searched for a tool at the workbench. I had to force myself not to look around while I worked, and it took an effort not to look back when I climbed the stairs. Sometimes my will broke, and I sprinted the top few steps and slammed the door behind me.

It was absurd, and at first I was more curious than dismayed. Except as a little kid at the river cabin, I'd never feared the immaterial before, there being plenty of the material to fear in the form of the old man. So I welcomed the fear, teased myself with it, let it swell like desire in my throat and heart and gut. It was, after all, a silly thing. I didn't believe in ghosts. Tim Harley wasn't walking. Whatever it was, it was in me, though sometimes it crept outside in the night to peer in at the window behind my easy chair while I watched TV, running light nails over the back of my neck until I took to closing the curtains at nightfall. Then it was trapped in the rectory with me, a fear of hearing not-quite-human footsteps come tapping down the upstairs hall toward my room some night, of seeing a garish face leap up the basement stairs from the darkness there.

Then being afraid was no fun anymore, and I slapped hurriedly at the light switch when I opened the basement door. I took to sleeping with Granddad's rosary wrapped tight around my fist and leaving a light burning. For a while a night-light would do, then the jug lamp on the dresser, and finally only the reading lamp on my bedside table, within reach, was enough.

24

THE LAST POKER GAME HAROLD CAME TO was at Saint Simon's, a bitterly cold Sunday afternoon under a high blue January sky. Fishing
shacks dotted the frozen lake and frost embroidered the windows.
It would be months before spring cast a green mist over the trees
on the far shore. Harold was bundled in blankets, propped up with
pillows in an easy chair, his head gaunt and huge on his wasted
body. "If I cough up a lung into the pot, don't bet on it," he said.
"It's not worth anything."

Danny Linz and Bill Snow were with him when he died. They
were in the living room watching the East-West Shrine game,
Harold in his hospital bed, and in the middle of the last quarter
Linz and Snow felt a change in the room and looked up from the
game to find him gone.

"I don't know why that surprises me, that we both looked up
at once," Linz said to me in the Outpost the day after the funeral.
He and I were sitting at the bar. Diana was at the far end, ignoring
us except to bring beers. She hadn't played poker lately, and I had
the feeling that whatever Mick had done to make their affair seem
okay wasn't working for her anymore.

"You getting Holy Sacrament?" I asked, watching Diana bent
over the sink beneath the bar, washing glasses, talking with Roger
Stonecutter. Stonecutter had written a nice extended obituary on
Harold—his years at the parish; his morning habit of dining at
the Dinner Bell Cafe with a circle of townsmen, Catholics and

Protestants; the time he'd successfully lobbied a multinational corporation not to close a local plant.

Linz gave me a wolfish, ironic grin. "No way the Chancery's going to turn over another parish to us ravenous Benedictines. There's a guy coming up from the Cities. Sterritt. Real gung ho." Linz tore a napkin into neat strips; he was trying to give up smoking. He went on. "Bell's Crossing is really growing. Sterritt's experienced, dynamic. But from what I hear, he's not good poker material."

Bell's Crossing was swelling with new construction, the latest and northernmost wave of commuters from the Cities. It had a rambling modern church building—I couldn't quite bring myself to call it a church—that incorporated "community spaces" and looked like a ski lodge. It would have been a big job for a young priest. And the turf battles between the archdiocese and the Benedictine fathers at Saint John's went back as far as John Ireland, who resented that the priests of the religious order weren't under his direct control. Still, I thought it a shame Linz hadn't been rewarded with Holy Sacrament. He'd handled the parish with grace and diplomacy while Harold was dying.

"It made me understand my vocation, taking care of Harold," Linz said. "He was peaceful at the end. Fulfilled. I think we all need moments like that to make us good priests."

I patted him on the shoulder, then walked down the bar to compliment Stonecutter on his piece about Harold. Diana went back into the kitchen as I approached.

"Ha!" Mick said, fanning aces and eights on the table. It was the last hand of the night. "Lookee here. Dead man's hand. Harold would've bet this up." In the months before his death, Lamplighter had gleefully bet the limit every time he drew the hand Wild Bill Hickok had been holding when he was shot in the back. Harold had a run of luck with it.

"They've gotta all be black," George said, turning up a low straight and stretching to curve his hands around the pot. "You're wrong on all counts, my friend."

Mick shrugged, began ordering his chips in stacks. "$10.20," he said.

George paid back Mick's original ten from the cigar-box bank, then flicked him two dimes. "Don't spend it all in one place."

Mick had ridden over from Blue River with George. "Give me a ride home, Dressler?"

"Sure," I said. I wasn't ready for bed yet—my rectory still spooked me. My night fears had grown worse since Harold's death. I couldn't sleep without a light on, but in my sleep I was dimly aware all night of the light burning in my room.

"What was Hickock's fifth card?" Danny Linz said.

George was dropping stacks of chips into his poker caddy. "No one knows. Might've been red, maybe a heart."

In the car, Mick scrubbed at the frost on the inside of his window with the side of a gloved fist. "Mind if I listen to the radio?" Outside of poker, we hadn't talked in months. I hoped the baseball season would change that come summer.

"It's broken." I drove under the speed limit, wary of icy patches and the whiskey and beer I'd had over the course of the evening. Mick and I were running along a straightaway that arrowed between two small lakes, though you couldn't tell that in the dark of the moon, just level gray plains out there that might have been fields save for their perfect flatness. Ahead, I saw Bill Snow's car turn off the highway in Kildare, where he was pastor at Saint Brigid of Ireland. Mick gazed out the window at the shuttered town as I slowed to creep through downtown, past a lone sheriff's car idling in the driveway of a boat dealership.

"Think you're over the limit?" Mick said.

I snorted. "After poker?" We were in the country again, on a stretch of road that ran straight toward the river valley. I nosed my speed up and clicked on the brights in time to see something gray flash across the road ahead. "Coyote?"

"Too big for a fox."

Silence.

"There's something."

"Where?" I tried to peer beyond the tunnel of the headlights.

"No. Chancery's transferring me to a hospital chaplaincy in Minneapolis."

"And Diana?"

Mick pushed his feet under the dash and the bucket seat creaked beneath him. "It's over. She's part of the transfer. Turns out the Chancery knew about her. George was in on that. Some friend, huh?" He laughed, and I remembered that when he and George had come in from the car earlier they'd seemed tense. Mick went on: "Anyway, Diana was fucking Stonecutter on the side. She doesn't know what she wants."

"Maybe she wants a man she can be with in public," I said.

Mick didn't answer, and we rode in silence down into the river valley, the bare black trunks along the roadside rising against the gray night and snow. When I parked by the side door of the Saint Christopher's rectory, Mick invited me in.

We went through the kitchen, and Mick grabbed a couple cans of beer from the refrigerator, then led the way to his study. He sat in his plush desk chair with the lights out, looking out into the dark river valley through the picture window behind his desk. He popped the tab on his beer and clinked the can against mine. "Cheers. There'll be other women."

"There shouldn't be," I said. "Stonecutter told me she was Sprenger's child."

"She told me that, too," Mick said. "But that has nothing to do with anything. Diana's a liar. Stonecutter, too."

"And George?" I said.

Mick swiveled toward me. "You're all the same. Even Harold would give me that tight little frown of his, like I'd personally betrayed him by bringing her to poker. But when she left the table, his eyes'd be on her ass."

I couldn't breathe. I stood and switched on the overhead light. "Don't talk about Harold." Mick tried to say something, but I cut him off. "George was right to call the Chancery." I was more than a little drunk, waving a finger around. "How's your life gonna look to you someday, Shankland? Your vows? What?—you have your fingers crossed that day in the Cathedral?"

Mick had stood with me, moved around the desk with a look of distress on his face, but at that last, his eyes widened. "Your vows did Tim Harley a lot of good," he said.

I hit him three times in the face before he realized he was in a fight. He sat down abruptly on the corner of the desk. I was backed into the door of his office, crouched like my old man with chin tucked and fists up, but Mick was an athlete, not a fighter, and he stayed where he was. His mouth and nose were bloody, and he'd have a black eye tomorrow.

"Get out of here, Dressler," he mumbled through puffy lips.

I got. Out in the car, I massaged my fists. My left was cut from hitting Mick in the mouth, and my great-grandfather's signet ring, which I wore on that pinky, didn't fit right. I worked something out from between my finger and the ring and held it up in the dome light. It was about half of one of Mick's front teeth.

The next Sunday, instead of driving over to Blue River after my last Mass, I puttered around the rectory with a basketball game on TV, then sat in my office getting ahead on work for the week. I kept glancing at my watch, more often as the afternoon wore on.

By five, I was standing in the back door twirling my car keys around one finger. The county was too small to go around avoiding Mick. So I went to the Outpost. Everyone but Mick was at the front table. Pam Dempsey, the owner, was taking dinner orders. I slipped into an empty chair next to Linz and ordered the walleye sandwich. After Linz ordered the same, he turned to me and said, "You know about Mick being transferred, don't you?"

"Yeah, I heard." I glanced across the table at George Martin, who regarded me steadily.

Pam Dempsey stood between Mullowney and Draper, clicking her pen. "Someone beat the crap out of him last weekend," she said. "Pardon my French, Fathers."

Draper twisted in his seat to look up at her. "Beat up Mick?"

"Julie in Doctor Wallbanger's office says Mick was in first thing Monday to get a tooth capped. Wearing sunglasses and with his face all bruised up." She slipped the order pad into her apron. "It didn't happen in my place."

Now George was looking at me. I played with the table setting.

"He was fine at poker," I said.

"Here's the man himself," Mullowney said.

Mick strolled in with his hands in his pockets, and took one of the two remaining chairs. The last spot at the table had belonged to Harold, and I wondered when Sterritt, the new man, would start at Holy Sacrament.

"Heard you had an accident," George said. There were still purple bruises under the inside corners of Mick's eyes.

"Walked into a door," Mick said.

"How's the door?" George asked.

"Sold it to a toothpick factory," Mick said. "Once they go bad, there's no living with 'em." He handed Pam Dempsey his menu. "I'll have the Angus burger. Make it a California and hold the pickle." She went back to the kitchen.

"So when's this transfer take effect?" Bill Snow asked.

George spoke up. "Next Sunday. Ken Sterritt starts at Holy Sacrament and Linz is free to cover Saint Chris."

"Quick," Mullowney said, nodding.

"You getting a raise for all this extra work?" I asked Linz.

He laughed. "Oh, right."

Everyone was quiet.

"I heard you let Diana go," Draper said to Mick.

"Does this mean she won't be playing cards?" Mullowney asked.

"She won't be playing cards," George said.

"Well," Mullowney said, "we're going to miss her." He gave it a beat. "Shankland we can do without."

At the end of dinner, Mick said, "Why don't we play at my place tonight? One for the road."

"Will we ask Diana?" Draper said. He looked around the bar. "She's not working?"

Mick stood up. "She's on vacation in Florida with Stonecutter."

"Oh," Draper said, then brightened: "They're back together, eh?"

Mick's rectory was mostly packed, boxes stacked everywhere, framed prints leaning against the bottoms of walls under empty nails—Chagall and Picasso, Paul Klee's *Golden Fish*. As we walked in, I heard Mullowney say to Draper, "This was quick."

With the others in the kitchen getting drinks or downstairs helping Mick set up the card table, I found myself alone in the living room, where the moving boxes and the furniture were all shoved out of the way at one end. The taped boxes brought back the day I'd helped Linz box up Harold Lamplighter's belongings to send back to his family in Cincinnati. I thought of the time in Harold's kitchen when he'd talked about being lonely, and I hoped that in the end his faith had been enough.

Mick came up from the rec room to the head of the stairs and called into the kitchen. "Let's play cards." He caught sight of me and started, then said: "C'mon, Dressler. You're too late to help with the packing." I was looking at a family photo I hadn't noticed before. Mick had five sisters, and they all looked like Homecoming queens. Probably he couldn't help it, being good with women.

I wanted a moment alone with him, but the poker ran late and I was tired. After I'd lost my buy-in, I went upstairs and sat on the couch amid the boxes in the living room. A roll of packing tape and a black marker pen on the box next to me caught my eye, and I drew a Kilroy-was-here face on one of the boxes. I would talk to Mick tomorrow. I would just sit here a moment with the smells of moving in my nose—marker ink and new cardboard and box dust—and then I would go. I'd just close my eyes for a minute.

Someone shook me by the arm out of a sound sleep. I was plastered to the couch, as though the earth's gravity had increased in the night.

"C'mon, Dressler, wake up."

I cracked an eyelid. In the dark, I recognized Mick's lantern jaw. "Go 'way," I said; "couch's comferble."

He shook me again.

"See you the Cities," I said to the cushion under my cheek. "Go to Twins game."

Mick chuckled. "At least use the guest bed."

"Sorry slugged you. Wanna stay here."

"My fault," he said. "I wasn't at my best that night." I heard his knees creak as he crouched beside the sofa. "I was out of line about Tim Harley."

I shook my head, still trying to crawl out of the deep well of sleep.

Mick paused, then said: "I miss Diana. I have this picture of her in my head, working her way along a ridgeline in front of me the one time we went hunting together."

"Christ, Mick," I said, my voice muffled by the cushion.

He stood. "We were after deer, and we never saw a one. Well, sleep tight." I felt a blanket settle over me, then heard Mick's footsteps on the stairs.

I woke up in the dark in a roomful of boxes, unsure of where I was until I stumbled to a lighted doorway and saw Mick's kitchen. Walking to my car while an owl hooted in the snowy woods down toward the river, I kicked an empty liquor bottle someone had left in the street, then picked it up and flung it across a vacant lot, a pinwheel of random glints in the moonlight followed by a thud. Above me, Cygnus and Cassiopeia glittered in front of the splash of the Milky Way like diamonds on snow. You don't see stars like this in the Cities, I thought. Stars were one thing the country had over the city. Stars and loneliness.

When I left Mick's, I drove to Saint Simon's and sat in a cushioned Adirondack chair on the rectory's front porch. George was an early riser, and I waited for a light in one of the darkened windows, watching my breath steam the air. It was a warm enough night for that time of the year, just above freezing, and I'd only been there a few minutes when the porch light came on. The door creaked open and George came out, bundled in a heavy flannel robe and moccasins. He didn't seem surprised to see me.

"Morning, Jim. You up late or early?"

"Early, more or less."

George sat down beside me and pulled a cigarette and lighter from his robe pocket. "What's on your mind?"

"I'm going to miss Mick," I said.

"Me, too." George leaned back and sniffed the morning air. A car motor turned over somewhere nearby.

"He and Diana were quits anyway. Or didn't you know that?"

"I knew." George lit his cigarette, shook out the match. "I might like Mick," he said, "but I'm damned tired of young priests making free with their vows."

He was looking at me with a sad, steady gaze—the rheumy brown eyes of a hound dog. *Good ol' George*, I thought, *he's loyal and true and has an unerring nose for other people's shit*. Then I thought I was being a little bit of a shit myself for thinking uncharitably about him.

"Linz is gay," I said.

"Linz is celibate," George said. "And I don't care who he's not sleeping with."

"I'm sorry I said that."

George waved it off. "Mick was following an old scent into a swamp, and I'd just as soon not watch it happen." He drew on his cigarette, let the smoke trail out.

"I didn't know you were so close to the Chancery," I said.

George's eyebrows went up. "The Chancery would be a lot happier if I were at the abbey baking bread," he said. He settled back in his chair at an angle, facing me. "Let me tell you a story: About ten years ago, there was a priest in Indian County who liked boys. I found out from one of my junior-high basketball players when I asked if he was going to basketball camp with Father Larry. *Father*, this kid says, *I don't want to spend two weeks with Father Larry*.

"Turns out Larry had a reputation among the junior-high boys. He'd start with a pat on the butt on the basketball court, an arm around the shoulder on the bench. The boys knew what he was up to, would tell each other, *Don't let Father Larry get you alone*, but all of them, with that remarkable pack instinct boys have, had kept it to themselves."

"So what happened?"

"Before I settled at Saint Simon's," George said, "I was stationed all over this country. Down South, Appalachia, upstate New York. I'd seen too many chanceries tell too many priests like my basketball-coaching friend to pray for guidance, then transfer them to some backwater parish where they kept up their ways.

"So I didn't take any chances. I went to Sheriff Johnson. He did an investigation. Larry went to jail. He'd been a friend of mine. Some priests in this diocese still won't talk to me."

"I'm sorry about Larry," I said. "But Diana's an adult."

"It's a sin of pride for me to see it this way, but I think of myself as high sheriff of this county. And I hate to see a young man who's made a bad decision run it into the ground. Mick doesn't belong in a parish."

A car slowed on the street in front of the rectory and the morning paper sailed onto the sidewalk with a thump, then skittered across ice and came to rest against a snowbank. "That's what I've been waiting for," George said.

I retrieved the newspaper and handed it to him. "Thanks for talking. It'd been on my mind."

George unrolled the paper. "Mine, too."

I left him on the porch and got into my car and drove north. The county roads were abandoned. The car floated above wisps of snow that were beginning to trail across the pavement as dawn stirred the air, and an icy mist rose from the snow in the fields. A small town appeared, a block of bare elms in each direction from a crossroads store with an orange neon *Closed* sign glowing in a window, one pale streetlamp drawing the town about it on the snowy plain.

Home, I let myself into the kitchen. A couple of unwashed dishes sat on the counter, and a spare key ring with a plastic tab advertising Stanfield's Super Service lay on the windowsill. Mrs. Gunther's sampler of the Prayer of Saint Francis hung crooked on the kitchen wall, and I straightened it. On the kitchen table was the RSVP card for Jacky's wedding dinner and dance, which I hadn't yet returned. I picked up a pen and filled in the blanks—*Father Jim Dressler* and *0* guests—and put a check mark by the steak, then put the card in the envelope, sealed it, and put it with the outgoing mail on my secretary's desk. I wasn't sleepy at all. The house was filled with furnishings that belonged to the parish: a beige sofa, armchairs with worn armrests, shaky pressed-wood tables and shelves, 1970s-issue inspirational posters with seagulls and rainbows, the odd coffee-table book about Rome or the Holy Land or the history of the Archdiocese of Saint Paul and Minneapolis. I walked through the rooms for a while, then poured a glass of orange juice from the jug in the fridge and sat at the kitchen table, playing a game of solitaire with an old poker deck.

25

DIANA AND STONECUTTER WERE MARRIED at Saint Christopher's in early March. Linz had done their marriage preparation, and George celebrated the Mass. He made his homily one of renewal; he said spring was coming and compared Roger and Diana to farmers who would be good stewards of the lands they were joining together today. He said he'd known Diana since she was a little girl and he was a young priest, and that few moments in his ministry had given him as much pleasure as seeing her happily married today.

I sat with Linz and Snow, and when I came down the aisle after Communion, I met the deep-set eyes of a man who'd sat in the very back on the bride's side and was slipping away without taking the sacrament. His lean face was familiar under longish gray hair and an unkempt salt-and-pepper beard, and after Mass I went up to the darkened hallway by Mick's old office, where the framed photos of Saint Christopher's pastors confirmed the man had been Michael Sprenger, Mick's ill-fated predecessor and Diana's father.

At dinner in the church basement, we priests had our own table. The whole poker group, or what remained of it, was there: George and Linz, Snow, Mullowney, and Draper. Families and children orbited around us: a little boy stopping to stare, people leaning in for greetings or business. Diana stopped at the table, serene in her long ivory veil, and hugged each of us. Roger was everywhere, red faced and awkward and happy in his black tuxedo. He and Diana, newsman and barmaid, had half the county at their wedding. Frank Harley pulled up a chair and told me he'd found a paving contractor willing to resurface the church parking lot at cost after the spring thaw; later, Mary McGlothlin, the history teacher at Our Lady of the Snows, introduced her fiancé, a tall, narrow-hipped Indian County rancher named Jarrod. Mary wore a blue silk sweater and paisley scarf with Carhartt jeans and a pair of hand-tooled cowboy boots, and she had the happy air of someone who has found herself a home in an unexpected and difficult place.

We priests finished dinner and watched the wedding-party dances. Roger led Diana with great dignity and no rhythm whatsoever. When the dancing got going in earnest, George stood and put on his black car coat. "Poker time," he said. We walked out as a group, waving and giving farewell benedictions.

In the dining room at Saint Simon's, Linz counted out stacks of poker chips while George set the sideboard with liquor and glasses. I phoned the answering service the county parishes subscribed to, checked messages, and told the operator where I'd be if I were needed. It was my month on call with the nursing home and hospital, a duty that rotated among all of us except Snow, who was excused because of his age. As I hung up the phone, I heard George say in a low voice to Snow, "You see Sprenger?" and Snow reply in the same tone, "Poor guy."

Before we sat down to cards, George poured a small glass brimful of Scotch for each of us and held his up to the light. "Here's to the people we marry and bury," he said. "Here's to the joy of being shepherds and to the great confraternity of the priesthood. May God grant you the strength and wisdom to serve your flocks and your brethren well."

I lifted my Scotch, its gold surface trembling in the light, and exchanged a glance with Linz over George's strange conflation of prayer and toast. Everyone was silent a moment, then "Hear! Hear!" Mullowney said, and we all clinked glasses.

That winter, with Harold dead and Mick transferred, Bill Snow getting older, and Danny Linz busy running Saint Christopher's, we had a hard time coming up with enough poker players. The game fell off to one or two Sundays a month, and, as I'd done the previous winter, I took to driving down to Saint Paul on those Sundays when George called and said the game hadn't made.

One Sunday night I saw Dad's car parked in front of John's Tap and went in. He was sitting at the bar, smoking a cigarette and watching the NBA, and he did a double take when I slid onto the stool beside him.

"The hell you doing here?"

I shrugged and ordered a beer from Cheryl, she of the black leather pants and custom pool cue. "No poker tonight," I said.

"That crummy little nickel-ante game? That ain't poker."

"We can't all be big players," I said. Not that the old man was. He bought lottery tickets and played bingo.

"Bunch of priests playing poker. That's gotta be a lively time. You're a live one, all right. Give me a shot of rye, Cheryl. This is my son, the hero priest." He'd started with the hero business after Tim Harley's suicide.

Cheryl, who had feathered black hair and too much eye shadow, gave me a tight smile. "Hi, Jim," she said. We knew each other. The introduction was an excuse to ride me. Cheryl went to the back to get a new bottle of rye. I turned on Dad.

"I told you, I'm not a hero."

He didn't look at me, talking instead to his reflection in the mirror behind the bar. "They called you that on TV."

"I'm no hero."

"Hero, hero, hero."

"Are you five years old?" I said.

He wouldn't look at me. "I've been tearing off a piece now and then with that Cheryl. She's a wildcat in the sack." He smiled around his cigarette. "Can see why Jacky liked it."

I finished my beer and set the glass down carefully. This was how he started fights. I imagined myself flat on my back on the barroom floor, my leather jacket open with the black shirt and Roman collar underneath, waking up with a crowd around me. "I'm out of here," I said. I put a five-dollar bill on the bar. "Make sure Cheryl gets that."

"What the fuck else would I do with it?"

It was March, and it started to sleet on my way back to Pretty Prairie, the highway darkening in my headlights. Maybe it was the non-conversation with my father replaying in my head, but I didn't pay enough attention to the road conditions. As soon as I hit the off-ramp to town I knew I was going too fast, even before I eased on the brakes and felt the road slide out from under me. The rear end of the car squirreled to the left and I slid sideways toward one of the reflective markers on the side of the ramp, which looked a lot bigger approaching the driver's side of my car at fifty miles an hour than it had from the road. At the last moment, I took my foot off the brake and hit the gas, counter-steering around the marker and a small tree that had been planted in the median. The car jolted through the grass just off the ramp, but somehow stayed upright. I took a quick glance in my rearview mirror, then steered back onto the roadway, the car bouncing hard as it hit the blacktopped shoulder. All in all it was some slick driving, and I was pretty proud of myself until I tried to turn right at the stop sign at the top of the ramp and the car went straight.

I slammed on the brakes and stopped just short of the access road into town. I backed up and started forward, slowly. I had no steering at all. Or rather, I had some; it just had little relation to the way I turned the wheel.

I backed up again and wobbled onto the shoulder, then put on the emergency flashers. Getting out into the sleet, I bent to look under the front of the car from about ten feet away. The wheels were splayed in opposite directions. I hunched my jacket up over my head, walked to the convenience store on the other side of the overpass, and called Dave Stanfield at home. He said he'd come with his wrecker.

Walking back across the overpass, I realized I'd jammed my thumb on the steering wheel when it jerked as I left the road. I put my head down in the sleet and worked the sore knuckle with my other hand as I walked, and I didn't notice Sheriff Miller's cruiser parked beside my car until I was on top of it.

Miller was walking back up the ramp from my skid marks in the grass. "Road move on you, Jim?" he said.

"Too slick," I said. "And I wasn't paying attention."

He got close enough to sniff my breath. "Been drinking?"

"One beer."

"I'll take your word for it. State patrol comes along though, and you're gonna take a Breathalyzer."

"That's okay."

"Everything else okay?"

"Fine. Hurt my thumb and my steering's gone."

He grimaced. "Tell you what, I'll just write you a warning for in-attentive driving. Something bothering you I should know about?"

"Everything's fine," I said. I cocked my head at him, standing there in his green leather sheriff's jacket, sleet gathering around the collar. "You wouldn't make a bad priest," I said.

Miller laughed. "Wife wouldn't like that," he said. "But we're both lawgivers, aren't we? Trying to help people, keep 'em in line."

"I guess," I said.

Dave Stanfield was pulling up in his wrecker, backing toward the front end of my car. He got out in a rain slicker and walked back toward us, peering down the ramp, where my skid marks made shadows in the yellow light thrown by the sodium lamps. He looked at me. "Road move on you, Jim?" he said. Miller chuckled, and I shook my head. "Pop the hood," Dave said.

Miller and I watched him while he shined a flashlight around under the hood, then leaned over and peered at something in the back of the engine compartment near the fire wall. He reached in and pushed and pulled, then looked up, the light catching the silver in his handlebar mustache. "Sheered the fucking rack and pinion right off the steering."

"How much to fix it?" I said.

He leaned his forearms on the fender and chewed his mustache for a minute. "Depends on whether there's anything I haven't found. Five hundred at least, a thousand tops. Ballpark. We can do it tomorrow."

"Okay," I said. There went my savings.

Stanfield got my car hooked up and gave me a ride. When he dropped me at the rectory, I stood on the front walk and watched my car go away, swaying slightly on the chains.

The bill came to six hundred dollars, and I put it on my credit card. God knows why, but driving around Saint Paul with a new front end the next Sunday, I stopped and went in again when I saw my father's car in front of John's Tap. He was at the bar, in a better mood. We watched another NBA game and talked sports. I didn't mention the accident, not wanting to bring up that Sunday. It was a pleasant evening.

The next two Sundays I ate dinner with Dad at John's Tap. The conversation was good, if nothing special: sports, Jacky's upcoming wedding (the old man pleased as punch about Mary Beth), his job. One week we had ham sandwiches, white bread loaded with meat and mustard, the next we had the Tap's pizza with its cardboard crust.

We were finishing the pizza when Dad started talking about Mom's parents, the Malones, who'd been older and both died when I was a little kid. "Roscoe liked his beer," Dad said. "So did Lil. They lived in a little house in the Midway they'd moved to after the Connemara Patch. Lil and the neighbor two houses down hated each other. Lil'd see that neighbor out gardening, and she'd go out in her own backyard and scream at her. Swore like a sailor." He chuckled. "She was a pistol.

"Roscoe was a carpenter, built that house himself. Taught me a lot about woodworking. They'd sit in their little kitchen with your mom and me summer evenings, drinking beer. Roscoe'd pour for Lil, and she'd say, 'Don't do me white, Roscoe.' She didn't like a head on her beer. She was German. German and Irish, just like your mom and me, but backwards. They got on, though. Your mom now, she's got a mouth on her. Times I'd like to bitch-slap her."

His mood had soured. I was getting ready to go, and I wanted to end the evening on a good note. I stood and reached for my black leather jacket, a dressy one with creamy leather that I'd paid three-hundred dollars for because I thought it went well with my priest's clothes. This was before I knew I was going to pay six-hundred dollars to get my steering fixed. I shrugged on the coat, smiled at Dad.

"I'm liking these dinners," I said. "I'm glad you're here every Sunday."

The old man looked at me sharply. "I'm not," he said.

I frowned. "Yeah you are."

"I'm not." His face was red.

"Okay, you're not." I had my coat on. "I've got to go." He'd bought dinner the week before. I took out my wallet. "Let me get this."

"I've got it."

"Let me. This once."

He slammed his hand on the bar. "Boy, I could buy you."

"Maybe you could," I said, slipping my wallet back into my pocket. "But it doesn't mean I can't buy once."

The old man nodded, his mouth open and working a little back and forth. His face was still red. Then: "Your mother's a cunt from hell."

I stood there. My chest felt all hollow. "Don't," I said.

The old man had swiveled his stool my way. He picked up his cigarette and held it upright between thumb and forefinger. Then, uncharacteristically, he hung his head. "Sorry," he said.

I stared at the top of his head, the bald spot mostly hidden in the center of his grizzled curls. My father had never apologized about anything, and it took the wind out of me.

"Okay," I said. I headed for the door.

"James," Dad called. I looked back. He was sitting on the bar stool, one hand on his thigh, the other still holding his cigarette. "See you next Sunday."

I waved and went out the door. But the next Sunday he wasn't there. I went a couple of more Sundays, but he never showed again. I thought about calling, but I didn't have his number.

"Father," my secretary said, coming down the stairs. "You have a letter here from the archdiocese."

I was taking a turn at the heavy bag after my morning prayers, and I pulled off my training gloves and toweled the sweat out of my hair. "Let's see," I said.

I ran a thumb under the flap and unfolded the Chancery letterhead. It said I was to report to Our Lady of the Trails in the southwest corner of the archdiocese by late May to be assistant to the pastor there. I sat down on the weight bench, pushing aside the boxing gloves. The letter said that Ken Sterritt would assume my duties at Saint Hieronymus in addition to his own at Holy Sacrament until a replacement had been found; I was to give him all necessary cooperation. The letter was signed by Monsignor Bell at the Chancery, whom I'd known when he was a seminary professor.

My hand started shaking, and I set the letter on the bench. My secretary, Mrs. Olchefske, stood nearby, looking concerned. "It looks like you're going to have a new boss," I managed. After she'd gone upstairs, I reached for the boxing gloves, then flung them into a corner of the basement and sat down again heavily on the weight bench, my head in my hands.

That afternoon, I phoned a friend from seminary who was stationed in Faribault and learned that Father Tanner, the pastor at Our Lady, was a petty tyrant and the parish widely viewed as a punishment assignment for priests who'd gotten out of line. After that, I called the Chancery and asked for a meeting with Monsignor Bell.

I parked in the shadow of the Cathedral and went up the Chancery steps like a medieval supplicant. The secretary let me into Bell's office to wait for him. The office was furnished in antiques, but the bookshelves were up to date, filled with recent and classic works in a wide range of subjects: anthropology, comparative religion, theology, medieval philosophy, child psychology, ethics, art history. There were several issues of *The Economist* on a side table. While I was waiting, I thumbed through some of the books without really seeing what was on any of the pages.

There was a knock at the door, as a doctor would do before entering an occupied examination room, then Bell strode in, a tall man with slightly stooped shoulders and a strong-featured but cadaverous face. Somewhere in his sixties, he still had all of his hair, and it was mostly black. "Sit down," he muttered, indicating a chair in front of his desk. "Sorry to keep you waiting." He was carrying a bottle of orange soda with a straw in it, and he set that on a maroon-colored desk blotter and took his seat. "What can I do for you, Father?" he asked, giving no sign he remembered me. His voice was cold and slightly nasal, and he enunciated words carefully. His students at the seminary had called him the Inquisitor.

"With all due respect, Monsignor, I've been pastor at Saint Hieronymus for two years and the parish is doing well—why am I suddenly getting farmed out to another parish as an associate?"

"Have you examined your conscience about this, Father?"

Diana? Surely not. "Nothing comes to mind, sir," I said.

Bell looked disappointed with me, and I felt a sympathetic disappointment with myself. He flicked open a manila folder I hadn't noticed. I saw my name on the tab, copies of reports I'd filed, my seminary transcript, a newspaper clipping about Tim Harley. And an envelope that had a familiar look about it. Bell picked up the envelope between thumb and forefinger, as if it were an object of some distaste. He laid it in front of me. There, in feminine handwriting, were the addresses of Diana's apartment and my rectory; the envelope was marked *Personal* in the same female hand. *Personal.* I wondered if it still had the faint scent of Diana's perfume about it. I thought of the rubber-banded batch of letters in the bottom of my sock drawer. I thought of Mrs. Gunther, my intrusive housekeeper, who would've seen the envelope on the mail table in the hall or maybe on my dresser, then looked for it later where she knew I kept personal mail.

I stared at the orange soda on Bell's desk, bright against his black shirt.

"Do you have anything you'd like to say about this, Father Dressler?"

I was silent. You couldn't tell from the letter that Diana and I had shared only a few kisses. It was immaterial now, anyway. I started to tell Bell that I'd made a confession about Diana, then thought better of it. Confession might have saved my soul, but it wasn't going to save my ass here.

"This young woman appears to have made the rounds," Bell said. Of course, he would have been involved in Mick's transfer, too.

"Not exactly, sir," I said. "Hardly anything happened between us. It was over before it began."

Bell's mouth drew into a tight frown. He picked up the Tim Harley clipping. "About the same time, wasn't it?"

A quiet chill ran down my spine. I shook my head. "I couldn't have saved Tim Harley."

Bell smiled. "Maybe not."

I saw what he was doing and made myself ignore it and go on. "I've got a good record at Saint Hieronymus."

Bell stared at me. When I wouldn't look away he settled back in his chair a little. "Ordinarily that would make a difference," he said. "We don't like transferring a man from a parish where he's done a good job." He fanned papers from my file across the open folder. "Since you've been at Saint H., attendance and collections are up. The youth group's growing, your outreach ministries are thriving." Bell neatened the papers, closed the folder. "But your housekeeper's quite a gossip, Father. If she hasn't started rumors already, she will soon enough. The transfer is best, for you and the parish."

He was right. So was Father Friedel, my spiritual director at seminary. The appearance of scandal was more than enough. Still, I didn't want to go to an isolated new post, far from family and friends and the community of priests George Martin had built in River County.

I asked if there wasn't a way I might stay at Saint Hieronymus, ride out the rumors about Diana, or whether he would at least demote me to associate at an inner-city parish in Saint Paul or Minneapolis, the sort of place my upbringing had prepared me for.

Bell hunched forward, eyes bright black. "If I could transfer housekeepers, believe me, I would," he said. "But don't mistake me,

Father: this is a punishment. You've done a disservice to your parish and caused me quite a bit of extra work. Your housekeeper—Gunner? Gunther?—is going to see you transferred to the far ends of the archdiocese. It may keep her quiet—that's my hope, and it's why I spent the good part of an unpleasant afternoon in her company. Father Tanner at Our Lady isn't the easiest man to work with, but you'll only spend a year or two there. It'll give you something to think about the next time you're tempted by a pretty girl." He stood and extended his hand. "Good luck," he said, and the interview was over.

After I left the Chancery, I went into the Cathedral and knelt in the south transept and prayed. In the ringing silence under the massive curve of the Cathedral dome, it came to me that the chain of events I'd set into motion by kissing Diana had come to fruition, and I bowed my head and numbered my sins while a nun from the Chancery moved about the altar, dusting the lectern and arranging cut flowers for Sunday Mass.

May almighty God bless you, the Father, and the Son, and the Holy Spirit.
I was standing on the altar at the end of eleven o'clock Mass. The column for next week's bulletin in which I would announce my transfer was half-written, locked in a drawer. I hadn't yet said a word to anyone, but already I saw my parishioners and the Saint Hieronymus church through the eyes of loss. The simple plaster Stations of the Cross, the creaky wood floor, the even creakier heating system in the basement boiler room, all were suddenly outlined in light in my mind's eye. I'd spent much of my spare time the last couple of days alone in the church, walking the aisles, running my hands over the worn wood of the pews, fixing a dozen little things I'd been meaning to get to, from a loose hinge on the tabernacle door to a broken kneeler. I'd even wormed my way into the steeple, rank with pigeon droppings and an old squirrel nest, to check for leaks in its cladding.

The Mass is ended, go in peace.

There was no closing hymn or procession today. I watched the congregation start to file into the aisles, Matt Miller in his sheriff's jacket guiding his wife with a gentle hand on her back, saw Steve Sullivan remind his rambunctious son Kevin to genuflect, and then saw George Martin, his overcoat buttoned around his throat, standing in the back pew. I nodded to him, then left the altar and went out through the sacristy door and along the sidewalk to greet people as they emerged from the church. Frank Harley stopped to shake my hand—"That paving contractor'll be by to sign a contract next week and set a date," he said—and beside him Verna smiled and said it was almost pie season. When the last people had trailed out, George Martin came down the church steps, hands in his pockets, and said, "Can I have a minute?" Ted Burkholder, the sacristan, on his way back into the church to make sure the candles were extinguished, paused with his foot on the step and cast a glance at us before he went in.

"I'll meet you in the kitchen in five minutes," I said, and went to the sacristy to change. When I came in the back door of the house, George was sitting at the kitchen table with the bottle of Jameson from the high cupboard and two rocks glasses full of whiskey and ice in front of him. He lifted a glass to me. "It is afternoon," he said.

I took a sip, swished the whiskey around in the glass to hurry the ice along. "Had lunch?" I asked, pulling bacon and eggs from the fridge. When George shook his head, I started toast and the coffeemaker, laid strips of bacon close together in the iron skillet and lit the burner.

George shifted in the chair behind me. "Heard anything from the home office lately?"

I looked up from adjusting the flame. "I'm being transferred," I said, and told him—without naming Diana—about the incriminating letter and my meeting with Monsignor Bell.

"I had a hunch," George said.

"Your hunches are usually pretty good," I said. George chuckled and looked pleased. I went on: "Thing I can't figure out is, I slip up a little and get transferred to the end of the world; Mick gets the girl and a trip to Rome." That was the other news of late: Mick had somehow wangled permission to take a doctorate at the Pontifical North American College. He was studying Italian and would leave for the Holy City come summer.

"You got the same girl, I hear," George said.

He was Diana's godfather. I sat at the kitchen table and picked up my whiskey. "I'm sorry," I said.

George tilted the bottle and topped off his glass. "There much to be sorry for?"

"Honestly?" I said. "Not much."

"How'd the Chancery get that letter?"

"Mrs. Gunther," I said.

"She's a dear," George said, reaching out to pat my knee. "Your bad luck."

I didn't say anything, and George scratched at the bristles in the cleft of his chin. "How was the meeting with Bell?"

"Rough," I said.

"Bell's a real dickhead," George said. "He's a very effective administrator."

"And you sicced him on Mick."

George rocked forward and stared at his feet. "Mick needed to know what kind of people he was going to be playing ball with."

"I don't get it."

He looked up. "Mick's going places," he said.

I sipped my drink, watched reflections from the room twist in the liquid. "He's going to Rome, anyway. And I'm going to Our Lady of the Trails."

George shrugged. "Mick's wrong, but he believes in what he's doing and he's smart about it. You're an idealist."

"And you're not?"

"I'm a good old boy. We get by any way we have to." He sighed. "You going to take the transfer?"

I went to the stove, flipped the bacon to the edges of the skillet, and broke four eggs into the sizzling grease in the middle. "I don't know," I said, when I sat down again.

George just sat there silently. He looked patient, like a hunter waiting for a rabbit to come out of the brush. "Mind if I smoke?"

I stood and got an ashtray from the cupboard, flipping the bacon one more time and turning down the heat under the eggs while I was up. When I sat down again, I said: "I don't know what to do."

George lit a cigarette. "Well, that's what I wanted to talk to you about. There's a history lectureship open at Saint John's that you'd be suited for." He turned the cigarette in his hand, watched the ash growing longer while I absorbed the offer. When I nodded, he went on. "My order would take you in for a year and give you a room at the abbey. Our particular callings are to prayer and work. You might be very happy." He paused, then said, "I think the bacon's ready."

While I plated the bacon and eggs and buttered the toast, George went on: "There's a practical side to this. Everyone who matters in the archdiocese knows what a posting to Our Lady means. It'll hurt your career. Go to Saint John's, and some other priest will get into trouble and sent to the woodshed with Father Tanner. A year from now, this little scandal of yours won't seem so important, even to Bell. The archdiocese may even offer you another parish of your own, if they think that's what it'll take to get you back from the abbey. They're too short of priests to stand on principle for long." George grinned around his cigarette, and I saw that he'd just slipped me an ace under the table.

"This is all a Benedictine plot to get your hands on me, isn't it?" I said, sliding a plate in front of him.

George raised his eyebrows. "Yeah, we're short of men who'll kiss the girls and beat up other priests, even ones who need it." He finished his drink, then went to the counter and poured each of us a cup of coffee. "But I don't want to see a promising young career ruined. If you're interested, write to the archbishop and ask for leave. I'll send a letter, too. He's an old fishing buddy, and I've got just enough pull"—he grinned again—"to get a man of uncertain morals into a classroom." He sat down and dipped a strip of bacon into one of his eggs.

"Let me sleep on it," I said, but I already knew that Monday I would write to the archbishop. I felt an overwhelming sense of relief and gratitude. It was grace of a sort: George had offered me an honorable way out of my predicament. I didn't deserve it, but I'd take it. After Jacky's wedding, I would try life at the abbey.

And so it came to pass that in May I boxed up my books and belongings under Mrs. Gunther's disapproving eye. She seemed always present in my last weeks, dropping plates of bland food, over- or undercooked, in front of me at lunch and dinner, vacuuming the front hall every time I sat down in my office to work. The rectory was hers, she was saying, almost daring me to bring up the stolen letter. I didn't bother.

I kept myself together through the parish farewell luncheon after my last Mass, and it was only when I was on the interstate heading south and caught a glimpse of the Pretty Prairie skyline in my rearview mirror—the gas station and fast-food franchises on the rise by the interstate, the grain elevator, the Saint Hieronymus steeple—that I had to pull over to the side of the road for a while.

VII

26

IN MY MOTHER'S KITCHEN, I TOLD ANNE everything: about Harold, and Mick and Diana and Tim Harley, even Betty and the abortion, which I thought no one in the family but Mom knew about. The last came stumbling out like a sinner from the confessional, but Anne just nodded. "Mom told me years ago," she said.

When I finished the whole story, long after midnight, Anne frowned. "So you're a Benedictine now?"

"Just staying at the abbey," I said.

"It seems like an awful fuss over one little kiss."

"Well, more than one," I said. "The point is, I gave scandal. Any priest knows better."

Anne rolled her eyes. "You're a wonderful priest," she said. "You think George Martin doesn't have his secret sins? Or that your friend Harold didn't?" She blew out her cheeks. "Mick sure does."

"Anyway," I said, "God brought me home for His own reasons." I rubbed at my eyes with thumb and forefinger. "It's up to me to understand."

"Why do priests," Anne said, "think God pays so much attention to them?"

I looked at her curiously. "God pays attention to everyone."

"Fair enough." She crossed her arms behind her head, stretched and yawned. "I am going to be so tired tomorrow."

"Today," I said. "Told you it was a long story." I got up and put the ashtray holding Anne's half-smoked cigarette on the kitchen counter. With my back to her, I said: "Is everything all right with you and Daryl?"

I heard the scrape of Anne's chair, and when I turned she was in the kitchen door, leaning back against the jamb with one hand on her belly and with the other tugging at one of the curls that was falling out of her hair. "What did she tell you?" she said.

"That you had a black eye."

"It's gone now." She disappeared into the hall, and I heard her going up the stairs.

I carried our pop and beer bottles out to the recycling bin on the porch, then went upstairs. Anne was clearing her bed of the Christmas stuff I'd piled there a week before. I joined her without a word, and then we found a set of wrinkled linens in a drawer and started making the bed. "Gotta love Mom's housekeeping," Anne said.

"I shouldn't have told you I knew," I said, pulling a corner of the fitted sheet tight.

Anne billowed the top sheet over the bed, tucked it in at the foot. "I can take care of myself," she said.

"You always could." I walked out into the hall. My sister had a quiet determination about her, whether she was a teenager bringing a pack of cigarettes to the dinner table and lighting up with our parents over coffee, or a grown woman with her hair in a bandana and her sleeves rolled up, clearing half her backyard for a vegetable plot.

Anne followed me into the hall and hugged me. I held her for a moment, hanging on to the solidness of her body, then let go and turned out the hall light. Anne went into her room and closed the door.

In my own room, I switched on the small lamp beside my bed,

undressed, and got under the covers. I lay on my back and stared
at the ceiling. For all the times Mom and I had dinner at my rectory, the one time she'd had something important to tell me about
our family, she'd done it in the confessional. Most priests have close
relationships with their mothers, but I'd always thought of myself
as the exception. Mine was a piece of work—no one else would
have married my father—and I held her at arm's length every bit
as much as she did me. But that was a relationship, too, the flip side
of a coin. I turned on my side, punched up my pillow, and did my
best to quiet my mind.

That night I slept badly, drifting on the ragged edges of dream
until I woke suddenly before dawn, to clammy sheets and the light
burning on my dresser, pale in the brightening room. I'd been on
the porch of the abandoned farmhouse where Tim Harley died,
a sapling stirring in the sweltering air and a fly buzzing against an
empty screen. But when I tried to find Tim I was in the Outpost
after closing, the chairs upside-down on tables and a streetlight's
shine through the windows and the brief taste of Diana's lipstick,
then I walked into the back of the bar and found a gaunt priest in
the yellow kitchen-light of a rectory who turned around to reveal
not Harold's face but my own, the eyes becoming Tim Harley's as
he lowered his mouth over the shotgun. Then the half-heard, half-
dreamed slam of a door somewhere in a house.

I got up in a sweat and went into the bathroom and bent over
the sink, resting my elbows on the edges and smoothing water
over my face and arms. After that, with the morning sun lighting
my window shade, I sprawled on the bed and fell into a sound
sleep, barely stirring when Anne stuck her head in the door to say
good-bye.

Later that day, when I came home from Mass—I'd gone to Saint
Agnes in Frogtown this time, still avoiding Father Phil—there was

a note from Mom to call Mick. When I reached him, he suggested we meet at Como Lake that evening for a walk. He'd just bought his plane ticket for Rome, was leaving in early June. After all the trouble with Diana, Mick had done only a brief stint as hospital chaplain before getting the assignment to study canon law. This summer, he was going to assist in one of the American offices at the Vatican.

Mick was waiting in his truck near the Como Lake pavilion when I pulled into the lot. There was a black-and-orange *For Sale* sign in the window of the camper top. I parked beside him, and we got out and started strolling along the paved walk around the lake. It was a cool evening, and we both wore windbreakers. The lake was like glass, the surface disturbed only by the spreading ripples left by feeding fish.

"Rome, huh," I said. "Your reward for being a bad boy?"

"Ciao, bella!" Mick said. *"Due cappuccino, per favore. Asciugamano. Sophia Loren. Spaghetti!*—Oh, I expect they'll keep a pretty close eye on me for a while."

I laughed. "And then?"

"The higher I rise, the more freedom I'll have."

At the south end of the lake, we paused, hands in our pockets, to watch a group of Hmong men on the fishing dock, baiting hooks, casting, joking among themselves.

"The North American College is a conservative boot camp," I said. "Full of the Pope's foot soldiers. You'd best watch your step."

Mick shrugged. He had the unabated confidence of a man who'd always been a star.

"Straight out," I said, "how do you justify the women?"

We started walking again, under towering cottonwoods whose pale, heart-shaped leaves rustled like running water at the slightest breath of the evening air.

"I struggled with it in seminary," Mick said at last. "I nearly quit when giving up women didn't work. And then I decided

I could have both. You've read your history—priests squiring devout heiresses around Rome and the Holy Land, Catholic U founded with money from a woman sleeping with the bishop of Peoria. There's room for men like me." He unzipped his jacket.

"God's own gigolo," I said, glancing quickly at Mick.

He answered evenly: "I'm just saying, plenty of successful clerics have had women in their lives."

"I hear the policewomen in Rome direct traffic in miniskirts and boots with three-inch heels," I said. Mick laughed. I went on: "Diana said once that you took everything in stride. Something in me admires that."

Mick looked at me appraisingly, then back out at the lake. We walked up the east shore. Flowers I couldn't name were coming up; the foliage on the trees was the new green of spring. We stepped off the sidewalk to go around an old Hmong woman walking slowly in a colorful traditional costume.

"I don't like breaking vows," Mick said, as we fell back into step, "but I'm willing to answer for it. The Church can fire me any time it chooses." We came to the narrow point that sticks out into the lake like a finger pointing at the pavilion, and we listened for a moment to a forties dance tune drifting across the water from an orchestra warming up for a show on the pavilion's wide promenade. "What about you?"

"I'm answering now," I said, "for a lot of things."

"A couple make-out sessions with Diana?"

We were walking out on the spit, gray quiet water all around us.

"I believe in absolutes," I said. "A broken vow is a broken vow. I wish Gunther wasn't a gossip, hadn't dug up that letter and turned it over to Bell, but I've been doing exercises in moral cause and effect since seminary, and when I trace things back, I hold myself responsible."

At the end of the point, we stopped for a moment. Across the water, the concession stand at the back of the pavilion was shuttered, waiting for summer. Mick hadn't answered what I'd said about vows, and I wondered if I'd offended him.

"I'm going further than you in the Church," Mick said abruptly, and I turned to stare at him. He was a big man, taller and broader than I, a five-o'clock shadow evident by midafternoon on his cheeks and jaw. I could feel the power and confidence he carried with him like the birthright of his size. He'd grown up in a doctor's household, had been told since boyhood that he could do anything. George Martin said Mick was wrong, but the truth was there always had been priests who were first and foremost politicians, career men. Mick's kind was as necessary to the workings of the Church as the other kind, the Danny Linzes who could talk at length and lovingly of the presence of God in their daily lives, speaking with wonder of how He worked through them. God working through Mick shouldn't have been a surprise. I might not have liked it, but Mick's hypocrisy wasn't unusual. He was willing to accept the moral compromises that come with running any large enterprise.

"It's the ruthless who run things," I said, the thought coming with the words. "You'll never be defrocked—you're one of them. And I'll never lead anything bigger than a parish."

"You're right." Mick gave me a long-jawed grin, and I felt something ease in my shoulders. George had called me an idealist, but I'd grown up around the old line: practical men like Father Phil and Harold Lamplighter, who excelled at the day-to-day work of a parish in the same way a born mechanic excels in the garage. For all I'd said about absolutes, I could see where Mick fit into the complicated engine that was the Church, how he had his own part in making things run.

And where did I fit? I wasn't particularly spiritual, not in the way Danny Linz was. For me, the priesthood was work made meaningful by ritual: God most present in the ceremonies of the Church, which begin as metaphor to make His presence tangible to man, then go beyond metaphor at the Eucharist when God becomes real and present in my hands, and I bring Him down from the altar to the people, where there is the intimacy of giving Communion to men and women whose sins and desires I know from the confessional. But I had let down the people I served, disturbed the smooth running of the engine and been cast aside, and now I said a prayer for God to guide me back into my proper place.

Mick was praying, too, some intention of his own—don't ask what told me this—and I crossed myself and started walking back toward shore. Mick tossed a stone into the lake and followed. In the still water in the lee of the point, a late-migrating flotilla of Canada geese bobbed like moored battleships. A half dozen more glided in from the west, splashing down to be greeted with honks and the beating of wings. Mick caught up with me, and spoke over the noise: "How's Diana?"

"She's happy," I said. "Turns out she and Roger were a good match."

"That's good," Mick said.

It was the wedding week, and Dad and I were prepping the living and dining rooms of the Frogtown house for painting. He surveyed the ceilings and pronounced them passable, and we went to work on the walls. We removed switch and receptacle plates, spackled cracks and nail holes, sanded and primed. Dad was in a good mood, horsing around, shadowboxing.

"Old man's still got it, doesn't he?" he said, straightening from his crouch and shaking a cigarette out of the pack in the pocket of his sport shirt. The flesh of his upper arms was beginning to slacken and take on the yellowish cast of age, but his biceps bulged like softballs when he cupped his hands to his face to light up.

"Bet you can't do this." I flipped up on my hands and hand-walked out the open front door onto the glassed-in porch.

Dad followed, laughing. "That's useful. Learn it in seminary?"

A minute later, standing on the front steps beside me, he said, "I'm streetwise." He rolled his neck, and vertebrae crackled. "'Course, what I'm saying is, I don't know shit." He nodded at the house. "You think I don't know Bob Nordyke's making money off me? Fifteen, twenty years from now, all that'll be left of me in this world is a cheap headstone."

It had turned out to be a hot day, and I was sweaty and tired. The old man had probably spent the night at the window of his apartment, smoking and brooding over the moonlight on Calvary Cemetery. "I'll buy you a pretty one," I said. "Marble and everything."

His head jerked my way, and something flickered behind his eyes. Then he snorted. "Some priest you must've made: 'Well, missus, I gave your husband last rites, so you can just as well stop the waterworks and get on with planting him.'"

After work Tuesday I put on my priest's suit, thinking I'd drive out to see Granddad. When I went down for dinner, I found Mom's boyfriend, Samuel, sitting at the kitchen table. He was sixty, chinless and balding, so that perched on a too-small kitchen chair with his lanky arms and legs splayed about him, he reminded me of a large frog.

"How ya doing, Reverend? Maura says you're eating her out of house and home." A hillbilly who'd moved north to work in the auto plants, first in Detroit, then Saint Paul, he spoke with a hoarse drawl.

Mom stood at the sink, the phone tucked under her chin while she ran water over a tray of ice cubes. "It's the Donovan-Dressler wedding," she said into the phone. "That's right, a 46. But he's got short arms. You got a 46 Stumpy? I don't know when he'll be in. You check on it." She heaved a sigh, the phone still tucked under her chin. "Your father."

"I don't like the way he comes and goes these days," Samuel said. He took the ice-cube tray from Mom, put a handful in a glass, and poured bourbon over them.

"Take it up with him," I said.

"Joe's free to see his son," Mom said. She shifted the phone to the other ear and put on a flowered oven mitt, slid a lasagna pan halfway out of the oven, sprinkled on a layer of shredded moz-zarella, then closed the oven door again. "Five minutes," she said. Then into the phone: "Thanks. I'll remind him." She hung up. "I'll never be free of that man."

Over dinner, Mom raised an eyebrow at my priest's suit. "Going to see your grandfather?"

"He's used to seeing me in this," I said.

"It won't be long for him," she said. "I hope." She drew on her cigarette, squinting through blue smoke.

"Seemed pretty bad to me the other night. Dad's taking it hard." I forked up a last bite of lasagna and went to the sink to rinse my plate.

"Give him a hug for me," Mom said. "And water his plants. Your father never does."

At the nursing home, I parked beside the old man's car. The sub-urbs were as quiet as Pretty Prairie; a warm breeze barely stirred the row of saplings planted along the walk.

I lingered by the entrance, toeing a dandelion growing where a chip had been knocked out of the sidewalk, its small leaves flat-tened to the exposed dirt. It came loose and left a green smear on the concrete.

"Hello, Father." A middle-aged man in a blue Izod shirt held the door. I went in. At the desk, a nurse I didn't know looked up and started. "Can I help you, Father?"

"I'm here to see my grandfather."

Somewhere nearby, an old woman kept up a singsong monologue. "Are you there, sir? Pleasesir, are you there, sir? Sir, sir, pleasesir, help me, sir. . . ." The voice faded into the gray carpet as I moved down the hall. There was no urgency to it, only compulsion.

Short of the hall's end I stopped, rubbed my cheeks. I'd forgotten to shave this morning. The old man was reading to Granddad. I recognized the title story of the Hemingway, the hunter dying of gangrene. What a choice. "It's Kilimanjaro"—Granddad broke in—"not Kimarjo. Lord, get the words right."

"Just then the—hyena—stopped whimpering in the night and started to make a strange, human, almost crying sound." My father finished the story, stopping to breathe at odd places the way people unused to reading aloud are prone to do.

A nurse came down the hall. I abandoned my eavesdropping. "How you doing there, Granddad?" I said, walking into the room. "Who's this, some volunteer from the library?" I took the book from the old man, thumbed to the table of contents. "You'd like 'Fifty Grand,'" I said. "It's about boxing."

"I like the other one just fine," Dad said. He fingered my shirtsleeve. "You're in costume tonight?"

Granddad, who'd been beaming at my black suit, looked puzzled for an instant. I shot Dad a dirty look, flipped the book onto the nightstand, and eased down into the wheelchair. It rolled back, and I set the brake. "You're looking bright-eyed and bushy-tailed, Granddad."

"Had a long nap this afternoon. Danged nurses left me alone for once."

"Good for them." I glanced sidelong at my father, who sat on the edge of the bed with his shoulders rounded, biting at a hang-nail on his nicotine-yellowed left thumb. "You having a nice visit with Little Joe here?" Dad's eyes started up to mine.

"Josephine?" Granddad said. His eyes grew brighter. "That one always was a squawker. Never napped, never slept but one night a month." His hand on the call button gripped and relaxed. "I'd carry him around the kitchen, dandle him. And do you know, when he started to get sleepy, he'd shake himself awake. Then he'd start to hollering. One night his mother threw a glass of water in his face."

My father got up and bent to the TV, his broad back hiding the screen. "Twins're on tonight," he said, searching through the channels.

"I leave it on Channel 4," Granddad said. "There's a show."

Dad found the Twins' pregame and sat back on the bed.

"That Channel 4?"

"Sure, Pop." Dad had the TV on 9.

"Twins on 4, now?"

"Yeah, Pop."

Granddad peered at the TV, then chuckled. "Next time his mother went to do that, he ducked. So she threw it in my face. And damned if he didn't laugh at that. Ha!"

"How old was he?"

"I don't know." Granddad drew out the last word, almost petu-lant. "He was a handful." He reared back and looked at Dad. "You regret all the grief you caused your mother?"

Dad ignored him.

"They put me in an oven when I was born," Granddad said.

I raised my eyebrows. "That so?"

"Nineteen-fourteen." Granddad nodded solemnly. "I was pre-mature, and they put me in a shoe box lined with cotton. Used the coal stove for an incubator. Every now and again, I'd turn blue, and they'd put a little whiskey on my tongue to get me going again. My German great-aunts would come over and say, 'Is he dead yet?' but Uncle Max's Irish wife would say, 'What a fine baby boy' and pinch my cheek. She used to read the papers for funerals and go sit in back of the church. Someone would take her for a long-lost cousin of the deceased and bring her to the cemetery and the funeral dinner. She had a whole set of ideas as to which denomination put on the best spread. I believe she preferred the Methodists."

Dad leaned on one elbow on the bed, watching the game. "Don't look at me." He rubbed his nose. "I never heard this one before."

"You never listened," Granddad said. "Turn the damn TV down."

Dad hit the mute button on the channel changer and rolled onto his back, throwing a thick forearm over his eyes. Granddad leaned toward him. "The Green Lantern boys would've made short work of you."

Dad's arm didn't move from his eyes. "Yeah? Well, they're dead. Didn't they turn that joint into a beauty shop?" His voice was soft and reasonable: "Seem to remember it when I was a kid. Downtown, and you standing in front of this window full of hair dryers, yammering on about the old days."

Granddad sank back and stared at the TV with stunned eyes. After a minute, he perked up. "During Prohibition, I'd come home drunk on bathtub gin, and my poor mother would follow me up the stairs, pounding on my back. And I'd say, 'What do you expect me to do, Mother? You gave me a taste for it at a tender age.' Heh."

Dad's breathing slowed.

"You're full of stories tonight, Granddad," I said.

My grandfather lifted the call button in front of his face and tilted his head at his clutching hand, as though it belonged to someone else. "Well, they're all dead now," he said.

He dropped his hands and sat there looking lost, his chin on his chest. Dad snored softly on the bed. I stood and pinched dried blooms off the mostly dead petunia in the window pot, then walked down to the nurses' station. Pretty, freckle-nosed Renee was at the desk now. "How was my grandfather today?"

"He had a nonresponsive episode this afternoon."

"What's that?"

"It means he was conscious and his eyes were open, but he wouldn't respond to anyone. We don't know why it happens, but it's not uncommon."

"For him, or for anyone?"

"For anyone in a nursing home."

"Pleasesir, are you there, sir? Can you help me, sir? Sir, sir, pleasesir, are you there, sir?" The singer was in an electric wheelchair and glided up to the station with an eerie smoothness.

"Knock it off, Dolores," Renee said.

"Knockitoffsir, pleasesir, are you there, sir?"

"Does she count as nonresponsive?" I asked.

Renee rolled her eyes. "She was a music teacher. Sometimes we get her playing the piano, and it stops for a while."

On my way back down the hall, I glanced into an open room. The drapes were pulled, and in the shadows I could see an old woman curled on a bed. She was shrunken to the size of a child, and her eyes stared emptily at the wall in front of her. I stepped into the room and waved a hand in her face. The expression didn't change. I blessed her and left.

When I stepped back into the hall, I bumped into my father.

"Jesus." He peered into the room. "She dead?"

"No," I said, and he gave me a look.

"Think he'll end up like that?"

"No," I said.

"Well, you're full of things to say, aren't you?"

"No."

We walked out together and stood by his car while he smoked a cigarette. The sky was solid gray and darkening. I'd watched it cloud over from Granddad's window, drifting clouds and spatters of rain and sunlight.

"I shouldn't have said that shit," Dad said, the words mumbled around his cigarette.

Surprised, I rubbed the back of my head. "Granddad pushes," I said at last. Dad nodded. It seemed as good a time as any to let him know about my coffee plans with Betty García. "I'm going to have to knock off about four tomorrow. I need time to clean up—"

"Guess you're not used to working a full day." The old man held his cigarette like a dart and the tip glowed in the shadowed curve of his hand.

"You sprung this on me Sunday, Dad. I've got Jacky's wedding this weekend—"

He dropped his cigarette and watched it roll across the pavement, then got into his Buick without a word and drove away. After the car went around the corner, I picked up a rock and flung it in that direction, then went inside to say good night to Granddad. I never made it. The call light for his room was on at the nurses' station, and I could hear him bellowing down the hall. "Jesus, God, help me! Somebody help me! Oh, Mary, Mother of God!" Renee and the other nurse were strolling down the hall, talking to one another. There was a whirring noise beside me, and I looked down into a pair of bright blue eyes.

"There he goes again," said the old woman. "I wish he'd shut up."

27

ON THE WAY HOME, I SWUNG PAST Mary Beth Donovan's Midway bungalow. I found my brother sitting on the glassed-in porch under a wall lamp, looking thoughtful in a pair of reading glasses. When I came up the walk, leaning into the wind that had sprung up, Jacky set his *Sports Illustrated* aside and laid the glasses on the cover. "You look like you had a rough day," he said.

"Just visited Granddad with the old man."

"Family night at the rest home," Jacky said. "I'll get you a drink. Beer or bourbon?"

"Beer." I didn't want to get started on whiskey. I followed my brother into the house. Storm sirens blared behind us, that rising wail. Jacky went on into the kitchen; I stopped and searched the TV until I found a map of the metro counties with the color-coded storm superimposed. The weatherman announced a severe thunderstorm warning.

Jacky came out of the kitchen with a bottle of beer for me and a bourbon on the rocks for himself, and we went back out on the porch. It was raining in, and we moved around closing the storm windows on the south and west.

"Where's your better half?" I settled into a wicker rocker. Mary Beth kept an awfully comfortable house for a woman with motorcycle dreams—one more sign, I thought, that the Donovans needn't worry about her. They'd put the down payment on this house in a decent neighborhood, so that even while Mary Beth was drifting she had an investment earning money. Families with money, families that were smart about it, didn't miss a trick.

"She's around. She'll probably be out later. Did I tell you she came down to the Tap last Saturday to say hi to you and found me and Cheryl playing pool?"

I raised an eyebrow. "Told you that was a bad idea."

"Hell, I was lucky she showed up. I only lost thirty-five dollars." He turned serious. "Mary Beth knows I wouldn't mess around with Cheryl again."

"Good for you." I was thinking about Dad and the letter from a law firm I'd seen at his place last week. "You know any reason the old man might be getting mail from a lawyer?"

"About a hundred." Jacky swirled his drink. "But, yeah, he beat up the wrong guy. Some idiot contractor wanders into the Gossip one night last month and gets into a conversation with you-know-who. The old man airs his opinion on the mayor, turns out this guy's a big fan. One thing leads to another, and Dad kicks the shit out of the guy. Beats him up real bad."

"Why didn't anyone tell me?"

"I'm the only one knows. I bailed him out—Mary Beth borrowed the money from her family. They think it's for the house."

"You keeping the old man's secrets now?" I said.

"Mom doesn't need anything else to go on about." Jacky took another drink, crunching ice. "Anyway, keep it quiet."

"I guess I'm surprised this didn't happen years ago." The old man was a throwback to a less litigious age. Then again, he fought mostly at the Gossip, where no one in their right mind went anyway.

Jacky shrugged. "Charges won't stick. Other guy swung first— you know how that works."

I did. Our father might have squinted at the contractor through the smoke at the bar as their argument grew heated and said something like "Show a little respect, son. I could've been your father, wasn't for that collie beating me over the fence."

Jacky was still talking. "Problem is, the guy's going to sue. Says he can't walk right any more."

"Dad hasn't got much to take."

"He's giving Mom hell on the alimony."

"So she says." I hid a sudden panicky feeling, wondering if I'd get paid for working on the house. I didn't have the savings to be doing charity work. The truth of the matter was that my father was a flake, his daily actions and his relations with his family governed by his whims and appetites of the moment. "Little brother," I said, as a cold draft from the storm chilled the porch, "do you think we're a family of irrevocable fuckups?"

Jacky furrowed his brow. "Who isn't?"

"Can we expect questions like that at our wedding?" Mary Beth stood in the doorway, barefoot in jeans and a gray sweatshirt. Even her feet were beautiful—long, with high, delicate arches. I stood and gave her a brotherly hug. She picked up my beer bottle and took a swig, then settled on the futon couch by Jacky, pulling an afghan off the back to cover her feet. "And how is our erstwhile priest?" she said.

"Missing the altar," I said. "Other than that, he's broke and at loose ends."

Mary Beth rested her head on Jacky's shoulder. "So, tell me about your plans."

Suddenly tired, I sat back in the rocker in the corner and put my feet up on the coffee table. "If you don't mind, I just want to have a drink with my brother and not think."

"You've come to the right place for that," Jacky said.

Mary Beth pursed her lips. "Fair enough." She started talking about the neighborhood: the ninety-eight-year-old Swedish woman next door had finally gone into a nursing home after falling down the basement stairs while trying to carry her geraniums in for the winter.

"I told her to call me to help her with that," Mary Beth said. "I miss her. She used to sit in her porch and watch the neighborhood kids play. When Lloyd came around in the fall to collect for the alley plowing, she'd call me over and warm up chocolate chip cookies for us in the oven. She slept with her windows open all year. She's still alive in that nursing home."

"You ever notice how long people in Minnesota live?" Jacky said. "I figure all the heavy snow shoveling wiped out the gene for bad hearts a few generations ago."

Mary Beth shifted closer to Jacky, and the wicker creaked beneath them. She moved on to the wedding—who might show up uninvited or drunk, who was mad at whom, who might pull something. These concerns focused on Jacky's side of the aisle.

The phone rang. Mary Beth went in and answered. "Well, I like the idea of the Jordan almonds, even if Grandma says they're too dago." Her voice receded into the back of the house. Jacky tilted his head and raised an eyebrow. "Women," he said, "are different."

"You're a brilliant observer of human nature," I said.

Rain and wind rattled the loose storm windows of the porch. Streetlights made raindrops glitter on the window glass.

"You think the old man knew he was an asshole while we were growing up?" Jacky said out of nowhere. Ten years after Jacky and I had moved out of the house, the old man still tended to crop up in too many of our conversations. The habit was founded in our earliest childhood, when we shared what was now my room and used to whisper in the dark across the narrow space between our twin beds, trying to figure out our father, the man who one instant called us his "*bone*-urges" and the next gave us the back of his hand. It was practical talk, two boys learning to predict a man's moods—what made him laugh, what set him off, how you could tell when it was time to run for cover.

"Most people think they're doing the best they can," I said. "If you asked the old man, I bet he'd say he was a good father."

Jacky nudged the coffee table with his feet. "Sometimes I worry," he said, "that I'll end up like him. When I have kids."

"If you're worried, you're probably okay," I said.

"I guess so," Jacky said, sounding unsure. He picked up the *Sports Illustrated* and studied the cover. "At least you've got that taken care of. I mean, being a priest and all."

"Sure." I had a sudden vision of Jacky's children: they would be lovely, with their parents' slender builds and black hair and dark eyes, and Jacky and I would teach them to throw a baseball and how the different systems of a house worked and were maintained; we would do all we could to make them strong and confident and able to take care of themselves. "Dad didn't do so bad with us," I said aloud to Jacky, who gave me a curious look in return.

Mary Beth appeared in the door. "I'm going to bed," she said. Then to Jacky: "Don't forget you have to work in the morning."

That was my cue. "So do I."

The storm was picking up again. Rain ran in waves down the street. "Want an umbrella?" Mary Beth asked.

"I'll just wait a few minutes and run for it."

We all said good night, and they went in. Mary Beth clicked over the lock, and I heard her say something about the wedding to Jacky. Somewhere nearby, a transformer exploded with a boom, and the streetlights went dark. I wandered to the porch door with my beer, waiting for the rain to ease. A flash of lightning revealed the well-tended house across the street: baskets of flowers hung from decorative coach lamps on the stucco garage, swinging in the wind.

Somebody was hammering on the door. "Wake up!"

Panicked, I rolled out of bed. "Wake up!" The old man. He rattled the knob. My stomach rose, floated on fear right up into my throat. "Wake up!"

Then Mom was out there. "Are you insane? I want that key back—"

I shivered in the cold dark, fumbling for my clothes. What on earth was he up to? The red numbers of the radio alarm atop my dresser read 5:15.

"He wants off early, we start early."

"I thought you moved out of here."

I pulled on a pair of jeans, stiff with dirt and sweat from the work yesterday. When I opened the door, Mom and Dad were standing in opposite corners of the landing.

"Whose car's out front?" the old man said in a low voice.

"I'm right here, Joe." Samuel appeared in the doorway to Mom's room. He was wearing an old flannel bathrobe, too short and exposing his knobby knees and a lot of fish-white thigh. For a moment, I took it for a castoff of the old man's and thought there would be blood for sure, but my father had never owned a bathrobe. Samuel leaned in the door and rubbed his face. He looked about half-awake to the danger he was in.

"Fucking den of fornication," the old man muttered.

Mom's tongue flicked once over her lips. Dad's fists were balled, his upper body swaying slightly, forward and back. I opened my mouth but shut it again without saying a word. Then Samuel yawned.

At that, Dad turned and went downstairs. The light from the landing at the bottom threw his distorted shadow, massive and lumbering, on the wall at the head of the stairs. Samuel let out a breath and ran his palm over the mottled pink skin of his skull to the back of his neck. Mom went to him and rested her head against his chest.

"Excuse me," I said. I crossed the landing to use the bathroom. By the time I was done, Mom and Samuel had gone back into her room. I considered the closed door, amazed my father hadn't hit anyone.

When I came out of the house, the old man was sitting in his car sipping a cup of coffee, the car's engine idling against the early morning chill. The storm had brought the cold back. The horizon was red, the sky pale and clear, but the sun wasn't up yet. "Fuck," I muttered. I stopped at the driver's side, pointed at Dad, and made a circular motion with my finger.

He glared back. Then, when I didn't move, he rolled the window halfway down. "What?"

"I'll meet you there."

"The hell you talking about?"

"I'm taking my car."

"Get in."

I started walking down the sidewalk, shivering and rubbing my arms. The street had been parked up last night, and my Chevy was around the corner. Dad idled alongside me, hanging his head and elbow out the window. "Get in!"

"My car's right down here."

"Get. In." He swerved to avoid a parked car.

I ignored him.

"Goddamn, what's with you?" He followed me all the way to the car. He should have got Jacky to help him, he said, forgetting Jacky's eight-to-five job. Jacky was dependable, used to hard work. By the time I rounded the corner to the welcome sight of my red Cavalier, the old man was quoting Obadiah: "And the house of Jacob shall be a fire, and the house of *Joseph* a flame, and the house of Esau a *stubble*—."

Esau slammed his car door on the rest of it.

We spent the day painting the living and dining rooms. I've always hated painting: slow, messy work that demands care and concentration. But the old man and I had worked together often enough that we fell into a routine that erased our predawn argument. Dad did the edging freehand with his steady brush; I followed with a roller. He was subdued all morning, keeping the radio in the middle of the floor turned low, carrying on a quiet debate with the AM talk-radio shows. He made an early lunch from the stock of staples in the fridge, and brought me a glass of iced tea to go with it.

Everything was fine until three thirty, when I set down my roller and got a couple beers out of the fridge. I waved one at Dad, and we went out on the porch, hot from the sun through the window glass. "Have a beer," I said. "Talk to me before I go."

"You said four. You said you'd work till four."

You'd think I'd martyred him. "We've been at this since sunup."

"Goddamn it, leave all the cleanup to me."

I left my beer on the window ledge. There was no talking to the man. "You'll live," I said on my way out the door, satisfied to have had the last word, and forgetting how dangerous that could be.

28

Hank's new offices, near Mears Park in Lowertown, shared a re-
stored brick building with artists' studios and lofts. I got there a little
after five and stopped in front of a heavy oak door in a tiled hallway. The door glass was fogged, with *Ramirez & García, Attorneys at
Law* lettered on it. I took a deep breath, then hitched up my khakis
and let myself in.

Hank was sitting at the receptionist's desk, his back to the door,
rummaging in a file cabinet. When the door clicked to, he swung
around. Surprise, pain, and distaste washed over his face in succes-
sive waves. We hadn't seen each other since Betty's wedding, and
we'd ignored each other then. Hank pushed himself slowly to his
feet. His curly hair and sideburns had gone gray and were cropped
short. His face was heavier, eyes sunken over puffy cheeks, and
there was a scar on his forehead that I hadn't noticed before.

"Hi, Hank."

"Thought you were a priest." He scowled at my casual clothes.

"I'm on leave."

"A man ought to be true to himself."

The hell with it. I stepped forward and offered my hand. When
Hank took it, I said, "I'm sorry about Hank Junior."

Hank blinked, then nodded. "Thank you," he said. "I'll get
Betty." He disappeared down a hall.

I looked around the office. It was neater and richer than the
storefront on Concord Street. The furnishings and carpet were

quality but well worn, solid without being fancy. Along with the standard diplomas, two blue satin United Auto Workers Local jackets with Hank's and Betty's names embroidered across the shoulders were pinned to the wall. I traced the letters of Betty's name with my forefinger, then started skimming framed newspaper articles. There was a recent one about Hank bringing a sex-abuse suit against the Church on behalf of some Hispanic men, now in their twenties—a different diocese, thank God, no unhappy surprises about anyone I knew. In a box quote, Hank said: "I love my Church, but sometimes it doesn't look out for its own best interests." In the story itself, a woman shrink said: "These young men come from a very masculine culture. It makes it easier for them to talk about what happened when a male role model like Hank Ramirez tells them it's okay."

I heard the click of Betty's heels and turned as if I'd been caught looking at dirty pictures. She glanced at the clipping, then back to me. "Hank's probably right," I said, then took a good look at her. Her black hair shimmered in a low ponytail held with a silver comb. She had diamonds in her ears, dark red metallic lipstick, horn-rimmed glasses that were professional and unobtrusive. She wore a pinstriped suit with a white blouse, charcoal gray hose, matching heels.

I whistled. "I want you on my side."

She grinned, the familiar lopsided one. "Damn straight."

Hank came out of the back and put his hand on her shoulder. "You mind if I walk out with you?"

Betty reached up and patted his hand. "Long as you don't invite yourself along."

Out on the sidewalk, the three of us stumbled over small talk. Betty, walking between Hank and me, made most of the effort, and every so often I saw Hank frown at her. I wasn't paying attention to where we were, so I was startled when I looked up and recognized the building where Dad worked. Just then, Bob Nordyke and the old man came out the front doors and turned toward us, deep in conversation. I stopped short and glanced at Hank, who had a peculiar expression, as if a bad dream had just walked into his waking world. Then Bob Nordyke shouted "Jimmy Dressler!" and hurried forward. "Jimmy D., Jimmy D.," he kept saying, pumping my hand. Bob was a smallish, gray-haired black man with a nickname for everyone. He'd been my father's boss and buddy for a quarter-century now, and I figured anyone who wasn't a blood relation and could put up with Joe Dressler that long ought to be canonized. Saint Bob of the Maintenance Shop.

The old man was looking warily at Hank and Betty, but at their clothes, not their faces. He didn't remember Hank. And why should he?—Hank was in a suit, not umpire blues, and the old man had been in Lord-knows-how-many fights since that summer. I made introductions. My father extended an awkward hand, bobbed his head. "Pleased to meet you," he said.

Hank shook his hand without saying anything. It was clear he wanted to be elsewhere.

The old man turned to Betty. "Girl, you dress like a million bucks," he said, opening his arms. His maroon work shirt was spattered with paint. There was a confused moment while Betty dropped her proffered hand and stepped forward to peck Dad on the cheek. A crafty look came over his face. "You didn't tell me you were seeing a beautiful woman," he said to me. He waved a hand at Hank and Betty. "See, the boy here's helping me work on a house, being on the outs with the Church, and mumbo-jumbo not being a transferable skill. I got a little hot with him for clocking out early today. But I see he needed time to pretty himself up for such dandy company from south of the border."

The smile Hank had been working on disappeared. Bob Nordyke got interested in a parking meter. Betty said, "You've got your geography mixed up, Joe. We're from the West Side." She gave him a cold-eyed smile. The old man's mouth opened and closed—he'd taken a shot at Hank for the silent handshake and it had been returned by a woman, and one he was fond of at that. I took Betty by the elbow and steered her away. When Hank followed, I hurried them along, spurred by the helpless feeling of being a grown man caught in the frayed webs of childhood.

Behind us, the old man called, "Don't keep him out late, Betty. He's a priest, you know."

We walked a little ways before Betty said, "What was that about?"

On the other side of her, Hank shook his head. But the years-ago fight had nothing to do with it. "Well-dressed people piss him off," I said. "So do I, on a regular basis."

"Some men need to take the world down a notch to buck themselves up," Hank said.

"And when one of them's your father, you take the bad with the good," I said.

Hank got the point. He stopped in front of a parking ramp. "This is where I get off."

I glanced again at Hank's gray hair, the puffy cheeks that had the red tinge of high blood pressure to them, the scar I was sure came from one of my father's steel-toed work shoes. I felt an affection for him I wasn't about to let show.

After Hank left us, Betty said she'd had a rough day and suggested drinks at the Saint Paul Grill. I started to walk, but she waved down a cab. "Heels," she said. "I'll pay."

"My car's just a couple of blocks that way," I said, annoyed by her assumption that a priest had no money, and even more that she was right.

"The cab's right here," Betty said. In the backseat, she slipped me a bill to pay the driver. I frowned, but we'd hardly settled in before the cabbie let us off in front of the Saint Paul Hotel.

The bar was on the ground floor, a business place, glittering mirrors and metal, crowded with well-dressed men and women, the air thick with deals and cologne. Betty stopped to shake hands with a couple of men, then found us a table for two along a wall covered with framed black-and-white photographs of famous Saint Paulites. I slid in beneath a Civil-War-era portrait of the lantern-jawed young John Ireland. Archbishop, politician, businessman, temperance leader. It appeared I couldn't escape episcopal oversight, even in a bar. Betty reached into her purse and came out with a Marlboro, which she twiddled between her fingers and then left unlit in an ashtray. Beneath the veneer of her makeup, she looked tired. When our drinks came, I handed the waitress my one credit card and told her to run a tab. "You don't have to do that," Betty said, crossing her legs with a slight scrape of nylon under the table.

"I can buy you a drink," I said. "Besides, that card's issued by a mission society. Little bit of each purchase goes to help build clinics and schools in Central America." George Martin had been put onto the card by a church-supplies salesman and talked everyone at the poker table into applying. He was quite taken with the idea of being able to indulge oneself and do good at the same time.

"The white fathers at work," Betty said dryly. She was in a bit of a mood. I watched business people mingle and wished I'd worn my priest's suit, which would have stood out but at least held its own. Betty belonged here. All the women were alike, put together in silk, nylon, and worsted wool, subdued eyeliner and lipstick, hairspray and expensive perfume. I wanted to unsettle Betty somehow.

I asked about her separation. Betty chewed the earpiece of her glasses, then admitted that her mother was frantic about it and still hopeful her marriage might be saved.

"Can it?" I said.

She gave me a pained smile. "What about you?" she asked. "You're on leave?"

Trying to distract Betty from the hurt I'd brought up, I told her about my own: Saint John's and the Benedictines, and Tim Harley and Diana. Betty's eyes flickered with amusement. "Your parish for a kiss?" she said, shaking her head. "You'd think she was Helen of Troy."

"It wasn't the kiss," I said, fiddling with my pinky ring. "I gave scandal. It's a priest thing. I'm not sure you'd understand."

"Sure I would," Betty said. "You wouldn't believe how the right detail can tip a jury." She caught me looking around the bar. "You don't like it here. Why don't you just admit that well-dressed people make you nervous? You're no different from your dad." She smiled, but there was an edge to the teasing.

"Do you ever let up?" I said.

"I'm just saying—" Betty began, then stopped herself. "You're right," she said. "I was in court today. Ethan and I used to call this The Zone—I'd come home still wound up and bite his head off over some little thing."

"And you wonder why you're getting divorced," I said, then grimaced.

But Betty laughed. "Touché," she said. She leaned on the table, clasping her elbows in her hands, and shrugged her head down into her shoulders, eyeing me from under her hair. "Why don't we get the hell out of here? Let me make you dinner."

I hesitated.

"I dare you. Women feed priests all the time." She mocked me, holding back a grin.

"Truer than you'd know. But you're asking in front of my arch-bishop." I jerked a thumb at the portrait that grinned over my right shoulder like an impish guardian angel.

"Oh, Ireland," Betty said. "Tell you what: I'm tired. Let's pick up food at El Mercado. We can eat there if you want. But the chairs are more comfortable at my place."

We caught a cab back to Mears Park, splitting the fare, then took our separate cars to El Burrito Mercado in the West Side's Mexican shopping district. Betty ordered several dishes in the cafeteria line while I counted the candy-bright *piñatas* hanging over the grocery aisles. Betty bantered with the counter help in quick Spanish, and when I tried to pay, shook her head. "This is lunch for the rest of the week. You can carry it."

Out on Concord Street, she pointed out new and old businesses, brightly painted in oranges and greens and pinks, and talked about the work Hank had done to help bring back a street that was pretty shabby a decade before. Betty was different here than she'd been in the bar—at ease in both places, but at home here.

"Your uncle's got his hands in everything," I said.

"He could win a seat on the city council," she said. "But he says you can get more done if you're not a politician."

"That why you're labor lawyers?"

"Two generations ago, our families were picking beets in the Red River Valley. A generation of union jobs later, and we're college graduates. Figure it out."

I mentioned Hank's "five niggers" comment at her quinceañera dance, which I'd never known how to bring up when we were younger. "It always surprised me he said that."

"Hank grew up in a shack in Swede Hollow, until the health department razed the place," Betty said. "A few drinks and he's a Mexican redneck."

"What's it like working with him?" I asked. We stopped in front of a Western-wear store, and I studied a cowboy hat on a black-haired, brown-skinned mannequin.

"You might look good in that," Betty said. Her reflection frowned beside mine. "I owe him everything. It's not ideal."

"Really."

She went on, her voice tight. "When push comes to shove in a tough case, he tries to treat me like the sweet little Mexican girl he sponsored for her quinceañera."

"Aw, c'mon. You never were that sweet."

Betty laughed. "Yeah," she said.

Betty's apartment was on the top floor of a brownstone up on the bluffs of the West Side. A skylight lit the stairwell in patchwork light. Some of the original glass had been replaced, making a hodgepodge of green and yellow and clear panes. I stepped out of my shoes and left them with the others lined up by the radiator at the top of the stairs, noticing a small pair of blue Keds sneakers with a hole in the toe.

Betty led me in and back to the kitchen. It was a typical brownstone two-bedroom, all the rooms in a line, a sunroom on the front, then living and dining rooms, and a long hall with the two bedrooms and bath, and the kitchen in the back. Betty had a lot of rugs down, hanging plants, throw pillows in warm colors. Onions and tomatoes on the kitchen counters, a braid of garlic over the sink. She nodded at the bedrooms on the way past, "This is my room, and Peter's is in the back, here." That door was shut, but hers was open and I caught a glimpse of a big low bed, a chest at its foot, piled with blankets and afghans and more throw pillows. There was a low double-wide chest of drawers with a mirror above it on the far wall. I was surprised at how settled the place looked, and wondered how long she and Ethan had been apart. But Betty had money, and I suspected she liked to live comfortably.

"So tell me more about being a priest," she said from the kitchen.

"What else do you want to know?" I said. In the kitchen, I helped her put the extra carryout away in the fridge. "There's Ash Wednesday, a little bit of ashes dribbling onto a pretty girl's nose. That the kind of detail you're looking for?"

"That's a good one," she said. "The girls are still pretty. Tell me more."

"My grandparents used to invite the parish priests and nuns to their cocktail parties. Granddad took a lot of pride in getting the nuns tipsy," I said. "But everyone had fun. It struck me as a full life. Now that I've lived it, it still does, but the world's changed: not as many priests, and we don't play as big a part in the life of the community. Mainly because there's not as much community, I suppose. If I could change anything, it'd be that." I caught myself preaching and waved a hand at the air. "Enough about priests. I'm supposed to be taking a break."

Betty turned from the counter where she'd been arranging re-fried beans and rice and tostadas on dishes. "No, really," she said. "I like hearing about your life."

"Well, it's a bit painful right now," I said. "You laughed about my parish for a kiss, but a priest's married to the Church. Vows, the whole bit. Right now, my wife's kicked me out, and I'm living at my mom's house because she—the Church—is also my employer. It's not just losing a job or having a relationship on the rocks. It's both at once." Betty had turned on the oven to warm our dinners, and I took the plates from her and slid them onto the oven rack.

"I don't feel very competent out in the world," I said. "Hell, I don't even know how to find an apartment. I've lived in church housing since seminary. My friend Mick says the Church has two thousand years of experience at control and the way she treats her priests—celibacy, low pay, rectory living—is meant to keep us stunted." I stopped. Betty was looking at me with a mixture of sympathy and embarrassment. "Enough of that," I said. "I'm doing okay. Even have a summer job working on a house with the old man."

"That's gotta be interesting," Betty said.

"*It's not just a job, it's an adventure.*"

She laughed and walked past me to her room, pulling the silver comb out of her hair as she went. "Be with you in a minute," she said. "You can pour us beers." The door closed softly behind her. I found two bottles of Dos Equis in the refrigerator.

Betty came out of her room changed into jeans and a flannel shirt, then padded barefoot up and down the hall, getting the food on the table. We ate in the dining room, tall burgundy candles flickering between us, amber beer in pilsner glasses.

"So, how does a priest live?" Betty said, raising her glass. The candlelight flickered in the beer and off the leaded-glass panes of the built-in buffet behind her. We were back to priests again. Given the chance, everyone I knew asked a million questions about life as a priest, as if they couldn't get their minds around our continued presence in the modern world.

"You've been in rectories. There's an emptiness to them, like any single man's place. Left to ourselves, we men don't tend to make things very cozy." I draped an arm over the back of my chair and glanced around the apartment. It was full of colorful wall hangings and Southwestern rugs somehow set successfully against a lot of dark, post-Victorian woodwork and wallpaper. "This is cozy," I said. "You have a decorator?"

"I couldn't have pulled this off on my own."

"It doesn't look like a lawyer's apartment."

"For that, you have to go to our—to Ethan's house. But this isn't real Mexican, either. It's a professional rendition, earthy and restrained, with just a note of kitsch."

I chuckled. "How do your folks feel about that?" I asked. "You dropping a bundle on looking Mexican?"

Betty bit her lip, trying to decide how to take that. "It had to be just right," she said. "Because I do occasionally entertain here." She went down the hall to the kitchen and came back with coffee and squares of cinnamon-flavored Mexican chocolate.

"Ethan's getting the house?" I asked when she sat down again.

She spilled a little coffee in her saucer and sopped it up with a napkin. "I have a feeling Ethan's getting everything," she said. Her voice was hard. "I had an affair with a judge. It was quite a scandal—a fifty-something WASP and the hot young Chicana activist. Ethan's going to win the custody fight, and he's already hooked up with a gushy little legal aide who wears bunny sweaters at Easter."

I waited for her to explain the affair, the extenuating circumstances, how she'd be unjustly served. Instead she blew on her coffee, holding the cup between her hands. Watching her cheeks hollow, her eyes downcast to the coffee, I began to think there might not be an explanation.

After dessert, I went into the living room to look at framed pictures of Jesus and Mary with the sacred hearts on their chests—Betty's parents and grandmother had owned identical sets, and I guessed these had been *Abuelita*'s. Betty had a couple of faux oil lamps lit on the end tables by the couch, and in the low light Jesus's upturned face seemed flushed. "You still think of your soul in your chest like this?"

Betty had followed me, and she was quiet a moment, then laughed. "I couldn't think of what you meant," she said. "I don't know, honestly. What about you?"

I stepped to a window. We had lingered over drinks and dinner and dessert. It was getting late, and outside the streetlights were coming on in the cold dusk. She'd earned everything she wanted and now was about to lose a good deal of it. "Are you okay?" I asked.

"That's kind of a big question," Betty said.

"Isn't this the time for Big Questions?" I said. "A few beers, nightfall—"

Betty went and sat on the couch and patted the cushion beside her. "I'm tired of talking," she said. "Sometimes that's all adults do. Go over the same old bullshit until there's no life left in anything." She sounded tired, and I turned from the window to sit with her.

Her hands were palm up in her lap, wrists white at the open cuffs of her shirt, a slim gold watchband glittering on the left. Her feet, crossed at the ankles, were small and brown, and her toenails were painted metallic red. I came to her as she'd asked, but instead of sitting, I knelt before the couch and took her face between my hands and kissed her. I drew away, but Betty reached for me with a look of such open need that I bent my face back to hers. We kissed for a long, slow time.

29

AT THREE IN THE MORNING, I WOKE in Betty's bedroom, in darkness that resolved into dim oblongs of light where the window shades were drawn. I was spooned around Betty, one hand cupped over her breast. I lay there a while, then slipped from the bed to use the bathroom. After that, I got a glass of water and padded down the hall naked to the living room, where I found my boxers and pulled them on.

I sat on the sofa among the rest of our discarded clothes, wrapping myself in a striped afghan. It was chill out here; shadows of tree branches cast by the streetlight broke the solid shapes of the furniture. My hand lighted on Betty's checked flannel shirt, and I brought it to my face to breathe her scent. The lace camisole she'd worn underneath was caught in one sleeve. At Diana's, after a single kiss, I'd had the urge to flee. But now I'd made love to Betty in her home, and the urge I felt was to confront myself. I was a priest and also, at least this night, Betty García's lover.

It was clear that I had a problem. It was not the Church's problem, and when part of me insisted that it was, that what the Church asked of her priests was unfair, another part answered, in the old man's voice, *Whoever told you the world was fair?*

There was a footstep in the dining room, a tentative voice. "Where are you?"

"Here," I said, and Betty came to me.

. . .

I woke again at five, the time I got out of bed in Pretty Prairie to say my morning office. Betty was curled against my back, one arm flung over my hip. I lay and listened to her breathing, felt the soft whisper of it against the skin between my shoulder blades. In Pretty Prairie, in the still hour between morning prayers and early Mass, I could get more work done than at any other time of the day. By the time I finished Mass, Mrs. Gunther would have my breakfast on the table, and then the phone calls and meetings began. Steve Sullivan might stop to ask if I'd coach a Little League team again in the coming summer. Out the window, Ted Burkholder, the sacristan, would have stayed after Mass to talk with Nels the groundskeeper about a line of saplings we'd planted along the church frontage. I'd watch them move from one slender tree to the next, gesturing, pausing to scrape a thumbnail over a leaf. Then the phone would ring and it would be a salesman of liturgical banners.

I became aware again of Betty's breath, the subtle movements of her forearm along my thigh as her rib cage rose and fell. I touched my hand to hers as if to touch the reality of what we'd done last night. At my touch, Betty stirred and rolled away. When her alarm went off, I listened to her get up and go to the closet, hurry to the kitchen to put coffee on, move from there to the shower. Once the shower started, I went to the living room and dressed. I sat a long time after I'd tied my shoes. It wasn't until the shower stopped that I thought to get up to check on the coffee.

The coffeemaker was done, and I poured Betty a cup, remembered that she liked it black, and brought it to the bathroom. The door was open, and Betty stood in front of the mirror wrapped in an oversized white terry-cloth robe, combing out her shoulder-length hair. "Thanks," she said. "I've never been a morning person." Her voice was tight.

She sipped her coffee and regarded me in the mirror. Neither of us knew what to say. Voices came from an air vent at Betty's feet. "Do you think we'll be millionaires?" a woman said eagerly. Then a man's voice, serious: "I hope so." This exchange was followed by bathroom sounds: someone gargling, the whirr of a hair dryer.

Betty pointed at the vent. "Just out of law school," she whispered. "The other half of the building's full of jazz musicians. I want to know what they talk about in the john."

"Gigs," I said, glad for the small talk. "Guitar strings. The manager's share, and whether he's worth it."

"Life's never as romantic as we think, is it?" Betty said. She turned and put a hand on the bathroom door. "I need to finish getting ready."

I went to get my own coffee. From the kitchen window at the back of the flat, I gazed over the roofs of houses lower on the bluffs to the sun striking downtown Saint Paul. I was sipping coffee at the sink and trying to pick out the building the old man worked in when Betty came in. She was dressed and made up.

"Nice view," I said.

She stretched up on her tiptoes beside me—the window was high for her, above the sink. "I guess there is one." She rustled open a brown paper bag and handed me a round pastry. "I don't usually bother with breakfast, but here's some Mexican sweet bread from when I had Peter for the weekend. Your old favorite."

I took it from her. Sweet bread is dry and chewy, and the sugar topping didn't appeal like it did when I was a teenage boy. "Do you ever think of what our child might have become?" I said. It slipped out, in the way things you want to say often do.

Betty turned her back on me and carefully set her coffee mug on the blue tile counter under the glass-fronted cupboards, then rearranged brushed-aluminum flour and sugar containers. Beside them was a framed photo of Peter, a smooth-faced, dark-eyed five-year-old in a Batman shirt. His father was out of focus behind him.

Betty picked up the photo. "Do you know that Peter really believes people think he's Batman when he wears this shirt," she said. Her hair hid her face, but I could hear the sadness in her voice.

"I should have gone with you to Chicago," I said.

She set down the photo, but left her hand resting lightly on the top of the frame. "That was so long ago." Then she stepped out of the kitchen and opened the door to Peter's room, inviting me to stand beside her.

It was bright in there, lit by the morning sun. The room was furnished with an aqua chest of drawers and a small bed against the far wall, under Vikings and Timberwolves posters. In a framed poster taken from the cover of a comic book, Batman leaped toward the window, fist out, jaw set. There was an electric racetrack on the floor, a red Dodge Charger and a blue Corvette at the starting line. A toy box at the foot of the bed. Stuffed animals that had belonged to Betty on the bedspread. One red-and-yellow plastic pickup truck upside down beneath a window. Betty crossed the room in quick, neat strides, picked up the truck, and dropped it into the toy box. She faced me, her hands brushing at the front of her skirt. She looked small under the room's high ceiling. "I've made a lifetime's worth of mistakes in ten years. And I think I'm in the process of making the worst one yet."

"If you lose, do you plan another custody fight?" I asked.

"I'm going to get the shit kicked out of me in this one," she said. There was a moment of unguarded pain on her face, then she composed herself. "I'd keep fighting if I thought it would do any good. But I'm an adulteress, and there's no point." The twist to her mouth suggested a lawyer's frank assessment.

"There's not a human being I know couldn't use a good dose of grace," I said.

Betty crossed the room and kissed me on the mouth. "Thanks, Dressler."

She pushed back and looked up at me. The maple floor creaked underfoot. "What happened last night—I didn't plan it." Her face was puzzled, not unkind. "It's important to me that you know that."

"No strings, huh?" I said.

Betty caught her lip in her teeth. "I know the cost of broken vows," she said. "I don't want to be party to someone else breaking theirs."

"I make my own choices," I said.

"Sure." Betty looked exhausted again.

"Will I see you at the wedding?" I could see where she might not want to be there—the divorce, and now last night.

"Before," Betty said. "The Donovans invited Hank and me to the lake." There was a wedding picnic there Friday. We stepped out of her son's room, and Betty closed the door. She took a deep breath, then said as if she hadn't made love with a priest the night before: "What's your day look like?"

I followed her lead. "Working on the house with Dad. He's going to be pissed I wasn't there at six."

"I see." Betty went into the living room and picked up her purse, and I followed her out. We said good-bye without touching at the curb.

I drove home over the new High Bridge, the sleek sweep of concrete that had replaced the rickety iron bridge of my childhood. For just a moment, I found myself longing for the vertiginous feeling of the old High Bridge, the steep views of the Mississippi that had so frightened me as a child. But then I saw the waking city spread before me: the Cathedral solidly at the crest of its hill overlooking downtown, and beyond it the Capitol like a model in a diorama.

Mom was on her way out the door for work when I got home. "Where have you been? Your father was looking for you this morning." Then she took in last night's clothes and couldn't change the subject quickly enough. "There's pancake batter in the fridge. Pick up some half-and-half at the store if you get a chance. And tell your father I still want that damn key."

She left in a hurry, and I busied my hands (*A little late about that, aren't you, boy?* Father Phil said dryly in my mind) with the details of the day—made pancakes with sausage and eggs, changed into work clothes—forcing myself to think only of the task at hand. It was the same discipline I practiced with the Liturgy of the Hours, concentrating on a set task and leaving my mind open to God. But God wasn't talking to me this morning.

When I got to the house in Frogtown about nine, the front door was open and the whine of an edger came from the dining room. Dad had started the floors. Five cuts through the living and dining rooms, beginning at 16 grit and moving up to 80. By the looks of the floor, he'd finished two passes with the drum sander already. He was wearing a dust mask, moving along the far wall of the dining room with the edger, unaware of me. I stopped to watch and instantly regretted not being there on time. Edging means hunching over a machine about as compact and heavy as a couple of bowling balls in a cylinder, elbows on your knees, fighting torque. It's young man's work, hell on the knees and back.

As I was thinking this, Dad tilted the edger back and killed the power. He used the window frame to pull himself upright and reached back to rub his spine. When he saw me, he yanked off the dust mask. "Where the hell you been?"

"Out."

"That's just fine." He worked a foam earplug from one ear. "I been at this shit since dawn while the priest makes the beast with two backs."

"Stick it up your ass," I said. I went to the covered radiator in the corner of the living room where there were dust masks and a box of earplugs. I compressed an earplug, twisted it into my right ear. The old man followed me, and I held up the second earplug in his face. "Good idea. Don't have to listen to the whining."

It took him a second to catch that. When he did, he reached out and gave me a little two-fingered shove to the chest. I stood my ground. When you grow up around a man like my father, you have a well-honed instinct for when he means business. This morning, he looked for all the world like a child trying to start a fight. "Gaahhh," he said at last, with a dismissive wave of his hand. "Run the edger."

"Good morning to you, too," I said. I snapped a dust mask over my nose and chin. "What are we on, 20?" I picked up a stack of sandpaper disks.

"It's ready to go," Dad said, wheeling the drum sander past me and into the dining room.

I got to work. The old man had marked up the floor with a pencil before starting: wide sweeps across most of it, a tighter pattern along the walls. After a pass with the drum sander, the pencil marks that hadn't been sanded away showed what needed to be edged. I did the living room, then worked the kinks out of my back and shoulders while I watched the old man run the drum in the dining room. He ran the sander forward from the middle of the room to the back wall, rocked the drum up so as not to gouge the floor, then backed away from the wall, kicking the power cord out of the way with a practiced sweep of his right foot on each backward step.

A little after eleven, I turned off the edger to find the drum standing idle in the middle of the living room and the old man's car gone. I took a couple of aspirin for my back, then made a bologna sandwich and ate out front, sitting in the cool breeze after the heat and dust of the house. Again, each time my mind wandered, I brought it back to the work at hand. We'd finished two more cuts;

the old varnish was gone from the floor and with each cut the exposed wood was more fresh and new. I washed down the last bite of my sandwich with milk, waved at the Hmong woman on the steps next door, who was studying a textbook while her kids played in the chain-link-fenced front yard, and went back to the edging.

By late afternoon, the floors were perfect, the red oak sanded smooth, the bare boards white with a delicate pinkish tinge. I crouched to run a hand over the wood, satin soft to the touch. It made me want to walk barefoot on it. My father came in from dumping a vacuum bag of sawdust out back. "After we take back the sanders, I've gotta run down to Seven Corners to have a look at power tools," he said. "They're on sale. If you wanna come along, I'll buy pizza."

"Sure," I said. "That the same sale they had on ten years ago?"

"Yup. Always worked with your mom." He deepened his voice: "'Gotta buy some tools at Seven Corners, Maura; they're on sale.'" While he talked, he took the handle off the drum sander, then picked up the base, umpteen pounds of steel and motor and drum that I could lift only with considerable effort. I held the door and watched him carry it across the yard, then tuck it under one arm while he fished for his keys and opened the trunk.

We returned the sanders, then ate at Cossetta's, taking an upstairs table that looked down on Seven Corners Hardware and the orange neon *Milwaukee Tools* sign in one window. The old man didn't mention my absence in the morning again, except to say, "Are you all right?" Then he tilted his head back to finish his beer so I didn't have to answer, and we went back to whatever it was we were talking about. At the hardware store, Dad bought a saber saw he'd had his eye on and put it in the trunk where it joined battery cables, flattened beer cans, and an open cardboard box that appeared to contain a set of dishes. He'd already moved a canvas bag full of softball equipment to the backseat to make room for the sanders. We left Seven Corners, climbed the steep hill to Summit, and cruised past mansions cut up into apartments. Dad hummed along to Roy Orbison's "Pretty Woman." At Lexington, he pulled to the curb in front of Saint Luke's and got out. I rolled down my window. "Where you going?"

"Light a candle for your grandfather." He crossed the sidewalk and went up the steps to the doors of the church. He tried a couple before finding an open one. After sitting in the car a few minutes, I went in, meaning to say an Act of Contrition. But the old man was kneeling at the bank of votive candles, and I came quietly up the side aisle and stopped to watch him, leaning against the end of a pew with my arms folded. Dad prayed with his eyes shut, forehead against his clasped hands. After a while he crossed himself and pushed stiffly to his feet. When he saw me, he started, then glared. "The fuck you want?"

When I got home, there was a message from Jacky reminding me of his bachelor party, just in case I'd changed my mind about going. I erased it, then remembered I was due in half an hour to see Father Phil and check that all was in order for the wedding. I took a hurried shower and dressed in my priest's suit, feeling like a man working his wedding ring back over his knuckles after an assignation with a lover. Before I left for Father Phil's, I knelt at my bedside and said a prayer for Mick, and the Act of Contrition that I hadn't managed all day. *O my God, I am heartily sorry for having offended Thee, and I detest all my sins because I dread the loss of Heaven and the pains of Hell, but most of all because they offend Thee, my God, Who art all-good and deserving of all my love. I firmly resolve with the help of Thy grace, to confess my sins, to do penance and to amend my life.* Then I glanced at the clock and crossed myself and rushed over to Phil's.

He was at his basement workbench, tying flies. When Cruikshank, the associate, sent me downstairs, my first glimpse was of Phil's ruddy bald head with the fringe of white hair above his rounded back. The hair was whiter and the back rounder, but he hadn't changed much since our ice-fishing days; he had slipped into the timeless old age of so many priests.

He turned at the sound of my tread on the steps, peered up against the light, then smiled and stood to shuffle toward me. "James, James, James."

As we shook hands, a frown replaced his smile. "But you're leaving," he said, going back to perch on the stool in front of his workbench. He gestured at a worn armchair beside it, placed so Phil could counsel without leaving his favorite spot.

I sat, and Phil adjusted the extensor lamp so it wasn't in my eyes. "I'm just taking a year off," I said. "Teaching for the Benedictines." I picked up one of Phil's unfamiliar fly-tying tools from the hardware scattered on the workbench and studied it.

"You don't work things out by running away from God's call." Phil's words jolted me, but his attention was elsewhere, his head tilted at the end of a nylon line he was holding up to a hook. "Why don't you mix us a drink?"

Part of the basement was finished into a rec room with a TV and a wet bar. There was a bottle of Vat 69 Gold sitting on the bar, and I made Scotch and waters. When I finished, Phil had moved to the sofa with the TV on, and I heard the plaintive theme song of *The Sportsman's Friend* with Harold Ensley: "Gone fishin', instead of just a-wishin'."

"So what's with this 'year off' crap?" Phil said.

"There was trouble with a woman," I said. *There is trouble with a woman,* I thought.

Phil didn't answer. On TV, Harold Ensley introduced Ted Williams, his fishing partner for the day, and then an ad for sonar came on. Phil hit the mute button. "Damn rerun," he said. He sipped his drink. "Need to talk?"

I shook my head. Where would I begin?

When I didn't say anything, Phil turned the sound back on. Harold Ensley and Ted Williams were motoring out onto an Arkansas lake. Ensley was explaining which lures the water conditions and crappie called for. For the next hour we watched Harold and Ted talk fishing and baseball. Phil didn't bring up my year off again, but when I mentioned borrowing the old man's season tickets for a Saints game, he said, "When I was a fresh-minted curate, Joe Dressler was the hardest working altar boy anyone ever saw. Jack Quinlan nearly had him recruited for Nazareth Hall, but then he hit puberty. We lose a lot of boys that way."

"I never heard that," I said.

"There were problems at home," Phil said. "Not that I blame Otto and Alexandra. They did the best they knew, with Joe and each other." He seemed to think he'd said too much, and got up to freshen his drink. "I've assigned you a couple good servers for Saturday," he said from behind me.

When we had everything set for the wedding, Phil walked me up to the back door. "Sacristan'll be at the church. I'm going to Duluth this weekend, got a charter."

"I thought you'd be around."

"Nah. Those Donovans are troublemakers."

"I hadn't thought of them that way." Jacky was marrying into a family of Catholic social activists. Mary Beth's aunts included a liberation theologian, an ex-nun married to a prominent Saint Paul civil rights lawyer, and a woman who'd formed a gay and lesbian support group in the Basilica parish in Minneapolis.

Phil patted my back. "I'm joking. I like arguing with the Donovan girls. But I've had this fishing trip lined up for a long time." Then he pulled me to him and kissed me on the cheek. "I love you, boy," he said, "like a son. Call me this summer."

30

FROM PHIL'S, I DROVE TO THE NURSING HOME. It was dark by the time I got there, and I leaned against the hood of my car for a few minutes, listening to the crickets. The air smelled of lilacs. There were only a few lights on in the nursing home, and from the outside it looked cozy, the long, low building put to bed for the night. I went in. A young woman aide, college aged, glanced up, did a double take at the collar. "Is there something—?"

"My grandfather's a resident here," I said. "I wondered if I could see him. Otto Dressler."

"He's asleep," she said. "We can't wake him. He yells at night." She stopped, as if she'd divulged a secret.

"I know," I said. "I don't need to wake him. I just want to sit with him."

"It's not usual." She looked doubtful.

I waited, and finally she nodded. "Do you need me to—"

"I know the way." I walked as softly as I could down the hall. The rooms were dark but not quiet: raspy snores and coughs and mutterings filled the air, along with the beepings of machines.

Otto was asleep. I settled into my customary spot in his wheelchair. Granddad slept on his back, the head of the bed elevated to keep fluid from collecting in his lungs. The oxygen machine hummed, and I wondered how it was that old people didn't dislodge their breathing tubes at night. Maybe they didn't move much.

A light in the courtyard lit the room faintly. I could see the square white shapes of the birthday cards on the bulletin board, the jumble of personal belongings and nursing-home paraphernalia on the bedside table, even the stubble of whiskers on Otto's cheeks. Mouth open, he snored roughly, snorting and wheezing. At times his breathing quieted and seemed to stop, almost, then he'd draw in a breath and start snoring again. After a while, I stood and looked out the window into the courtyard. I'd never seen one of the residents out there, only staff on smoke breaks.

I turned back to Otto. His eyes glinted in the dim light. He was awake, and his gaze followed me as I bent over the bed.

"Otto?" I tried in a low voice, but he didn't answer.

"Otto?" I laid a hand on his forearm. Still no answer, but this time his other hand clamped over mine. Startled, I tried to draw away, but he clung to me as if hanging on to more than a hand. I reached back with my free hand and found the wheelchair, pulled it under me, and sat. Otto's grip tightened. I stroked the back of his hand. His eyes were wide open now. "Granddad?"

His grip relaxed, and I lifted his hand and set it on his belly. He kept watching me silently. "Do you want to say the Rosary, Granddad?" I said, picking up Gram's rosary from the bedside table and arranging it in my hands. Granddad yanked the rosary from me and clutched it to his chest.

"Help!" he yelled. "Help me!" He picked up the call button and fumbled with it, then started punching it repeatedly.

"Shit," I muttered.

"Help! Help!"

I stilled an impulse to put a hand over his mouth. "Quiet, Granddad!" I hissed.

An older nurse rushed into the room, then turned on the young aide from the desk. "What's he doing here?"

"I didn't do anything," I said, sounding guilty as hell. "He just woke up."

"It's his grandfather," the aide said. "He wanted to sit with him."

"You never let anyone in a sleeping patient's room," the nurse said. Then to me: "And you should have known better, Father."

"Help!" Otto yelled.

"Shit," I said.

"We can't have them stirred up," the nurse said. The aide moved behind her, bending over Granddad and trying to talk with him.

"There's nothing I can do?" I said.

"You should leave."

I bent to Granddad, kissed him quickly on the forehead, and smoothed back a wisp of white hair. He stopped yelling as suddenly as he'd begun and glared at the three of us as if he was realizing for the first time that we were in the room. "What the hell's going on?" he said.

"Nothing, Boss," I said. "We were just leaving."

The nurse looked at me curiously, but the words satisfied Otto. "Fine," he said. "A man can't get a good night's sleep around here."

Outside the room, I waited for the nurse. "Don't blame the girl," I said. "It's hard to say no to a priest."

She gave me a disgusted look. "Every one of you thinks you walk on water."

"You're right," I said. "Good night."

"And that," the nurse was saying to the aide as the front doors closed behind me, "is why you never break the rules."

31

I HADN'T BEEN TO THE DONOVANS' HOUSE on Forest Lake in fifteen years. The drive was marked by a weathered board carved with *Donovan's Back-acher* and nailed to the mailbox post, and as soon as I saw it, I remembered the sign, its spot on the county highway, and the gravel drive hidden in the trees.

The Dresslers and Donovans had a long history. My grandfather and Gerard Donovan were childhood friends, but the families lost touch over the years. Alexandra unjustly blamed Otto's Irish buddies for his drinking, and on their part there had probably been some resentment of her settling influence on the golden-haired rogue of their youth—again unjust, because the war changed him as much as marriage did. And then there were children. Gerry fathered a houseful of vibrant girls, while my grandfather's son was, well, my father. Sometime in the late 1950s, Joe, a sullen, curly-headed boy with cigarettes in his dungaree jacket, would have stopped coming to the lake. By the mid-1960s, when Donovan gatherings were full of news of the girls' successes at a string of private colleges, promising engagements, and progressing careers, Otto could report that his son had settled into a maintenance job that would allow him to support his young wife and three children. There had been a brief resurgence in the 1970s, when Otto could trot out his growing grandchildren, but the old man begrudged our trips to the lake, and we'd never fully taken to that life of sun, swimming, and waterskiing.

Beyond the belt of trees that sheltered the property from the county highway, there was a wide garage partly shaded by a huge and decrepit apple tree. I parked in the ditch along the drive, which was already crowded with cars. Mary Beth had family arriving from across the country: New Mexico, Arizona, and Brownsville, Texas; Washington state and Washington, D.C.; Madison and Sheboygan. Among the rental cars and out-of-state plates, I spotted Betty's Mustang and the old man's Buick. Mom wouldn't be here; she said she couldn't get off work.

I walked down the steps from the garage and past a clothesline hung with swimsuits, to the screened-in porch at one end of the house. Inside there was a picnic table filled with midwestern bounty—potato salad, cold cuts, soft white rolls. There were coolers along the walls, and open bottles of Chablis and white zinfandel on a TV tray. The cushioned porch chairs were full of old people I didn't recognize. I was in summer uniform—a short-sleeved black shirt with my black slacks and shoes—and they perked up when I came in.

"Aren't you Otto Dressler's son?" asked a woman in a red-and-white sweater set, with the peculiar aggressiveness of the old. "I'm Ruth Wilmar, Gerard Donovan's sister. I've been a widow thirty years now."

"His grandson," I said, helping myself to a Styrofoam cup and coffee from a percolator.

"This is Otto Dressler's son," she said to a white-haired man beside her. "Sit down, Father."

I excused myself and ducked into the kitchen to say hi to Mary Clare Donovan, Gerard's widow. Clare was a handsome, white-haired woman, still vigorous in her early eighties, her skin tanned a light mahogany from years of living at the lake. She leaned against the counter, near a small maple kitchen table crowded with fruit pies. School portraits of grandchildren and great-grandchildren lined the window ledge. I squeezed her shoulder. "How's your grandfather?" she asked right away. "Not good," I said, and we talked about him before I went to join the party.

Outside, there was a lawn at the lip of a steep hill down to the lake, another flat down there, and then the boat dock. I spotted Hank standing at the end of the dock, talking to a little boy with a fishing rod. The speedboat was out, two of Mary Beth's willowy aunts were rigging a sailboat, and on the other side of the dock, an uncle cranked the catamaran down into the water. The upper lawn was full with people eating and visiting at a picnic table and in lawn chairs, Jacky was off on the side lawn playing Frisbee with a couple of Mary Beth's teenage cousins, and William Reilly, as lean and tanned in his eighties as his sister Clare, stood nearby, eyes shaded by a visor, demonstrating a golf swing for my father.

I went down to the dock, where Hank stood in linen slacks and a polo shirt. At his feet, the little boy sat with his chin on his knee, watching sunfish circle his bait in the clear water. He squinted up at me, pulling the brim of a Twins cap down against the sun. "Hi, Father," he said.

"What's your name?" I said.

"Willy."

"Well, Willy, I think you're about to get a bite."

"Taking the day off?" I said to Hank. It was Friday around noon, the lake empty except for the Donovan speedboat. At our feet, there was a brief splashing as Willy played a bluegill enthusiastically, then ran from the dock to show off his catch.

Hank had on Wayfarers, and the tan knit collar of his shirt showed against his dark skin. "Hard to clear the schedule, but we managed. Glad it didn't rain after all that. I see you're back in uniform."

The white square at my neck wavered in the black lenses of Hank's sunglasses. "Showing the flag." I wondered whether Betty had said anything about our evening. "Where's your niece?"

He pointed out at the lake. The Donovans' speedboat, a husband in a droopy-brimmed hat at the helm and one of the aunts half-turned in the seat beside him to keep an eye on the skiers, chopped over the surface. Behind, crisscrossing the wake, Betty and Mary Beth skied in black one-piece racing suits, hair flying, the lines of their bodies supple against wind and water. As I watched, Betty turned her head to shout something at Mary Beth and her hair blew across her face.

"She's beautiful," I said unconsciously.

Hank looked at me in surprise, then smiled. "That she is."

I watched the boat make a turn, the girls swinging expertly behind, and grow smaller as it headed for the far end of the lake.

"Your father doesn't remember, does he?" Hank asked.

"He's been in so many fights," I said.

"He taught me a lesson, that's for sure," Hank's voice was pained. "Everyone ought to have the shit kicked out of them at least once in their life."

I thought of Betty using the same words to describe her upcoming custody fight and was annoyed with Hank. "Well, that's terrific," I said. "Life's just full of lessons."

Hank took his sunglasses off, twirled them by an earpiece. Then he nodded. "I suppose you're right."

After taking my leave of Hank, I joined the old man at one end of a picnic table full of Mary Beth's uncles by marriage. They were my father's age, but sported varying combinations of beards and wire-framed glasses, held white-collar jobs, and kept themselves busy with music classes, volunteer work, and cross-country skiing and bicycling clubs. Father Phil called them "guitar Catholics," and fittingly enough, when I sat down the subject was music. Ross, one of the uncles, remembered Bob Dylan going electric. "I was outraged," he said. "We were so damned serious in those days."

The old man was fidgety, brushing at his hair, shifting on the picnic bench. He'd gravitated to the one gathering of men on the hillside, but it wasn't his crowd. When there was a break in the conversation, Dad leaned into the table, stubbing out his cigarette on the wood and dropping it in the grass at his feet.

"So I was fucking this coed," he said.

Silence from the rest of the table.

"Summer of 1960. I worked construction at the university, and I hooked up with this sweet little thing. Philosophy major, I believe."

"C'mon, Joe, you were seventeen," Ross said. They'd gone to high school together.

"I was precocious," the old man said. "So. We're in this Dinkytown coffeehouse—her idea, mind you—with this God-awful folk singer. 'Course, I didn't know a folk singer from a harp seal in those days, just sounded like this fellow wanted to save the world and was depressed about it. His set finally ends, and after I use the john, I find him in front of the place having a soulful talk with my girl. As I step out the door, he reaches up and brushes a strand of hair out of her eyes. Very tender."

The old man paused, knocked a cigarette out of his pack and stuck it behind his ear.

"Well, the long and short of it is, I broke Bob Dylan's nose."

Silence.

"That's why it's so damned big."

Men studied their hands, splinters in the table, the birds in the sky.

"Joe, he's Jewish," Ross snapped.

The old man leaned back and peered at him. He took his cigarette from behind his ear and tapped it on the table. "What are you, anti-Semitic?"

"Yeah, Joe, that's it," Ross said. He swung one blue-jeaned leg over the picnic bench. "Anyone besides me want a beer?" Faces turned away and several conversations sprang up.

The old man glared at me. "You got something to say?"

"Me? No, not me." I patted his shoulder. "Hell, maybe you're to blame for his voice."

"Huh?"

Jacky came up in the middle of this and said, "Pop, Clare needs someone to run into town for more ice, and I just volunteered you."

After the old man had gone, Jacky said, "Well, he's colorful. Looks like the boat's coming in."

The speedboat swung by the dock, and Betty and Mary Beth let go of the tow ropes and slalomed into the shallows, sinking as they lost speed. They bobbed in the water, talking while they plucked their skis off, then clambered onto the dock. Jacky and I ambled downhill into the glare of the sun coming off the water and the smell of gasoline from the motorboat. The girls dropped their life jackets on the dock and came to meet us, toweling their hair, laughing together, barefoot.

Mary Beth put her arms around Jacky and kissed him on the lips. Betty stopped and looked over my black slacks and shirt. "Wow," she said, and all three of them looked at me.

"Not exactly boating wear, is it?" Jacky said, and I noticed with surprise that my brother was wearing Topsiders. Suddenly filled with the irrational fear that Betty had said something, that they somehow knew, I glanced at my brother and his fiancée. But their faces showed nothing beyond the open happiness of two young people on the eve of their wedding.

"How was the bachelor party last night?" I asked. "Tie one on?"

"Hell, no," Jacky said. "You think I wanted to wake up on a bus to Cleveland with my dick painted orange?"

"He's not entirely housebroken," I said to Betty and Mary Beth.

"Thank God," Mary Beth said.

. . .

The four of us loaded plates in the screened porch, where the old people were discussing the slots at Turtle Lake, then sat down to eat on the narrow veranda on the lake side of the house. Mary Beth and Betty talked waterskiing, with Mary Beth lamenting being out of practice, Betty saying she herself was just plain out of shape and would surely be sore tomorrow, and both of them agreeing that the water was too damned cold this early in the year. Then I told everyone about my disastrous visit to the nursing home.

"What'd you go out there for?" Jacky said.

I paused over a forkful of cherry pie. "Some notion of reading him a bedtime story. Sweet scene in nursing home, dutiful grandson, that sort of thing."

"I like the part about walking on water," Mary Beth said.

"Can you?" Betty asked, widening her eyes in mock earnestness.

"You know, I think I could," I said, holding up my pie fork, "—if that boat pulled me fast enough."

"My aunt Maureen can ski barefoot," Mary Beth said.

"Ow," Jacky said.

"Miracles don't come easy," I said.

When Jacky and Mary Beth went to talk to the aunt who would be doing the first reading at the wedding Mass, Betty and I slipped into the house and sat down in the living room. The room was paneled in knotty pine, with windows that let in a pleasant play of light from the large shade trees surrounding the house. There was a fieldstone fireplace, a TV, and, on an inner wall, a four-foot-long wooden sailing ship model built by Gerry Donovan.

"Where do you know Mary Beth from again?" I asked, filling the uncomfortable silence that had ballooned between us as soon as we were by ourselves.

"High school. We actually met in Model UN," Betty said. "What about you?"

"Our families go way back, but we lost touch. Jacky met Mary Beth in a bar." I swiveled the upholstered rocker I was sitting in

and ran a fingernail along the lines of the ship's planking. I had
a vague memory of seeing Gerry working on it in my childhood,
tweezers and glue and thick black glasses. "My brother's changed
in ways I never imagined for him."

Betty crossed her legs. She'd brought her towel in and was sitting on it to spare the sofa. Her bare thighs were shapely and beginning to tan, and even without sun her skin had a cream and
gold undertone. I smelled water and sun and tanning lotion again.
"What are you thinking?" I asked.

"That here I sit with my boyfriend who became a priest." She
had her head resting on the back of the sofa and was fiddling with
her engagement and wedding rings.

"Why are you still wearing those?" I said.

"Why do you wear that?" she answered.

"I'm a priest."

She held up her hand and turned it so light glinted off the
diamond. "I think I wear these as punishment. How Catholic of
me, right?"

I stood and looked at the clock on the mantelpiece, one of
those glass ones where you could see the workings inside.

"What happened with you and that judge?" I asked.

Betty patted the couch beside her, and when I sat down, she
sighed. "After law school, Ethan and I discovered that what we'd had
in common was law school. The judge and I worked on a Minnesota
Bar committee together. Lots of late nights. Ethan was into his career,
and he didn't have too many late nights left." She ran the edge of her
hand over the couch fabric, brushing the nap one way and then the
other. "What I didn't count on was Ethan being able to use it against
me in court. On his wanting custody." She brought her hand down
on the arm of the sofa. "I didn't count on me being stupid."

"But trying to take a child from its mother——" I said, making
things worse.

"Ethan's a good lawyer." Betty's voice was cool, with only a slight tremor underneath. "He hired a private investigator. A typical adultery, thoroughly documented, is pretty damning. This one sank a prominent judge, and it doesn't help that the guilty party is an uppity Mexican."

Then she forced a smile. "I'm Mexican, I'm privileged." It was a saying she'd liked to trot out when we were kids and she was trying to have her way over something, but she always said it, even back then, with a hint of irony.

I imagined the coming trial: hale, grave-eyed Ethan, erect and righteous in the witness stand, calmly repeating the facts of Betty's adultery while she had to sit there with a brave face, twisting her hands about the knowledge that her child would be taken from her. I put my arm around her shoulder and squeezed. She looked up at me. "Do you always do that after a confession, Father?"

"Never."

"It's remarkably effective."

"I didn't mean to ask about that."

"I know."

Then I had a sudden vision of myself standing at the lighted window of Betty's apartment just before we'd made love, of the two of us walking out of the building together the next morning. "That detective—" I said.

Betty shook her head. "He's gone," she said. "Ethan has everything he needs." She looked at me again, then away. "Don't worry, you won't be on the front page of the paper."

"That wasn't what I was worried about," I said, unsure myself.

Betty excused herself and went down the hall to use the bathroom. I thumbed through magazines from the rack by the fireplace, glancing briefly at the latest issue of *Commonweal*. Gerry Donovan had died in this room, in his chair in front of the TV. His last glance was possibly out the window at the lake he loved, framed by the hanging boughs of a shade tree and the curved hull of a small sailboat stored cockpit-down on sawhorses in front of the window. I wished such a view for Otto, who would die, like Alexandra, staring at the ceiling of a nursing home.

"Come here." Betty's voice sounded funny. I went down the hall and found her in one of the back bedrooms. She stood between twin beds with cotton honeycomb spreads that were scattered with children's backpacks and clothes. We had the house to ourselves. Voices and laughter drifted faintly from the lawn like a memory of childhood. Here there was silence and birdsong and a cool north breeze through the window and the sound of the leaves of the trees. Betty's nipples poked through the material of her swimsuit, and her bare toes curled in the carpet. The ceiling fan thrummed above our heads. When we kissed, her lips were cool and tasted of lake water and lemonade.

We both stepped back.

"What the fuck are we doing?" I said.

"I can't do this," Betty said. "It's the clothes."

"It's more than the clothes." I brushed at the front of my shirt, the black buttons.

"You're . . . separate."

"It's sort of a relief that you see it that way," I said, thinking of Diana, who hadn't.

Betty shook her head as if she were trying to clear it. "This is confusing the hell out of me, James."

I pulled her into a tight hug. She wrapped her arms around my waist and relaxed into me, and I closed my eyes against the sight of the room's twin beds and children's things.

Betty spoke against my chest. "I got carried away the other night. It's been a long time since I was with a man." A moment later she laughed and said, "Jesus, you're a priest. Like I should be complaining."

I shrugged, still holding her against me. "I have a different perspective," I said. "Mostly I don't miss intimacy."

She stepped back to look up at me, her hands at my waist. "It goes so fast," she said. She started to say something else, then rushed past me and out of the room. I went to the door in time to see her disappear around the corner of the hall, and I knew that she was leaving and I shouldn't stop her. I went back and sat on the bed in the quiet room. What God wanted was no longer obvious to me.

A little while later I looked up and found Jacky leaning in the doorway, holding a can of beer. He frowned. "She doesn't need you confusing her right now."

"Get the hell out of here," I said.

After some trouble finding the lights, I led the rehearsal that evening without a hitch. Everyone ran through their paces, and it appeared we wouldn't embarrass ourselves tomorrow.

The rehearsal dinner was at the Lexington. My great-aunt Marie Therese and her husband had arrived from northern Wisconsin late in the day and were at the dinner, sorry to have missed the lake. Mom came alone. Samuel would be at the wedding, she confided, and if the old man pitched a fit tomorrow night, well, that was his problem. I threw myself into the role of convivial priest, moving around the table before and after dinner with a beer in my hands, visiting with everybody, telling jokes.

But after dinner, as the family walked along Grand and stopped in front of Wuollet Bakery, where the wedding cake was being prepared, Marie Therese put her arm around my shoulder and said: "Jimmy, as your godmother, I have to ask: Why are you turning your back on God?" When the news of my leave got out to the family, I'd received a card from a shrine to the Virgin Mary in Illinois, where Marie Therese was having a novena said for me.

Instead of answering, I twined an arm around her waist and asked: "Have you seen Otto since you and Paul came down?"

After Forest Lake, I'd gone to the nursing home, where I found Granddad in his recliner with his hands folded in his lap, the call button forgotten on top of the oxygen machine. He seemed a bit out of it, but happy, blinking and nodding while I told him about the lake and his old friends. He didn't remember my visit from the night before, and looked at me strangely when I apologized for waking him.

"We stopped on the way in," Marie Therese said. "I wish we lived closer."

"He'll be happy to have seen you." I gave her a peck on the cheek, asked if they needed anything at the motel, and said good night.

Later, I lay in bed listening to the mechanical noises of the Burlington Northern transfer station on Pierce-Butler: the thrumming of semis and diesel locomotives, a loudspeaker, the warning beeps of backing machines. Ever since I was a child, I'd been lulled to sleep by the sounds of men working. Summer nights then, under cool sheets, I listened to the Twins on the radio. Kaat or Perry on the mound, Carew, Oliva, or Killebrew at the plate, the names become an incantation in the announcer's measured voice: *Two balls and a strike. Perry leans in, takes the sign. Campaneris off the bag at first. Perry looks him back. Here's the stretch. And the pitch. Change-up at the letters. Strike two.*

If I couldn't sleep I would pray the Rosary. I had a cheap, plastic, glow-in-the-dark rosary my grandfather had received for making a donation to Saint Joseph's Indian School in South Dakota. On my nightstand, its milky white beads gave off an undersea luminescence, faint green pearls when the lights first went out. If I were awake long enough, around midnight I might hear my father's key rattle the front lock and feel the house's slight shudder as he closed the door behind him. Other nights I'd hear him outside, stumbling against the siding. From my window, I could watch him weave into the backyard in the light of the full moon. He was young then, and the bulk of his shoulders rose like a toppling wave above his slender waist. He would wander about the yard, check the tomato plants, stop to look at the full moon, which lit his broad brow and curly hair, then make his way to the weedy back corner of the lot and urinate against the garage wall.

Tonight, every time I started to drift off, I saw Tim Harley die. I prayed for his soul, and I prayed to Harold Lamplighter, asking him to intercede for me. No priest should behave as I had with Diana and Betty. But still I couldn't imagine quitting. I couldn't imagine telling George Martin, or him at the poker table, relaying the grim news to Bill Snow and Danny Linz: *They say it's his high-school sweetheart. Now he's working for Catholic Charities, behind a desk in a tie and Levis.* Then I felt again the brush of Father Phil's lips against my cheek—*I love you like a son,* he'd said.

I'd received my First Holy Communion from Phil, and, wide awake now, I remembered my first-grade class preparing for it on a darkly overcast day in December 1970, wind blowing leaves and litter across the playground out the classroom windows, low rushing clouds, and Sister Mary Cornelius telling us a story about an Eastern Bloc country where the Communists shut down the Catholic Church. At one parish, the soldiers burst into the church during Mass, ordering the people out and seizing the priest. The ciborium was dashed to the stone floor, scattering the consecrated Hosts about the altar. Sister Mary Cornelius told it so that I could see the desecrated tabernacle, the fallen candlesticks, smashed votives and stained glass, spilled wax cooling, the flame of faith guttering.

But the story didn't end there. The next Sunday, a young girl crept into the darkened, silent church. She approached the altar like a fawn, and knelt to pick one of the Hosts from the floor. I saw the white circle of unleavened bread, inscribed on each side with a cross, upraised between her slender thumb and forefinger. "The Body of Christ," she whispered. And "Amen." She placed the Host on her tongue. Swallowed.

Every Sunday after that, the young girl returned to the abandoned church and knelt at the altar among the scatter of Hosts that made a swirl of white stars on the dark floor, and she took Communion. Then one Sunday, a Communist soldier waited in the shadows. He shot the girl as she came to the altar, and she died on the sanctuary steps, still trying to reach Jesus.

And then Sister Mary Cornelius asked: Would we give our lives for Christ, as that young girl had?

In seminary, I told this story one day in Liturgy class. On break, most of the class went outside to enjoy one of the rare warm days that spring. We were a mixed group, not uncommon in seminaries by the 1980s: men studying to be priests and deacons, lay men and women preparing for liturgical positions with the master of arts in pastoral studies, even a couple of Protestants. Kate, a fortyish Episcopalian, lit a cigarette and approached me. "What a horrible story to tell seven-year-olds."

"It didn't seem horrible," I said. "When you're seven, you're powerless in all things. What a great gift to be told that you could die for God's Son, that God might think enough of you to ask such a thing."

But in truth the story was probably apocryphal, and to a liberal intellectual like Kate it was hard to understand. Now, trying to sleep in my childhood bed four years after my ordination, I remembered something I didn't tell Kate that day in seminary, if only because I didn't remember it then myself: The dying young girl had lived brightly in my mind for years. As a child, I imagined soldiers shutting down our parish church, saw myself following the girl's example and dying for my faith. When I hit puberty, the girl, who was of indeterminate age in Sister Mary Cornelius's story and had aged with me, became part of the story. Sometimes we died side by side, other times I died trying to save her.

I got out of bed and dressed warmly, then made a nightcap of whiskey and went out and sat on the back patio.

The oak tree rustled in the night breeze. It was three in the morning, and after pacing around the patio with a whiskey, gesturing to an unseen audience, I set the empty tumbler on the planter, its bottom grating against some fossil caught in the limestone. Then I knelt, resting my elbows on the planter. I felt the roughness of the stone under my elbows and the cold of the concrete patio through the knees of my jeans, and it brought back the old ache of kneeling on something unyielding. I clasped my hands and rested my forehead against them and prayed again—for Tim Harley, for Harold and Sister Mary Cornelius, even for the girl who never existed, whom I saved night after night in my childhood. Then I stood and walked out into the abandoned garden and pissed on the garage wall.

32

WHEN THE PHONE RANG SATURDAY MORNING in the middle of my second cup of coffee, and the old man's voice said, "I'm at the nursing home. I need you," it was as if I'd been expecting it. I hung up, left the coffee on the counter, dressed in my priest's clothes, and collected my stole and the small stoppered bottle of oil.

At the nursing home, I could hear my grandfather bellowing even before I opened the front door, his voice carrying down the long hall and through two sets of doors. Inside, the sound clarified to words I'd heard before—"God help me! Mary, Mother of God, help me!"—only louder and more urgent. Old people disturbed by the noise wandered the halls or clustered with whispers and accusing glances. I felt a rush of anger at the dumb passivity they shared in the presence of death. "He's worse than usual this morning, Father," the singer in the wheelchair solemnly reported after steering to place herself squarely in my path. "You're worse than usual," I snapped, then caught myself at the look of stunned hurt in her eyes. "God bless you," I said, making the sign of the cross and touching her forehead.

"Godblessyousir, helpmesir, pleasehelpmesir." Her chant started behind me as I walked down the hall.

In the room, Renee prepared a dropperful of medicine. The old man stood by the window, fists in his pockets, staring out at the other wing of the building, across a landscaped courtyard with a fountain and goldfish pond.

Granddad bellowed, caught his breath, bellowed again. He was on his back, the head of the bed raised, and he yelled without any apparent effort save for the intake of air into his lungs marked by the rising of his thin chest.

Renee stooped over the bedside. Granddad's eyes focused on the dropper; he lifted his head from the pillow and opened his mouth, eyes shut, head and neck scrawny as a baby bird's. His mouth closed around the dropper, then his head fell back against the pillow. His eyes opened and settled on me. He gathered himself. I bent near to listen.

"Help!" he yelled. "Help!"

My ears rang. The old man left the window and walked out of the room. I stepped to the door in time to see him go out the fire door at the end of the hall. The alarm went off.

"I'll turn it off," Renee said beside me. "Go on out."

When I got outside, my father was pounding on the brick wall of the nursing home with the meaty side of his fists, blood running down his wrists. I wrapped my arms around his thick chest and upper arms and drove him a step back from the wall. An instant later the day exploded into stars and I was on the ground. Dad stood over me with his fist raised. The alarm was ringing and then stopped ringing. "Help!" Granddad's voice boomed from inside the walls. Renee came out the door to say something and stopped with her hands over her mouth. "I'm calling the police," she said.

I swallowed blood. "Don't. We're fine."

Dad was slumped against the bricks. He raised his torn hands to his face.

I tried to get up, but toppled sideways onto the lawn. I felt like a little kid who'd spun himself silly. Renee reached to help. "Give me a minute," I snapped. She jerked her hand back.

"Help!" Granddad had one word, and he kept repeating it.

"I'm going in," Renee said, looking back and forth between us. "If anyone hits anyone again, I'm calling the police. You can both go to jail." The old man rolled his eyes. She glared at me. "Do you understand?" She let herself back inside, and I saw her turn a hex key in the crash bar to keep the door unlocked. I forced myself to my feet and went and leaned with both hands against the wall. I dropped my head between my arms.

Dad's voice: "You okay?"

"I don't think so," I said. I felt the world go away again. I tried to hang on to the wall. My fingertips scraped over the rough bricks and the spaces between the bricks.

I opened my eyes in the dark. I couldn't see. I put my hands to my face and found a wet washcloth. I was lying on a bed in an empty room. The light was out and the shades were pulled. There was daylight behind them.

Someone was yelling for help.

I sat up. I couldn't remember what had happened, but I was sure it would come. My left eye was throbbing and wouldn't open. I stopped myself short of touching it. Instead, I stood and tested my balance. The air in the room was cool on my skin.

"Help!"

Granddad. I found myself still holding the washcloth. I left it on the bed and walked out into the hall and stood blinking my good eye in the light. Old people milled around slowly. Two policemen were talking to my father and brother. The older one turned to me. He stared at my face and whistled. "Do you want to press charges?"

I looked at Dad and Jacky and remembered what had happened. I waved a hand at the cops. "Go away."

The younger policeman started to say something, then clamped his mouth shut. I looked down. I was dressed in my priest's clothing.

We were standing near the room where the staff brought soiled linen on its way to the laundry, and a sudden whiff of piss, shit, and disinfectant made me gag and reach for the wall.

"You probably have a concussion, Father," the older policeman said gently. "You don't have to make a decision right away."

"Go solve a crime," I said.

Jacky hid a grin.

Mom came down the hall and stood beside Dad. "Listen to my son," she said.

The older cop looked like he'd had enough. "Let's go," he said to his partner. Then to me: "I've seen better priests."

"Tell me something I don't know," I said.

Mom took my arm. "Let's sit you down," she said, and steered me away to a small dining room that families used for private dinners. I felt better with a chair under me.

Granddad's kidneys had shut down, Mom said. The doctor told Dad there was an outside chance dialysis might restart them. Without it, Otto would live a day, maybe two. Dad had planned to ask my opinion, then slugged me instead. Mom looked at her watch. Her hair and makeup were done for the wedding, but she was in a blouse and jeans. It was ten in the morning. Dad had been called to the nursing home at eight. When he arrived, Granddad was sitting up in his recliner. He hadn't gone to breakfast and was a bit confused, but he wasn't unhappy. The nurses asked Dad if he wanted his father moved to the bed, and Dad thought it was a good idea. The move had started the yelling. It wasn't unusual for my grandfather to yell for a while in the morning, but this time he didn't stop. Now they were giving him morphine, in case he was in pain and in hopes of calming him. The old man blamed himself for the yelling and wanted to try dialysis, although the doctor had told him the move to the hospital would be painful and almost certainly futile. The doctor was available by phone.

"No dialysis," I said. My head throbbed, and I lowered my face into my hands.

"Is it euthanasia if we don't?" Mom asked. "Honey?"

"No," I said, still holding my head, grateful for George Martin's advice in a similar situation in River County. "In his condition, dialysis is considered an extraordinary measure."

"Tell your father," Mom said. "He'll listen to you."

She went to get Dad. Jacky came in and sat down. "How are you?" he said.

"Weak as hell. Jesus, no one's ever hit me that hard." My voice was a bit slurred. I forced myself to sit up straight, tried to will away the pain in my head. I needed to think clearly.

"Mary Beth wants to postpone the wedding," Jacky said.

Mom came back in time to hear this. "Do you have any idea how many people the Donovans have in town?" she said. "No way."

Jacky shrugged. "Whatever. But she really means it."

Dad came in and sank into a chair, giving me a concerned glance before facing Mom.

"Maybe we should try the hospital," he said.

"The doctor discouraged it," Mom said. "It's the Catholic doctor."

Dad turned toward me.

"He's had a catheter in since February," I said. "He can't breathe by himself or use the bathroom without two nurses. His mind's half gone."

"He's asking for help," Dad said.

"He does that every day. This morning his routine's been disturbed and he doesn't know why. Dad—" I reached for his hand, then thought better of it "—if you let them, they'll keep him alive until he's lying in bed crapping himself like a baby."

The old man looked at Jacky. My brother nodded. "Jimmy's right."

All morning, old people appeared in the doorway of Granddad's room, drawn by the noise. The woman in the room across the way was in a wheelchair and senile, and she kept wheeling across the hall. We'd look up and she'd be rocking her chair back and forth in the middle of the hall or in the door to the room, like an uncertain animal approaching the light. She wore pop-bottle glasses and behind them the whites of her eyes were visible all the way around the irises. Once she got up to the foot of the bed before Mom turned to find those eyes. "Oh!" Mom cried, and Jacky grabbed the old woman's chair by the handles and wheeled her back across the hall. He put her on the other side of her bed for good measure. "Stay there, Mina," he said, looking at the nameplate by her room, but she was back in our doorway in a few minutes. "Someone set her brakes," the old man muttered.

I gave Granddad extreme unction with the family and Mina looking on. He stopped yelling as soon as the oil touched his forehead, but grew agitated as I finished. "Help," he cried softly in a despairing voice. "Help."

I tried to talk to him then, but he wouldn't acknowledge any of us, except to ask for water after he'd yelled himself hoarse. Someone would lift a glass to his lips. He'd drink, then let his head sink into the pillow again. "Help!" he'd yell.

Jacky and I stepped out in the hall.

"You'd think he could at least say hi," Jacky said. He'd just held the water glass for Granddad. "How's your head?"

"Better," I said.

"That black eye's a real beaut. It'll go with my tux. Maybe Mary Beth can put some makeup over it."

Mina rolled across the hall behind Jacky.

I ran over and captured her. "Mary Beth's got enough to do." I deposited Mina back in her room. "Why don't you call Mary Beth again, let her know what's up. Then go home, have a drink, get dressed. There's nothing more you can do here."

Jacky went to call from the relative quiet of the nurses' station. The old man came out in the hall. He shook his head. "I told him he was dying," he said. "I told him he was dying right before you got here. I thought he'd want to know. Hell, I'd want to know. That's when he started yelling."

"The Church'd say you did the right thing," I said. "You gave him a chance to make his peace with God."

In the room, Granddad yelled again. "Doesn't sound peaceful to me," Dad said. His face was pale, and he leaned back against the wall and ran a hand over his hair.

"No one's ever died on you before," I said. My grandmother had guarded her privacy so closely that the family hardly knew when she went into the hospital. Granddad made all of the decisions about her last illness by himself. "Did he ever tell you what he wanted?" I asked.

"Nah," the old man said, staring at the opposite wall. "We never could talk."

My grandfather yelled for five hours. I fought to get him more morphine, finally insisting the nurses call the doctor, who gave his okay. It was early in the afternoon, a half-hour after another dose, when Granddad quieted and shut his eyes. By then Mom had gone home to finish getting ready for the wedding. Jacky stayed, saying, "Hell, all I have to do is put on a damn penguin suit." A few minutes after Granddad quieted down, Marie Therese and her husband Paul showed up—we'd forgotten about them, and Mom had called their hotel from home. They offered to stay with Granddad through the wedding. The old man was confused. He wanted to see his son married, but didn't want to abandon his father.

"He'll have family with him," my great-aunt said. "He had all of you with him this morning when he needed you." We didn't tell them how little good that had done, but, with Jacky and I insisting, Dad agreed to go to the wedding.

I held Granddad's hand for a few minutes before leaving. His fingers were curved as if they still wanted the call button, but there was no response to my grip. The skin was cold and waxy.

VIII

33

JACKY DROVE US HOME IN MY CAR. I didn't trust myself behind the wheel yet. Besides, he wanted his car hidden for the wedding; he had that kind of friends. While he changed, I sat down with the homily I'd been working on. It was passable as it stood, which was good because my concentration was shot. It didn't help that I was trying to write while holding a slab of frozen sirloin over my eye. I revised the draft I had without improving it much, then worked in a few words about Granddad and left it at that. The steak helped the swelling, though, and while the eye was still numb, Mom dabbed concealer over the bruise before she left to pick up Samuel.

With Jacky on the porch looking at his watch, I went upstairs and made sure all my wedding vestments were in the clothing bag I was bringing to the church. Then, after a moment's consideration, I added a change of clothes. Usually I stayed in my collar at receptions and put up with the people who thought all any priest wanted to do was talk about God, but tonight I was brother and son as well as priest, and the civilian clothes meant privacy to be with my family. I carried the clothing bag out to the car, and Jacky drove us to the church.

It was a cool, gray day, threatening rain. We sat in the car near the sacristy door and watched people with light overcoats over their dress clothes go in the front of the church. "I can't believe we were at the lake yesterday," Jacky said. He pulled at the lapels of his tux. "I hate all this attention."

"Shit," I said. "You're marrying Mary Beth Donovan. No one's even going to see you."

Jacky smoothed his mustache in the rearview mirror. "I'll never get used to hearing you cuss in those clothes."

"Come on," I said.

I led him across the lawn to the rectory and went in the front door, nodding at the kid at the receptionist's desk. It could have been me fifteen years ago, covering the phones on a Saturday. We went downstairs to Phil's bar, and I put two shot glasses on the water-stained wood, then rummaged in the liquor cabinet. "Drink?"

"You bet."

I brought up fifths of Evan Williams and Jameson, poured shots.

Jacky held his drink in one hand, rested the other on the bar.

"Here's looking at you, kid," I said, and tossed back the Jameson. Tilting my head quickly was a mistake. I leaned on the bar until the room stopped spinning.

"All right?" Jacky asked.

"Mary Beth's a better woman," I said, "than you deserve."

"You got that right." Jacky downed his bourbon.

I lifted a bottle. Jacky nodded. We had another shot.

"Grandpa's dying," Jacky said.

"True." I put the bottles away, rinsed the glasses and left them in the sink. "So we do the wedding partly for him. Because it's all about family and ritual and carrying forward."

Jacky stared at the floor. "When I was little, I asked him if he killed anyone in the war, and do you know what he said? That he hoped not." He shook his head and rubbed at an eye with his wrist. "I never thought to ask him why he yells every morning at the nursing home."

"Neither did I. He probably couldn't tell us anyway." I gave Jacky a one-armed squeeze. "Let's go."

We crossed the lawn to the sacristy. I stepped out onto the altar. Everything was in order. I left my homily on the shelf below the lectern, weighted with a hymnal. One of the altar boys, a tough-looking, freckle-faced kid with a cocky strut, moved around lighting candles. The other, taller, more serious, already in his robes, came out, and they whispered together, the taller one glancing at me. I remembered the anxiety of serving Mass for a visiting priest. I walked over. "Jim Dressler," I said. "Kevin and Rob?" I saw Rob, the tall one, glance curiously at my bruised eye. Up close, the concealer didn't hide it. "Got slugged this morning," I said. "How's it look?"

"Pretty bad, Father," Rob said.

"Who hit you?" Kevin said.

"A man who was upset because his father is dying." I changed the subject. "You guys play football?"

They nodded.

"Let me guess: end"—I indicated Rob with a forefinger—"and defensive back."

"Linebacker," Kevin said.

"Little guy like you?" I said. "You must be a hardnose." He puffed out his chest.

The church was filling up. "I served Mass here when I was a kid," I said. "If I need anything, I'll tell you. Otherwise, just follow my lead."

Jacky was chuckling with his best man and groomsmen in one corner of the sacristy. "You idiots have the ring?" I said. The best man fumbled in his pocket and held it up.

I went over to the mirror and vested, starting with the amice, letting it rest briefly on my head, then arranging it around my shoulders. I tied the cincture about my alb. *Purify me, O Lord, from all stain, and cleanse my heart, that washed in the Blood of the Lamb I may enjoy eternal delights.* How many priests had reassured themselves with this prayer that they were worthy to celebrate the Mass? Well, this one needed it. The stole next, and last the heavy white wedding chasuble. I flipped it over my head, then stood in front of the mirror, smoothing a hand over the gold embroidery on the chest. Two interlocking rings above a stylized chalice and Host. *Granddad's dying,* I thought. Then: *Betty will be on Mary Beth's side of the church with Hank. If she shows.* Then: *It's Jacky's day, not yours. Relax.* I glanced over at my brother, who stood in profile by the sacristy window, translucent gray now with a steady rain. His best man stepped in front of him and straightened his tuxedo jacket. I adjusted the chasuble, felt my heart lighten with anticipation of the Mass.

One of Mary Beth's aunts stuck her head in the door. "They're ready, Father," she said.

The bride's side of the church was filled with tall, well-dressed people; Donovans alone occupied the front quarter. Jacky's side was full of his buddies from the street department and the three softball teams he played on. In front, Mom sat with Samuel, then Anne and her family, and, finally, my father glowered at the far end of the pew next to Daryl Sr. I stood in the center of the altar with Jacky beside me. When the last bridesmaid reached the altar and the wedding march began, Jacky struck the typical groom's pose, legs slightly apart, one hand clasped over the other. I watched him watch his bride coming up the aisle. He was handsome and clear-eyed, and I rested a hand on his shoulder for a moment.

Mary Beth took her place at the altar, and I spread my hands in greeting. "Friends, we are gathered here today to witness the marriage of Mary Elizabeth Donovan and John Joseph Dressler. Let us call upon God to be with us as we celebrate this union of two into one. In the name of the Father, and the Son, and the Holy Spirit."

With the greeting, the dull ache at my temple receded, along with the worries about Granddad and Betty and what I would do tomorrow, and I felt, as on so many Sundays, that I was a vessel for the words of the Mass, that I had stepped aboard a boat that would carry me safe to some far shore, if only I in faith followed the compass points of the liturgy.

The introductory rites and the readings swept by. One of Mary Beth's aunts read First Corinthians, and then I was at the lectern, reading from the Gospel of John. When I finished, I rested my homily on the cover of the lectionary. "As most of you know by now, our grandfather, Otto Dressler, is very ill. His sister and her husband are with him now. The family invites any friends who might wish to say their farewells to visit at the nursing home after Mass." In the second row on Mary Beth's side of the church, Clare Donovan whispered something to her brother, William Reilly, who tugged at his ear and nodded.

"The sacraments mark the stages of our lives. Last rites mark the last step of this life. We cannot know, but it's our faith to believe, that, as with the other sacraments, last rites prepare us for the next stage of existence. The poet John Keats said we are not put in this world to save our souls, but to make them. My grandfather made a good soul in this world. Many of you on both sides of the aisle today know Otto Dressler. You know of his heroism in Normandy. And some of you probably thought he should have been awarded another combat medal for raising my father."

Laughter. At the far end of the front pew, the old man chuckled and looked pleased.

"My grandfather, like the rest of his generation, bequeathed a good life to each of us here: the chance to make our own souls. So it's fitting that today we mark the union of his grandson with the granddaughter of his old friends Gerry and Clare. They start a new family today, a start that calls them to build on what the older generation built for all of us." The old man had leaned forward, hands clasped, and was studying me with his head tilted. His eyes glittered.

I paused, then went on to the homily I'd prepared before this morning.

"'Faith, hope, and love, and the greatest of these is love', says First Corinthians. Think of the different vocations to which God calls us. Faith symbolizes the religious vocations, those individuals who give up earthly rewards in the service of Heaven. Hope," I paused, "might belong to those called to the single vocation"—the congregation tittered—"and love belongs to those who are called, as Jacky and Mary Beth are today, to marriage." In the congregation, someone shifted, and I spotted Hank Ramirez sitting with his eyes cast up to the stained-glass windows. Betty was beside him, half-hidden by the man in front of her.

"Love is the greatest of these, for it's from the marriage bond that children come, and they represent our hope for, and our faith in, the future of God's people. Love calls for the greatest sacrifice from the individual. People, especially priests, often say that priests make the greatest sacrifice"—there was more laughter at this— "but married couples, in raising their children and in accommodating one another's wishes and needs, make a greater one. And they're often rewarded with the greatest growth. If the clergy is the head of the church, and those called to single life are its arms and legs, then the family is its heart and soul." Now I could see Betty, leaning into the aisle for a clear view, one hand cupping her chin.

"Marriage calls for patience and growth. Patience on Mary Beth's part and growth on Jacky's." I waited until the laughter died. "It calls for faith and hope: faith in one another, hope in children and in Jesus Christ. And, finally, as the word *love* is often translated in this passage, marriage calls for *charity.* Not charity in the sense of gifts to the poor, but charity in the sense of Christian love: love that is given selflessly, with no thought of personal gain, and love that, in the course of even the best marriages, calls upon one partner or the other to make a lenient, merciful—charitable—judgment upon their spouse. And so, as we watch Mary Beth and Jacky pledge their love to one another, let us also pledge faith, hope, and charity to ourselves, our loved ones, our Church, our God, and our world."

The sun briefly broke through at the start of the marriage rite; the stained-glass windows glittered for a few moments, then the light faded as if it had been drawn from the church, leaving a hush.

Jacky and Mary Beth stood before me, hand in hand, my brother solemn and handsome, his bride grave and beautiful—the way, I thought, it ought to be.

Since it is your intention to enter into marriage, with your hands joined, declare your consent before God and His Church, your family and your friends.

"I, John Joseph, take you, Mary Elizabeth, to be my wife. I promise to be true to you in good times and in bad, in sickness and in health. I will love you and honor you—" Jacky's voice caught "—all the days of my life."

Mary Beth repeated the vows in her smooth alto, then surprised everyone by impulsively leaning forward and kissing Jacky on the lips.

"You're getting ahead of yourselves," I said.

This is the Lamb of God who takes away the sins of the world. Happy are those who are called to His supper.

I waited at the head of the center aisle while the ushers took their places and the family members in the front rows filed out for Communion. Anne and her family stood and stepped into the Communion line, and my father and mother, along with her Baptist boyfriend, joined them. I hadn't covered this in rehearsal, taking for granted that here, as in Pretty Prairie, I would stand by Church practice, denying Communion to Protestants and remarried Catholics.

I'd always gone by Harold Lamplighter's reasoning at poker, that even if I disagreed with the Church and had my own failings, on the altar I represented something bigger than myself, one holy Catholic and apostolic Church to which I had freely given vows of obedience. So now, by turn, I gave Communion to Mom and blessed Samuel with the sign of the cross, saying: "May the Lord bless and keep you." I did the same for baby Kelsey in Anne's arms—*aren't we all children of God?*—and my sister took Communion by mouth and smiled beatifically. The old man watched all of this and dropped his hands and hung his head. He stood before me. I raised my hand to bless him as well—and saw him as he had been at his father's bedside this morning as Otto yelled for help over and over. I froze with my hand in the air, then lifted a Host.

"The Body of Christ," I said.

"Amen," he said, and I pressed the Host into his cupped hands. Our eyes met. My father put the Host in his mouth and smiled. He turned from the altar, and I watched him return to the pew, the silvering hair, the shoulders that strained his suit coat.

Only a few people stopped by the nursing home afterward, Donovans and Reillys, other old friends. Otto's generation was mostly gone. Jacky and Mary Beth were in the room with him now, the door closed. I'd brought consecrated Hosts with me and given Communion to Marie Therese and Paul. While I described the wedding, the old man stepped up. "Why don't you two go to the dinner and dance? I'll stay out here."

"We've already eaten," Marie Therese said, "and we don't dance. You enjoy Jacky's wedding day and come back tonight so we can go to bed."

"I'll be out, too," I said. "A priest at a dance isn't good for much once the food's gone."

Jacky and Mary Beth came out of Granddad's room, and I walked them down the hall to where Jacky's best man waited to drive them back into town. Old people craned their necks at Mary Beth's wedding dress, but Jacky hurried her along. "And I thought it was bad at church," he muttered.

"You loved it," Mary Beth said, hitching her dress up above her shoes. "Got to walk out in front of all those people with a beautiful woman on your arm. Slow down. Let these people have something to talk about."

"You okay to drive now?" Jacky asked me.

"Fine. I'm gonna tell the old man he's losing the snap in his right."

"You washed your face," Mary Beth said, indicating the purple bruise under my eye. I'd rinsed away the concealer after the wedding photos.

"It'll give people something to talk about," I said.

When Granddad's room was empty for a moment, I went in and stood at the bedside. The oxygen machine hummed. The rise and fall of Granddad's chest was barely perceptible. I sat down and held his hand. Then I took my rosary—the one he'd given me—from my pocket and twined it in his fingers. "You borrow this tonight." I smoothed his shaggy eyebrows, which Gram used to trim for him, and bent and kissed his forehead.

Renee came in and lifted the sheet at the foot of the bed. "No discoloration in the feet yet," she said. "You usually get some by now." Granddad's feet were short and broad with yellow nails.

"Was he in pain with all of that yelling?" I asked.

"Your grandfather yelled every morning," she said. "Sometimes he quieted down on his own, sometimes we sedated him. The only difference was this morning we used morphine."

The last time he'd had morphine was in Normandy. This morning as it was finally taking hold, he would drift off for minutes at a time, then shake himself awake like an infant fighting sleep, yelling again for help. Dad and Jacky and I took turns talking to him, holding his hands, rubbing his shoulders, but we might as well not have been there. His attention was fixed on some awful fear.

Alexandra had refused medicine the last week of her life, spent her last night in a coma with Otto at her bedside. In the morning, after he'd gone home to freshen up, she woke, heard from the nurse that Otto had been there all night, and winked. Then she settled into her pillow and died. As a priest, I'd long ago learned that some people accepted death gratefully while others fought it all the way. But I didn't know what tipped the scales of faith and fear, whether it was the sum of a life or one moment that came to outweigh everything else. I didn't know why my grandfather spent his last hours of consciousness yelling for help that his faith and books and family couldn't bring, or why he fought so hard against the comfort of the morphine even as he craned his neck to receive it. I wanted to think I would be braver in the end, but I knew better than to trust the power of resolution. No one knows what old wound or weakness might break us. All I know is that my grandfather, who had a medal for valor in Normandy, slipped from the conscious world calling for help that did not come.

Back at the church, I started toward the sacristy to change clothes for the dinner and dance. My leave had officially begun. But I didn't want to take off my priest's suit. I would still be in the public eye tonight.

After the dinner and the toasts, the clinking on glasses to make Mary Beth and Jacky kiss, the tossing of garter and bouquet, and the wedding-party dances, Betty and I stood to one side of the floor in the parish hall, watching Hank waltz with his wife. He was a graceful dancer, a big man who'd learned to move smoothly to save his wind and his knees. Donovan aunts and uncles danced to the polka band as if they were in a ballroom. At a table, Daryl Sr. bottle-fed Kelsey, while Anne skipped in a circle with Chrissie and the twins, all four of them holding hands. Junior slouched with a couple boys, ignoring a nearby cluster of girls. Mom and Samuel were at a table smoking cigarettes and drinking beer, and, in one corner, the old man monopolized two of the groomsmen, gesturing, mugging, shrugging his shoulders.

"So what now?" Betty asked.

I made a face. "Dad and I are about done with the house. I need a job for the rest of the summer."

"One of the caring professions?"

"I was thinking of something where I could work with my hands. Same kind of thing I'm doing with Dad, but saner company."

"A carpenter?"

I caught her barely suppressed grin. "Hardly." Then I frowned at her. "Did you mean 'what now' about the other night?"

Betty bent her attention to untying the narrow white ribbon around the neck of a net bag of Jordan almonds. When she looked up again, her face was serious. "I was thinking about my trial, James."

"Oh hell," I said. "Thing about being a priest, you get used to thinking too much about yourself. Isn't that funny?"

"Not really," Betty said. "Here. For luck." She slid all five almonds off the net into my hand, then took one for herself.

Ruth Wilmar, Gerry Donovan's sister, hobbled by with a cane and a beer. She stopped and stared at me. "You were out at the lake," she said. "Otto Dressler's son. Your father was a fine man. Never thought his son'd be a priest, though."

"It doesn't seem likely," I said. Ruth moved on.

"What—?" Betty said.

"She's confused," I said.

We stood there awkwardly, a priest in a black suit and a Mexican woman in an elegant blue dress. The candied almonds softened in my hands. I busied myself with crunching them one by

one. "Here." I held the last almond up between thumb and forefinger. Betty smiled and tilted her chin up, mouth open. I aimed
the almond, and she caught it and coughed.

"Bull's-eye," she said.

"Luck," I said. "You wanna dance?"

Betty shook her head, indicated my collar. "Not with a priest,"
she said. She let out a tired sigh. "I'm going to leave in a little while,"
she said. "I still need to pick up Peter from his father, and I can't take
much more happiness." She walked over to Anne's table, where she'd
left her purse. She rummaged for a cigarette, put it to her mouth,
then changed her mind. She talked to my sister for a moment. Anne
reached up to fix her hair, and Betty tucked a strand into place for
her, then walked quickly into the crowd in the direction of the bar,
weaving in and out of sight. I stood between the dance floor and the
tables, undecided whether to sit down.

"Look, Father." One of Jacky's friends stopped beside me and
pointed at the dance floor. The dollar dance had started. The old
man stepped up to Mary Beth and made a slight, awkward attempt
at a bow with his hand on his belly. She rested her hands on his
wide shoulders while he pinned a bill to her dress. She glanced
down, looked again, and said something. Her father, standing near,
said something, too, and clapped the old man on the back, and
then Dad and Mary Beth started dancing. He led her in a stiff-
kneed polka, a big grin on his face.

There was a stir in the hall, a ripple that spread from Mary
Beth's father. Mom and Samuel sat up and took notice, and Mom
spoke angrily, stabbing the air with her cigarette. Jacky, who'd been
over with them, walked quickly across the dance floor. He stopped
beside me with his hands in his pockets, trying to hide a grin. "Old
man just pinned a brand-new thousand-dollar bill on Mary Beth,"
he said. "Mom's really pissed."

"Everybody's gonna want to dance with Mary Beth now," I
said to Jacky. "You'd best keep an eye on her."

Jacky looked around. "Where's Betty? I thought I saw her a minute ago."

"I don't know," I said. "She was talking to Anne, then disappeared."

"Too bad she's missing this." Jacky watched Dad polka by with Mary Beth, then turned his attention back to me. "You still going out to the nursing home?"

"Soon." I looked again for Betty. "I'll catch up with you in a few minutes."

I left the hall and cut across the lawn to the sacristy. Nearby, a circle of Jacky and Mary Beth's friends stood under a tree. The scent of pot drifted over, and I saw the brief orange flare of a joint. The night was wet, the evergreens by the sacristy door dripping rain. I lingered a moment on the steps, then let myself in.

There was a night-light on above the sink, where the cruets were drying upside down in a dish rack. The clothing bag that held my wedding vestments and change of clothes hung from a coat tree in the corner. The sacristy was quiet and shadowed, and I left the lights off, stepped out into the church, and knelt in one of the pews to the side of the altar. At first I bent my head and closed my eyes, then I rested my chin on my hands and stared at the single electric candle burning in the sanctuary. But I could not pray. Out in the suburbs, Granddad was dying. In high school, when Betty's grandmother had died, Betty and I had slipped away from the funeral dinner to *Abuelita's* empty house. Betty had a key and we let ourselves in, thinking we were looking for a quiet place to talk. Lust caught us unawares, and we made frantic love on the slipcovered living-room couch, still in all of our funeral clothes except for Betty's heels and hose. After, we stared at one another in disarray and confusion, wondering why the heady adult smells of cologne and sex so reassured us.

I crossed myself. Would a life of the world, among women, offer anything more than the comfort of the body? Did I want that comfort? Darkness gathered around the sanctuary light and the silence was immense, heightened by an occasional creak from some joining of wood or metal. I went and stood at the altar, thinking of the lines of communicants that filled this church every Sunday, how the shades of all of our dead relatives shuffled forward among them. How ritual, repeated over the centuries, brought generations of Catholics into communion with one another.

Then I squeezed my eyes shut. I was twelve years away—a million stars over a lake after a skating party. Back on shore, a few late drinkers stoke the remains of a bonfire until it flicks orange fingers of light onto the ice. Betty glides back and forth at the very edge of the fire's glow while I swivel to follow. We've been keeping warm with a pint of schnapps. "Come on." "We don't know it's solid." "It's been solid for days." A cold autumn with little snow has left the lake ice bare save for wind-blown lines of snow that look like wisps of clouds against the reflected stars. Betty sweeps a little further out. "I'll race you." She gathers herself and is off, gone into the night. I dig hard after her, fear helping me build speed—I watch for open water, but it's the thin spots that get you. I see myself catching Betty, roughly grabbing her arm, but when I do catch her, halfway across the lake, I sail by, dizzy with stars and schnapps and speed. We race to the far shore, where the snow climbs away up a hill into the night, and we stand under winter-black trees and kiss until our frozen faces are flushed with heat.

At the altar, I opened my eyes. Betty was my first lover, and longest and deepest, and when I took my vows, her face was the face of the world that I turned my back on. In that moment it was clear to me that I had taken the Mass for a whole life and it could no longer be so, even if a part of me would always regret that. I genuflected, head lowered between my arms, and a prayer came: *Lord God, forgive me for what I'm about to do. Forgive me for wanting communion with one woman over that with the people you called me to serve. And forgive me most of all for wanting a son of my own, for not finding your Son to be enough.* Then I got to my feet, unlocked the tabernacle, and drew out the ciborium. I gave myself Communion, made the sign of the cross, and left the sanctuary.

When I came in from the parking lot, after changing and putting my clothing bag in the backseat of the Chevy, I paused in the door of the parish hall, my eyes adjusting to the glare of the ceiling lights. The dance was in full swing, the Flying Dutchman, then a schottische while people caught their breaths. Women kicked off their shoes and kids were openly sneaking beer from the keg while parents pretended not to notice. Amid the dancers, I had glimpses of Jacky shaking hands with Mary Beth's dad, the best man dodging across the floor with his bow tie loosened and a beer in each hand, and Hank leaning on the cash bar talking to Betty, who sipped a glass of wine and answered, jiving a little to the beat, fluorescence flashing off her glasses. Dad sat with Bob and Erma Nordyke, sweating and smoking a cigarette, his shirttail untucked and his tie long gone. Caterers cleared wreckage from beer-soaked tablecloths. A groomsman staggered up, cross-eyed with drink, and stared at my blue oxford-cloth shirt for a moment before placing me. "Father," he said, "where's Jacky's car?" I shook my head. "It's a confessional secret." Anne and Daryl laughed now with Mom and Samuel, while twelve-year-old Junior stood next to a girl about his age, their heads averted, both of them dying to talk. Next to me, three couples made plans for after, the wives clutching matchbooks and cocktail napkins with Jacky and Mary Beth's names on them. The sounds of two women arguing came from the ladies' room to my right, and the old man had Bob and Erma laughing, his own gruff *haw-haw* audible now and again at a break in the music. Outside the high windows of the hall lightning flashed. Rain was moving across the Cities, falling in long

shafts between the skyscrapers of downtown Minneapolis, spatter-
ing the Lake Street bridge and the Mississippi and the little sand
beach there below the seminary, running up Summit past the rich
people's houses, beating against the lit windows of the church hall
and going on to darken the green dome of the Cathedral.

Soon I would excuse myself from the dance and go with the old
man to sit beside Otto a last time. We would arrive too late: out in
the suburbs, Marie Therese and Paul had sat up at the first near
flash of the storm and checked Otto's still chest, and even now
Marie Therese sat with her head bent in the silent recognition that
she was the last of her generation of Dresslers. Tuesday I would say
Otto's funeral Mass. He would be buried in the Dressler family plot
in Calvary Cemetery, down the hill from the slab of granite that
covers John Ireland's grave. The early bishops and archbishops of
Saint Paul lie beside Ireland, and the ranked graves of priests and
nuns wait in neat rows, all the stones of each order uniform.

But downhill in the Dressler plot, there's plenty of room for
eccentricity among the maiden aunts and drunks. In the crowd
around Otto's coffin, after the last prayers are said and some
VFW representative hands the old man a folded flag, I will look
for Betty's eyes, wanting, in the hard knowledge that I will never
lead a congregation in prayer again, to go to her place and make
love in her big bed, two adults not surprised at all this time to find
themselves rutting in answer to a death.

If Betty is there. I'm still standing in the doorway to the hall,
and while I can see Hank at the bar, she's disappeared again. One
of Mary Beth's aunts says something to the bandleader, and the
music quickens into the "Beer Barrel Polka," the *tiki-tiki-ta* of the
accordion rising over the rapid tap of the drums. Dad swings into
view, doing the polka with Anne in his stiff, rocking gait. He says
something in her ear, ending with *haw-haw.* Anne pats his shoulder,
and they are gone in the mix.

There's lightning outside, and the ceiling lights flicker. The accordion falters, then picks up the beat. Now, in the midst of the dancers, I can see a young Otto in his gangster hat, huddled with Alexandra at a cocktail table with a lamp in the middle. There's thunder, and Alexandra murmurs in Otto's ear, excuses herself from the table, and goes to find her grandson James, frightened in bed. *It's just the angels bowling in heaven,* she says. *Say a prayer.* And then it occurs to me that I would instinctively comfort a child of my own with the same words, that all I've forgotten and never understood of my parents' and grandparents' lives would come back to me.

At that, I take a step into the hall, looking for Betty, and see that Daryl Jr. has finally asked the cute girl standing next to him to dance. And just like that, another prayer comes. *Glory be to you, dancers; to hawks for their many names; to baseballs for falling into green outfields and waiting mitts; to white nights, the slice of skates, the evening light on the Mississippi. Glory be to the great city at its head, to Saint Paul and the working men who built its churches and taverns, unloaded its steamboats, and laid down its trolley lines and its railroad to the Northwest. Praise be to my father, bent to some task of joinery in an old house; and to Betty's son, I want to teach him to swim and water-ski, to skip happily over the deep green waters of Forest Lake.*

And now, glory be to his mother, who's working her way through the crowd on the other side of the floor. She looks tired, but there's something in her eyes when she sees me, and then she's crossing the dance floor, hair falling like black silk about her shoulders. "Dance with me?" I mouth, and still halfway across the floor, she nods and stretches forth her hands. And I rejoice when I take tight hold of them, and we step forward into the confusing whirl of dancers, as it was in the beginning, and is now, and ever shall be, world without end.

THANKS FIRST TO EVERYONE AT MILKWEED EDITIONS—Daniel Slager, Ben Barnhart, Patrick Thomas, Jessica Deutsch, and all, for their expertise and enthusiasm. Special thanks to Christian Fuenfhausen for the cover.

Thanks for generous support and encouragement go to Robert Hedin and the Anderson Center for Interdisciplinary Studies; the Jerome Foundation; the Minnesota State Arts Board; Nat Sobel and Judith Weber; J. Michael Lennon and the James Jones Fellowship Contest; the Napa Valley and Sewanee writers' conferences, particularly Alice McDermott and everyone in her 2009 Sewanee fiction workshop; and the Loft Literary Center and McKnight Foundation.

Thanks to the lovely and talented literary community of the Twin Cities and Minnesota.

I studied writing at the University of Kansas School of Journalism and in the University of Arkansas MFA Program; thanks especially to Rick Musser at Kansas and the late James Whitehead at Arkansas.

Thanks to the Cooney, Harrison, and Morrissey families, who welcomed an old friend's son to Saint Paul; to Charlie Kuhl, who answers my questions about the city; to Don Luna, who talked to me about the West Side; and to Fathers John Malone and John Estrem, who gave me their time and insights into the priesthood.

Thanks to my family: to my brother Mike; and to my parents, the late Carl and Maxine Reimringer, who gave me everything in the world.

And, most especially, thanks to my wife and best reader, Katrina Vandenberg, and to my other best reader, our best man Michael Downs.

About the Author

A former newspaper editor and a graduate of the MFA program at the University of Arkansas, John Reimringer lives in Saint Paul, Minnesota, with his wife, the poet Katrina Vandenberg. *Vestments* is his first novel.

More Fiction from Milkweed Editions

To order books or for more information,
contact Milkweed at (800) 520-6455
or visit our Web site (www.milkweed.org).

The Farther Shore
Matthew Eck

Ordinary Wolves
Seth Kantner

Driftless
David Rhodes

Montana 1948
Larry Watson

Milkweed Editions

Founded in 1979, Milkweed Editions is one of the largest independent, nonprofit literary publishers in the United States. Milkweed publishes with the intention of making a humane impact on society, in the belief that good writing can transform the human heart and spirit.

Join Us

Milkweed depends on the generosity of foundations and individuals like you, in addition to the sales of its books. In an increasingly consolidated and bottom-line-driven publishing world, your support allows us to select and publish books on the basis of their literary quality and the depth of their message. Please visit our Web site (www.milkweed.org) or contact us at (800) 520-6455 to learn more about our donor program.

Milkweed Editions, a nonprofit publisher, gratefully acknowledges sustaining support from Emilie and Henry Buchwald; the Patrick and Aimee Butler Foundation; the Dougherty Family Foundation; the Ecolab Foundation; the General Mills Foundation; John and Joanne Gordon; William and Jeanne Grandy; the Jerome Foundation; Robert and Stephanie Karon; the Lerner Foundation; Sally Macut; Sanders and Tasha Marvin; the McKnight Foundation; Mid-Continent Engineering; the Minnesota State Arts Board, through an appropriation by the Minnesota State Legislature, a grant from the Wells Fargo Foundation Minnesota, and a grant from the National Endowment for the Arts; Kelly Morrison and John Willoughby; the National Endowment for the Arts, and the American Reinvestment and Recovery Act; the Navarre Corporation; Ann and Doug Ness; Jörg and Angie Pierach; the RBC Foundation USA; Ellen Sturgis; the Target Foundation; the James R. Thorpe Foundation; the Travelers Foundation; Moira and John Turner; and Edward and Jenny Wahl.

MINNESOTA
STATE ARTS BOARD

NATIONAL
ENDOWMENT
FOR THE ARTS
A great nation
deserves great art.

TARGET.

THE McKNIGHT FOUNDATION

The Editor's Circle of Milkweed Editions

We gratefully acknowledge the patrons of the Editor's Circle for their support of the literary arts.

Interior design by Connie Kuhnz
Typeset in Baskerville
by BookMobile Design and Publishing Services
Printed on acid-free 100% post consumer waste paper
by Friesens Corporation

ENVIRONMENTAL BENEFITS STATEMENT

Milkweed Editions saved the following resources by printing the pages of this book on chlorine free paper made with 100% post-consumer waste.

TREES	WATER	SOLID WASTE	GREENHOUSE GASES
121	55,587	3,375	11,542
FULLY GROWN	GALLONS	POUNDS	POUNDS

Calculations based on research by Environmental Defense and the Paper Task Force. Manufactured at Friesens Corporation